WON'T YOU SAVE ME

A gripping and addictive crime thriller

WENDY DRANFIELD

Dean Matheson Book 3

Revised edition 2023
Published in Great Britain by
Choc Lit
A Joffe Books company
www.choc-lit.com

First published in Great Britain in 2020

This paperback edition was first published
in Great Britain in 2023

This book is a work of fiction. Names, characters, businesses, organizations, places and events are either the product of the author's imagination or are used fictitiously. Any resemblance to actual persons, living or dead, events or locales is entirely coincidental. The spelling used is American English except where fidelity to the author's rendering of accent or dialect supersedes this.

Cover art by Nick Castle

ISBN: 978-1-78189-638-9

This one is for all the other cat lovers out there.

CHAPTER ONE

Dr. Sheila Didcott is working alone in the morgue. It's late, and the only sound is the heavy rain hammering the single window in the room, but she can't leave work just yet. A corpse has been brought in by an ambulance crew, and she's waiting for someone from Maple Valley Police Department to come take a look.

With her back to the contents of the zipped-up body bag, she selects her clean autopsy instruments: bone saw, forceps, scalpel, suture needles, rib cutter, and scissors. She lays them out on the steel tray in front of her and checks her watch with a deep sigh. It's almost ten o'clock on a cold Sunday night at the beginning of March.

Sheila's hoping she can refrigerate the body overnight and perform the autopsy tomorrow because she's itching to get home to her fiancé and slip into a hot bathtub to wash off the lingering smell of decomposition.

As she unties the elasticated band holding back her long red hair, the fly control unit on the wall above her head flickers on and off. She hears a high-pitched buzzing noise that doesn't last long. The unit has done its job. A large black fly drops to the floor. Sheila likes to keep the morgue clean, so she bends down to pick it up by its wing. As she does this, she hears someone cough.

She stands and looks toward the closed door. “Finally, they’re here,” she mutters.

She throws the fly into the medical waste container and takes the last sip of her lukewarm peppermint tea. She turns to the door and waits. But no one enters the morgue.

“What the . . . ?”

Sheila walks to the door and opens it, looking up the dark stairwell beyond. The morgue is next door to the police station and she’s in the basement. The stairwell’s single lightbulb failed months ago so she can’t see much, which is fine because she’s not afraid of the dark.

The stairwell is empty.

“Could’ve sworn I heard someone cough,” she murmurs.

Silence fills the room while she stands still, looking up and listening for footsteps.

There’s nothing.

She slowly releases the door handle, allowing the door to swing shut, but she doesn’t move. Something doesn’t feel right to her. The atmosphere has changed in here and the hairs on her arms stand on end.

A rustling noise behind her makes her blood run cold. She breaks out into a sweat. There’s no one in here but her and the corpse.

Sheila doesn’t believe in ghosts and she’s not afraid of the dead, but as she slowly turns around to face the noise of a zip being undone, she uncharacteristically screams.

The bag is open. The badly beaten body, almost unrecognizable as a human, is sitting up. And it’s staring at her.

CHAPTER TWO

It's early on Monday morning and already Dean Matheson's day is not going well. He slept through his alarm, and now he can't find his house keys anywhere. He's going to be late for his first day back in law enforcement at Maple Valley Police Department.

As he spins around, searching the living room for his keys, the doorbell rings. His stomach flips with nerves. The time has finally come to start the job he's always wanted. He walks to the hallway and opens the front door.

"Time to see what you're made of, Matheson."

Dean smiles as Detective Eva Valdez walks into his house. She's tall and slim with long brown hair and brown eyes. She can be quick to anger but this morning she looks amused.

He closes the front door behind her. "I've lost my keys. Can you see them anywhere?"

Eva casts a critical eye over him.

"What's the matter?" he asks.

"Aren't you a little overdressed?" she says. "You're a detective, not a bank manager."

He's wearing a black suit that he bought specially for the occasion. Detective Harry Jones, Dean's old mentor and colleague at MVPD, always wore a suit to work before he recently retired for the second time. Whereas Eva has mastered the smart but casual look in jeans and a shirt. As it's still winter, she's also wearing a waterproof jacket.

"I just want to make a good impression on my first day," he says. "Don't you?"

She raises her eyebrows. "Are you saying I'm underdressed?"

It's her first day too. They met in Colorado at the end of last year after working on a particularly messed up missing persons' case together while Dean was a private investigator and Eva worked at a local PD. Once that was over, Eva helped Dean return home to New Hampshire. He was wounded and couldn't manage the journey alone. She took a liking to the place and decided to stick around when she was offered a job at MVPD. Dean knows she has little reason to return to Colorado after everything that happened.

It's been two months since Dean left the hospital, so he's had plenty of time to recover, although most of that time has been spent trying not to tear open his stomach wound. After being shot twice in the same month — once in the stomach and once in the shoulder — he was ordered by his doctor to take things easy. That wasn't difficult as all his body wanted him to do was to catch up on sleep.

Today is their first day as partners. At thirty-two years old, Eva may be almost five years younger than him, but she's more experienced. Dean's first attempt at playing detective failed miserably so this time he's got something to prove, which only adds to his nerves.

"No, not at all," he says. He looks down at his suit. "Maybe I am overdressed. Should I change?"

She picks up his untouched coffee. "I'm not here to style you, Matheson. You have the time it takes me to drink this to get ready. Then I'm out of here, with or without you."

He runs upstairs to change into a pair of smart jeans. He keeps his pale blue shirt on, along with a dark blue tie, but he swaps his black suit jacket for a more relaxed one, which conceals his holstered weapon. Once changed, he spots his missing keys on the dresser and grabs them.

True to her word, he can hear Eva opening his front door to leave. He knows she has little patience. He runs downstairs and locks up behind them.

* * *

When they arrive at the police station, Dean has flashbacks of the last time he was here. It was at his leaving party, after New Hampshire's worst female serial killer had finally been convicted and sentenced. He thinks about how he'd made the decision to leave his job as a police officer to become a private investigator once the trial was over. That adventure lasted just over a year, thanks to the devastating case he worked on in Lone Creek, Colorado. He never dreamed he'd be back at MVPD so soon, and definitely not as a detective.

He and Eva walk through the front desk to the offices behind. Jenny from dispatch greets him with a wave and an enthusiastic smile from her desk before approaching them. Dean notices she's in uniform.

"When did this happen?" he asks, pleasantly surprised. He was always impressed by how professional Jenny was in her previous role. She even saved Detective Miller from dying once and if that doesn't show professionalism, he doesn't know what does. He knows she'll make a great cop.

"While you were away, I took all my tests and graduated from the academy," she says.

"That's great. But why didn't you tell me before now?"

"I wanted to surprise you."

She seems pleased with herself, and rightfully so. She's young, only in her mid-twenties, and Dean knows she comes from a poor background. Her father was in prison for most of her childhood for beating her mother so severely that Jenny and her brother were young carers. He eventually got himself killed in a prison brawl. Her brother turned to alcohol to cope and eventually moved away, leaving Jenny with sole responsibility for looking after her mother. Despite that, she was determined to achieve something.

"Well, I look forward to working with you, Officer Lawson."

She blushes and returns to her desk.

Captain Brown appears from his office and approaches Dean and Eva. He shakes their hands. "Good to have you back, Matheson. Welcome to the team, Valdez."

"Thanks," says Eva.

"These will be your desks."

Dean realizes he has his old desk back. He doesn't know whether that's a good thing or not. A lot went down while he was an officer, so he was hoping for a different desk to signal a fresh start but, whatever, he'll deal with it. Eva's desk is opposite his; their computer monitors are back-to-back.

"I may have to send you out on your first job already," says Brown. He checks his cell phone. "I'm just waiting for Sergeant Dalkin to update me on something that happened last night. But in the meantime, you have all the usual paperwork to sign because it's your first day."

Dean nods. "Let's get the paperwork out of the way."

"Not yet," says Eva. "First things first, where's the coffee machine?"

Jenny offers to show Eva the kitchen facilities as Captain Brown returns to his office. When they've gone, Dean looks around and spots Carl Miller arriving. He's not looking forward to working with him again. At least Miller's been demoted from detective to officer. Dean knows that couldn't have gone down well with him.

He's shocked at how much weight Miller's lost since they last saw each other. According to Detective Jones, he had gastric bypass surgery soon after his heart attack. He looks much older too, with newly sagging jowls. It doesn't look like the weight loss has made him any healthier — his skin is pale and mottled and his eyes have heavy bags under them. He looks strange in a police uniform. Too old for it. Dean's used to seeing him in a cheap brown suit.

He figures it's time they bury the hatchet and try to get on, so he cautiously approaches him. He's hit by a strong smell of nicotine. "Hey, Miller. How's things?"

Miller's eyes narrow. "Well, well, well. Look what the cat dragged in. I hear you got yourself shot the minute you left town with your tail between your legs. Twice, in fact."

Dean shakes his head. The urge to punch this jackass is overwhelming. Instead, he remains calm. "I did, yeah, but I didn't die, unfortunately for you. I got your job instead."

Miller's face reddens.

Dean spots Officer Marty Swan arriving for his shift. Marty stops to chat on his way past but he must notice the tension between Dean and Miller because he closes his mouth and stands still.

Miller leans closer to Dean, making sure the captain can't hear them from his office. "Listen, asshole. Captain Brown's going to regret what he did to me and I'm going to get my job back, so don't get too comfortable playing detective. You'll be back to giving road safety classes to elementary kids before you know it."

Marty whistles at the put-down. He looks at Dean for a reaction but he won't get one. Dean has plenty of insults he could throw back at the guy but he decides against it. They have to work in the same department so he's determined not to let Miller ruin this job for him.

"I see you guys have picked up where you left off," says Marty, trying to make light of the situation.

Eva walks up to them and hands Dean a mug of coffee while sipping her own.

"Where's mine, honey?" asks Miller. He talks to her chest.

She looks at Dean with raised eyebrows, and then she looks at Miller. "Did you just call me honey?"

Miller rolls his eyes. "Oh great, you're one of those easily offended snowflakes. Just what we need."

Dean tries not to smile at Miller's mistake. He holds out his hand as Eva gives him her coffee. He's half-expecting her to pull her weapon. Instead, she pulls out a small notepad and pen from her back pocket and reads aloud what she's writing. "Day one at MVPD. March 4th, 2019. 9:30 a.m.," says Eva, as she writes. "Officer Miller demands I make him coffee and calls me *honey*. Incident witnessed by Detective Dean Matheson and . . ." She looks over at Marty.

"Officer Marty Swan, at your service, ma'am."

They've met briefly before, at the hospital before Dean was released, but his name must have escaped Eva.

"Thank you, Marty." She continues reading aloud what she's writing. "I was made to feel uncomfortable because of the gender stereotype Officer Miller was projecting onto me, especially because it was in front of our male co-workers and he was talking to my breasts at the time."

"What the hell are you doing?" asks Miller, with a stupid smirk.

Eva pockets her notepad and pen. "I'm keeping a log of every inappropriate comment you make so that when I sue you, my attorney will have a full list of examples to cite in court. The more examples I have, the more money I'll be awarded. So you keep going, *honey*. I need a new car this year."

She takes her coffee from Dean and walks over to her new desk.

Dean turns to Miller. "You better be careful. The last man who treated her like a piece of meat bled out from his groin."

Marty whistles again and crosses his legs.

Miller looks incredulous as he turns away. "You two are batshit crazy."

Dean smiles to himself. It's going to be fun working with Eva.

Marty leans in and whispers, "Are you for real? She actually shot someone in the balls?"

"Yeah, he was trying to rape her," says Dean. "I wanted to warn you, actually. You can't make your stupid jokes anymore, Marty. She'll rip you a new one."

Marty considers it for a moment. "Is she single? Please tell me she's single?"

Dean looks at him. "Marty, you're married."

"Actually, no, I'm not. We separated while you were away playing Magnum PI." He grins. "I'm single and ready to mingle, my friend!"

Dean shakes his head in exasperation. "I'm so pleased for your wife. I always knew she could do better."

Marty laughs like it's the funniest thing he's ever heard. "Welcome back, man. I've missed you around here. You're the only person I've ever met who's unluckier than me."

Dean watches as Marty walks over to Eva and holds out his hand.

"It's a real pleasure to work with you, Detective Valdez. I hear you stopped our friend here from dying out there in Colorado. That's a real shame but I won't hold it against you." He laughs at his own joke.

Dean cringes. He knows how Marty normally finishes that sentence . . . "Unless you want me to." Thankfully, Marty might have grown up over the last year because he doesn't say it. Maybe he's heeding Dean's warning.

"Thank you, Officer," says Eva. She doesn't invite further conversation. Instead, she stands up and checks her cell phone. Marty takes the hint and heads over to dispatch.

As Dean sits down to turn on his PC for the first time, Captain Brown emerges from his office again.

"Matheson and Valdez, you need to get to the hospital. Sheila's having a problem with a corpse."

Dean looks at Eva and smiles. "We have our first case."

CHAPTER THREE

Danny Mallory falls hard onto his knees and cries out in pain as the gravel from the playground tears open his pants and scrapes off the top layer of his skin. He sits down, stunned. Just seconds before, he was standing up, watching some of the other kids playing catch. Big, fat tears well in his eyes as he tries really hard to hold them back.

Within seconds, his classmates circle him and laugh. This isn't how he wanted Monday recess to go. He looks up at the boy who pushed him in the back: Johnny Laverne. He's smiling like a wolf and standing way too close.

"Hit him, Johnny!" shouts April.

Danny's surprised as he thought she was his friend.

"Stand up and fight properly," demands Johnny.

Danny really doesn't want to stand up. He knows what will happen next but he doesn't know how to stop it. Although Johnny's the same age as him — seven — he's taller and meaner. That's why the push stunned him so much. Danny looks down at his knees and can see blood. They sting so bad.

Suddenly, the crowd parts, and his favorite teacher pushes her way toward him.

"Johnny Laverne!" she shouts. "Go and stand outside my classroom right this minute!"

She pushes Johnny in his back, hard, and he almost goes flying himself. But because he's heavier than Danny, he's just able to maintain his balance. Johnny walks away, looking like he wants to report her for pushing him. Teachers don't normally do that around here.

Danny smiles up at her, more relieved than she'll ever know.

"Everyone else, get back to class and open your books," she says. "You better have read at least five pages by the time I return."

They do what she says and scatter. She's a strict teacher who even shouts at their parents when they're running late for drop-offs or pick-ups, but Danny's not scared. Since she started as a substitute teacher she's always looked after him and some of the others. The ones who get picked on by other kids or by their parents. In his opinion, she's the best substitute teacher they've ever had.

She crouches down next to him and rubs his back. "Are you okay, Danny-boy? Do you need some candy?"

Danny wants to cry again, but not because he's scared this time. He just doesn't understand how his teacher can be so good to him when his parents aren't. He nods his head. "Yes, please."

She pulls him off the ground and hugs him to her. "Don't worry, Danny. I'll take good care of you. If anyone ever hurts you, you just let me know. Deal?"

He smiles into her neck. "Deal."

CHAPTER FOUR

When they eventually track Sheila down at Mercy Hospital, Dean notices she's visibly agitated, pacing back and forth in the hallway and talking to herself. She ties her long red hair into a ponytail and then shakes her hands out, as if she's anxious. He's never seen her like this before. As a medical examiner, she's usually calm and controlled. She doesn't even notice when they approach.

"Hey, Sheila," he says.

She jumps. Then she laughs nervously. "Am I glad to see you two. Last night was insane. Steve was here until he got another call-out, but I just can't relax. How did I get it so wrong?"

Eva takes her by the arm and leads her to one of the visitor chairs in the hallway. They both sit. "What happened?" she asks.

Sheila takes a deep breath. "Okay, so this young woman was brought in last night, at around eight-thirty, just as I was hoping to finish up. The ambulance crew didn't know anything about her. They found her by the side of the road near that big new church just past the woods." She turns to Dean. "You know the one I mean?"

Dean had noticed it a couple of weeks ago. He's driven past a few times since he got out of the hospital. It's just past Frankie's Diner, on the edge of town. You wouldn't know it was a church from the outside but you can also just kind of tell. It's called the Hope Center. Frankie told him all about it.

"I know the one," he says. "Frankie said it's for some kind of cult and it's getting popular. He said they sometimes stop by his diner after their sessions and talk about 'happy clappy crap'."

Sheila doesn't laugh. "Well, this poor woman was badly bruised all over her head. Like, seriously bad. Her face was black, blue, and yellow. She had lumps all over the place, as well as swelling so bad she looked like a watermelon. Her face was too big for her body. The ambulance crew weren't even called out to her; they were just driving back to the hospital and noticed her body. They tried to revive her at the scene and got a weak pulse, but she slipped away in the back of the ambulance before they even started the engine." She pauses to take a deep breath. "So, because she passed away, the paramedics were told to bring her straight to me. I checked her clothes for ID, but she wasn't carrying any. She had nothing on her at all. Eventually, I bagged her up and I was waiting for someone from your department to come and see her when . . ." She hesitates. "Well, when she woke up on my table."

Dean leans forward. "Wait, what? What do you mean she woke up?"

Eva visibly shivers. "You can't be serious? She's *alive*?"

Sheila nods, wide-eyed. "She sat up on my slab and she unzipped the body bag. I think I lost ten years of my life in a split second."

Dean and Eva share a look.

"I know what you're thinking," says Sheila. "I should've seen that she was still alive, but her lips and fingernails were pale when she arrived and her injuries were so severe, I wasn't expecting her to have survived them."

"And the paramedics told you she was dead," says Dean. "You'd expect them to be right about something as serious as that. This isn't your fault, Sheila. She must have some kind of weird condition."

Sheila nods. "That's what the doctor here said. There's a rare condition where some people's pulse is so faint, it's undetectable. She's seen it once before with a man, years ago. They didn't actually bag him up before they realized he was still alive, though." She hugs her arms to her chest. "Oh, God. That woman's going to have nightmares about waking up like that for the rest of her life. So will I. Anyway, she's been admitted, but her condition is . . . well, strange. I had to get out of her room. She was creeping me out."

"Can we see her?" asks Eva.

Sheila hesitantly leads them into the woman's room. As Dean enters, he's shocked at what he sees. The woman is sitting up in bed, leaning back against the white hospital pillows and facing the TV on the wall opposite. Her whole head looks badly swollen, like it's bandaged even though it's not. Her face is so battered he can barely locate her eyes among the bruising. Her dark hair is greasy and scraped back. She doesn't move when they enter.

Sheila steps up to her and touches her hand. "Hey, sweetie. These are the detectives I was telling you about. They're here to help you, okay?"

The woman barely nods her head but she still winces with the pain of it. Dean thinks she must be really thin under those covers because there's not much of an outline to her body. He tries to age her but it's impossible.

"Hi, I'm Detective Matheson and this is Detective Valdez. We just need to ask you a few questions, then you can get back to resting, okay?"

She doesn't respond but she is watching him. He thinks her eyes are brown but the left one is fused shut and the other is swollen, so he's not certain.

"First of all, can you tell us your name?" he asks.

She slowly shakes her head, but it's barely perceptible. "I can't remember." Her voice is croaky.

He's not surprised she can't remember anything. She must be on a lot of pain medication and the beating could have affected her memory.

"That's okay," says Eva. "How about you pick a name that you'd like us to call you for now, until your memory clears a little?"

The woman appears to think about it. "My favorite singer's called Taylor. I like that name."

Eva smiles at her. "Perfect."

Dean starts to wonder if this woman is more likely a teenager. "What's the last thing you remember, Taylor?" he asks.

She licks her dry lips, so Dean hands her a cup of water with a straw in it from her nightstand. She takes a sip and gives it back to him.

"I remember feeling like I was in a sleeping bag, almost being suffocated."

Sheila quietly groans and turns away.

Dean feels for her. He knows she'll always blame herself for mistakenly bagging and tagging this girl. Her usual clients are dead by the time they get to her, so she never gets to know them. She never gets to know their back story. He envies her in a way. Policing involves trying to build up a picture of the victim and their lives, so you always get to know them and their family, whether they're alive or not. It makes him think about Jodie Lawrence and the appalling way she died in Lone Creek. He dreams about her sometimes, about the lengths she had to go to in order to escape her horrific situation.

"I pulled it open and sat up. That's when she screamed." She points to Sheila. "Then I went dizzy and passed out until I woke up here."

Eva leans in. "What about before you woke up in the room with Sheila? Can you remember what you were doing up by the church?"

Taylor gasps. "What? Where was I?"

Eva looks at Dean, clearly worried, before continuing. "You were found by the side of the road, outside the church. Do you remember what you were doing there?"

Taylor starts crying and looks truly terrified. "Oh my God!" She scrambles to get out of bed but she can't move well enough yet. "You've got to get me out of here!" She starts screaming.

"Why?" says Dean, quickly moving toward her. "Taylor? Who did this to you?"

She stills for a minute as she tries to think, before turning to Dean. "I . . . I can't remember."

She starts hyperventilating. Eva runs to get assistance.

"Calm down," says Dean. "It's okay. You're safe here."

She's not listening. A doctor runs in and administers a shot of something. Within a minute, Taylor is placid and drowsy. She collapses back onto the bed.

Sheila's trying to hold it together but Dean can tell she's upset. She's shaking and she can't stand still.

He turns to the doctor. Her ID tag shows her name is Jean Armstrong. "Is she going to survive her injuries?"

The doctor looks at him. "Not if you don't leave her alone. She's obviously in no condition for whatever you said to her. She's not strong enough for questioning, not if it's going to invoke this kind of response. She's still traumatized and hasn't even had a psych evaluation yet."

Sheila steps forward. "They were just trying to find out what happened to her, Jean. The sooner we know who did this, the safer she'll be. Earlier, you told me she's experiencing amnesia?"

"Right," says Dr. Armstrong. "It's likely post-traumatic amnesia. She also has internal injuries and swelling of the brain. I'm hopeful it will clear when she's had time to heal but she'll be in here a while."

"I hate to ask," says Dean. "But was she sexually assaulted?"

The doctor looks uncertain. "She let me perform a rape kit and there's evidence she's had penetrative sex recently, but

I couldn't say how recent and there was no semen present. There's no bruising around the area but she is bruised up and down her legs. They're older bruises though, not related to last night's attack."

Eva looks at him. "It would be worth checking whether any local sex offenders have been released recently."

Dean nods in agreement, happy to take any direction from her.

Dr. Armstrong looks at him, concerned. "If you think she's at risk of a follow-up attack I can keep security nearby."

"I think that would be a good idea," says Dean. "In your opinion, was she beaten with some kind of instrument?"

The doctor looks down at Taylor, who's sleeping now, and they all follow her gaze. It's an uncomfortable scene.

"If they had used some kind of weapon, there would be lacerations and blood."

"I agree," says Sheila. "This was done by hand. It looks like the kind of beating that isn't planned in advance, because they usually involve a weapon of some kind. This is the result of someone losing their shit unexpectedly and fast." She stops for a second. "Whoever did this has serious anger issues and is extremely dangerous."

"Are we looking for a male or female?" asks Dean. "*Could* a female do this much damage with her fists?"

The two doctors share a look before Sheila says, "Anything's possible. But the kind of rage that caused this—" she gestures to Taylor "—is more likely to be displayed by males, in my experience."

Dr. Armstrong nods thoughtfully. "It would be easy to assume it was a man because of the damage caused, but I'm reserving judgment because we can't be sure."

Dean should feel the excitement of having a new case, but looking at Taylor's injuries just makes him feel sick. "Okay, thanks."

He's relieved to follow Eva out of the hospital and into the cold, fresh air.

CHAPTER FIVE

On the ride back from the hospital, Dean and Eva are both silent at first. The only noise is the hard rain that's pelting against the windows. The weather has been like this for three days straight, and it's looking like the sun isn't going to make an appearance any time soon.

Dean wonders how someone could beat another human being so badly.

"I don't even know what to say," says Eva, keeping her eyes on the road as she drives.

He looks at her. "I know. It's crazy how someone can hate another human being that much. He must've assumed she was dead and just left her in the street, like roadkill."

"Nothing she could've done warranted that attack," she says.

Dean thinks about how hysterical Taylor became when they mentioned the church. "We need to go to the church and see if anyone from the congregation was around when it happened. There could be witnesses. I mean, she wasn't found that late at night."

Eva agrees. "She seemed pretty shocked when she found out that's where she was discovered. Maybe she's a regular there herself."

The exhaust on Eva's car noisily splutters and Dean sees black fumes spitting out behind them.

Eva shakes her head. "This car's a piece of crap!"

"Where did you buy it?" he asks.

"From a used car dealership your pal Frankie recommended to me. It was the cheapest they had."

Dean resists the urge to tell her you get what you pay for. He knows she's broke.

"I wish George was here," she says. "He'd be able to fix it. He's great with cars." George Hobbs is Eva's foster dad. He still lives in Colorado.

Suddenly Eva accelerates. "What the hell was that?" she yells, panicking.

"What?" Dean looks behind them and spots a clown standing at the side of the road next to a bicycle with yellow balloons tied to its handlebars. It's waving at them and laughing. "It's just a guy dressed as a clown. There must be a carnival coming to town." He looks at Eva, but she's shaking her head.

"No way. I do not do clowns!" She shudders.

He laughs. "Eva, slow down. It's just a guy in fancy dress. What's wrong? You're not scared, are you?"

"Of course I'm scared! Who does that? Who dresses as a figure from people's nightmares and stands by the side of the road waving at them?"

Dean's not too surprised by her reaction. In Colorado, she had let on she was afraid of the dark. "I thought you told me you loved horror movies?"

She looks at him. "They're in my TV, Matheson. Not in my damn town!"

They pass a large billboard by the side of the road advertising a new year-round extreme haunted house attraction that's opening up nearby.

"You gotta be kidding me," Eva whispers, as she slows the car to read it.

Dean tries to read it all. It says it's opening tonight, in the women's correctional facility he used to work at.

"The prison closed down?" he says, surprised. "I know it was marked for closure years ago but I never thought they'd actually do it."

Eva looks at him again as she speeds up. "Really? That's what you take from this? Not that this means there's going to be hundreds of freaks in town dressed as clowns, demons, and who knows what?" She shakes her head. "I can't believe you talked me into moving here. I would never have come if I knew this kind of thing would open."

He can't help but find her reaction amusing.

"The people who run these places take horror to the extreme!" she continues. "They don't just jump out at you and say *boo*! They do everything just short of murdering you."

He laughs. "Come on! They can't do anything illegal."

She rolls her eyes at him. "Oh my God, Matheson. You're so naive!"

He looks away, keeping his opinions to himself. As they approach his side of town, he checks the time. "Can you drop me at my house before you head back to the station?"

"I guess. Why?"

"I've got a realtor coming to look at my house."

She looks across at him. "Really? You're selling up?"

"Maybe. This realtor approached me, saying she's got young families looking for a home in my area." He shrugs. "I thought it wouldn't hurt to see how much I could get for it. I mean, it's just me now and I don't need a three-bedroomed house. I don't even need a backyard now Rocky's gone to spend his retirement living with Jones."

He thinks about Rocky, his unofficial K9 partner. He's missed the huge rottweiler these last couple of months. It still feels strange being home alone. Dean's house is full of reminders of things he'd rather forget.

He unbuckles his seatbelt as they pull up outside his house. "Thanks. When I'm done here, I'll take my car and meet you at the church in about an hour?"

"I'm going to swing by Frankie's for lunch so meet me there," she says. "You want me to pick anything up for you?"

When Eva first moved here, she stayed with Dean, but only for two weeks. He wasn't surprised when Frankie almost immediately offered her the apartment above his diner. It had been empty for over a year and he needed the extra income. The only problem is neither Dean nor Frankie told Eva who had lived there before her: Lizzie Glover. New Hampshire's notorious female serial killer.

Frankie didn't want to put off a prospective tenant and Dean didn't want to spook her, plus he's hoping Lizzie will never return to Maple Valley. The trail has gone cold since she escaped from the secure psychiatric unit just before Christmas and now the FBI is officially in charge of the case. Maple Valley PD has been told to leave it to them. Part of Dean wants to find her before they do and make her pay for what she's put everyone through, but he has to admit it would be a relief if the Feds found her and dealt with the problem.

"Yeah," he says. "Grab me a club sandwich and a decaf coffee. I won't be long."

She grimaces at the word *decaf* and he watches her drive away. Her car's exhaust appears to be fine now.

Within minutes of getting back, Dean's doorbell rings. He opens the door and Camille Richards, the realtor, looks up at him. She's petite and blonde with blue eyes and a friendly smile. Dean thinks she's around his age, mid to late thirties.

"Hi again, Mr. Matheson." She holds out her hand and he shakes it.

"Call me Dean. Come on in."

She walks into his living room and looks around. "Thanks for letting me take a look at your house. Like I said when I knocked on your door the other day, I have a lot of interest in this part of town right now so I've been trying to find people willing to sell." She smiles at him and removes her coat.

"No problem," he says. "I've got to be honest upfront, though. I'm not sure if I want to sell. I'm just testing the water to see if it'll be worth it."

She leans in and touches his arm. "That's what they all say, but once I tell people how much their house is worth, they quickly become serious."

He laughs. "I bet. Want me to show you around?"

"Sure."

He leads her around the house, answering her questions as they go. He tries to hide the damage Rocky made to one of the doors, back when Dean used to try to keep him out of the bedroom.

Camille measures the rooms and says all the things he'd expect from a realtor: good-sized bedrooms, bathroom needs updating, great plot, and so on, before they find themselves back in the living room and her questions turn more personal. "So what do you do for a living if you don't mind me asking?"

"I'm a detective at MVPD." He gets a kick out of saying that. It's still new to him and he's proud he finally made it.

Her eyes light up. "Really? How long have you been a cop?"

"I was a police officer first, then a private investigator, and today's my first day as a detective."

"Wow, you lead an interesting life!"

He smiles. He notices she doesn't have a New Hampshire accent, but he can't place hers. "How about you? Have you always been a realtor?"

"No, I've done all sorts. But I like this job. I can work my own hours and I work from home most of the time. Although it's a pretty boring job compared to yours."

"Trust me," says Dean, "sometimes boring is good."

"I guess." She laughs.

He checks his watch. "Sorry I can't offer you a drink but I've got to get back to work. Have you seen everything you need to see?"

She looks at her notes. "I have for now. I'll need to come back to take photos if you decide to go ahead and list it for sale." She pulls her coat on. "I'll give you a call when I've done some research and come up with a listing price."

"Great."

Once she's got her things ready to go, she looks up at him and reaches for his hand to shake again. "It was a pleasure, Detective Matheson." She smiles at him in a way that suggests she's interested, holding onto his hand slightly longer than necessary.

He wasn't expecting that. He walks her to the front door and watches her drive away. He's not really thinking about dating right now, he has enough on his plate with his new job. Besides, he doesn't have a great track record with successful relationships.

CHAPTER SIX

Eva's seated by the large glass window in Frankie's Diner, waiting for Dean. The club sandwich she bought him has gone cold, and she's eager to get to the church to interview people. She's thinking about leaving without him when the waitress comes over and refills her coffee cup. "Thanks, Rachel," she says. "It's so dark outside again today. Does this weather ever make you depressed?"

Rachel sighs. "All the time. You'll get used to our weather once you've been here a while though. You'll love it in the fall. It kind of makes up for this." She gestures to the rain hitting the window.

Eva doesn't know whether she'll still be here in the fall. She's finding Maple Valley a little dull so far and if this haunted attraction takes off, she'll never be able to relax. She curses herself for watching so many horror movies over the years. She can't seem to resist them, even though they give her nightmares.

"Is there a movie theater around here?" she asks.

"There used to be, but it closed down about four years ago. The nearest one is about sixty miles away now."

"That's a shame."

"So what's it like working with Dean?" asks Rachel. "I bet he's nervous today. I was so happy for him when he told me he was offered the position." Eva knows Rachel used to date Dean's older brother, well before he took his own life.

She looks at her watch. "Well, he's not great at time-keeping so far. I'm early for everything, so it's annoying. I guess time will tell whether he makes a good detective."

Her cell phone rings and her foster dad's name flashes up. "Hey, George. How are you?" she says as she watches the parking lot.

Rachel leaves to serve some customers.

"Hey, yourself. I'm not good," he says. "But you already know that. An old man shouldn't be living alone hundreds of miles away from his only remaining family. When can I move in with you?"

He's been asking her this for weeks. She doesn't mind him moving here but she doesn't want him to live with her. She's thirty-two years old and recently widowed. She needs her own space and her own life.

"I've already told you, I'm living in a sleazy one-bedroom apartment over a tacky diner. There's no room for you here yet."

Frankie Lorenzo, the owner of the diner and her apartment, is walking past with his hands full of dirty dishes. Unfortunately, he overhears her comment. "Sleazy? That's the thanks I get!" he mutters, shaking his head.

She'll have to apologize to him later, he's a super sensitive person. It's not really a sleazy apartment, it's just a little dated and could desperately do with a make-over.

"Then I'll stay in a hotel for a few months," says George. "There must be hotels in New Hampshire?"

"George, I'm not having you live out of a hotel room. I said I'd try to find you a place but I need more time. I'm busy right now."

"Okay, okay," he says. "Just don't forget about me out here, all alone. I could fall down the stairs and no one would find me for weeks, you know. I'd be just a puddle on the floor dripping through to the downstairs apartment before anyone noticed I was missing."

"I'm sure your lady friend would notice you missing before then." She smiles. She knows he has a casual girlfriend, a sixty-year-old neighbor from the apartment next door to his. George never admits it because he probably thinks Eva would feel he was cheating on her foster mom, Mary, who passed away a few years ago.

"Are you kidding me? I don't have the energy for a lady friend. I'm too old," he says. "Anyway, tell me about your first day at MVPD. I was looking at their website earlier but it's not very up-to-date. You're not even listed as an employee yet!"

Eva laughs. "Give them a chance, George." She spots Dean's car entering the parking lot. He blasts his horn. "I've got to go. I'll fill you in later."

"Of course you're too busy to speak to your old man."

She smiles as he ends the call. She knows he's only teasing her. He's not weak or frail — quite the opposite in fact. Until a month ago he ran a soup kitchen for the homeless and he's still got his wits about him, but she knows he's lonely. It does play on her mind.

She pays Rachel, who passes her a fresh decaf coffee, and then she runs out to see Dean, pulling her hood over her hair as she goes.

"You're late," she says, as he winds down his window and smiles at her. She passes him his sandwich and coffee.

"Yeah, sorry about that," he says. "I'll eat this on the way. Let's go."

Eva gets in her car and follows Dean out of the parking lot.

* * *

When they arrive at the church, there's only one other car in the parking lot: a dark blue Ford pickup truck. It looks brand new. Presumably, as it's the only car here, it belongs to the owner of this place. Eva gets out of her car, rubs her cold hands together, and looks up at the building. It sits under thick, dark rain clouds, and the only thing that makes it different from every other building around here is that it has a new red sign on it that says the Hope Center.

"This place is huge," she says, as Dean approaches. "Why would they need so much space? I heard on the news that church attendance declines year on year."

"They must run a lot of community activities," he says. "Churches have to adapt, I guess."

"Well, whoever built this has some money, that's for sure."

Eva looks around and grabs Dean's arm as she spots a yellow balloon tied to a railing on the other side of the parking lot.

Dean puts his hand on hers. "What's the matter?"

She nods to the balloon. "Go and get it," she says. "Keep it inflated so we can get fingerprints off it."

He frowns. "Why would we need prints off it?"

She turns to him. "In case one of those clowns turns out to be the person who beat Taylor."

"Eva, they're just promoting the new attraction." He dutifully retrieves it anyway and, as he tries to hand it to her, she backs away.

"I don't want it!" she says. "Put it in your car. I bet you fifty bucks we're going to need that at some point."

She can tell Dean wants to say she's being ridiculous, but he wisely keeps his mouth shut and does what she says. In her experience, if it's related to clowns, it's trouble.

They head to the building's large glass entrance and Dean holds the door open for her. She walks up to a reception desk and rings the bell. The inside is as impressive as the outside, and it's warm. Everything is pristine and there's a distinct new carpet smell. There are a couple of comfortable break-out areas, with a small coffee shop and children's play area nearby, with lots of doors suggesting individual rooms behind them.

The bulletin board next to the reception is filled with children's drawings and posters for exercise classes and leisure activities. If Eva wanted to, she could take a writing class on a Monday night, a flute class on Tuesdays, a yoga class on Wednesdays . . . There's a lot going on.

She hears someone open a door behind the reception desk and clear their throat. A tall white male is standing there. He looks like he should be in a men's fragrance advert with his strong bone structure and thick head of blond hair. He appears happy to see them, with a welcoming smile. She's instantly suspicious.

"Good morning! Or is it afternoon now?" he says. "I've been so busy I've lost track of time. How can I help you?"

"Hi. I'm Detective Valdez and this is Detective Matheson." She doesn't bother flashing her badge and she notices Dean discreetly sliding his back into his pocket, following her lead. "We'd like to ask you some questions about an incident that occurred outside last night."

The man looks concerned. "Of course. Let me come over to you." He walks around the large desk and joins them in the lobby area. "I hope no one was hurt?"

Dean points to the chairs nearby. "Let's take a seat." When they're all seated, he turns to the man. "Can I get your name?"

"Jacob Andrews, but I prefer Jake. I'm the owner and manager here. We have lots of part-time employees and volunteers but I'm here more than anyone else."

"Does that mean you live here?" asks Eva.

"Yes, I have an apartment upstairs."

"Would you have heard any commotion out front, on the road?" asks Dean. "Is your apartment near the front of the building?"

Jake appears to think about it. "My apartment does overlook the front of the building, but I don't remember hearing anything. What actually happened? And what time are we talking about?"

Eva isn't sure how much to tell him, but he seems genuinely concerned. She takes over from Dean. "A female was found outside, in the road, just after eight-thirty. She was in a critical condition."

"I'm sorry to hear that," says Jake. "Was she hit by a car?"

"No. Actually, she was badly beaten by someone."

He looks shocked. "Beaten? I thought Maple Valley wasn't that kind of place. Is she okay now?"

"She's in the hospital, but she's not doing well. She doesn't remember why she was outside your church, so we were hoping to find some witnesses."

Jake runs a hand through his hair. "I didn't hear anything, but I would've been down here tidying up. Sunday's our busiest day and our last activity ends at eight. It was a karate class for the kids. They were pretty loud and wound up when they left."

Dean looks at her. He must be thinking the same thing. There would have been lots of witnesses leaving this place just before Taylor was found by the EMTs.

"I have to ask," says Eva, "do you have anyone who could vouch for you? That you were here, tidying?"

Jake doesn't hesitate. "No, I'm afraid not. Obviously, everyone would have seen me here until the end of the class because I locked up after the last person left at about eight-fifteen. But after that, I was alone. I took a shower before settling down in front of my laptop to work. The sound of the shower probably blocked out the sirens."

"There weren't any sirens," she says. "She was found by a passing ambulance. We'll need you to get us a list of everyone who attended that class. Someone could've seen something on their way to their vehicles, or on their way home."

Jake nods. "Of course. That won't be a problem."

"Also, do you have any CCTV anywhere?"

He rubs his face. "Not yet. I mean, I've got the cameras installed but they're not live yet. There was a disagreement about the price originally quoted, so I'm currently negotiating with the security firm. They must think a place like this has money to burn so they're trying to pull a fast one."

"That's a shame," she says. He could be lying of course. She stands. "Thanks for your help. We may be back at some point."

Dean and Jake follow her lead.

Jake holds out his hand. When she shakes it, she feels something. Some tiny spark that she doesn't want to believe is attraction. He's the opposite of her late husband, but she gets a good vibe from him. He appears to be genuine and his good looks don't hurt.

She passes him her number. "If you hear anyone talking about it, please get in touch."

"I will. By the way, we're not a church."

Eva raises her eyebrows. "You're not?"

"No. It's a common assumption, and I can see why people would think that." He smiles. "But I'm not religious and the purpose of this place isn't to study the bible or anything like that. We're here for educational and recreational purposes."

She looks him in the eye. "Good to know."

She follows Dean out of the building.

CHAPTER SEVEN

After his first day at work, Dean has a joint retirement party for Detective Jones and Rocky to attend. It was Marty's idea to include Rocky seeing as he's retired too, thanks to his recent arthritis diagnosis. It's being held at the Tavern; the closest bar to the police department and therefore everyone's favorite place for drinks.

It took Dean a while to convince Eva to come along because she's not a sociable person by nature, but when she heard Sheila was going, she finally agreed. Dean knows from speaking to his friend and sergeant, Steve Dalkin, that Sheila's enjoyed getting to know Eva. They've even had her over to their house for dinner a couple of times. He's relieved she's settling into life in Maple Valley so well.

He pulls into the parking lot. His headlights illuminate the tacky blue and red balloons tied around the Tavern's doorway. He snorts. "How original."

Someone pulls up next to him and Dean spots Detective Jones. Jones may be retired but Dean still considers his first name to be detective. He doesn't think he could ever bring himself to call him Harry. It just doesn't suit him.

"Hey. Good to see you," says Jones as he gets out of the driver's side. "Is Rocky going to be okay inside? A lot of people are coming tonight so it could get noisy."

"Are you kidding me?" says Dean. "He'll love the attention." Dean peers into Jones' car and hears Rocky bark from the backseat. He hasn't seen the dog in three weeks so he's nervous. Rocky can obviously see him as he's starting to scratch the inside of the door.

"Let's bring him out before I've got no door left," says Jones.

Dean crouches down, ready. When Jones opens the car door Rocky carefully jumps down to the ground. His arthritis must be hurting him as he used to be a lot quicker. Somehow Dean had forgotten how large he was. His torso is the shape of a barrel and his head is huge.

Rocky stands where he lands and eyes Dean without moving. After a minute's hesitation, he wags his tail and barks. Then he lunges for him.

Dean has just seconds to consider how painful this is going to be before Rocky flattens him with his body. He's pushed back awkwardly against his own car and his face is covered by Rocky's huge tongue.

"Whatever aftershave you're wearing, it sure works!" says Jones, laughing.

Dean struggles to stand up. "Hey, boy. It's been a while."

He can't help feeling guilty that he sent Rocky to live out his last year or two with Jones. Rocky started showing signs of aging on their last assignment, and when the veterinarian told him he needed to live a quiet life for his final years, Dean instantly thought of Jones, who not only retired recently but also lost his wife at Christmas. He reasoned they could keep each other company.

"You're getting me all teary-eyed over here," says Jones.

He's much more in touch with his feelings since Barbara passed away and, now he's retired, Rocky's almost all he has. Jones has coped better than Dean expected, but he suspects he's putting on a brave face in public.

When Rocky's satisfied with the attention he's received from Dean, he sits next to his new master.

"So, come on!" says Jones. "Tell me how your first day as a detective went."

Dean smiles. "It's been interesting. We've had an attempted homicide already."

Jones leans forward. "Tell me more."

Dean fills him in with the short version of his day before changing the subject. "Anyway, how have you been?"

Jones sighs. "It's quiet at home without Barb. Thank God for Rocky, that's all I can say. Taking him out for walks keeps me fit but he's not one for the cop shows on TV. And I'm probably talking to him too much." He pauses. "I miss her, Dean."

Dean feels for him. When you've been married to someone all your adult life it must be terrible when they go before you. Even worse when they're murdered. But Jones is only approaching seventy this year. He's too young to give up on life.

Something Eva told him earlier springs to mind. "Are you in the market for a roommate?"

Jones looks wary. "I've already taken your dog in. Are you telling me *you* want to move in next? I'm not a damn homeless shelter, Matheson!"

Dean smiles. "Not me. Eva said her dad's desperate to move out here to be closer to her. How about he stays with you until he finds a place? I'm sure he'd pay his way."

Jones thinks about it for a second. "What if we don't hit it off? How do I get rid of him?"

"I've never met him but he was a foster carer and now he volunteers, so he's got to be a stand-up guy."

"What did he do for a proper job before that?"

"I think Eva said he was in the military. I'm not sure of the details."

Jones looks impressed. "Ex-military? So he'd be neat. I'm not cleaning up after anyone."

Dean can tell he's seriously considering it.

"I wonder if he likes cop shows?"

"Probably. His daughter's a detective, after all."

Jones nods. "I'll speak to her about it. Then I'll do a background check on him, you know, just online."

Dean smiles. Jones loves researching things.

"Is Eva coming tonight?"

"She said she is," says Dean. "But to be honest she could've agreed just to shut me up."

"You sound like an old married couple already."

Ever since he brought Eva to Maple Valley, Dean's had to put up with a lot of jokes about them being a couple. They're not and they never have been. He likes her, but he's pretty sure she just puts up with him. At some point Dean's going to have to tell everyone to quit it with the assumptions.

"I found out today that the women's correctional has shut down," he says. "You never told me about that while I was away."

"Didn't I?" says Jones. "It only recently closed. That place should've been condemned a long time ago; it's practically falling down. They've moved the inmates and employees up to the state prison near Cedar Falls. It's huge. I know the employees weren't happy about being moved away from town, but what can they do?"

Dean thinks of Pete and Toad, his old co-workers from when he was a corrections officer at the prison. He probably won't be seeing them around any time soon. "Did you know someone's turned the building into a haunted attraction?"

Jones shakes his head. "Ever since the murders, this town has become a macabre attraction for weirdos who want to live in their own horror movie. It doesn't surprise me that someone's already profiting from it."

Dean looks at the entrance to the Tavern. "We better go in. They'll be waiting for you."

Jones sighs. He's not looking forward to being the center of attention tonight, but it's a ritual all retired cops have to go through. "Do we have to?" he asks.

"Yes. It's Rocky's party too, remember."

Jones laughs and looks down at the dog. "Well, in that case . . ."

* * *

Within an hour, the whole place is packed and people can barely hear themselves speak over the sound of jukebox music and the heaving, drunk crowd. Dean looks around. There must be over a hundred people here. Not just cops, family, and friends, but also perps that he knows Jones helped to put away. He was always fair with everyone so few people hold a grudge against him.

Jones is on the other side of the bar, surrounded by people. He's drunk already, which makes Dean laugh. He's never seen Jones drunk before. Someone has lined up three shots of whiskey in front of him, and he doesn't look like he's going to object.

Dean's glad to see such a good turnout. He just hopes some of these people stay in touch with Jones when the party's over. It's not unheard of for retired cops to die from loneliness. Usually with the help of their own guns.

Dean feels a warm hand on his back, so he turns around.

"I believe you still owe me a drink for saving your life in Colorado," says Eva.

He raises his eyebrows and smiles. "You *almost* saved me."

"Almost?"

"Well, I still got shot, didn't I? If you'd have been a little quicker with the trigger, it would have saved me multiple operations and a long, expensive hospital stay."

She laughs. "Whatever, Matheson. You're still alive to annoy me. That's the important thing to remember."

Dean smiles. "What would you like to drink?"

She leans over his shoulder to see what's available. "Awesome," she says. "They have my favorite tequila."

He thinks about the last time they drank tequila together. They were trying to keep warm in a remote ski lodge during a power outage with a psychopathic child killer on the loose. Something like that will help you bond with a person.

He shouts his order over the music to the bartender. "Two tequila shots, thanks."

"What's this? You're actually going to drink?" Eva smiles at him. "Careful, Matheson. Someone might take advantage of you."

He enjoys her jokes. Probably because she's normally so serious. He passes her a shot and is about to ask if she wants to get a booth, but she's suddenly pulled away by Sheila, who looks ready to party.

Marty joins him at the bar instead. He claps Dean on the back. "Now you're back in town are you going to join our bowling team?"

Dean had noticed the bowling alley downtown had been re-opened. He's surprised by how many changes there were in his absence. "Are you for real? Bowling? What are you, twelve?" He swallows his shot of tequila. "There's not enough booze in the world to entice me onto your bowling team. Sorry, man."

Marty puts his empty beer glass on the bar. "Jeez, you're so happy these days. I think I preferred it when you were miserable. It was easier to make fun of you."

"Yeah, well. I'm a detective now. It's easy to be happy when you finally get what you want."

"Oh sure," says Marty. "Like that's the only reason."

Dean knows what's coming but he still asks. "What do you mean?"

Marty nods to where Eva's sitting with Sheila. "It can't possibly have anything to do with the striking brunette you brought home with you like an expensive vacation souvenir?"

Dean looks over at her briefly. "Shut up and buy me a welcome home drink."

Marty laughs.

CHAPTER EIGHT

The next morning, Dean gets a text from Eva telling him he's on driving duty today as she's exhausted. He's not surprised because she stayed behind when he left the Tavern at midnight. She was dancing with Sheila and they were attracting a lot of male attention. Everyone in there must know Sheila's engaged to Steve, so they were probably interested in Eva. He wonders how long it will be before someone hits on her. Knowing this town, it won't take long.

When he left the party, Jones was doing a terrible rendition of a Frank Sinatra medley on the bar. He'll regret that this morning, especially as so many people had their cell phones out, recording it.

Dean smiles at the memory as he pulls into the diner's parking lot and texts Eva to let her know he's arrived. It's still dark out as it's only seven a.m., and it's raining lightly. The diner is lit up and he can make out Rachel serving the early breakfast customers behind the condensation on the windows. He looks up at the apartment above and can see the lights are on in there too. As he waits for Eva to appear, he notices a head bobbing up and down behind a car door a few feet away. It looks like someone's trying to stay hidden.

He swings open his door and walks toward them. "What do you think you're doing?"

It's a teenage girl. Her hair hangs in front of her face and she's dressed in faded jeans and an oversized sweater, but no coat. She must be freezing. Her eyes widen when she sees him and she immediately spins around to run away, but Dean has fast reflexes. He grabs her arm and pushes her against a vehicle. She almost squirms out of her sweater.

"Stop squirming or I'll have to cuff you." He forces her hands behind her back until she stops trying to get away.

"Get off me!" She starts screaming, "Help! I'm being raped!"

"Don't be ridiculous, I'm a cop. If you stop trying to hit me, I'll let go. Deal?"

She finally stops squirming and stands still.

He spins her around to face him. When he realizes who it is, he lets go and takes a step backward, stunned. He didn't recognize her at first. She's two years older and about six inches taller than when he last saw her.

"Emily?"

She looks at him like she wants to kill him. "Yeah, so what? What do you care, *Officer Dean*?" She says Officer Dean in a mimicking voice, but it's her younger self she's mimicking.

He instinctively pulls her toward him for a hug. He's genuinely pleased to see her.

At first, she softens and almost hugs him back, but then she pulls away from him. "Get off me!"

Dean's shocked at her anger. "Emily, what's wrong with you? What are you even doing out here this early?" The large scratch on the side of the car door suggests she was trying to get in it. Surely she's not capable of hotwiring a car? He notices the crowbar that's been discarded near the trunk.

She spits on the ground. "Have you got a cigarette?"

He shakes his head. He can't believe how downtrodden she looks. "What happened to you? Are you still living with Simon and Julie?" He thinks of the foster carers who took her in after her mom, Tammy Gordon, was murdered.

They were great with Emily but they wouldn't take her dog, Rocky, which is why Dean ended up rescuing him. Emily's mother was a drug addict who neglected her. Dean had tried to get her removed from her mother's care many times but then Tammy was murdered, which solved the problem. He assumed all Emily's problems were behind her so he's shocked to see how she's behaving now.

"It's none of your business," she says. "Why do you even care?"

He's surprised she has to ask. "Of course I care," he says. "Didn't I always?"

She hesitates before explaining. "They kicked me out about a month ago. Those two up-tight assholes were just looking for an excuse to get rid of me."

Dean never met Simon and Julie but Derek Jackson, Emily's social worker, only had good things to say about them. Dean knows the life of a foster child isn't easy and it frequently takes more than one placement to get the right fit, but he doesn't understand why they would just kick her out.

"How old are you now? Sixteen?"

She rolls her eyes. "Seventeen soon. What does it matter?"

"I'm just trying to think where I can get you a bed. Are you sleeping rough?"

Eva joins them. She's wearing sunglasses, even though it's still dark out. She's carrying two tall takeout coffees from Frankie's. "Hey. Who's this?" she asks, looking at Emily and quickly assessing the situation. "Coffee?" She hands Emily one of the cups.

Dean's grateful she doesn't make a big deal about this unkempt girl who's out here in the rain at this time of the morning, clearly for the wrong reasons.

Emily hesitates for a second and then takes the coffee. "I have to go." She walks away, fast.

Dean shouts after her. "Let me give you a ride somewhere?"

"No! Leave me alone."

He watches her practically run away from them. She turns left, heading downtown. His heart sinks. He needs to know what's going on with her. He'll give Derek a call later to catch up.

As they get into his car, Eva asks, "Who was that?"

He sighs as he starts the engine. "It's a long story." And it involves Lizzie Glover. He still hasn't told Eva everything that happened with Lizzie, just the basics. He knows he'll have to at some point if they decide to ignore the FBI and go after her. He just doesn't want Eva to lose any respect she might have for him.

"Let me guess, a result of the care system?" she says.

He looks at her as she blows on her coffee. He remembers she's also a result of the care system, but one with a happier ending. "I'll tell you about it sometime," he says. "But for now, we need to go and see Taylor."

* * *

When they get to Taylor's room at the hospital, she's sitting up in bed watching a music channel on TV. Her face is still blue but the swelling has gone down considerably from when they saw her yesterday. It looks like she's taken a shower as her dark brown hair is clean today. They were warned by Dr. Armstrong before they entered that they weren't allowed to upset her again.

"Morning," says Dean. "How are you today?"

She doesn't smile. She looks like she's still in a lot of pain. She's wired to several machines and not able to move much. "I'm okay. Do you know who did this to me yet?"

Eva takes a seat next to the bed and removes her sunglasses for the first time. She looks a little tired. She pulls out a bar of chocolate she bought from the vending machine outside and gives half of it to Taylor, who willingly accepts it. Eva starts eating the other half. "Not yet, but we're working on it. Has anything come back to you yet?"

Taylor, with her mouth full of chocolate, shakes her head. "When's my mom going to visit me?"

Dean feels sorry for her. The only visitors she's getting right now are doctors and cops. Still, he's glad to hear she has a mom. He needs to get a photo of Taylor out to the press so they can run a story on her and find her family.

"We can't track down your mom until we know your name," says Dean. "Has that come back to you yet?"

She makes a thinking face. Then shakes her head.

"Do you know how old you might be?" he asks.

"I'm supposed to be in high school, but I dropped out. I don't remember when."

Eva looks at him. He knows what she's thinking; if Taylor's meant to be in high school, she could be anywhere between fourteen and eighteen. Dean would guess sixteen.

Eva's obviously wondering what kind of asshole could do this to a teenage girl because she's shaking her head in disgust. When they first saw Taylor yesterday, she seemed older, and Sheila said she'd aged her at about twenty-one when she was brought into the morgue. The injuries made it difficult to tell. He needs to contact Child Protective Services because this girl needs a social worker. He can mention it to Derek later.

"Do you remember which high school you dropped out of?" he asks.

She finishes the chocolate and licks her fingers. "Nope."

"Do you have a cell phone?"

"I did. But it's not with the clothes I was wearing. My keys are gone too."

Whoever did this to her has taken anything that could identify her. "Do you know your cell number off by heart?" Dean thinks it's worth a shot.

She tries to think. Then shakes her head. "No, but I'm pretty sure I've never known that."

Eva smiles. "Me neither."

"What about social media?" Dean presses, determined to jog at least one memory. "Are you on any social media? Do you remember any of your usernames?"

Taylor yawns. She'll be asleep again soon. "I'm pretty sure I'm on Instagram. But I don't remember my username or password. Sorry."

"No problem. I know it's hard. Do you mind if I take a photo of you?" he asks. "If I can get that out to the media, your mom will see it and come forward."

Taylor looks confused. "But won't she already be looking for me? I've been in here two days now. Hasn't anyone contacted you guys to say their daughter is missing?"

Dean checked this on Monday afternoon and again when they were on their way to the hospital this morning. Steve told him there have been no reports of a missing girl. At the moment, Taylor's mom clearly isn't worried about her. That could mean that Taylor was meant to be staying over with friends and her mom doesn't know she's missing yet, or that her mom knows but doesn't care.

"Not yet, no," he says. "We could wait for her to come forward but it would be quicker if we get your photo released. Would that be okay with you?"

Taylor picks up a hand mirror from her nightstand. She winces at her reflection. "But I look terrible."

Eva jumps in. "We all look terrible at this time in the morning, and none of us like having our photo taken, trust me. But your mom will be able to tell it's you and that's all that matters right now."

Taylor puts the mirror down and agrees. "Okay then. I mean, I guess."

Dean pulls his cell phone out as Taylor plays with her hair. "Ready?"

Taylor nods and Dean snaps five photos in succession. "Great. We'll get something out to the media today. Keep watching as you might be on the news later."

Taylor smiles and looks up at the TV in awe.

"If you remember anything at all, get Dr. Armstrong to call us, okay?" says Eva.

"I will." She lies back, exhausted by their short conversation.

They leave the hospital. As they drive back to town, Eva tells him she's hungry.

"First, let's get the list of people who were at the church Sunday night," he says. "Then I'll treat you to lunch."

"It's not a church, remember?" she says.

"If you say so."

They ride along in silence until Eva says, "Whoever did that to Taylor is seriously twisted. I mean, she's a *teenager*." She looks over at Dean. "You know everyone in this town. Who do you think did it?"

Dean's taken aback. "I don't know everyone in this town! It's not that small, Eva. And I was gone for a year, remember? It could be someone who was passing through, looking for an unsuspecting victim to take his rage out on. Or she could've been on her way home from a friend's house when she was randomly attacked, unlucky enough to be in the wrong place at the wrong time. Steve told me nothing was found at the scene that could be used as evidence. Maybe she didn't even get attacked where she was found."

Eva shakes her head. "No, I don't think this was random. Remember, Sheila said whoever did this was full of anger toward her. He must've been, to take it so far. She must've upset him somehow, in his own mind if not in reality. I don't think someone would do this to a random person. This was personal."

"Maybe you're right," he says. "I wonder if there's any DNA under her fingernails. We should get forensics to check. Maybe Taylor fought back."

Eva looks at him. "I really hope so. They could take her prints too. You never know, she might have a criminal record."

Dean nods. "Let's see if the church guy recognizes her first."

CHAPTER NINE

When they reach the Hope Center, Jake's already there, talking with a group of teenage girls. Dean notices they're all hanging off his every word. It makes him think of those cult leaders who were popular in the seventies. He looks around to see if there are any teenage boys anywhere, but there aren't. Could that be because boys are less likely to use a center like this, or because Jake doesn't cater to boys on purpose?

When Jake spots them, he excuses himself and then walks straight over. "Morning, detectives. How are you today?"

Eva smiles at him and removes her sunglasses. "Good, thanks. How are you?"

Dean's surprised she's making small talk. She's not a small talk kind of person.

"I'm good. Would you like a drink? We have an excellent coffee shop here and drinks are free for detectives." He smiles at her.

Eva makes a beeline for it, leaving them both behind.

Dean turns to Jake. "Do you have that list of names we asked for?"

"Sure, I'll just grab it for you." He leans over the reception desk and pulls out a sheet of paper. As he hands it to Dean he says, "Everyone was so shocked to hear what happened. I asked around to see if anyone saw or heard anything as they were leaving the center that night, but no one did. I told them to expect a call from your department."

Dean glances at the piece of paper. It has a printed list of twelve names on it. "Were they okay with that?"

"Oh, sure. They want to be able to help."

"Good. We've just come from the hospital and I took some photos of our victim." Dean pulls out his phone. "Do you recognize her at all? She's of high school age, around sixteen. Unfortunately, she doesn't remember her name right now."

Jake winces and Dean can tell he wants to look away. Some people would lean in, get a good look, and then tell all their friends about it in graphic detail, but Jake clearly isn't like that.

"We have a lot of teenagers who use our facilities," says Jake, "but I don't recognize her. Although I doubt her own mother would recognize her like that. Maybe once she's looking more like herself we could pass a new photo around here, see if anyone else knows her?"

Dean nods as he slips his phone into his pocket together with the piece of paper. He's hoping it won't take that long to ID her. He looks around the center and wonders whether this is the kind of place that could help Emily Gordon get back on her feet. "On another matter," he says, "I know a teenage girl who might be sleeping rough at the moment. She has no family and she was recently asked to leave her foster home. Do you know of anywhere that could help her?"

Jake enthusiastically nods. "Absolutely. I assume she already has a social worker?"

"She does. Can I give him your contact details?"

"Of course. We have lots of programs here she might be interested in. And we offer free lunches two days a week. We could put her in touch with families who would be willing to help her with clothes and toiletries. Anything she needs, really."

Dean's surprised. Do people really do that for strangers? Cuts in government funding mean there are few services left that offer this type of support, so he's glad to hear a place like this is plugging the gaps. "That sounds perfect. I can't guarantee she'll be interested in coming here, but it's worth a shot. She's a good kid."

Jake smiles. "Sometimes it takes people four or five visits before they're willing to accept our help. But we're always here for them, and eventually they embrace the benefits. I need to know, though, does she use drugs or alcohol?"

"Not that I'm aware of." Dean hopes not. "She smokes cigarettes, but that's it as far as I know. Why? Are people less inclined to help those most desperate for it?"

"It's not that," says Jake, letting the dig slide. "I just want to make sure I match her with the right people. Some people who come here have lived more sheltered lives than others, you know? Some are intimidated by addicts and alcoholics, or they don't want them around their kids, but we have plenty who are the opposite, so it balances out."

"Fair enough," says Dean. "So you're not an actual church then? The name of this place — the Hope Center — is a little ambiguous."

Eva joins them with a steaming cup of coffee. She didn't get Dean a cup, and he's glad. He can't drink as much caffeine as she can.

Jake smiles. "We're definitely not a church. It's named after my late fiancée, Hope. We're more of a community center or meeting place for people to get together. I think people assume we're a church because we offer similar things: friendship, support, classes. But we're here to meet the community's needs. I gather churches haven't done well in Maple Valley, if the lack of them is anything to go by. The only one I've seen is the derelict one on the other side of town. I guess young people are moving away from traditional churches, which is why I thought they needed something else."

Dean can't help feeling suspicious. It sounds too good to be true. "Who funds this place?"

Jake reddens. "I do."

Eva raises her eyebrows as she sips her coffee.

Jake notices. "I made a small fortune when I was in my twenties and I felt guilty about how easy it was. My job left me feeling dead inside, and I realized I wanted to do something more meaningful."

Eva scoffs. She's cynical by nature. Dean hopes Jake doesn't take offense.

"I know how it sounds," says Jake. "Cheesy, right? I'm the kind of person I roll my eyes at."

Eva laughs again. "It does sound a little cheesy. How did you make your money?"

"I designed a financial planning website that became popular, and I sold it for a good price. Now, when I'm not working down here, I write motivational books upstairs in my spare time."

Eva seems interested. Dean notices her lean in. "What kind of motivational books?" she asks.

"Oh, all sorts. I write books about how to deal with things like grief, sadness, loneliness. That kind of thing. I lost my fiancée when she was just twenty-eight. It put things into perspective, you know?"

"Sorry to hear that," she says.

Dean can tell Jake's won Eva over. He feels a little jealous.

"Why bother working all day and even in your spare time if you already have money?" she asks. "I assume you could probably afford to retire?"

Dean used to be shocked by Eva's directness but he's getting used to it.

Jake doesn't seem bothered by it. "I could, but I like to keep busy. It stops me thinking too much. Plus, 'idle hands are the devil's workshop', as the saying goes."

Dean frowns. "I thought it was 'the devil finds work for idle hands'?"

"Yours is a variant of the actual scripture. Mine would probably be more accurate."

"So you *have* studied the Bible at some point then?" says Dean. He feels Eva's eyes on him. "I thought you said you weren't religious?"

Jake smiles but it doesn't extend to his eyes. "I think we all pick up random quotes from the Bible over the years, don't we?"

Dean doesn't reply. He's wondering how much it would take to get a reaction out of him and see the real Jake Andrews.

"Well, thanks for your time," says Eva. "If we need more information, we'll be in touch." She drinks the rest of her coffee and hands her empty cup to Jake.

Dean follows her to his car. He looks back before getting in, but Jake has disappeared from view.

"What do you think?" he asks, as they buckle up. "Do you buy all that 'wanting to give back' crap, or could it be a cover for something?"

"I'll tell you what I think." She slips her sunglasses back on. "I think I need that lunch you promised me."

CHAPTER TEN

Back at the station, after what was an expensive lunch for Dean, they sit at their desks as Steve tells them they're to be on the lookout for a missing seven-year-old boy from Cedar Falls, a town north of Maple Valley.

"His name's Danny Mallory," says Steve. "Detective Briggs from Cedar Falls PD says the boy went to school as usual yesterday, got involved in a playground fight at first recess, and arrived home after school with nothing to suggest he was unhappy. His mother, Shannon Mallory, says she fed him dinner and then he went to play in his room. When she went to wake him for school this morning, he was gone. He left a note on his pillow explaining he'd run away."

"Did it say why?" asks Dean.

Steve looks at his screen. "I've emailed you a copy, but it says he was unhappy because he felt like no one loved him. He says not to look for him because he's never coming back."

"Poor kid," says Eva. "Let's hope he hasn't hurt himself."

Dean nods. The news is full of kids taking their own lives these days, something that was almost unheard of when he was younger. But social media wasn't around back then. You could leave the bullies in the playground and get some respite at home. Although, if he's feeling unloved, Danny's bullies may be his parents. "Do they think he might come this far south? Does he have any relatives here?"

Cedar Falls isn't that far away by car, probably just over an hour's drive, but it would be a long way for a child to travel alone.

Steve looks up from his notes. "Nothing to suggest that, no. His principal's being interviewed as we speak and the local PD will keep me informed. Here." He hands everyone in the room a photo of Danny.

Dean looks at the boy. He's small for seven. Skinny too. He has brown hair, blue eyes and is wearing a Marvel T-shirt. He looks like any other kid, and will be hard to spot. "We'll keep an eye out for him," he says. "Keep us posted."

Eva's arranged for forensics to take Taylor's fingerprints and fingernail scrapings. Now she gets to work calling all the people on Jake's list, to see if any of them witnessed Taylor being beaten or dumped outside the Hope Center on Sunday night.

Dean transfers the photos he took of Taylor to his computer. He winces as he opens them. Her bruising looks even more painful up close. He needs to put together a statement to release to the press but he struggles with it. How much detail is too much? If the perp happens to read it, Dean doesn't want him getting off on the long list of injuries she has. And if he left her thinking she was dead, will he come back to finish the job once he finds out she survived? Unfortunately, it's a risk they have to take if they want to locate her family. The family should be able to fill in the blanks about where Taylor was that night and who she was with.

He puts together just the bare facts and emails them, together with the best photo he has of Taylor, to Captain Brown.

Now he needs to call Emily Gordon's social worker. He knows her life is none of his business, but he can't just leave her to fend for herself. They have history.

He calls child services and asks to speak to Derek Jackson. The switchboard operator surprises him.

"I'm sorry, sir. Derek left CPS last summer. Moved to Minnesota."

"Oh, okay." He's disappointed. Derek was great with Emily. He wonders whether that's why she's gone downhill. Derek's yet another person who's left her. Dean wishes he'd checked up on her while he was working away in Vegas and Colorado. "Who's taken on his caseload?"

"Let me just check," she says. "Er, Ryan Scott, apparently. Want me to put you through?"

"Before you transfer me, would you give me his direct number so I have it for future reference?"

She does. The line rings out for a long time. Dean's about to hang up when someone answers.

"This is Ryan." He sounds harassed.

"Hi, this is Detective Matheson from Maple Valley PD. I understand you're the social worker for Emily Gordon?"

Ryan sighs as if he's used to getting these calls. "What's she done now?"

Dean's irritated by his attitude. Emily's a good kid. "Nothing. I'm just looking for an update on her situation. I'm an old friend of hers."

"Really? You're not related, are you? I'm trying to find her somewhere to live."

Dean thinks about his two spare bedrooms and feels guilty. It would be crossing a line to let Emily stay with him. They're not related and she's only sixteen. It wouldn't look good. Plus, he's hoping to downsize.

"No, not related. I knew her when she was younger. I was the one who found her mom dead."

"Oh, right. I've heard her mom used to beat her."

Dean thinks back to the frail young girl who was too timid to answer the door to him and Derek. She's not that timid anymore, which he hopes is a good thing. "Right. I bumped into her this morning and I was a little surprised by her circumstances. She said she's been kicked out of her foster home. What gives?"

"Well, Emily's a nice kid and all but she's easily led astray," says Ryan. "She's not doing so well at the moment which makes her hard to place. Any potential foster carers just see her as trouble."

"She's not using, is she?"

"What, drugs? No way. Emily tries to be good. She just fell in with the wrong crowd."

Dean's disappointed. He wanted a better outcome for her. "She was trying to break into a car outside Frankie's Diner this morning. When she saw me, she acted like I was a piece of shit. Why's she so angry?"

Ryan hesitates. "She's angry with everyone; don't take it personally. She's at that age, and she feels like the whole world's against her. To tell you the truth, she's probably right. It's just that she's learning this now. Most of us at least get to enjoy childhood before we find out life's a bitch."

Dean's not so sure it's a general issue. Emily seemed particularly pissed at him. "I was at the Hope Center earlier today. You know the building on the edge of town, past the diner?"

"The church?"

"It's not a church, apparently. No religious affiliation, just some rich guy who wants to help people. Anyway, I mentioned Emily and he said there might be people there who would be willing to help. With clothes, toiletries, classes, that kind of thing."

"That sounds too good to be true," says Ryan. "What gives?"

Dean smiles. Being in their jobs, you have to be cynical. "It seems legit. The owner's trying to plug a gap in services, I guess. He's doing a good job from the sounds of it. Would you take Emily there sometime? See if she takes a liking to the place? They do free lunches and classes."

"Absolutely, we'll check it out. It might be good for some of my other kids too. Thanks for the heads up."

"No problem." Dean thinks about Taylor and wonders whether she could be known to CPS. "I don't suppose you're missing anyone at the moment? A teenage girl?"

Ryan takes a minute to think about it. "Not that I know of. I mean, I don't know where all my kids are at any given moment, but I check in with them regularly enough. No one's currently flagged up within the department as being AWOL."

"Okay, it was a long shot." Taylor asked after her mother, so it makes sense she wouldn't be known to child services. "If I can help with anything for Emily, call me." Dean gives him his cell number.

"It's nice to know you care, man," says Ryan. "These kids I work with are forgotten by everyone except us."

"Tell me about it."

"So, if you work at MVPD I'm surprised we haven't crossed paths before, what with all the kids I have to collect from you guys."

"I'm new," says Dean, feeling a little self-conscious.

"That'll be why then. I'll keep you updated on Emily."

"Thanks."

Dean ends the call just as Eva finishes hers.

She takes a deep breath and drops her pen. "When did everyone become so self-centered? Not one person noticed anything out of the ordinary that night, and no one knows anyone who's missing a daughter."

Dean thinks about it. "If she was found by the ambulance crew at around eight-thirty and the people you called were leaving the center at around eight, it must mean she was beaten elsewhere and dumped outside the center on the perp's way past. Funny place to dump her, though."

"Not really," says Eva. "Think about it; when you're brought up by a strict religious family and you get pregnant at thirteen, where do you leave the newborn baby?"

"Outside a church."

"Correct. Her attacker could be someone who thinks they were doing her a favor by dumping her outside the community center, because they might have thought it was a church, like the rest of us. They might have felt guilty after the beating and assumed she'd get help there. Could've been a boyfriend who took it too far this time."

He takes a sip of his coffee. “Have you thought about the alternative?”

She waits for him to tell her.

“Maybe the person who dumped her there isn’t the same person who beat her. Maybe they were trying to save her.”

Eva shakes her head. “Then they should’ve dropped her at the hospital, not left her in the road to get run over.”

“Well, sure, but they could’ve panicked. Maybe they know Jake and thought he’d help if he found her.”

Eva thinks about it. “Hmm, maybe. Have you sent the press release out yet?”

“Yeah, it’s with the captain.”

“Good. I need to speak to you about something important. Let’s grab some coffee.”

Dean agrees. He’s ready for a break.

CHAPTER ELEVEN

Eva leads Dean to one of the station's small interview rooms. It's windowless and freezing cold because the tiny wall mounted heater has a handwritten *out of order* sign on it. She rubs her hands together.

Dean looks nervous as he places his drink on the table. "If you've brought me in here to question me, I just want to start this interview with a denial." He holds his hands up. "I swear I didn't touch your special coffee."

She scoffs. "I know you wouldn't dare." She closes the door behind him as he takes a seat. She sits opposite him and isn't sure how best to approach what she wants to say.

It's only their second day working here, and they have Taylor's case to focus on, but equally important is catching Lizzie Glover — something Dean had asked her to help him with when they were first partnered, and before the FBI took over the case. But, so far, Dean hasn't even mentioned the woman and it's driving her crazy. As Eva's not one for sugar-coating anything, she comes straight to the point.

"Listen, it's time to talk about Lizzie. About you and Lizzie, specifically."

He takes a deep breath and then sips his coffee. He doesn't look surprised or uncomfortable which suggests he's been waiting for this conversation to happen.

"What do you want to know?" he says. "I'll tell you anything."

She sits back in the hard, plastic chair. "Dean, I already know everything. Frankie filled in the gaps."

Now he looks surprised. "He's been talking about me behind my back? I thought he was a friend."

"He is," she says, softening her tone. "He worries about you. He was sympathetic to you as he was telling me. Well, apart from saying you were thinking with 'little Dean' when you fell for her. He said that's why you couldn't see what she was doing."

Dean leans forward in frustration. "But no one did, Eva! Frankie was her *landlord*, so he's one to talk!"

It's Eva's turn to be surprised. "He was her landlord?" It suddenly dawns on her. "Are you saying she lived in my apartment before me?"

He nods. "Looks like Frankie didn't tell you everything."

She shakes her head and shivers. "That's just creepy." Then she thinks about it. "You didn't have sex with her in my bed, did you?"

Dean surprises her by laughing. "Oh shit. You know what? We did. I hadn't thought about how weird that is until now."

She should probably be annoyed, but she likes seeing him laugh. He spends so much time in his head normally, overthinking things and dragging around guilt for everything Lizzie's done.

"Are you finished?" she asks.

He stifles his laugh. "Sorry. Go on."

"I don't want to bring you down but you asked for my help to catch her, so we need to plan where we're going to start. What did Jones and the Feds find out about her escape?"

Dean finishes his coffee and gets serious. "We know she escaped from the secure unit at some time on December twenty-second. The employees don't know what time exactly, but when they unlocked her door for dinner at five p.m., she wasn't there."

"So how did she get out?" asks Eva.

"She must've had someone working with her."

"An employee?"

He nods. "It must be because her room was locked. Someone let her out and then locked it up after her to make it appear as if she was still inside. Also, don't forget that Jones' wife was volunteering in the mother-baby section of the unit just before Lizzie escaped, which means the same employee who let Lizzie out must've been the one to poison Barbara's drinks."

Eva knows Jones opted not to have an autopsy performed on Barbara because her doctors had enough evidence to be certain she died from ingesting antifreeze that was added to her energy drinks. He couldn't bring himself to let them cut her open unless it was absolutely necessary.

Dean continues. "Almost as soon as Barbara started working there, her health declined. Lizzie must've been instructing this employee every step of the way."

Eva shakes her head in disgust. "I can't believe she managed to talk someone into doing that for her."

"She's good at what she does, Eva. When she worked at the women's correctional facility, she talked an inmate into killing herself."

Eva leans back. "We need to interview everyone on the medical team who worked with her."

"The Feds already have," says Dean. "They've done a lot of work already, but Steve says they've cut us out of the investigation and we're not meant to get involved. But if she's still in New Hampshire, she's our problem. If she hasn't already killed anyone else, we could stop it from happening again if we can catch her, because she *will* kill again. Whether that's here or somewhere else, she'll do it again because she believes in her reasons for killing."

Eva thinks about it. "The real reason the Feds haven't tracked her down yet is because they don't know her. They can't appreciate how she works and what she's thinking." She pauses. "They can't possibly appreciate her feelings for you, either. We have one big advantage; you know her. You're probably the only person who does."

Dean shifts uncomfortably in his seat. "I don't think anyone really knows her. I mean, she killed her own mother and sister so even they didn't know her well enough to see that coming."

"What about the guy who shot you at Barbara's funeral at Christmas?" she asks. "Did you get a good look at him?" Eva wasn't there but Dean had been taken by surprise at the graveside. The shooter put a bullet in his shoulder, but chose not to kill him. Instead, he delivered a message from Lizzie and then fled before anyone could detain him.

"No," he says. "I passed out too fast to see his face. I probably wouldn't recognize his voice either, I was pretty distracted by the pain. All he said was, 'Lizzie says welcome home'."

Eva's disappointed. "If he was one of the unit's employees you might recognize him if you saw him in person. Maybe we should go visit that place, if they'll let us. Have there been any reported sightings of Lizzie since her escape?"

Dean shakes his head. "Not even one. So she's either left the area or she's in hiding. Personally, I think she'll be long gone by now. She's not stupid so I don't think she'd risk her freedom by returning to Maple Valley any time soon."

"Doesn't she have a score to settle with you?"

"Not really," he says. "She did far more to me than I did to her. And she's already killed Barbara out of some twisted need for revenge. Now that she's managed to escape her sentence, any score she wanted to settle should be settled. She knows that if she gets caught again it's game over for her. She'll go to a maximum-security prison next time, not a secure hospital."

"Why did she hate Barbara enough to kill her?" asks Eva.

Dean runs a hand over his jaw. "Because she hates Jones. Jones was the one who figured out who she really was and what she was up to. Before she came here, she was locked away for murder in a secure unit in the UK until they deemed her fit for release."

Eva's surprised. "They voluntarily released her?"

He nods. "That's how good she is at manipulating people, even the professionals. Honestly, Eva, you'd never know she was capable of murder if you met her on the street. She had a charming, intelligent demeanor on the outside. I was completely fooled."

Eva knows Dean was in a sexual relationship with Lizzie while she was killing people. Something he'll never forgive himself for.

"She's obviously good at what she does," she says. "But why on earth did she set her sights on *you*?" As soon as she says it, she realizes it came out wrong. Dean's actually a good-looking guy, and she can see why Lizzie would be attracted to him. What she's curious about is why Lizzie wanted to drag Dean down with her.

He leans back in his chair, looking ashamed. "I was an emotional mess when I met her. It wasn't a good time for me. She must've known she could easily manipulate me while staying close to the investigation into the murders at the same time. If I hadn't been distracted, I would've been able to prevent some of the damage."

Eva touches his hand. "Don't do that to yourself, Dean. She could've picked anyone on the team to manipulate. Miller, for example." She grimaces. "At least she didn't sleep with Miller. She's obviously not that crazy."

He laughs.

She thinks it's time they read the progress reports Lizzie's doctors kept during her incarceration at the hospital. She pulls them out from a file and looks down the list of doctor's names: Hibbert, Livingstone, McCloud, Creed . . . She realizes just how many employees are involved in one patient's care. Is it worth the cost when offenders like Lizzie refuse to accept their help?

She looks at Dean, who looks like he's figured out what they are. "I assume you haven't read these yet?" she asks.

He leans forward and he looks like he'd rather be anywhere but here right now. "No. I don't know anything about her incarceration other than a few things Jones told me."

"Are you ready for it?"

He doesn't hesitate. He grabs a handful of reports, leaving her with the rest.

CHAPTER TWELVE

Eva and Dean sit in silence for an hour, reading all the reports from the very beginning of Lizzie's sentence. They have one detailed report for each month, with briefer updates in between, all obtained by Detective Jones before the Feds took over the case. Occasionally, one of them gasps at something they read.

Certain words and phrases jump out at Eva.

> *The patient thinks she's in control and I allow her to believe that for now . . . She uses a variety of techniques for gaining trust and manipulating those around her. These would be hard to detect for most . . . Highly intelligent . . . Severely harmed by her mother's actions in childhood . . . At times unable to distinguish what's real and what isn't . . . No remorse for any of her actions, despite what she tries to portray . . . A superiority complex that is compensating for an inferiority complex and used as a method of escape from her reality . . . Fixation on certain people due to an inability to accept responsibility for her actions . . . Patient is not a self-harmer or at risk of taking her own life. Quite the opposite. She only really values her own life, finding everyone else to be just an extra, as in a movie.*

Eva gets goosebumps on her arms when reading the disturbing statements. As she moves on to the more recent updates, she can sense a change in the observations.

Lizzie is progressing well. She has accepted some responsibility and not just at face value . . . She has made some friends on the unit and genuinely appears to have feelings for them . . . Helpful with employees, offering her own, rather insightful, opinions into the mental health of the other inmates which are often surprisingly accurate. She's obviously well read with regards to psychological theories . . . Finally able to attend group therapy sessions without upsetting the others . . . Working through the trauma and the impact of her mother's Munchausen by Proxy disorder.

It all looks unexpectedly hopeful to Eva. Until she reads the final paragraph of the most recent report.

Just one delusion persists. She is convinced that her former lover Dean Matheson, who is a significant victim of her crimes, is in love with her and wants to marry her. Nothing to suggest this is actually true since he has not visited or interacted with Lizzie and he was an important witness at her trial, leading to her conviction. This is highly unusual behavior. Usually, offenders will want to forget those they wronged, to avoid feelings of guilt or anger. I will persist in working with her on this matter. Having a special rapport with Lizzie makes her trust me to a certain degree and I feel this final delusion can be quelled. I have weaned her off of her asthma inhaler, making her see she does not suffer with the chronic condition, or indeed with any physical ailment. This was difficult due to her mother's persistent lies. Lizzie's condition and the effects of her mother's control don't excuse her actions, but they do help us to understand them. Overall, it is my opinion that things are moving in the right direction.

Eva sits back in her chair, takes a deep breath, and pushes the papers away from her. "That woman has serious issues."

Dean looks up and indicates he's also read enough by pushing his papers away from him.

"It might be best you don't read this last report," she says.

He rubs his face and looks at his empty coffee cup. "Let me guess. She's waiting for me to marry her?"

Eva's surprised he already knows.

"Jones gave me a heads up after his last visit to her."

She can tell he's disturbed by the thought of it, so she tries to lighten the mood. "How did you propose? Down on one knee? Gun in one hand, ring in the other?" She smiles.

He doesn't. "You know what's really screwed up? Right up until she killed Barbara, I felt sorry for her. Even after everything she did, I still pitied her. But for the last year she's had free access to all the help she could ever need: all kinds of mental health professionals, medicine, therapy, everything! Yet she refuses to use any of it to get better."

"Mental illness isn't a choice, Dean."

"I know it isn't, and that's not what I'm saying, but she seems to get off on what she's done. Surely, that's a choice? She's not just ill; she's evil."

Eva thinks about it and knows he's right. Lizzie chooses to hurt Dean by killing those closest to him. That can't be blamed on her upbringing or her illness. It's a choice.

"So how do we end this?" she asks. "Where's she likely to be hiding?"

He looks at her with despair in his eyes. "I have absolutely no idea."

* * *

Back at their desks, they don't mention Lizzie again, but Eva knows they're both thinking about her. They work late into the evening, still following up on Jake's list of potential witnesses from the community center. Dean leaves work before her and Eva only stays an hour longer. It's dark outside when she finally heads home. The rain is heavy tonight and her windshield wipers struggle to keep up. She thinks about dinner. Frankie's food is expanding her waistline so instead of calling in at the diner on her way up to her apartment, she intends to eat whatever's in her refrigerator.

She parks her car and runs up the external wooden stairs with her purse over her head, trying to keep dry, but her hair is drenched by the time she gets her keys out. As she turns to let herself in, she notices a single yellow balloon tied to her door handle.

At first, she hesitates. Then she spins around to check whether anyone's watching her. She can't see anything through the rain. What if one of the clowns from the new haunted attraction is a serial killer? What if he wants to terrorize the local detectives? It would be easy for him to locate where she lived. That's the problem with living above the diner — someone is always watching her come and go and everyone knows what she does for a living.

She decides to ignore it. She won't be intimidated by anyone, and Dean would say she's overreacting.

She opens her front door and walks in. Immediately she can smell that something's wrong. When the door closes behind her, a smell hits the back of her throat and makes her gag.

She reaches for the light while putting her other hand over her nose and mouth. The light illuminates something on her couch. When her eyes adjust, she realizes it's a mutilated corpse.

"Shit!" Eva swings around to look for the killer as she struggles to comprehend what she's seeing. Most of her living room is covered in dark red blood spatter.

Horrified, she drops her purse and pulls out her weapon.

CHAPTER THIRTEEN

Emily Gordon can't stop shaking. She's involved in something she can't control and it's too late to back out. She's made a deal with the devil and that can't be undone. She knows it was wrong, but she didn't have much choice. Besides, she's got to take care of herself because no one else will.

She hides behind a parked car and pulls out a pack of cigarettes from her coat pocket but it takes four attempts before she can light one. Not because of the wind or the rain, but because of her trembling hands.

As she takes a deep drag of the cigarette and waits for the nicotine to calm her down, she thinks about her mother for the first time in months. Her mother had loved her, she truly believes that, but she wasn't emotionally able to convey it. She had a temper that was made deadly by the drugs and alcohol she consumed. She would've killed both Emily and Rocky eventually.

Emily stares at the smoke from her cigarette and tries to ignore the craving creeping through her bones. She's recently started injecting heroin. Not for recreational purposes, but for necessity. It helps numb her senses to the things she does for money, detaching her from reality long enough to get the job done.

She wonders whether she'll end up like her mother and is surprised when tears roll down her cheeks. Is this why her mom turned out the way she did? Was she numbing the pain of whatever she'd gone through in her life? Emily's thoughts turn to her future children. Are they going to end up victims of *her*? Or can she break the cycle now before she goes too far? She's not so sure she has any control over the horror she's caught up in.

She wipes her eyes with her dirty sleeve and looks up when she hears sirens approaching. She can't cope with this life for much longer so there may not be any children for her to worry about. What she witnessed tonight will stay with her forever.

She creeps backward into the dark wooded area to stay hidden from view.

CHAPTER FOURTEEN

It's late when Dean arrives home from work, and he's exhausted. The physical impact of his recent gunshot wounds is still taking a toll on his energy levels, although the wounds themselves have healed well. He can already tell being a detective will mean working long hours. He just wishes he was working at a hundred percent fitness.

He showers, changes into a T-shirt and sweatpants, and crashes on his couch. It's right about now that he usually starts missing Rocky. Before he can think about it there's a knock at his door. When he opens it, he's surprised to find Camille standing there.

"Hi. Did we have an appointment?" he asks.

"No, sorry. I was passing and I saw your lights on, so I thought I'd stop by on the off chance that you have time to discuss the house sale?"

He doesn't feel he can say no. "Sure, come on in."

She smiles as she passes him. "It's much warmer in here!"

She stands in front of him instead of taking a seat, so close he can smell her perfume. "Can I get you a drink?" he asks.

She waves the suggestion away. "No thanks. I won't take much of your time. I just wanted to know if you'd thought any more about the sale? I sensed you weren't that into the idea when we discussed it yesterday. It's just that, if you would like to move forward, I'd need to take photos."

Dean thinks about it, about the memories wrapped up in this house. A new house or apartment would give him a chance to start over. After all, not only did his wife and Rocky live here, it's where his relationship with Lizzie developed. The thought of her not knowing where he lives appeals to him after reading those psychiatric reports earlier.

"Actually, I *am* ready to move. So go ahead and do whatever you need to."

"Great!" she says. "When can I swing by and take photos?"

He thinks about it as he leads her to the front door. His job is so unpredictable he doesn't think he could give her an accurate time when he'll be around. He has a spare house key in his car's glovebox from when Eva gave it back to him. "I'm not sure when I'll be available over the next few days so let me give you my spare key."

He walks past her, into the rain and over to his car. He opens the passenger door and leans in, rummaging until he finds it. Once he's locked his car he says, "You could swing by tomorrow to take your photos and then drop it at the station's front desk for me after."

He briefly wonders whether giving access to his home to a stranger is dumb, but it's not like he owns anything worth stealing, and she already knows he's a detective so would she really be stupid enough to try to scam him? He's already run a criminal background check on her which came up clear. He doesn't want to be untrusting of everyone just because of what happened with Lizzie Glover, but he *has* got to be realistic, as he's determined not to make the same mistake twice.

The rain quickly soaks his hair and T-shirt.

Camille steps out from under the porch. She takes the key from him and smiles. "You know, you didn't even ask how much I charge." She says it with a flirty look in her eyes.

He smiles. "I can't ask a lady about her rates in public at this time of night. A cop can get into a lot of trouble for that."

She laughs. "Don't worry, my fees are reasonable. And yes, I can do tomorrow." The rain is persistent so she pulls the hood of her raincoat up. "I need to go before this weather gets worse. It was nice to see you again, Detective." She maintains eye contact longer than necessary.

Dean watches her drive away until his cell phone rings. "Hey, Eva. What's up?"

"You need to get to my apartment. We have a situation." She sounds shaken.

He doesn't ask for any details. "On my way."

* * *

When Dean arrives at the diner, he notices a police cruiser with its lights flashing and Sheila's old Honda Civic already parked outside. His heart beats a little harder.

Eva's apartment is cordoned off with yellow tape and a couple of onlookers are trying to get a glimpse of what's happening. They shout questions at him but he doesn't respond.

The heavy downpour has stopped, but he pulls his raincoat on anyway. He ducks under the police tape and runs up the steps to Eva's apartment where he finds the door wide open and the apartment lit up. He spots the blood that covers the walls before he notices who's in there.

"Oh my God. What happened here?" he asks. He looks around for Eva. She's standing next to Steve. She doesn't look harmed, just shaken.

Sheila's leaning over the couch, taking photos. All of them are wearing protective suits and latex gloves, not just to preserve the scene, but to avoid getting blood on their clothes. There's so much of it.

Eva nods to the couch. "Take a look at the body."

Before he gets a chance, Sheila stands up and runs for the door. She only just makes it outside before she loudly vomits over the side of the staircase. Dean looks at Steve in surprise.

"Well, she's never done that before," says Steve.

They watch her come back inside, wiping her mouth.

"Sorry. It's not the blood, it's the smell," she says. "It just turned my stomach for a minute there. I'll be fine." She sighs. "I think someone outside took a photo of me throwing up. That better not make the news."

Dean's worried about her. Sheila's been around numerous corpses and performed hundreds of autopsies, but she's never reacted like this. He wonders whether Taylor waking up in the morgue has knocked her confidence.

He takes the protective gear Steve hands him, slips it on, and walks over to the body while trying not to step in any blood, which is difficult because it's everywhere. The body, a white male, is starting to smell already, probably because it's been opened. Dean holds a hand to his nose as he leans in. A large incision runs all the way down the front of the guy's torso and it looks like some of his organs have been disturbed.

"Jeez." Dean's never seen anything like it before. He swallows back some bile.

The victim looks to be in his early thirties, with thinning red hair. Even though he's on his back, Dean can tell he's tall. He's also completely naked and a little overweight. Dean doesn't recognize him. He looks around for the guy's clothes but they're not here.

He turns to Sheila. "Was he killed here?"

She nods. "Sure was. Hence the amount of blood."

"Do we know how long he's been dead?"

Sheila thinks about it. "I'd guess no longer than five hours, but I'll know more when I perform the autopsy."

Eva steps forward and looks at Dean. She has her arms crossed and he can tell she's seething. "You and I both know there's only one person who would do this here. In this particular apartment."

He shakes his head. "There's no way, Eva. This isn't Lizzie's MO. For starters, she's only ever killed women. And she's not this violent. She made all her murders appear to be suicides. She never cut someone open like this. And how would she overpower a man of this size? She's shorter than you."

Steve agrees with him. "This doesn't feel like her. She was sneaky about the way she killed people. This looks more like it's some kind of warning."

"What do you mean?" asks Eva.

"Well, think about it," says Steve. "You're investigating the attempted murder of a girl who was so badly beaten she's unrecognizable. Whoever did that is the kind of person who's capable of gutting a man, don't you think? Maybe he knows you're trying to get him for what he did to the girl, so he's warning you to back off."

Dean thinks it makes sense. "In that case, we know whoever did this is watching us. And he thinks he's powerful. He doesn't like being investigated."

"Maybe he is powerful," says Steve. "Maybe he has money, or a powerful job."

Eva shakes her head. "I don't know."

Dean says, "You know you can stay with me until this is cleaned up, right?"

Eva rolls her eyes. "I'd rather stay in a hotel."

Steve gives him a look that suggests he's in trouble, but Dean doesn't know why she's mad at him. He genuinely doesn't think this was Lizzie Glover, so how can he be to blame?

"And how do you explain this?" She points to the balloon tied to her front door. It's swaying in the breeze.

"Where did that come from?" he asks.

She rolls her eyes at him again. "Obviously it comes from that stupid haunted attraction. It was here when I got home. Is it supposed to be funny, or is this how they mark their next victims?" She gestures to the body on the couch. "Is this how clowns work these days?"

"Come on," he says. "They're probably just a bunch of high school dropouts promoting a new attraction. You can't assume anyone from there had anything to do with this just because of a balloon, Eva."

She shakes her head, irritated. "Well, it's either someone who works there, the person who beat Taylor, or your psychotic ex-girlfriend. Which is great because none of those options particularly appeal to me."

"I've seen those promo balloons all over town," says Steve. "So I wouldn't assume it's linked to this."

Dean looks closer at the front door. "No sign of forced entry. Could you have left your door unlocked?"

Eva glares at him. "Look at the lock, Dean. A child could pick that with a hairpin. It's ancient."

She's right. The door could definitely do with upgrading. The windows too.

"And look at this mess! How am I supposed to even begin cleaning this up?"

Dean looks again at the blood that appears to be sprayed on every wall.

"Let me call some cleaners," says Steve. "The people I'm thinking of are awesome at their job. You won't know this ever happened here by the time they're done. Laurie could have it all cleaned up in two or three days."

"Who's Laurie?" asks Eva.

"She runs *Scene It All* cleaners. They exclusively clean up crime scenes and offer very reasonable rates considering what they have to do."

"Fine," she says. "Thanks, Steve. Hopefully Frankie will split the bill with me."

Dean asks Sheila if she needs them to wait for her team to arrive. They'll take what's left of the body to the morgue for her.

"No, that's okay," she says. "Maggie's on her way. She'll want to dust for prints and the rest of it. I think the captain's coming too."

Dean hasn't met Maggie Summers, their new forensic technician, yet. They didn't have one when he worked at MVPD previously.

"You two get going," says Sheila. "I know you've already had a long day. Just leave me your keys, Eva. I'll get them back to you when we're done here."

"Frankie has a spare set, Eva," says Dean. "You can use those in the meantime."

Eva silently heads into her bedroom to collect some items while he waits for her.

Steve searches the room for evidence. Normally, Dean and Eva would help, but Dean thinks it's best to get her out of here. He'd be shaken if this happened in his house.

Eva says thanks to Sheila and Steve as she walks past them with a full backpack.

Sheila gives her a hug. "Try not to worry about this. Call me if you need anything."

After removing their protective gear, Dean leads Eva outside. She pushes past the gathering crowd of onlookers and ignores their questions. It looks like they've come out from the diner to see what's going on as some of them have even brought their food with them. One man starts filming Eva on his cell phone. Dean's not surprised when she grabs it from his hand and throws it across the parking lot.

"Get out of my face or I'll arrest you," she says.

"Hey! You can't do that to my phone!" he protests.

The crowd makes disapproving noises and part to let Dean and Eva through. Dean follows her to her car. "Where are you going to stay?"

"I told you. I'm going to a hotel. I need to sleep."

Dean's disappointed, but it's up to her. She doesn't say goodbye as she drives away.

He decides to stay and look around outside to see if he can find any more balloons or clues as to what happened here tonight. He knows he's being watched and probably recorded, but he has to ignore the onlookers. He's just glad the media haven't arrived yet, although that's just a matter of time.

Officer Jenny Lawson turns up in another police cruiser. She rushes over to him. "What can I do?"

"We have a dead male upstairs," he says. "A homicide. I need you to question everyone who was eating in the diner about what they saw. Get their contact details."

Jenny looks up at the apartment. "Is Eva okay?"

"She's fine. She's staying at a hotel. Can you also tell Frankie to close the diner early? It's the quickest way to get rid of these guys."

"Sure. No problem." She heads to the crowd, opening her notebook.

Dean pulls out a flashlight from his trunk and uses it to search the parking lot. He doesn't find anything out of the ordinary, so he makes a note of every vehicle's license plate for future reference. He walks into the woods on the edge of the lot. After twenty minutes of searching, once he's in the thick of the trees, his flashlight reflects off something.

He moves forward and crouches down.

It's a large knife. And it's covered in blood.

CHAPTER FIFTEEN

The next morning, Eva's already at her desk when Dean arrives at the station shortly after eight a.m. She's concentrating on her computer screen, analyzing photographs of the victim from her apartment. She doesn't acknowledge his arrival until he speaks.

"Morning," he says.

"Hi." She doesn't look up.

Dean checks to see if she has coffee yet. She does, alongside a half-eaten pack of cookies.

"What's wrong?" he says. "Have I done something to piss you off?"

She finally looks up at him and sighs. "I don't know."

He smiles. "You don't know what's wrong or you don't know if it's me?"

"Both." She doesn't smile back.

"How was the hotel?"

"Expensive."

"Jeez, this is hard work," he says. "Are you just going to give one-word answers to everything?"

"Probably."

Dean sits at his desk and switches his computer on. "You could've stayed at my place, Eva. You've been there before, and I know you can't afford a hotel right now so I don't know why you went there."

She finishes her coffee. "Sheila's invited me to stay with her and Steve tonight, so it doesn't matter."

He tries not to show his disappointment, but it feels like something's changed between them. "Guess what I found in the woods last night?" he says.

She looks interested. "What?"

"A bloody knife. It could be the murder weapon."

"Great. Is it being analyzed?"

"Yeah. I met Maggie Summers, the forensic tech, for the first time. She arrived just after you drove away last night. She's interesting."

"Interesting, how?"

"She's funny. But I can tell she won't take any shit. I just hope Marty behaves around her." He hesitates. "She reminds me of you actually. I think you two will get along."

"Well, I'm sure I'll meet her soon enough," says Eva.

"She's going to get the knife tested for DNA and she'll check for prints too." He pauses. "I gave her the two yellow balloons we have too, but they've both deflated so it might be tricky getting something off of them."

Eva raises her eyebrows. "Why test the balloons if you think I'm being stupid?"

He smiles. "Because you're more experienced than me, so I'm willing to follow your lead."

She looks away, but Dean thinks he sees a hint of a smile on her lips.

"Maggie will let us know if she gets anything useful," he says. "Jenny and Marty are checking your apartment for anything else that could tell us who killed that guy. They're going to interview Frankie and the waitresses too, in case they or last night's diners saw or heard anything."

"It'll be interesting to see whose knife it was," she says, with no enthusiasm at all.

"We need to visit Taylor again today. Hopefully she's starting to remember something." Dean's cell phone rings and he sees Camille's number appear. He answers it. "Hey, Camille."

As he says her name, Eva looks up at him with interest. When she sees him notice, she immediately looks back at her screen.

"Hi, Detective," says Camille.

"Seriously, call me Dean."

"No! I've never had a detective in my phone book before. I like it!" she says with a laugh.

Dean stands up and walks away because he doesn't want Eva to see him smiling. "Are you calling about today?"

"Right. What time do you want me?"

"I'm not going to be able to get away, so go ahead and let yourself in with the spare key."

"Sure," she says. "I'll be there around one o'clock if you find you can spare some time."

"I'll see what I can do."

When he returns to his desk, Eva says, "You'll have to visit Taylor alone this time. I've had a call from Jake so I'm heading to the community center to see what he wants." She stands and pulls her jacket on. "Catch you later."

Dean watches her walk away.

* * *

Taylor's sitting up in bed eating a small bowl of cereal when Dean arrives. When she sees the flowers he's holding, she beams. "Are those from my mom?"

Dean shakes his head. "No, sorry. She hasn't gotten in touch yet. I'm assuming she's out of town for work, or maybe on vacation. These are from Sheila. She still feels guilty about mistaking you for a dead body."

Taylor watches as he places them on her nightstand.

"So how are you feeling today?" he asks. "Can you remember anything yet?"

Her bruising looks the same but the swelling's gone down some more. It's more obvious now that she's a teenager, not a young woman. She's still pinned down with wires, so she can't be out of danger yet.

"I'm so bored in here," she says. "I just want to go home, but I still can't remember my name or address."

Dean sits in the armchair next to her bed. "Okay, let's play a game. I've been thinking about this and you never know, it might work. I'll run off a list of people and places, and you tell me whether you know their names. Sound good?"

She puts the cereal bowl on her nightstand and readjusts her position, ready to play. "Okay."

"Just shake your head if you don't know," he says. "Okay, here we go. What's the name of . . . your dad?"

She shakes her head.

"Your mom?"

She tries hard to recall something before shaking her head again.

Dean quickly runs through other potential people in her life: a brother, a sister, any extended family, her doctor, any pets she might have, her high school. But it's no good. She doesn't remember the names of any of them.

He tries to reassure her. "You just need more time to recover. Don't worry, I'm sure it'll all come back to you eventually."

She leans back into her pillows, already tired.

"We ran your picture online last night," he says, "but we haven't had any credible leads yet. It'll be shared on the news later so make sure you're watching. In fact, I'd watch the local news as much as you can because it might trigger some memories if you see your old school, or church, or whatever."

He deliberately uses the word *church* to see if she reacts negatively again, but she doesn't. He doesn't want to push her on it because Dr. Armstrong wouldn't be happy with him. It's still early days in Taylor's recovery so he has to be patient. It's hard when her attacker is still out there and a risk to others. Especially if he's the one who killed the guy in Eva's apartment.

"And I'm going to visit the local high schools to see if anyone there recognizes you. Can I take a new photo now you're looking a little more like yourself?"

She nods, so Dean snaps a couple with his phone.

She suddenly leans forward and spits into her hand. She looks down at it and then up at him. She's lost a tooth. "It was cracked the other night, but I didn't think it would actually come out."

Dean can tell she's trying to hold back tears and he feels terrible for her. He takes her tooth away and passes her a drink of water.

"I'll send Dr. Armstrong in to check your mouth. Is there anything I can bring you tomorrow? Magazines, music, a book? You know, in exchange for your tooth, like a tooth fairy."

She doesn't laugh. Instead, she struggles to talk without crying. "I need a cigarette."

He sighs. "If I bring you cigarettes Dr. Armstrong will kill me. You realize that, right?" He gets up, ready to leave.

She almost smiles. "Okay. Just bring me chocolate then, while I've still got teeth to eat with."

"Sure thing."

By the time he returns from the hospital, it's just after lunchtime so he swings by his house to see if Camille's still there. He notices her red Nissan parked outside as he pulls in. He tries to tell himself he's not checking up on her. He's just there to answer any questions she has about the house.

She's approaching the front door when he enters.

"Oh, you made it. Great," she says. "I've taken all the photos I need so I should be able to write it up by the end of the week and get it to you for checking. Here's your key."

As she hands it over Dean tries not to notice her curvy figure. She's dressed in yoga clothes and sneakers. He wonders if she's heading to the gym next. "Thanks. I'll see you out."

As she leaves his house she says with a smile, "Have a great afternoon catching bad guys, Detective."

He laughs as he locks up. She's definitely flirting with him.

CHAPTER SIXTEEN

Eva drives to Sheila's house after work. She glances at the bottle of vodka on the seat next to her. It's been a crap day. She feels horrible for being moody with Dean earlier, but she needed some alone time. Every now and then she just can't deal with people.

This afternoon she concentrated on phoning the list of people who were in the diner last night in case anyone saw who killed the guy in her apartment, but it seems as if no one saw a damn thing, just like with Taylor. She's starting to think small-town mentality is at play. People might not be forthcoming because they all know each other and half of them are related. Either that or they walk around with their damn eyes closed, or on their phones. She's finding small-town life incredibly different from city living, and she's not sure she can get used to the slower pace.

She's also not sure why she's so annoyed at Dean, but after seeing that body on her couch and all that blood everywhere, it made her wonder what she's gotten herself into. Logically, she knows Lizzie Glover can't be back in town because she'd have been spotted by now, but she wishes she'd known the woman lived there before she moved in. It's not surprising Frankie didn't want to tell her because he wanted a tenant in the place, but Dean should have told her sooner.

As for the balloon tied to her door, that's too close for comfort. She went sleepwalking last night at the hotel. She used to do it a lot as a kid but thought she'd grown out of it. Just like she thought she'd grown out of teenage acne, but that seems to have made a comeback too. She knows it's the thought of clowns being in town, not the crime scene at her house, that's making her sleepwalk. They stress her out for reasons she doesn't want to think about right now.

Eva's planning to pay the new haunted attraction a visit tomorrow to find out who tied the balloon to her door. She's seen several clowns around now, dressed menacingly by the roadside and waving at passers-by. Even if it wasn't one of them who killed the guy on her couch, they could've spotted who was hanging around her apartment when they tied the balloon to her door. They could have witnessed something.

Her mood today also hasn't been helped by finding out Jones is happy for George to move in with him. He phoned George to introduce himself and apparently, they got on so well they're already planning a vacation to Gettysburg together. She loves George, but she could just do with some space while she settles in here. He reminds her of her old life in Colorado, of Frank and McArthur PD. She hasn't thought about Detective Garner and that whole sorry mess at the ski resort for a few weeks, and she doesn't want to.

It's dark as she pulls up outside Sheila's house. Steve's still at work. She knows because she left him chatting to Captain Brown. She hopes he doesn't mind Sheila inviting her to stay the night.

Sheila appears at her front door and waves her inside.

Eva holds up the vodka bottle. "I brought company. I hope you don't mind."

"Awesome, just what I need after my day," says Sheila. "I meant to head to the liquor store on my way home, but I've been so forgetful lately. I think it's the hours I'm putting in.

Steve says I need to cut back because he's sick of repeating everything twice." She laughs.

They grab some glasses from the kitchen and settle on the couch in the living room, in front of the TV. Some trashy reality show is on, which surprises Eva as she didn't think Sheila would watch this kind of thing.

"I need to decompress by watching something light," explains Sheila. "I have enough crime and death in my life, so I don't want to watch it at home too."

They both down a shot of vodka.

Eva's planning on taking it steady. The last time she was properly drunk was in Colorado. Dean was nursing her better after she was attacked. The memory makes her smile. It was the moment she realized she could trust him. "Do you have anything to eat? I'm starving."

Sheila jumps up to get her phone. "What do you fancy? I don't feel like cooking, but we can order anything we want."

* * *

After sharing a huge, spicy takeout pizza, and more vodka for Eva, she feels relaxed for the first time since she found the body in her apartment. She learns Sheila's not good at holding her liquor. She's only had two shots and a small glass of wine and she's already a giggly mess, with potato chips all down her shirt.

"Now, Eva. Tell me honestly." She puts her wine glass down. "What do you really think about Dean?"

Eva knew this question was coming at some point tonight. She knew people would assume they're probably sleeping together. "He's annoying."

Sheila looks surprised. "No, he's not! He's just misunderstood. He's had a tough time. I'm not sure how much you know about that?"

"Frankie filled me in."

Sheila laughs. "Don't believe everything Frankie tells you! Some things are lost in translation."

Eva snorts. "Yeah, I noticed. How long have you known Dean?"

"Ooh, let me think." She unnecessarily counts the years on her fingers. "About five or six years, I think. Ever since he joined MVPD as a rookie cop. He worked at the prison before that, but I'd never met him then."

"What was he like as an officer?"

Sheila looks at her. She's clearly drunk. "One word. Hot!"

Eva laughs again. She wasn't expecting that. "You think he's hot?"

"He *is* hot!" she says. "He used to look great in uniform. That's the worst part about him being promoted to detective, he doesn't have to wear a uniform anymore." She leans forward with a finger over her mouth as if she's revealing a secret. "Did Frankie tell you about me and Dean?"

"No. What about you and Dean?"

"OMG, Eva. I assumed you knew! I hope you don't think any less of me when I tell you this, but I want to be honest with you." Sheila hesitates and checks over her shoulder, even though they're alone in the house. "We had a very brief affair. While he was married."

Eva's not easily shocked by people and their affairs, after all, her own husband was cheating on her before he died, but she can't imagine Dean being the cheating type.

"It's not as bad as it sounds though, because his wife was cheating on him at the same time," explains Sheila. "Their marriage was practically over already, and our affair happened right after his brother killed himself. You know about that, right?"

Eva nods. "How long did your affair last?"

"Oh, not long at all. He felt so guilty about it, but I was single and I enjoyed every minute of it. Is that wrong?"

"Kind of. But it depends. Were you friends with his wife?"

Sheila screws her face up. "No. Linda wasn't very friendly toward me. I don't want to speak ill of the dead, obviously, but Dean could've done much better. They weren't a happy couple during the last two years of marriage. That woman made him miserable if you ask me. Not that he'd ever speak poorly of her, dead or alive. But she wasn't a girl's girl, like you and me."

Eva shakes her head as she considers it. "I can't imagine Dean cheating on someone. He doesn't seem the type."

"He isn't. But his brother's death devastated him. They only had each other because their parents are already gone. Then Linda died immediately after telling him she was pregnant with his child."

"*What?*" Eva had no idea. She sits up straight. "He didn't tell me she was pregnant when she died! The poor guy. No wonder he hates talking about all that."

Sheila leans in like she's telling another secret. "But Linda was lying."

"What do you mean?"

"I did her autopsy. She wasn't pregnant at all. She must've said that to trick him into getting back with her after their break-up."

Eva's even more shocked now. "That's a terrible thing to do!"

Sheila nods. "I told you she wasn't very nice."

"How did Dean react when you told him she wasn't really pregnant?"

Sheila takes a deep breath. "I never told him. How could I? It would've messed him up all over again. Other than Dean, only me, Steve, and Captain Brown know anything about the supposed pregnancy. And only I know it was fake."

Eva can't believe she kept it from him. "But he's been grieving for a baby that never existed. You need to tell him it was all a lie!"

Sheila shakes her head. "I can't speak badly about Linda to him. It'll break his heart. He carries so much guilt for cheating on her that he's put her on this pedestal. To find out she lied about the baby will devastate him all over again."

Eva feels terrible for him. She wants to change the subject as she knows Dean would hate to find out they were talking about him. She also needs to sober Sheila up because she's going to regret telling her all this when she wakes up with a hangover tomorrow. That's if you can get a hangover with the small amount Sheila's managed to get drunk on.

"Okay, enough about Dean," she says. "What do you think about those creepy clowns hanging around town? Would you go to that stupid haunted attraction?"

Sheila waves the question away like it's not interesting enough to talk about. "Oh please. If those kids want to be scared, I can scare them. Give them five minutes in my morgue with that body I took from your couch and they'd be running for their mothers." She scoffs. "Never mind those clowns; tell me something interesting!"

"Okay," says Eva. "I got asked out on a date today."

Sheila smiles from ear to ear. "I'm not surprised; you're gorgeous!"

Eva rolls her eyes. "I'm hardly gorgeous with all these spots on my face. Who'd have thought I'd still get teenage acne at almost thirty-three?"

"It'll be the stress you've been through. I read somewhere it takes three months for a stressful situation to show on your face."

Eva thinks about her husband's death and her last case in Colorado, which both happened three months ago.

"But you're still gorgeous," says Sheila. "I mean, someone asked you out, didn't they? Who was it?"

"Just a guy we went to talk to on Monday, where Taylor was found. You know that new community center past Frankie's?"

Sheila nods.

"Jake, who owns it, asked me out. Sheila, he's so attractive he could be a runway model, I'm not even kidding." Eva thought he'd asked her to visit him so he could tell her about a potential witness to Taylor's injuries. Instead, he had taken her by surprise.

She hears some movement outside the house and tries to listen.

"You're not going to go out with him though, are you?" says Sheila.

Eva frowns. "Why wouldn't I?"

"Because of Dean. Come on, I've seen the way he looks at you. He never looked at me that way, I can tell you that much."

"Don't be stupid," says Eva. "He doesn't look at me any kind of way. Besides, I think he's already seeing someone." She thinks about his phone call earlier, with someone called Camille. He clearly didn't want her to listen in on it.

"I doubt it," says Sheila. "He hasn't dated anyone since his wife died. I know because he told Steve at the party the other night. You know, you've never actually told me anything about your husband. I know he died in the line of duty, but you don't seem like you're in mourning, or is that a terrible thing to say?"

Eva sips her drink. "I was at first, before I found out who he really was. But once I got over the revelations, I stopped wasting my energy. I've always moved on quick."

"Was he cheating?"

"Oh, please! Cheating, scamming, embezzling. You name it, Frank was doing it. I didn't find out until after he died. But you're right, I don't miss him as much as I thought I would. Maybe it's the result of being raised in foster homes but you learn to move on fast. If you get too attached to anyone, you're going to live your life in a state of perpetual heartbreak. It might sound callous, but I'm ready to move on."

Sheila grins. "Let's drink to that!"

They clink glasses and down their drinks.

Sheila leans in again. "Can I tell you something?"

"Why not?" says Eva, smiling. "You're on a roll with disclosing secrets tonight."

Sheila playfully slaps Eva's arm. "We're friends now, I can tell you anything! Including the fact that Dean Matheson was the best I've ever had." She pauses before adding, "You know, in bed."

Eva drops her head into her hands. "Seriously, Sheila, that's too much information! How am I supposed to look him in the eye now without picturing him naked?"

Undeterred, Sheila continues. "I'm serious. He was so intense. When I was with him it was like I was the only person who mattered to him. When he looks at you with those gorgeous blue eyes, he's hard to resist. Just you wait. I don't regret our affair at all and if that's wrong then God strike me down now!" She holds her hands up in a surrender pose, laughing.

Someone clears their throat behind them.

Eva's stomach flips with dread. She doesn't want to look but she has to.

Steve's standing there. He must have heard what Sheila just said.

Sheila visibly shrinks into the couch as she says, "Hey, Steve's home!" She launches into a coughing fit before adding, "Honey? I think I'm going to throw up."

Eva tries not to outwardly cringe.

Steve looks unimpressed. He doesn't move as Sheila bolts for the bathroom.

CHAPTER SEVENTEEN

Dean's planning to head to Frankie's for breakfast but he has to wait for Camille. She's stopping by with an update on his house sale. When his doorbell rings, he puts his coffee down and opens it.

Camille greets him with a smile. "Morning!"

Dean wonders how she always appears so positive. He leads her into the living room.

"Well, I definitely have people interested in your house already," she says. "Isn't that great? Here's my suggested listing price."

When Dean reads the figure, he's surprised. It's much more than he paid for it. But a sense of dread tells him things are moving too fast.

"The next step is to hold an open day," she says. "But only if you're sure you want to sell."

Dean takes a deep breath. "To tell you the truth, I think it's a little soon for that. I'm still getting used to the idea of moving. I haven't even started looking for a new place yet."

She nods. "I had a feeling you'd say that. But that's fine. We'll go at your pace. I have somewhere I need to be but would you mind if I use your bathroom before I go? It's a long drive to my next appointment."

"Of course." He moves aside and she heads upstairs. He's washing his cup in the kitchen when his doorbell rings again. He opens his front door to Eva. She has two tall take-out coffees in her hands.

"Morning, partner," she says with a smile. "Want to car share today? I'll drive."

He's surprised. He thought she'd still be upset about what happened at her apartment.

Just as he's about to answer, Camille comes down the stairs with his detective badge in her hand.

"I guess you're going to need this today," she says. "It's a little wet from falling in the shower."

Dean inwardly cringes as he notices the look on Eva's face. She's going to think he's sleeping with this woman.

"Hi, I'm Camille." The realtor holds her hand out to Eva, who reluctantly shakes it.

"Pleasure," says Eva. Her face doesn't agree. She looks at Dean. "I'll wait in the car." She disappears.

Dean says goodbye to Camille on his doorstep as he grabs his coat and runs to Eva's car, trying to avoid the rain. He has a feeling that if he hesitates for just one minute, she'll drive off without him.

As Eva pulls away, Dean buckles himself into the passenger seat and takes a sip of coffee so she can't pour it over him. He can't seem to do anything right at the moment.

"I know what it looked like," he says. "But it's not what you think."

"Hey, it's none of my business who you sleep with." She doesn't sound annoyed but she also doesn't sound happy.

"Eva, she's my realtor. She went upstairs to use the bathroom. Trust me, she's not my type. She's too happy. You know I only go for women with deep psychological issues," he jokes.

"Good to know," she says.

They drive on in silence for a couple of minutes. Dean realizes he cares about her opinion and he doesn't want her to think he's sleeping with his realtor.

"Eva?"

"What?"

"You have the wrong impression of me."

"I don't think so. She's cute. I recognize her from somewhere, but I can't think where. Anyway, you'd make a good couple. She looks as wholesome as you."

He's taken aback. "*Wholesome?* Okay, that's it. Pull over."

She glances at him before pulling into a liquor store parking lot. It's currently empty due to the early hour. The wind rattles the car's windows as the rain gets heavier.

Eva turns the ignition off, and they watch the rain on the windshield for a minute.

"Doesn't it ever stop raining here?" she asks. "I think I prefer snow to this."

He turns to face her. "How about we get real with each other right now?"

She looks like she knows what he's talking about. Dean's heard Marty's taking bets on how long it'll be before they sleep together, so if he's heard that, she must know about it too.

"I can handle that, if you can," she says.

"Great, I'll start. It can't have escaped your attention that everyone's talking about us as if we're a couple," he says. "Am I attracted to you? Of course I am, Eva. You're everything I like in a partner: honest, determined, and you have a great sense of humor, when you're not pissed at me. I know you're a good detective and I respect the hell out of you."

She blushes but she doesn't look away.

"I actually look forward to coming to work, and not just because I'm a detective at last."

She blushes harder and self-consciously touches her face where she's broken out in a few tiny blemishes.

"But I know you're not interested in me," he says. "So you don't have to worry about me making a move on you. I can be professional, despite what everyone must've told you about me. We'd make a terrible couple because you think I was stupid to be blind to what Lizzie Glover was doing and, let's be honest, you respect me a little less for it. And I'm not your type. You like macho, confident men who give as good as you in an argument. Men who lift weights every day and bring their buddies home for card games."

He knows this because Eva told him a little about Frank when they were on their road trip back to New Hampshire after leaving Colorado. "I'm not like that," he says. "I'm too aware of my weaknesses. Hell, I'm not even sure whether I'll make a good detective or whether I should've been in uniform for longer. I have many insecurities . . ." He stops, aware that he's probably being too honest.

She looks at him. Is that disappointment he sees in her brown eyes, or is that wishful thinking on his part?

"You shouldn't talk about yourself in that way, Dean. You'll make a great detective. Especially if you listen to me."

He smiles.

"You want to know what I think about our situation?" she asks.

He nods. He wants nothing more than to know what she thinks.

"Okay, here's the deal." She takes a deep breath. "I hate it when I watch a long-running TV show and the two main characters, who've always worked perfectly well together as friends, suddenly start screwing each other, then fall in love and marry. It's such a cliché. Why can't people just work together and not sleep together? What's wrong with friendship between a man and a woman?"

He tries to hide his disappointment, even though this is what he expected. "I think spending so much time together makes it inevitable sometimes," he says. "Especially as cops. I mean, we spend more time at work than at home. But, yeah, I agree it's a cliché."

"I liked working with you in Colorado," she says. "After I got used to the idea. You can be a little annoying sometimes . . . And you're *always* running late, which is infuriating." She sighs. "Am I attracted to you? You're okay to look at, I guess. But I haven't had sex in a while so I'm not the best judge of character right now." She smiles at him.

He lets her make her jokes.

"Relax, I'm kidding!" she says, playfully punching his arm. "You're right, you're not my usual type, but you're easy on the eye. You know, in Colorado your smile annoyed me, because you seemed too nice and wholesome, so I assumed it was all an act. I've never spent much time around men like you. Men who don't have an ulterior motive. I mean, you met Detective Garner, right?" She scoffs. "He wasn't just a crooked cop, he was a lowlife who did whatever it took to save his own skin. That's the kind of guy I was used to being around. And let's not even get started on my husband. So yeah, I assumed it was all an act. But the more I get to know you, the more I realize it's not. This is just you. And to be honest, that's scary to me. I don't know how to deal with people like you."

He feels shame burning his face. Does he really seem wholesome to her? If only she knew. "You don't know everything about me though." He hesitates before adding, "This wholesome guy you think I am cheated on his wife, just months before she died."

Eva leans in close. He can smell her perfume.

"I know, Dean. Sheila told me about your affair."

He looks away, ashamed. He can't blame Sheila for telling her. He just wishes it had never happened. It's not something he'd ever done before or would ever consider doing again.

"Don't worry about it," she says. "I'm usually attracted to assholes, so that just made me more attracted to you in a screwed-up way." She laughs. "But we work together, Dean, so it can't happen. It would ruin everything. Let's not be that tired TV cliché. Deal?"

He watches the rain on the car's windshield. He knows she's right. "It's like Mulder and Scully," he says. "When they got together in *The X-Files*, it ruined the show. There was no chemistry anymore."

Eva snorts and leans back in her seat. "You watched that show?"

He looks at her. "Sure! It was a good show for the time. You seriously never watched it?"

"I guess I'm a little younger than you, so I missed it. I spent my youth watching badass horror movies." Then she quietly adds, "And countless re-runs of *The OC*."

It's his turn to laugh. "You're telling me Detective Eva Valdez used to watch *The OC*? That annoying show about privileged white Californian kids with the bad soundtrack?"

She cringes. "Yeah. I was in love with Ryan, the tough kid from a poor family."

He grins. "See, I told you I'm not your type! I don't ride a BMX. But if that's what it'll take . . ."

She rests her hand on his.

Dean can feel the electricity in this car right now, despite what they've both agreed. The windows are steamed up and he's not convinced it's because of the weather. He puts his spare hand on hers, leans in, and whispers, "Maybe we should just sleep together anyway. You know, to get it over with?" He's only half joking.

She looks at him like she's seriously considering it. "If I didn't work with you, Matheson, it would've happened already."

Dean would actually consider giving up his detective badge to sleep with Eva right now.

She pulls her hand away and starts the engine. "Okay, so we agree?" she says. "It's never gonna happen, so we can stop thinking about it. You can sleep with your cute little realtor, and I can sleep with Jake."

He laughs, then stops and looks at her. "Wait a minute. Who's Jake?" It takes him a few seconds to place the name. "No way! The priest guy?"

She rolls her eyes at him and then looks both ways to check for cars. "He's not a priest! He's a witty, intelligent millionaire who just happens to look like a male model."

She pulls out of the parking lot, leaving Dean lost for words.

CHAPTER EIGHTEEN

As they drive toward the diner, Eva changes the subject.

"We're going to pay a visit to that haunted attraction today. Just so you know."

He's surprised. "I thought you hated those places?"

"I'm not going for fun, Matheson. I want to know who tied that balloon to my door in case they're the killer, or in case they saw the killer or the victim while they were doing it."

"Why don't I visit Taylor at the hospital while you're there," he says. "So we get more done today?"

She takes her eyes off the road and stares at him, incredulous. "You'd actually make me go there alone? One minute you're telling me you want to sleep with me and the next you're leaving me to take my chances with a bunch of killer clowns, like some kind of sacrificial virgin!"

"Okay, okay! I'll come with you." He laughs. Although she's tough, and not afraid of dangerous criminals, she's genuinely afraid of clowns. He adds that to the list of other things he's learned she's afraid of so far; spiders and the dark.

"Damn right, you will." She shakes her head and turns her eyes back to the road.

Just as they're about to turn into the parking lot at Frankie's Diner, Eva gets a call on her cell. Because she's driving, she hands it to Dean.

It's Steve.

Dean says, "Hey, Steve, it's me. Eva's driving."

Steve doesn't answer.

"Steve?"

"Captain Brown wants a briefing ASAP. Are you on your way?" Steve sounds annoyed.

"Understood. We'll be there in ten minutes."

Steve hangs up without saying goodbye.

Eva doesn't need to be told. She turns the car around in the parking lot and drives back the way they came.

"That was Steve. He sounded weird," says Dean.

"Oh shit, yeah. I should probably warn you about something." Eva hesitates. "Actually, you know what? I'm not really in a position to explain what happened."

He doesn't understand. "What does *that* mean?"

"Erm . . . how do I say this? I was with Sheila last night, at her house. We were drinking and Steve walked in on us."

Dean leans in. "Is this going where I think it's going?"

"Where do you think it's going?"

He doesn't want to say. "Never mind."

"Basically, Steve overheard Sheila talking about you two." She takes her eyes off the road for a second to look at him. "About your affair."

He cringes. "What did she say?"

"Oh, you don't have anything to worry about." She grins. "Sheila was *very* complimentary."

Dean wonders what Sheila could have said about him to upset Steve.

"But Steve wasn't happy," she says. "He asked me to give them some privacy, so I got banished to the spare room. I was too anxious to come out all night. I don't like getting caught in other people's relationship drama. I could hear them arguing and it looked like Steve slept on the couch. I really don't want to stay there again tonight."

"Wait, I'm confused," says Dean. "Steve already knows we had an affair; it was before they were together, so why would that bother him?"

Eva clams up. "Because of what he overheard her say."

"Which was . . . ?"

"I can't tell you. Sorry. Girl code."

She pulls into the station's parking lot and Dean's more confused than ever. "Great. So I'm walking into the lion's den with no idea why he's mad at me. Thanks, partner."

"No problem. I just wish I had popcorn." She laughs, clearly enjoying the predicament he finds himself in.

They walk into the station and look for Steve. He leans out of the conference room and signals them over. He doesn't greet either of them.

Captain Brown is already inside.

"Morning, guys. Take a seat," says the captain. "Let's see where we're at. Any progress with Taylor yet? Does she know who she is?"

As Dean saw her yesterday, he answers. "Unfortunately not, Captain. I visited the local high schools yesterday afternoon with a recent photo of Taylor, but none of the admin teams recognize her. That's not too surprising, given her injuries. And the principals didn't want to risk upsetting the students by showing them Taylor's beaten face."

"That's understandable," says Brown. "But if her family doesn't come forward soon, I'd say go back and do it. In my experience teenagers love looking at anything ghoulish. My nephew googles crime scene photos. Can you believe that? Idiot. It's not like he wants to be a cop or work in forensics; he just does it to pass the time. When I was his age, I was signing up to law enforcement to protect people, not sitting on my damn PlayStation all day and spending my nights googling dead bodies." He shakes his head. "He wouldn't know a hard day's work if it crapped in his lap."

Dean suppresses a smile. Captain Brown's in his late fifties and old school.

"No response from the press release or the news feature?" asks Brown.

Steve speaks up. "Nothing at all, Captain, which is pretty odd. Usually there's at least one crazy who would come forward to claim a teenage girl."

"No psychics even?" asks Dean.

"None," says Steve. "It's a little eerie. Who is this girl?"

"That could mean she's not from around here," says Eva. "Maybe this proves she was dumped here after being abducted from somewhere else."

"Or it could mean she's a runaway and unwanted," says Dean. He thinks of Emily Gordon and how she has no parents and no foster parents, just a well-meaning social worker. And Jodie Lawrence from his last investigation out in Colorado, who left home never to be reported missing by a single member of her family. No one ever came forward to bury her, even after what happened was all over the news.

"It's time to push her then," says the captain. "Check with her doctor first but try to trigger her memory. The doctor must have suggestions based on how they deal with other patients suffering from amnesia. It sounds harsh but we can't worry about upsetting her. She'll be more upset if she gets released from the hospital with nowhere to go and no one to protect her from another attack."

Dean reluctantly agrees.

Eva says, "Maggie's taken her prints, but she doesn't have a record."

Captain Brown nods. "Okay, let's move on to the victim found in Eva's apartment. Maggie's had the DNA report back from the blood on the knife."

Dean raises his eyebrows. "That was quick!"

"I think the guys at the crime lab are afraid of her," says Brown. "She's pretty fierce when she wants to be."

Eva snorts. "Can't wait to meet her."

"She says a match has been found on the national database," says Brown. "The blood belonged to the victim. We have the photo from his driver's license on record."

Dean and Eva look at each other.

Steve takes over. "His name's Connor Peterson. He was on the system for various misdemeanors. His address is registered as no fixed abode."

Captain Brown says, "We need to find the clothes he was wearing that night, and his wallet and cell phone. His phone might tell us who he was meeting. I've asked Marty and some of the other officers to conduct a search of the area." He hands Eva a sheet of paper. "Follow up on Connor Peterson. Find his family and notify them of his death. Find out who his enemies were."

She nods before clearing her throat. "Captain?" she says. "I don't know if you've noticed but there have been some clowns hanging around town recently. They're scaring the community."

"I have noticed," he says. "They seem harmless enough. One of them was waving at me this morning. I was so surprised, I found myself waving back."

"Well, with all due respect, Captain, they're not harmless," she says. "In fact, there was a yellow balloon tied to my front door just before I found the victim on my couch."

Captain Brown looks amused. "You think a clown killed this man? You want me to put out an APB for Pennywise?" He chuckles to himself.

"No, sir. But with the homicide in my apartment and the attempted murder of Taylor occurring around the same time that this new attraction is opening, I think it's worth considering that one of their employees could be acting out his sickest fantasies. I mean, they're all walking around the place fully masked. They could do anything and never be identified. So I'm just letting you know that Matheson and I are visiting the attraction today to check it out."

Brown thinks about it. "Okay, fine. Where is it?"

"The women's prison."

He looks surprised. "Someone bought that dump? They must have more money than sense."

Dean thinks of Jake Andrews. He's new to Maple Valley too. Could the haunted attraction be another of his business ventures? One he's not inclined to admit to owning?

Eva looks at him. "We'll go there as soon as we've seen Taylor."

He nods.

CHAPTER NINETEEN

Danny's snug on the couch in his new pajamas. He's under a thick blanket, with a hot chocolate and a bowl of cereal next to him for breakfast. He feels happy. He's a little uneasy about not having seen his mom and dad for three days, and he hopes they're not upset or anything, but his teacher's house is so cool it makes him forget he shouldn't be here.

He still can't believe she lives in a house big enough for a library. It's only a small room, but it's almost completely full of books about the human body and what happens when it goes wrong. The books have long words he can't pronounce. There's even a skeleton! Not a real one, of course. Well, he doesn't think so. He's guessing she wants to be a high school biology teacher one day.

As he listens to her cleaning the dirty pots in the kitchen, he thinks about the night he ran away from home. After he left his goodbye note on his pillow and snuck out of his house after dark, his teacher picked him up from their meeting place outside the school. She was real nice to him. She took him to a McDonald's drive-thru and bought him everything he wanted. He'd heard about that place, but he'd never been there before. Mom always says her welfare doesn't pay for things like fast food, but it pays for her cigarettes and adult drinks, so Danny's never really understood that.

His teacher watched him eat his food the first time they went, like she wanted some for herself, but she didn't have any. He's since found out it's because she's on a diet. She mostly only eats fruit and vegetables.

When they arrived at her house that first night, he quickly realized he could be really happy here. It's much better than his tiny home. She made him cozy on the couch and let him watch whatever he wanted until it was bedtime. She even has more channels on her TV than he has on his. He decided very quickly that he's going to be as good as gold while he's here because if he upsets her, he'll have to go back home to his cold bedroom and angry parents.

"Are you okay in there, Danny?" she shouts from the kitchen. "Do you need anything?"

He turns to her voice. "I'm good!"

He has everything he's ever wanted now. The only thing ruining it is a weird smell. But he doesn't want to think about that. Instead, he smiles to himself as he finds a cartoon to watch on TV.

CHAPTER TWENTY

Dean persuades Eva to stop at the diner on their way to visit Taylor at the hospital. Frankie is so pleased to see them, he comes out of the kitchen to hug them.

"Here are my favorite two detectives in Maple Valley!" he exclaims.

"Frankie, we're the only two detectives in Maple Valley," says Dean, as he picks a seat at the counter.

Frankie looks at them both seated side by side. "You two would make beautiful babies. I can see it now! And I'd be an uncle at last."

Rachel hits him over the head with a dishcloth. "Shut up, Frankie. You're making them uncomfortable."

Dean and Eva share a smile.

"Okay," says Rachel. "Maybe you're not making them uncomfortable."

Dean thinks that, after their blunt conversation this morning and the deal they've made not to ruin their working relationship, they can handle all the innuendo now.

"Hey," says Frankie to Eva. "That Laurie woman is amazing. She's almost finished cleaning your apartment already, can you believe that? I'm thinking of offering her a job cleaning our freezer seeing as that's practically a crime scene. I can't find anyone who does a good job and Rachel threatens to sue me when I ask her to do it."

"Does that mean I can move back in soon?" asks Eva.

"Really?" says Frankie, looking relieved. He mops his brow with the grease-stained towel he keeps tucked in his apron. "You're happy to return?"

Dean nudges her gently. "I'd play harder to get if I were you, Eva. Cut him a deal; free breakfasts for you and your partner for at least a month. You know, because of all that happened up there. It's a very stressful time for you. You may even have complex PTSD . . ."

Eva smiles. "If I eat any more breakfasts here, I won't fit into any of my clothes anymore."

"Well, *today's* breakfast is on the house for both of you." Frankie turns to Rachel, who's just finished serving a family. "Rachel, take their order. It's on me."

Dean orders his usual breakfast of pancakes with blueberries on the side and a squeeze of maple syrup. Eva orders three types of eggs with hash browns, bacon, and an espresso.

"Get ready with a latte too," she says. "For when I finish the espresso."

Rachel laughs. "I don't know how your heart takes the amount of caffeine you drink."

"Trust me, it works harder when I don't drink it."

Dean leads Eva to a booth and they sit opposite each other, their knees touching. Frankie hasn't renovated this place in years so it's a little tight because he keeps adding more and more seats, thinking one day he'll be catering for the masses. It almost happened during Lizzie Glover's murder trial because the town had an increase in visitors. Morbid tourists wanting to see where the famous serial killer committed her crimes. But that didn't last long once the media attention wore off.

Something catches Eva's eye and she grabs Dean's wrist. He follows her gaze. A man wearing a Michael Myers mask and a blue boiler suit walks into the diner and takes a seat at the table next to them. He doesn't speak a word. He just stares straight ahead.

Eva looks at Dean. "Are you going to let him get away with that?"

"With what?" he says. "Even Michael Myers has to eat!"

She kicks him under the table, clearly not in the mood for a joke.

"Okay, okay." He turns to the man. "Hey, buddy. Why don't you remove your mask for me? You can't look that bad underneath, surely?"

The guy turns to face Dean, stares hard for a few seconds, and then turns back, ignoring him. Dean has to admit, it's pretty creepy.

Eva's pissed. She gets up and walks over to him. She pulls his mask off as he tries to hold it on, but he's not quick enough. The mask is hiding a spotty teenager underneath.

"Hey! What do you think you're doing?" he yells.

She keeps the mask and sits back down. "You're acting like a serial killer, you crazy freak."

"It's called performance art, lady! Give me back my mask."

She throws it at him and flashes her badge. "If you don't get out of here in thirty seconds, I'll throw you in jail and you can perform some art on your cellmates."

The guy catches his mask and looks scared. He walks out of the diner, mumbling something under his breath.

"Seriously, Dean. I can't live here if this attraction takes off. It's them or me." She sighs.

Rachel brings their food over and as they tuck into it, a woman enters the diner and speaks to Frankie. Dean watches her with interest. She's petite, about five-foot-two, and she has bright pink hair and lots of piercings. Frankie points over to them with a big smile on his face.

As she walks over, Frankie shouts across the diner, "This is Laurie!"

Dean puts his cutlery down and shakes her hand. "Hey. Dean Matheson." He realizes too late that he probably shouldn't have shaken her hand given what she's doing upstairs. He discreetly wipes it on his jeans under the table.

Eva moves across the worn faux leather seat to make room for her. "Eva Valdez."

"Oh no, that's okay. I can't sit down," says Laurie.

She has a strong New Jersey accent and carries an eye-watering smell of bleach on her clothes. Dean tries not to react to it.

"I don't want to disturb you. I just wanted to say we're almost done upstairs. I need to know whether you want to keep the couch or not? I gather that's where the poor guy was found so I didn't know if you'd ever feel comfortable making out there again."

Dean smiles.

Eva looks a little taken aback. "Well, I haven't made out there with anyone yet, but I wouldn't let what happened stop me."

Dean's shocked. "Eva? Seriously, you can't keep the couch. Get a new one. I don't want to sit on that thing now."

"Who says you'll ever be invited over?" she says.

Laurie smiles. "You two are adorable."

Eva ignores the comment and looks at her. "Seriously, I can't afford a new one. Unless you think you can't get the blood out?"

"Oh, the blood's easy," says Laurie. "It's the stomach juice that might linger for a while. Just the smell. I have industrial sprays, but they smell worse than the juice. I can try it, but it's up to you. They might bleach the fabric."

Eva looks down at her scrambled egg which is covered in ketchup. She drops her fork on her plate and pushes it away. "You know what? I'll treat myself to a new couch. If Frankie doesn't mind it going in the dumpster. I mean, he owns it, not me."

Laurie surprises them by shouting loudly across the heads of the other diners. "Hey, Frankie? Can we throw your couch away? It's covered in stomach juice and blood."

Frankie looks aghast. "You do what you gotta do." He puts his dirty towel to his mouth.

The other diners look equally disgusted.

"Okay, we'll take it away," she says. "In that case, we should be done with the clean-up by Saturday lunchtime at the latest. You won't ever know someone was gutted in there." She says it with a big smile on her face, completely unfazed by what she's been cleaning.

"Great, thanks," says Eva. "How do I pay you?"

"Any way you like. I'll leave an invoice on your coffee table."

"Thanks, Laurie."

"Pleasure. Think of me for your next crime scene." She hands them both business cards. "Nice meeting ya."

She walks away, whistling.

Dean looks at Eva and knows she's worrying about how to afford a new couch and her half of the cleaning bill. Frankie's agreed to pay the other half.

"I can loan you some money," he says. He would never ask for it back, but he knows she won't take it if it's not a loan.

"I've got an armchair up there. I'll just use that for now," she says. "I'm waiting on Frank's life insurance money coming through. Once I get that, I'll be fine."

Dean suspects she won't want to use her dead husband's insurance money to buy furniture, but it's none of his business. "At least stay with me tonight. You can't stay at Sheila's, and you can't afford a hotel."

"I could ask Jones?"

Dean's exasperated. "You've stayed with me before so why are you hesitating now?" He leans back and smiles. "Unless you think you can't trust yourself around me."

She rolls her eyes. "You wish, Matheson. Listen, I just don't want to fuel the rumors, that's all."

"Eva, the rumors are already lit up like a Fourth of July celebration."

She picks up her latte and downs it. "Okay, fine. I guess it's just for one night."

He smiles. He wants her to know she can trust him. He has no intention at all of ever coming on to her.

Eva's cell phone rings and when she answers it, her smile fades. "Oh my God. We'll be right there."

* * *

Dr. Armstrong greets them in the hallway outside Taylor's hospital room. She looks grief-stricken. "I'm sorry. It happened so fast."

She told Eva on the phone that Taylor succumbed to her injuries.

Dean's still in shock. She was doing better yesterday so he didn't expect her to die. He's pissed off that this could happen to someone so young. She didn't even get to see her mom before she died. It's gut-wrenching.

Two nurses appear from the room, pushing machines and keeping their eyes low.

Dr. Armstrong leads them in to see Taylor. She's lying still with her eyes fixed on the ceiling. Evidence of the resuscitation attempt is all over the room.

Eva looks away. It's a distressing scene.

Dean swallows. "What happened?" he asks.

The doctor pulls the white sheet over Taylor's face, covering her glassy stare, then turns to look at them. "A nurse was with her and said she saw Taylor reach for her head before becoming visibly upset. Taylor explained she felt a sharp stabbing pain behind her eye, and within a minute she slipped away. We worked on her for twenty minutes before calling it."

Eva shakes her head but remains quiet.

"It must be her internal injuries," says the doctor. "She could've still been bleeding. Or maybe it was an aneurysm. I wouldn't be surprised considering the head injuries she sustained. Do you want to notify Sheila, or should I? Because this young lady's going to need an autopsy."

"Oh, God," says Eva. "Poor Sheila."

Dean nods. He knows Sheila will take this hard. "I'll call her."

The doctor leaves and Eva moves to the bed to hold Taylor's hand as Dean calls Sheila. She's not available so he leaves a message with one of her team, then sighs as he slips his phone into his pocket.

He goes to Eva. "Are you okay?"

She lets go of Taylor's hand and nods.

They wait for Sheila on the chairs outside the room.

After a few minutes' silence, Eva says, "Why is it always girls? Men are such lowlifes to take their issues out on young girls who can't defend themselves. I'm sick of it!" She swallows back a sob.

Dean rubs her back. He knows as well as she does that it's not always girls. Plenty of boys fall victim to this type of crime too, just not as many, so she's right about that. He knows she's just frustrated.

She falls quiet and stares at the floor.

As Dean checks his cell phone, he feels like he's being watched. At first, he doesn't bother looking up because he's replying to a text, but the feeling doesn't ease, so he stands and puts his phone away. He looks left. There's no one there but busy medical staff, so he looks right and just catches a man in a black coat walking away and turning down a hallway to the exit. Dean's about to go and check him out, but Sheila arrives from the other direction and she looks flustered.

"Hey," she says. Her eyes are bloodshot. She's been crying.

"She's in there," says Dean. "Do you want us to stay with you?"

"No, it's fine. I can handle this. After all, it's my job. You go and find whoever did this to her."

He nods. "Sure. Let me know if you need anything."

He watches as she enters Taylor's room and pulls back the white sheet that covers her lifeless body. Sheila stares silently at Taylor's pale face.

Dean walks away. He wishes they could have done something for her. She was too young to die.

CHAPTER TWENTY-ONE

Eva has a mug of coffee in her hands, which has stopped them from shaking. To distract herself from thinking about Taylor, she's come to sit in Maggie's office, as she bumped into the forensic tech in the kitchen and Maggie introduced herself.

Her office is small, but it's warm and full of interesting stuff. MVPD sends most evidence away to be analyzed by a professional team at the state lab, but Maggie's able to perform some tasks, saving them time. Her walls are covered with photos of blood spatter patterns and research papers about recent DNA developments. Among all that are a *lot* of cat photos.

Maggie catches Eva looking at the felines. "The tabby is Joey. He's a doll but he'll try to screw your leg, or your head, come to think of it; he's not fussy. I had his balls chopped when he was a kitten, but I think he has a third one floating around inside somewhere. That boy's insatiable, God love him. The caramel-colored one is Sookie." She pauses. "You ever watch *True Blood*?"

Eva nods. "The vampire show? I did, actually."

"Sookie's named after Sookie Stackhouse. She'll love you once she's known you a few years, but you can't pet her any time before that if you value your life. She has trust issues. She recently had kittens actually, even though the shelter assured me she was neutered when I rescued her." She turns back to the photos. "And the orange one?" A smile breaks out across her face. "Well, that's Teddy-bear and he's just downright insane. He weighs almost seventeen pounds because he's a Maine Coon. He looks like the sweetest creature on earth but he's a hunter. He's always bringing me animals, from birds to wild rabbits. He once brought me the cooked chicken from my neighbor's dining table, or what was left of it after he ate his share. But that's better than getting gifts from some jerk who's just trying to get into my pants, right?"

Eva smiles. Maggie must be almost sixty, with a gravelly voice and a smoker's cough. She has dyed purple hair and wears glasses that hang off the end of her nose. She reminds Eva of the actress who played Molly Brown in the Titanic movie. She's already earned a reputation at the station for being opinionated, so Eva doesn't want to get on the wrong side of her. "I guess," she says.

"Oh, don't be coy," says Maggie. "I've heard you're a real ball-breaker. You're not that keen on men either. Am I right?" She raises a hand in a gimme five gesture, before noticing Eva's reaction.

Eva's genuinely shocked. She can't understand why she'd get that reputation. "Really? Who told you that?"

"Miller and Marty were gossiping about you when I was making coffee earlier. Miller said you shot a man in the balls just for coming onto you, and he died. He thinks you're gay."

Eva shakes her head. "No, that's not how it was at all. Well, I did shoot him in the groin. And yes, I guess he died, but not because I hate men."

"Shame. We could've had some fun."

Eva realizes Maggie's flirting with her. She laughs, which eases her tense shoulders. "Sorry, Maggie. I was actually married to a guy until recently. His name was Frank, but he died four months ago."

"Sorry to hear that."

"Thanks. He was a cop and he died on the job. But I know who killed him, and now they're dead."

"Whoa! I wouldn't want to mess with you!" Maggie tries for another high-five.

She thinks Eva killed Frank's killer in retaliation. Eva's about to correct her when Dean walks in.

"Hey," he says to them.

He looks as depressed as she feels.

"Detective Matheson," says Maggie. "Glad you could join us. So I guess you guys want to know about the blood on the knife that was used to kill that man in your apartment?"

Dean speaks up. "Actually, the captain told us the blood belongs to the victim, Connor Peterson. We need to track down his family."

Maggie nods. "So, Detective Matheson, I hear you're a dog person?"

Eva smiles. Dean's about to get a roasting from a crazy cat lady.

He frowns. "What?"

Eva watches as he notices the cat photos on the wall for the first time and it slowly dawns on him.

"I like cats too," he says. "I used to have one, actually, before I had a dog. Her name was Bella."

"Oh yeah?" says Maggie. "And what happened to little Bella?"

Dean suddenly clams up. He's struggling to come up with a suitable answer.

Eva's intrigued by his reaction. He must know what happened to his damn cat?

"Er, she went to live with her aunt by the coast." When that doesn't satisfy Maggie, he adds, "Only because my wife and I were thinking of divorcing, and she was kind of my wife's cat."

Maggie shakes her head. "The pets are always the ones to suffer."

Dean makes eye contact with Eva behind Maggie's back and motions to the door. He wants to get out of here. "Thanks for the update, Maggie."

She turns around to face them. "Before you go, are either of you in the market for a kitten? I've got just two left from Sookie's litter and I can't find anyone to take them. One's orange and one's black." She looks at them as if she's fully expecting them to say yes.

Dean struggles to find a suitable answer so Eva answers for both of them. "Sorry, Maggie, but we don't have time for cats. We're always at work."

"That's perfect!" she says. "Cats want the house to themselves. You just need to open the food can twice a day and worship at their altar. They're not soppy like dogs, who follow you around the house all day." She claps her hands together. "That's settled then. I'll get them ready for you to collect tonight. Here's my address."

She writes it down and hands Eva a scrap of paper.

Dean tries to protest. "No, Maggie, you don't understand. I have a rottweiler. He'd eat a kitten alive. Or he'd sit on it and squash the poor thing."

Maggie eyeballs him over the top of her glasses. "Are you lying to me, Matheson?"

"No, of course not!"

"Then how come I heard you offloaded your dog to retired Detective Jones? If the dog's not living with you anymore, you have an empty house. You're not allergic to animal fur, so what's the problem? You want to see these kittens *die*?"

He looks like he wants to escape, and Eva has to stifle a smile. She likes the idea of having a kitten, so unless Dean can get them out of it, she'll go with the flow.

"Why would they die?" asks Dean, confused.

"It's a rhetorical question, Detective," says Maggie. "Like I said, I'll get them ready for you to collect tonight."

Dean admits defeat and looks at Eva. "I guess we're getting cats."

Eva laughs. "I guess we are!"

"I can't guarantee what time we'll be able to collect them," says Dean. "We might not finish until late, and I wouldn't want to wake you."

"Wake me?" Maggie laughs. "That's a joke. I'm menopausal. I haven't slept in five years. Now, back to business. You haven't asked if there was anything else on the knife." She looks at her notepad. "There were fingerprints all over the handle. One set."

Dean steps forward. "Do you know whose?"

"No. I've been busy. Want me to check now?"

Eva doesn't hesitate. "Yes."

Despite what Dean and Steve said after the body was discovered at her apartment, Eva suspects Lizzie Glover lured that man there somehow and killed him. She knows Lizzie's prints are already on the system, so she's expecting a match. She's looking forward to seeing Dean's reaction when he realizes she was right.

Maggie turns to her computer and within minutes the database is searching through its records of prints and convicted felons. Dean leans over her shoulder to watch.

"Well, it was worth a try," says Maggie.

Eva's surprised. "You mean there's no match?"

"Nope. Not on here."

Maybe Lizzie got someone to do it for her.

Dean looks at her. "I know what you were thinking," he says. "But it obviously wasn't Lizzie. At least now we have fingerprints on record for whoever killed him. It'll make our job easier when we do catch him."

Eva hides her disappointment. "Thanks, Maggie," she says. "Catch you tonight, I guess."

"I'll be waiting." Maggie doesn't look up as they leave.

CHAPTER TWENTY-TWO

Dean drives them to the old prison to visit the haunted attraction. Eva seems sure it's no coincidence that Taylor was beaten and Connor Peterson was killed soon after the new attraction came to town, bringing with it people who like to dress up as murderous villains. But Dean's not convinced.

"I bet everyone who works there has a criminal record," she says, looking across at him while he drives. "Who else would that kind of job attract but freaks and felons?"

He nods. He's trying not to think about the last time he was here, back when he was a police officer.

As he pulls into the parking lot, he notices the women's correctional signs have all gone, and there's a huge build-up of furniture and waste off to one side of the building, presumably waiting to be removed by a private hire firm. Any signs of it once being a prison may be vanishing but the razor wire fence remains. The looming brick building now bears a large graffitied sign calling itself *The Haunted Asylum*.

Dean shakes his head. The kids who work here wouldn't last five minutes in a real asylum. Lizzie Glover would eat them for breakfast.

The attraction looks exactly how he'd expect it to, with clown and horror mannequins everywhere, lights flashing in all directions, and loud metal music playing on speakers dotted around the site. It'll look pretty impressive once the sun goes down, but it's only late afternoon now. The attraction doesn't officially open until tonight so there's no one out front.

They get out of the car and Eva pushes him ahead of her, through the open gates. "You can lead the way." She's probably expecting to be ambushed by clowns.

Dean walks toward the entrance, which is no longer glass-fronted. It now consists of two heavy black wooden doors covered in more graffiti. He knocks loudly. Nothing happens, so he pounds harder the second time.

Eventually, someone without a mask appears. He steps out of the building, holding the door open with his foot so it doesn't close behind him. "We're not open for another five hours yet, guys," he shouts. "I like how keen you are, but you'll have to wait."

"Can you shut the music off?" shouts Dean. "It's too loud."

"If I could, I would, but the system's malfunctioning. I've been trying to fix it. Everything's linked: the music, the sound effects, and the lighting. That'll teach me for paying peanuts."

Eva pulls out her badge and shows him. "We're police. We want to look around."

The man sighs. He turns the nearest speaker to face the wall, making it easier for them to hear each other. "Seriously? Why do you guys always assume there's something shady about these places? This is the third one I've run and I've never witnessed anything illegal, despite what the guys on social media say about the last place I worked at and my 'alleged involvement'." He makes air quotes with his fingers. "Can't you give us a break?"

Dean steps in. "We're not here to cause you any problems. In fact, I used to work here, when it was a prison. I'd be intrigued to look around and see what you've done with the place." He holds his hand out. "I'm Detective Matheson, this is Detective Valdez."

The guy accepts the handshake. "I'm Matt. I know your name from somewhere."

Dean inwardly cringes. People sometimes recognize his name from the news reports from when Lizzie Glover was on trial.

When he doesn't volunteer any information, Matt continues. "We only used part of the prison for this attraction. It would be too expensive to fill all of it. But are you for real? You used to work here? Do you know if the rumors are true?"

Dean feels Eva looking at him quizzically.

"What rumors would they be?" she asks.

"You haven't heard?" says Matt. "This place is supposed to be legitimately haunted! By the ghost of the inmate that serial killer brainwashed into killing herself. The inmate was called Shania Riley. According to the book, she was a nasty piece of work which is why she haunts this place, seeking revenge for her death. Why do you think I agreed to work here?"

Dean hopes he's misheard him. Surely there's not a book about the murders?

Eva turns to face him. "Is it true? Is this place haunted?"

He takes a step back, feeling like there's no reasoning with either of them. "Eva, come on! You don't seriously believe in ghosts?"

"Hey, man. They're real!" says Matt. "I've seen more than one myself. I almost caught one on camera too."

The man who was wearing a Michael Myers mask in the diner arrives behind them, still wearing his boiler suit and clutching his mask. He looks at Eva and rolls his eyes. "Are you following me?"

Dean's cell phone rings. He pulls it out. "Hello?"

"Dispatch has taken a call about a dead body," says Steve. "Where are you?"

"At the Haunted Asylum."

"That's where the caller said the dead body is." Steve sounds confused.

"You're kidding?" Dean turns and walks away, not wanting Matt to hear any details. "What do we know?"

"All the caller said was that a teenage boy was killed in the Haunted Asylum last night and they've left his body there to be discovered by customers tonight. It's to boost numbers apparently. Some wise guy came up with the idea that a real murder victim in this place would help it go viral online and bring in more visitors."

Dean can't believe what he's hearing. "Who called it in?"

"It was a male," says Steve. "He hung up before giving any personal details."

"Okay, we're on it. I'll let you know if we find anything, but you might want to send backup, just in case." Dean ends the call and turns to Eva, gesturing for her to come over to him and out of the employees' earshot.

"Steve says they just received a tip-off about there being a dead teenage boy inside this place, to help drum up business, apparently."

Her eyes widen. "You're kidding?"

"Nope." Dean sighs. "How should we handle this?"

"I'll tell you how we handle this, Matheson." She pulls her weapon from under her jacket and holds it up and out in front of her as she advances on the two employees. "Get down on the ground with your hands behind your heads *right now*!"

The two men are so shocked they immediately do as she says.

Eva cuffs the Michael Myers wannabe as Dean cuffs Matt. "Is there anyone else inside?"

"I don't think so." Matt sounds flustered. "The others aren't due for another hour. But they'll probably be arriving early like Tim did." He nods to Michael Myers.

"So what's the screaming I can hear from inside?" asks Eva.

"I was in the middle of testing all the lights and audio. I was going to do a run-through with the actors next."

He could be lying. There could be someone hiding in there. Dean leads both men to his car and pushes them into the back. "More police are on the way so if you try to run you won't get far and even if you did, you'd never get those cuffs off." He opens a window and locks them in.

"But we haven't done anything!" says Tim.

Dean doesn't respond because Eva's already ahead of him, entering the asylum. He follows her in and lets the doors close behind them. Eva hesitates when she realizes it's pitch-black inside.

Dean takes her arm and positions her behind him. "You'll be fine. It's all make-believe. Just don't shoot me if someone jumps out at you. I don't think I can take another bullet."

He heads further into the asylum.

CHAPTER TWENTY-THREE

The first room they enter is pitch-black until what must be a sensor-activated light show begins. Green strobe lighting flashes all around them, encouraging a disoriented feeling. Dean can't see what's in the room so he pulls out his cell phone to use the flashlight. Eva copies him, but their lights have little effect and the hissing smoke machine makes visibility even poorer.

He can just about see a coffin in the middle of the floor, surrounded by spiderwebs, and his gut tells him what's going to happen next. Sure enough, the coffin lid opens and a mannequin dressed as a vampire shoots upward, near to their faces.

Eva screams and pushes it away.

Dean can't see any other bodies — real or fake — in this room so they continue onward, through a dark, narrow hallway.

As they walk, he can feel thick spiderwebs hanging down, brushing against his face. He can hear Eva tearing them all down behind him.

"If any of this contains real spiders I'm burning this place down," she yells.

It's hard to hear her over all the sound effects of people screaming and doors opening and closing, but at least the music from outside is quieter here.

Someone grabs Dean's hand. He jumps and instinctively pulls his hand away. "What the hell was that?" he says.

"What? Dean, *what?* Don't tell me there are people in here?"

Eva sounds on the verge of losing it, so he brushes it off. He must have touched another mannequin. It couldn't be real. But it felt warm.

"Aren't you going to play with me?" says a young girl's voice. At first, it sounds like she's right next to them and then her voice fades. Dean can feel the floorboards vibrate as someone runs away.

He doesn't think that was a mannequin.

Eva grabs his shoulders. "Dean. We need to get out of here. We should've waited for backup to arrive."

"But what if the boy's still alive?" Dean knows they're too far in to turn around now. These places aren't designed to let you out the same way you enter. They're designed to confuse you into pressing forward and seeing everything, just like those Ikea stores. "We're fine, Eva. It's all designed to mess with our senses. That's why people enjoy coming here. They like not knowing what's real and what's fake."

Eva shudders behind him and lets go of his shoulders.

Dean's flashlight goes out. His phone battery must have died. "Shit." He pockets it and continues.

Along the hallway, various windows light up as they walk past, depicting empty chambers. Some are fitted out to look like nightmarish operating theaters and Dean can just imagine the actors hamming it up in there tonight.

Something runs by their legs as they walk through the long hallway. It must be motorized. Eva actually jumps behind him and groans. At the end of the hallway they come to some steps that lead down to the floor below. Dean didn't even know this place had a basement. He dreads to think about what it was used for when it was a prison.

He leads them down, using his hands to move aside anything that's hanging down. At one point he feels a large bug of some sort scurry down the neck of his shirt, down to his back. He knows that was definitely real. There's nothing he can do about it, so he continues forward. He hears Eva taking a deep breath behind him before she moves him aside so she can walk in front with her flashlight. She's either adapting to the darkness or trying to conquer her fear.

They reach the lower level and wind through the maze of rooms. There are so many motorized mannequins mixed in with the décor that it would be difficult to locate a real body in here without emptying the place and switching on the lights. It's hot down here and claustrophobic. Dean just wants to get out now. Eva's right, they should've waited for backup.

Suddenly, Eva pauses in front of him, causing him to walk into her. He rests a hand on her waist. "Eva? What's wrong."

She drops her cell phone. It must land face down as the light no longer illuminates the path ahead of her. "I just saw a girl."

Dean leans over her shoulder. "I can't see anything."

Eva crouches down to retrieve her phone and as she brings it up, light facing forward, they both see a young girl standing at the end of the hallway, staring at them.

"What's wrong with her face?" asks Eva, voice shaking.

The girl's head is white and shiny, with a small painted mouth and no hair.

"It's just one of those porcelain doll masks," says Dean. "It's probably just another mannequin under there. Try not to freak out."

But the girl slowly starts walking toward them. "Will you play with me now?" She raises her hand toward Eva.

Eva stumbles over him as she tries to get away from the girl. She's screaming in genuine fear. Dean moves in front of her.

"Hey, what's your name?" he says. "Do your parents work here?"

The girl stops walking toward them and thinks better of it. She turns and flees, quicker than Dean can follow her. He tries anyway, leaving Eva behind.

He runs through dark hallways until he's forced to stop in front of three doors that are lined up next to each other. They each have one word on them: Painful, Gory, Quick. He assumes they're pretend murder rooms. He doesn't know which door the girl went in, so he opens them all one by one. The first two rooms are empty, and no bigger than a closet.

As he opens the last one, someone jumps out at him; a large male dressed as a zombie lumberjack and carrying what looks like a real axe over his head.

He runs past Dean, laughing menacingly, heading back in Eva's direction. Matt must have been lying to them. There are people already in here, and they must think this is the dress rehearsal for tonight.

He runs after the guy but gets lost in the maze. The flashing lights are disorienting. It takes him longer than he'd like to find Eva. He calls her name as he goes.

After a couple of minutes of searching, someone runs up to him in the dark and he braces for impact. He receives a hard slap to his face.

"You *asshole!*" yells Eva. "Why did you leave me there like fresh bait? I told you I hate these places!"

He rubs his face, amused. "I'm sorry, but I didn't know if that girl was here of her own free will or not!" Blue strobe lighting starts up. He looks down at the floor and notices the huge axe. Then he spots the man who was holding it. He's also on the floor, trying to sit up.

"Hey, lady! What do you think you're doing punching me like that? That's assault!"

Eva approaches him. "You're lucky I didn't shoot you for coming at me with an axe!"

"It's my job! Why are you here if you don't want to be scared?"

Eva leans into his face. "Get us out of here, *right now*."

The lumberjack stands up. "Fine. Follow me."

He knows his way around and quickly gets them outside, where Eva shoots the speaker, which blows the power, making everything that's electrical shut off at once. It's a huge relief to Dean's ears and might help ease his emerging headache.

Steve has turned up with Jenny and Marty, so he lets them deal with Matt and the other employees. More of them have arrived for work, all dressed and ready to scare people, but Matt's been ordered to let the officers conduct a proper search of the building. He'll have to delay opening night by one day, and he's not impressed.

While Marty and Steve are inside, Dean sits next to Eva in his car and they watch the employees hovering outside the entrance. Most of them are smoking and occasionally they point to Eva and laugh.

Eva doesn't respond. She just keeps eyeballing them.

"Why won't that girl take her mask off?" She nods to the young girl they saw inside. She's still wearing the porcelain doll mask and every now and then she turns to stare at them.

"She's messing with you," says Dean. "Ignore her."

He's got to admit they look like a creepy bunch of ex-offenders having some kind of reunion. He can't understand why they'd want to do this for a living, and he'd bet Eva's right about at least one of them having a criminal record.

After twenty minutes, Steve comes out of the building and walks over to their car. Dean gets out to meet him. "Anything?"

Steve shakes his head. "Nothing. Must've been a hoax call. Maybe one of the locals isn't happy about this place and they tried to get it shut down. I can't say I'd like to live near this."

Eva joins them. "Can we get them for anything?"

Steve raises his eyebrows. "Like what? It's just an attraction. They're not breaking any laws."

"It's just a matter of time," says Eva. She sighs and looks at Dean. "Let's get back to the station. I'm sick of this place." She walks around to the passenger side and gets in the car.

"She okay?" asks Steve.

Dean nods. "She's just afraid of the dark, and clowns."

"Really?" Steve frowns. "She doesn't seem the type."

Dean looks at her. "Yeah, she's complicated."

CHAPTER TWENTY-FOUR

Ryan Scott waits for Emily Gordon outside the Hope Center. She's late and it's raining. Not hard, but that fine mist that makes you wish you'd never bothered getting out of bed in the morning. Although working as a social worker will do that too.

When she finally turns up, she drags her heels.

"Come on, Emily," he says, finishing his cigarette. "I don't have all day. I'm a busy man."

Normally, she'd smile at this, but today she doesn't. She's getting soaking wet and her clothes are dirty. She's tied her hair back in a messy ponytail. He wishes she would take more care of her appearance. She walks past him without a word and swings the entrance door open. She doesn't even hold it for him, so it closes in his face.

Ryan rolls his eyes. "Charming."

When he catches up to her inside, she's talking to a tall guy. Ryan notices he's dressed head to toe in designer clothes.

"Hi, are you Ryan?" asks the tall guy.

"The one and only," he says. "And this is Emily."

A look passes between the guy and Emily. Ryan's gut tells him they don't need introducing.

"Are you Jake?" he asks.

"I am. It's good to meet you." They shake hands before Jake says, "Let me show you around the place."

He signals to the woman behind the tiny coffee shop counter for three coffees.

Ryan won't complain about getting a free coffee while he's here. There aren't many perks to his job, and it might melt the cold from his bones. Thanks to his kids, he spends a lot of time outside. Mostly looking for them.

As Jake leads them around the impressive building, he hands them both a schedule showing what classes are on offer. Emily could learn just about anything she wanted and for a subsidized fee. Some classes are even free. But she still hasn't even said a word. Ryan's used to stroppy teenagers, so it doesn't faze him. "You okay, Emily? Cat got your tongue?"

She nods. "I'm just cold."

"Have you been here before?" he asks.

She looks at Jake before answering.

Ryan stops. "Why do I get the feeling you two already know each other?"

Jake looks awkward and leaves Emily to answer. She pulls her shabby coat tighter around her thin body.

"Sometimes Jake lets me have a sandwich or a free coffee when I need it. But we don't really know each other."

Ryan's pissed. Why is he wasting his time introducing her to someone she already knows when she could've told him she's been here before? And why did this guy go along with it? "Any reason neither of you felt like telling me that before now?"

Jake leads them to a table near the coffee shop. Their drinks arrive. "It's my fault," he says. "I don't know Emily well, and I try to keep out of other people's business, so I wasn't sure whether she'd already told you or not. Sorry."

Ryan relaxes and tries his coffee. It's bitter so he adds sugar. "No problem. But you gotta keep me in the loop, Emily. You're supposed to trust me, remember?"

She shrugs and warms her hands on her cup.

"So who pays for this place?" he says, looking around. "I've heard rumors you're a millionaire."

Jake laughs self-consciously. "Well, never believe rumors. But, yeah, I'm funding it for now. Maybe one day the government would like to help contribute to the social care we provide."

Ryan scoffs. "Don't hold your breath."

As they chat about what's on offer that Emily could benefit from, he watches their body language. Emily is leaning back, away from Jake, and Jake focuses on her as he talks. Ryan could be imagining it, but he thinks they're keeping something from him.

He sighs. Maybe he's been a social worker too long.

He figures he'll give the guy a chance and let Emily start using the center. At least then he'll know where she is. But he thinks it wouldn't be a bad idea to keep an eye on Jake Andrews from now on.

CHAPTER TWENTY-FIVE

When they're back at the station, Dean and Eva spend what's left of the day trying to track down anyone who knew either Taylor or Connor Peterson but, so far, there are no leads on either of the victims.

Dean checks for any sex offenders living in the area who have recently been released from prison. He makes a list of four. He contacts the parole officers responsible for them to check their whereabouts the night Taylor was assaulted and is told they'll call him back when they've looked into it. Taylor's doctor didn't think she'd been raped so her attack might not have been sexually motivated, but he still thinks it's worth a try.

He rubs his eyes, sits back in his chair, and looks around the station. The dispatchers — Carrie and Susan — are in their cubicle, gossiping about something while the phones are quiet. Officer Miller is seated at his desk reading a newspaper. Since being demoted from detective, Miller never seems to go out on patrol or do anything useful. Dean wonders if Captain Brown has given up trying to get any work out of him. Maybe he's working on getting Miller fired.

Dean checks his watch. It's after eight and he's thinking about calling it a night and heading home. Eva walks to her desk with a fresh coffee. Steve follows her.

"I've just had Detective Briggs on the phone from Cedar Falls PD," says Steve. "Shannon Mallory, the mother of their missing seven-year-old boy, has told them she thinks her partner's missing now too. He's Danny's biological father. We need to be on the lookout for a male in his mid-thirties with short, red hair. She thinks he's about six foot four inches tall. She also thinks he might have taken the boy with him. It sounds like they have a lot of domestics and the boy's caught up in it all."

"I thought Danny went missing on Monday?" says Eva. "When did the father go missing?"

"The next day," says Steve. "Shannon thought he was just on a drinking spree, but he isn't usually gone this long, and with Danny missing too she's starting to think that he took their boy and fled the state. Maybe the dad made him write the goodbye note, to buy them some time."

Dean stands up. "The kid's name's Danny Mallory, right?"

Steve checks his notes. "Yeah. Dad's name is Trey."

"Trey Mallory?" asks Dean.

"Let me check." Steve returns to his computer screen.

"If his wife thinks they've left the state," says Eva, "why are we being updated? They're probably long gone by now. The Feds will have to get involved if Trey crosses the state line with his son."

"Detective Briggs isn't convinced the father took his boy," says Steve. "There wasn't a custody battle going on and the parents are still living together, on and off, but not married. Danny dropped some hints to his teachers that all wasn't well at home. He described feeling neglected. Told one teacher the family dog gets more attention than him. Sounds more like the kid has just run away for a few days. He's probably hiding at a friend's house."

"Could Trey have killed his son?" Eva asks.

Steve takes a deep breath. "Anything's possible, but Briggs isn't going down that route yet. We've just been asked to keep an eye out for either of them, same as the other PDs around the area."

Eva looks at Dean. "What do you think?"

"You said Trey's red-haired?" says Dean. "Do we have a photo of him?"

Steve shakes his head. "Not yet. Looks like he doesn't share Danny's last name; his is Peterson."

"Trey Peterson?" says Dean. "The guy found on Eva's couch is called Connor Peterson. He was a redhead, and tall too."

"Could they be brothers?" asks Eva.

Dean looks at Steve's computer screen. "Says here our murder victim has a middle name, but only an initial is given. Connor T. Peterson." He looks at Steve. "Get Cedar Falls PD to email us a photo of Danny's father. He might go by his middle name."

"Sure." Steve picks up his desk phone.

"You really think they could be the same person?" asks Eva.

Dean shrugs. "Why not?"

"It's a long shot. And what would he be doing in my apartment if he's from Cedar Falls?"

Steve leans back in his seat, holding the phone away from his mouth. "They're emailing me a photo."

Dean and Eva stand behind Steve's chair. When the email comes through Steve clicks on the attachment. All three of them stare at the image.

"Well, I'll be damned," says Eva. She looks at Dean and smiles. "Looks like you're right, Matheson. Our victim and Danny Mallory's father are the same guy: Connor Trey Peterson. Looks like he prefers to go by his middle name."

Dean's relieved. "But now we need to tell Shannon Mallory he's dead. And where's her son? Why wasn't Danny with Trey?"

Eva thinks about it. "Maybe whoever killed Trey took Danny, or maybe Danny really did run away on his own. We can drive up to see Shannon first thing tomorrow. It's too late now."

Dean nods. Cedar Falls is an hour's drive away, and it's already late. He's exhausted. It's been a full-on first week so far and tomorrow is supposed to be his one day off. He'll have to take it another time.

With a glance at her watch Eva says, "Oh crap. We're meant to collect the kittens!"

Dean sighs. "Do I really have to home a kitten? Can't you take both of them?"

"No way!" she says. "I can't afford to feed *two* extra mouths."

Steve stands. "I'll update Detective Briggs. You don't want Briggs to notify Shannon of her partner's death?"

"No," says Dean. "I want to see how she reacts. Besides, Trey was killed here so Briggs won't have all the facts."

Steve nods. "Sure. See you guys tomorrow."

As they walk away Dean asks Eva, "Are you still crashing at my place tonight?" He notices Miller looking at them with a sickening grin on his face.

"I was right," says Miller, shaking his head.

"Oh yeah?" says Dean. "Right about what?"

"You two. It's embarrassing for the department for you to be screwing each other. You'll bring your domestic problems to work with you."

Dean feels his face redden. "No, asshole. You're the only embarrassment to this department." He starts forward, unable to contain himself when it comes to Miller. It's not just because he's a prize-winning asshole; it's because he took such delight in arresting Dean for the murder of his wife after she died. Dean will never forgive him for that.

Eva steps in and pulls Dean away. "Come on, lover boy. Save your energy for me in the bedroom." She surprises him by winking at Miller. "At least we're getting some tonight, *Officer*. You think about us when you're alone in the shower, desperately trying to get it up."

They walk away, grabbing their coats as they leave.

"Doesn't that bother you?" says Dean. "What they're saying about us?"

"We've got bigger fish to fry," she says. "Come on, let's get out of here."

CHAPTER TWENTY-SIX

The drive to Maggie's house is quick as the roads are empty. It's a cold night, but it's stopped raining at last. They take separate cars, which gives Dean time to consider what could be happening with Danny Mallory and his family, and what they need to do next. He wonders whether it's in any way related to what happened to Taylor, but other than the fact both crimes occurred in the same week and in the same town, there's nothing else to suggest a link.

Maggie appears at her front door before they're even out of their cars. Dean pulls his jacket on and approaches her door behind Eva. She leads them into her small living room. It's filled with cat trees and pet beds with various cats curled up inside them.

Eva's straight on her knees, looking at the two kittens in a box who are emitting high-pitched cries. "Oh my God, they're adorable. Dean, look!"

He kneels down next to her. The kittens look tiny and he wonders whether Rocky actually *would* eat them if he met them. Eva picks up the orange one, so he picks up the black one.

Maggie says, "That one's a girl, Eva. Matheson has the boy."

Eva's girl purrs gently, looking up at her in awe. The boy scratches Dean with razor-sharp claws as he tries to get away.

Maggie laughs. "Yours is a bit of a live wire, Matheson. He'll be fun, that's for sure."

"Shit!" He didn't realize how sharp their claws could get. The kitten makes it onto his arm and pulls himself up toward Dean's shoulder, leaving a trail of kitty-claw destruction behind on his jacket.

Maggie plucks him off and places him in a pet carrier. Eva kisses the top of her kitten's head and gently places her next to the boy. Maggie closes the door so they're secured.

"I have food, litter boxes, bedding, and toys for you to take," she says. "They like wet pouches. I haven't been able to get them interested in dry food yet, but it's just a matter of time. Don't feed them human food if you don't want to live in a state of constant regret, especially chicken."

Dean raises his eyebrows in question.

"They'll get a liking for it and never let you enjoy your food alone again," she explains. "You'll need to buy some bowls for food and water, unless you have something suitable from the kitchen."

Dean thinks of Rocky. He ate from an old pasta dish for the entire time they lived together.

Eva gets up off the floor and picks up the pet carrier. "Thanks for this, Maggie. I promise we'll take good care of them."

"You better. No giving them up behind my back." Maggie looks at Dean. "I'll know if you do."

Dean wouldn't dare. Maggie escorts them out of the house and waves as they pull out of her driveway. Dean has a feeling she's waving goodbye to the kittens, not to them.

* * *

When they enter his house, Eva places the pet carrier on the floor in the living room. Dean looks in at the cats. They're asleep, curled up together. He's got to admit, they're sweet. He's still not sure this is a good idea, though.

"Can I take a quick shower?" asks Eva.

"Sure. I'm going to make dinner. Is pasta okay?" It's all he can be bothered to make this late.

She nods before taking her backpack upstairs.

Dean looks for a jar of pasta sauce in the kitchen and his eye is drawn to one of the drawers near the sink. The one he keeps his mail and paperwork in. It's open a little, with a letter poking out. That's weird; he doesn't leave drawers open. Not ones he doesn't go in very often, anyway. He pushes it closed.

By the time Eva appears, in sweats with wet hair and no makeup, dinner's ready and the kittens are awake.

"This looks great, just what I need," she says. She lets the kittens out and eats while sitting on the floor, letting the kittens walk all over her.

Dean screws up a piece of junk mail and flicks it. The black cat runs like the devil to catch it, throwing it into the air and entertaining himself. Amused, Dean watches as he eats his pasta.

"What are we going to call them?" asks Eva.

"I think I'm going to call mine Bullet," he says.

She puts her fork down. "You're not calling him Bullet, Dean."

He laughs. "Why not?"

"It's too clichéd for a cop's pet. Let me try to think of a name."

They both go quiet for a minute.

Dean grins. "I've got it!"

She looks up at him.

"We can call them Mulder and Scully!"

Eva laughs at first, but her smile quickly fades and she looks almost on the verge of tears.

"We don't have to," he says. "It was just a suggestion."

She whispers, "Dana Scully." She appears to get used to the idea. "Scully!" she calls. Her kitten stops what she's doing and walks over to her, tiny tail held high. She starts purring when Eva touches her face. "She likes that name. Okay, then. Scully it is."

Dean looks around for his kitten. It takes a while to spot him because he's halfway up the drapes. "Mulder! Get down!"

Eva laughs as he tries to pull Mulder off the thick material. He's holding on with his claws.

When she's finished her food, Eva stands and grabs a fluffy pet bed from the pile of things Maggie gave them. She picks Scully up with her free hand. "I need to sleep."

"I'll be going up soon too," says Dean. "It's meant to be my day off tomorrow, but I'll postpone it now that we've had a break in the case."

Eva thinks about it. "How about you take the morning off and then I take the afternoon off? Frankie told me Laurie's almost done with my apartment, so I'd like to go and check it out after work and arrange for better locks to be fitted before I move back in. You can visit Shannon Mallory at lunchtime if you want to be the one to break the news to her."

Dean would rather they both went to see Shannon, but as MVPD only has two detectives, it's a balancing act. "Sure. Try not to wake me when you get up in the morning. I'm exhausted and could do with a few extra hours' sleep."

"Roger that." She heads upstairs.

Dean turns back to the living room. "I guess it's just you and me tonight, Mulder." He looks around but Mulder's nowhere to be seen. "Shit."

CHAPTER TWENTY-SEVEN

Danny's scared. He hasn't seen his mom and dad in four days, and he's beginning to think he's made a mistake. Sure, his parents are either screaming at him or ignoring him, but that's better than watching someone unravel in front of him. Aren't adults supposed to be calm?

His teacher has left him alone in the house. He's glad but he doesn't know when she's returning, so he can't relax completely. He knows she would've locked the doors and windows behind her, because she caught him trying to get out yesterday. He wishes he could find a book in her library about how to make someone normal. Because she isn't acting normal anymore, and that's why he wants to go home.

He's not quite in full-on panic mode yet, like when he knows Johnny Laverne's about to punch him, but he's getting there. It turns out his teacher is a completely different person at home than she is at school. She's started talking funny at home. It's an accent he's only ever heard on TV. It makes him nervous because he doesn't know why she does it.

He's also noticing she cleans things over and over again, like she's afraid of germs. She makes him shower twice a day, saying that kids have more germs than adults, and she cries at really random times. She looks so sad when she does that, it almost makes him cry. She talks to her mom a lot too, even though it's just them here. He's afraid she's talking to a ghost.

Danny wishes he'd told people in his running-away note where he was going.

But it's too late now.

He takes his dirty glass into the kitchen. He doesn't like the kitchen because that's where the smell is coming from. Not a food smell, more of a gone-bad smell. He looks at the door that leads to the basement. It doesn't have a lock on it, but it does have a wooden chair pushed against it. He suddenly wonders whether there's a way out down there. His basement at home has a small window that's always left a little bit open. His dad says it's to stop the mold from getting worse. Danny thinks he could squeeze through a window like that.

He thinks about what to do. If Miss Livingstone comes home soon, she'll catch him down there. He doesn't think she'd hurt him, but he's not certain so he hesitates. The overwhelming urge to go home and see his mom spurs him into action. He easily moves the chair out of the way and grabs the doorknob, praying it's not locked.

It turns in his hand, so he opens the door. His first reaction is to run away. The foul smell is a million times worse now and it attacks his throat. He turns around and throws up his dinner all over the floor. He can still recognize the peas he ate, along with the large red vitamin pill Miss Livingstone makes him swallow every day.

Afterward, his skin crawls and he feels shaky. Something's not right down there. But he wants to go home so bad. Maybe it's a dead animal. He's seen plenty of those by the side of the road before and he knows they can smell bad. But what if there's a rat family down there and they're all eating the dead animal?

April Parker from school told him that rats eat each other. She had a mommy rat who gave birth to seventeen baby rats and the mom ate every single one of them. April showed him a photo of what was left of them. Just skulls and tails, basically. He'd had nightmares for days after seeing that and just thinking about it now makes him feel like he might throw up again. He retches.

Danny knows he has to be brave because Miss Livingstone could be back any minute. Although he still likes her, he doesn't like living with her and he'll explain that once he gets out of here and returns to school. He hopes she'll understand.

He tries to find a light switch for the basement and succeeds. He pulls the string, but the bulb doesn't go on. With shaky legs, he slowly walks down the steps, making sure there's a step below each one before placing his weight on it. He'd hate to fall through a gap and die down here with that smell. He has to cover his mouth and nose with his T-shirt, but he still gags the closer to the bottom he gets.

When he feels he's near the floor, he puts his foot out to find it. His foot finds something soft and squelchy. When he puts his weight on it, the object splits apart with a weird popping noise. A disgusting smell comes out and his foot warms.

Danny screams as he pulls his foot back and tries to see what he stepped in, but it's so dark down here. After standing still for a minute or two, his eyes adjust and he suddenly wishes they hadn't. He gasps.

It's a man.

He's just lying at the bottom of the stairs. His face is turned away from Danny. Danny looks at his stomach and realizes that's what he put his foot in. He starts crying and wets himself at the same time.

"Danny Mallory!"

He spins around and sees a dark figure at the top of the stairs, backlit by the kitchen light.

"What on *earth* do you think you're doing down there?"

It's Miss Livingstone. She sounds really mad. He's trapped between her and the dead man. As the man's blood runs off Danny's wet foot, he realizes he'll never see his parents again.

CHAPTER TWENTY-EIGHT

Dean's woken from his deep sleep by the sound of the doorbell. It takes a few minutes to realize what it is. He looks at the time: it's just after ten a.m.

"She must've forgotten something," he murmurs, getting out of bed wearing just his dark blue pajama bottoms. He thinks about putting his T-shirt on but the doorbell rings again. He'd forgotten to give Eva the spare key. Mulder is fast asleep on the bed next to him in the pet carrier, with the door open. He kept Dean awake last night with his playful antics.

When he opens the front door it's not Eva standing there, but Camille.

"Oh, sorry! Did I wake you?" Her eyes drift downward to his bare chest.

He's confused. "Do we have an appointment?"

"I texted you last night," she says. "I said I'd be dropping by this morning to get your approval of the photos I took for the listing."

Dean runs a hand through his hair. "I haven't seen your message yet, sorry."

She looks disappointed so he feels like he should at least invite her in for coffee. Despite it being obvious he's only just woken up, she accepts. They head to the kitchen and Dean remembers he left Mulder upstairs.

"Give me one second," he says, as Camille takes a seat at the breakfast bar. He doesn't want the kitten to wake up and fall off the bed trying to get to him, so he runs upstairs to pull on a T-shirt and get the cat. When he enters the kitchen with a sleepy Mulder in his arms, Camille appears surprised.

"Oh my goodness. That's so cute!"

Dean notices she doesn't make a move to stroke the cat.

"I have allergies," she explains. "Cat fur is one of the worst. I can only appreciate a kitten from afar."

He places Mulder on the breakfast bar and empties a small wet pouch of kitten food onto a saucer. He reads the back of the pack. Surely this can't be all he needs? Rocky would eat ten times this amount. Mulder starts purring as he eats.

"You look half asleep," says Camille. "I feel guilty for disturbing you."

Dean notices his reflection in the microwave. He has two days' worth of stubble and his unruly black hair is sticking up all over the place. He could do with a haircut. "Don't worry about it. I probably should've been up by now anyway."

He starts the coffee machine and selects some mugs from the cupboard.

"You drink coffee?" he asks.

"Whatever you have is fine."

He tries to find out more about her. "You're not from around here, are you? Your accent doesn't sound local."

"I'm from LA actually, but I moved here a few months ago. I'm just renting at the moment. I'm not sure if I'll stay."

"What made you choose the east coast?"

"I had to go where the work was and I thought it would be safer than LA. What about you, have you always lived here?"

He nods. "I grew up here. I spent last year living in Vegas, but it was too hot for me."

"It must be nice to come home and have your family around you?" she asks.

He doesn't know what to say. His parents are dead, and his brother killed himself, so there's only Dean left. He doesn't know Camille well enough to tell her that.

When the coffee's ready, he pours it and joins her at the breakfast bar with a carton of milk in one hand and the mugs in the other. She looks dressed-up, like she's going somewhere special later. He spots her looking at Eva's hairbrush on the dining table. It's obviously not his as it has long strands of dark brown hair sticking out of it.

"I hope I'm not interrupting anything?" she asks, nodding to the hairbrush.

"That's my co-worker's. She had to stay over last night because of a problem with her apartment." He finds himself wondering why he's explaining this to his realtor.

"I still have some of my ex's stuff," she says. "I should probably dump it because we've been apart for a year now. I haven't dated anyone since."

He's surprised. She's attractive and outgoing. He thinks a lot of men would react to that in this town. To change the subject, Dean asks to see the photos she took of his house. She hands him her camera.

"Speaking of exes, my ex was a fireman," she says. "I guess I have a thing for men in uniform." She leans forward and puts her hand on Dean's thigh.

Dean suspected she might be interested in him, but he didn't expect her to act on it this quickly. He hasn't decided whether it's a terrible idea to get involved with his realtor or not.

"Just for the record, I like you, Detective." She puts her coffee down and looks at him. They're sitting side by side.

Dean can't pretend he's not tempted. It's been over two years since Linda died and he's not been with anyone since. And the house is empty, and he has the morning off. The conditions are perfect. But there's so much going through his head right now. Eva, primarily. He knows what they agreed and it's not like he's saving himself for her, but she'll never let him live it down if she finds out he slept with his realtor.

Camille slides her hand up his thigh and leans in to kiss him. She tastes good. But after a few seconds, Dean pulls away. He puts his hand on hers to stop it going any higher.

"This isn't a good idea. We don't know each other very well."

She smiles. "Isn't that part of the appeal?"

He laughs. "Maybe. But we should probably keep this professional. Otherwise it's going to mess with Mulder's head." He tries to keep the mood light, but he can see surprise on her face.

She leans in again and whispers, "Are you sure?"

She lightly kisses him again and it takes every ounce of willpower he's got to pull away. For some reason, he just doesn't want to get involved. Not right now. Maybe it's because of what happened with Lizzie Glover or maybe she's just not the right woman, he doesn't know. He could easily take this further because he's attracted to her, but he doesn't want it to end in tears.

"You're very tempting, but I'm sure."

She sits back on her stool. "No problem. I understand. You're a cop, you're married to the job. It's probably for the best." She takes her camera and smiles at him. "Thanks for the coffee."

"Sure." As he watches her leave, he has a feeling he won't be hearing from her again.

He looks at Mulder. "You'll never know how much strength that took, boy."

Mulder ignores him and continues eating. Dean's cell phone rings. It's Captain Brown.

"Matheson? You need to come to the station *immediately*."

Dean stands. "Is everything okay?"

"Not really," says Brown. "I need you to get here before the shit hits the fan."

Dean swallows. "I'm on my way."

CHAPTER TWENTY-NINE

Before Dean can even check his desk for messages, Captain Brown's door opens and Eva appears from inside his office. She looks tired and pissed off.

"Dean? Can you get in here?" she says.

He enters the office and finds Steve and the captain already inside. The atmosphere is tense. "What's happened?" he asks.

Eva closes the door behind him.

Captain Brown takes the lead. "We had some information come into us about an hour ago about the man found on Eva's couch."

"And?"

Captain Brown shares a look with Steve before saying, "The caller claims they saw the killer."

Dean frowns. "Surely that's good news?"

Eva faces him. "The caller said it was me, Dean. They said that *I* killed Trey Peterson."

"What?" He looks at her, incredulous.

"I know, right?" she says.

"Why would someone say that?" he asks. "Did the caller give their name?"

Steve speaks up. "That's what's even more messed up. It was Emily Gordon."

Dean's mouth falls open. He can't believe it. Why would Emily lie about something like that?

Steve takes a deep breath before explaining. "Dispatch transferred the call to me. Emily wouldn't give her name at first. She said she wanted to report a violent crime above the diner. The way she tells it, she was hanging around outside, smoking a cigarette, when she saw Eva arrive home with a tall man who had red hair. She said he was wearing a brown jacket and blue jeans."

Dean looks at Eva. "We don't have his clothes, do we?"

She shakes her head. "Whoever did this took his clothes with them. Obviously, because they'd be covered in DNA. There was no cell phone, wallet, or ID either."

"Emily said the pair were making out at the top of the steps, really going for it apparently," Steve continues. "It looked like they couldn't wait to get inside the apartment. Then, once the front door was closed, she heard the man yelling from inside. That's when she hid behind a car in the parking lot, so she could watch what happened next. She said after almost ten minutes, Eva came out, walked past the cars, and entered the woods. She had something in her hand but Emily couldn't make out what. She did, however, notice the woman's hands were covered in blood."

Eva rolls her eyes. "How convenient."

"How would Emily know there was a knife in the woods if she's lying?" mutters Dean, trying to figure out her motives.

Steve says, "Apparently, Eva returned to the apartment. She was in there for another ten minutes before I arrived at the scene, responding to Eva's call. Emily said she ran away when she saw the police cruiser. She didn't want to get dragged into it as a witness, at least not at first."

Eva shakes her head. "This is bullshit. She's lying. If it was me, what did I do with his clothes? You would've found them still in my apartment."

"Didn't you pack some things to take to the hotel with you?" asks Steve.

Eva glares at him.

He holds his hands up. "Sorry, I'm just playing devil's advocate. The prosecution could claim you took his clothes away in your backpack, right in front of us, and then disposed of them elsewhere."

Her eyes go watery, and Dean can tell she's afraid they don't believe her. "Eva, we know you didn't do this," he says.

"But if the press hears this my name will be dragged through the papers!" she says. "This is just the kind of salacious crap they'd print."

Captain Brown tells everyone to calm down. "Matheson, why would Emily do this? You know her better than anyone here."

"Did she actually name Eva or does the woman she saw just fit Eva's description?" he asks. There is a possibility, no matter how small, that this could have been done by someone who looks similar to Eva, and therefore Emily could be telling the truth. That's what he wants to believe, anyway.

"She didn't use Eva's name but she said it was the same woman who lives in the apartment," says Steve.

So she *is* accusing Eva. It's personal. Dean thinks about it. Emily seemed pissed at him when he caught her trying to break into that car a few days ago. "She met Eva outside the diner the other morning, so Emily knows she's working with me, and I think she's mad at me for some reason. But she's not normally a liar."

Eva spins around to face him. "So you believe I killed that man?"

He reaches for her arm, but she pulls away. "That's not what I'm saying. I just don't understand why she'd lie about something so serious."

"Well, the best way to stop this getting out to the media is to not talk about it outside of this room," says the captain. "But in case it does get out, we need to take your fingerprints, Eva, to compare them with the prints found on the knife. Just so we can be ready with the denials."

Eva's shocked. "Is that really why you want to take them, or do you believe the girl? Because I'd rather you were honest with me from the beginning."

Captain Brown clears his throat and looks at her sternly. "I'm in the business of policing, Detective Valdez. If I have to take an officer's fingerprints to rule them out as a suspect, then that's what I'll do. Now go and see Maggie. She can take them. Unless you want Sergeant Dalkin to do it out there, in front of everyone?"

Steve looks at the floor and Dean can tell he's hoping he doesn't have to do it.

Eva storms out of the room and slams the door shut behind her so hard the glass rattles in its frame.

Dean has no idea what's going on in Emily's head but he needs to find out. He doesn't follow Eva to Maggie's office. He knows the fingerprints won't be a match, and Eva probably doesn't want him there anyway. First, she thinks Lizzie Glover's after her, and now Emily's making these outlandish allegations. The one thing that links them all is him, so he doesn't blame her for being annoyed at him.

He walks outside to his car to make a call in private. It's raining again.

Emily's social worker picks up almost straight away. "This is Ryan."

"Hi. It's Dean Matheson."

Ryan sighs. "I was expecting a call from you. Sorry, but Emily really doesn't want to speak to you."

Dean's disappointed but not surprised. Emily knew that accusing his partner of murder would result in questions from him. "Why not?"

"She says you'll try to intimidate her so that she doesn't testify against your partner."

Dean shakes his head. "That's not her talking. She doesn't speak like that, in those terms. She won't have to testify because Detective Valdez didn't do what Emily is accusing her of. That'll be cleared up in about ten minutes, so what she alleged is irrelevant. I need to speak to her. She's either being manipulated by someone, or she was mistaken about who she saw that night."

"Hey, I wish I could help," says Ryan, "but she was adamant. Even went so far as to say she was afraid of you. I don't know what your history is but she does not speak highly of you, my friend."

Irritated, Dean says, "Ryan, listen to me. Someone's controlling Emily. She's not the same girl I used to know. Who's she been hanging out with lately? Anyone new? You said she fell in with the wrong crowd."

Ryan lets out a long breath. He's obviously thinking about it. "Well, let's see. Her BFF hasn't been around for a while so everything's been quiet on that front. And I took her to that church place you told me about. She liked it there. That Jake guy was good with her, I guess, and she's going to stay with one of the families she met at the free lunch. I visited their home with her, to make sure it was all above board and not some people trafficking set-up. They're a nice, religious family who've fostered a bunch of teens before, although they're not registered foster carers for us. Emily clicked with their kids right away. She knew them from school but always kept her distance because she knew they were religious, and she wasn't raised that way." He sighs. "She's sixteen now and it's her choice where she stays. All I can do is look out for her as best I can. Which means respecting her wishes about you."

Dean ignores the comment. "What are their names? The family. I need to speak to them in case it was one of them who put her up to it."

"Whoa! You can't go spoiling this for her," says Ryan. "If you mention she witnessed a murder, they might not want to help her out anymore. The thought of cops and court cases can put people off, trust me. Besides, they only just met her. How could they be involved in this?"

Dean feels like he's banging his head against a brick wall, but Ryan's right. He can't question them. They're trying to help Emily. "Can't you speak to her?" he says. "Try to find out if she's holding a grudge against me and taking it out on my partner? She needs to know I'm not mad at her. I just want to know what's going through her head."

Ryan hesitates. "That's not really my job, man. I'm *her* social worker, not yours."

Dean watches Marty pull into the parking lot.

"Have you considered Emily might not be lying?" says Ryan. "Let's not assume the foster kid is the one in the wrong here. I mean, is there a chance your partner *did* kill someone? How long have you guys actually worked together?"

Dean wonders how much Ryan knows about the homicide. The press release was obviously in the papers and it was all over the news, but Eva's name was kept out of it. The location was just noted as the apartment above Frankie's Diner. But Emily obviously knew it was Eva's apartment as she's been hanging around. It sounds like she hangs around outside the diner a lot. He doesn't want to think about why she does that. He's hoping she's not turning tricks to earn money.

Neither she nor Ryan knows how Trey Peterson was murdered and what effort the killer went to. That wasn't mentioned in the press release. No one would consider Eva capable of it if they'd witnessed the crime scene.

"There's no way she did this, trust me."

"Whatever you say," says Ryan. "But you know what? I'll give it a shot. With Emily. I'll try to find out what's going on in her head. I just can't guarantee you'll like what she has to say."

Dean's relieved that Ryan seems to realize the potential trouble Emily could cause by lying. "I can take it," he says. "It's not fair to drag my partner into whatever games she's playing."

"I'll be in touch." Ryan ends the call.

Dean takes a deep breath and tries to concentrate on what they need to do next. He slips his phone into his pocket and looks up. He notices a man staring at him from the other side of the road, opposite the station's parking lot. He's tall but he has his hood up so Dean can't see his face or hair. He's partially obscured by a large tree trunk. The man suddenly turns and walks away, disappearing behind traffic.

Dean's stomach flutters with nerves, which is stupid. But he feels like he knows him, even though he didn't get a good look. There's something familiar about him. About the way he walks. Could it be one of those actors from the Haunted Asylum, following him? Is this the same guy who was watching him in the hospital?

His phone buzzes with a message. It's from Steve.

You better get back in here.

CHAPTER THIRTY

Eva's fuming. She can't stop shaking her head. But part of her is afraid too. How does she prove her innocence?

Dean squeezes into Maggie's office to join the rest of them. "What's going on?" he asks.

Everyone simultaneously looks to Maggie for her to deliver the bad news.

"There's only one set of prints on the knife and they're a match," she says. "It would appear that Detective Valdez held the knife that killed your guy."

Eva notices Maggie uses her full title instead of just her first name. The captain did it earlier too. Is this what happens when you suddenly become a suspect? Are they trying to de-personalize her to make it easier for them to arrest her?

"This is ridiculous!" she says. "I'm obviously being framed by someone. I don't even know the dead guy. I don't know anyone in this damn town!"

Captain Brown leans on Maggie's desk. "Is the knife from your apartment? Have you ever seen it before?"

"I don't know," she says. "Dean found it after I left the scene and he gave it straight to Maggie, so I've never actually seen it."

She starts feeling hopeful that she can easily explain why her prints are on it. As the murder happened in her apartment, it would make sense if the killer used one of her kitchen knives. But there would be more than one set of prints on it. Unless they wore gloves.

"Maggie? If you would be so kind," says the captain.

Maggie looks up at Eva with sympathy in her eyes as she pulls open a lockable drawer and brings out a bagged knife. It's a large carving knife, with a black handle. Eva didn't bring any kitchen items with her when she moved. The apartment came almost fully furnished. "I can't say with one hundred percent certainty that it's mine because I don't own anything in my kitchen, but it looks like an everyday kitchen knife so it could be from my apartment."

Captain Brown sighs, clearly disappointed that they can't be sure. "Okay, so who would want to frame you for this? Who stands to gain from it?"

She's only been in town for two and a half months and she hasn't made any enemies yet. She hasn't gotten off to a good start with Officer Miller, but it's nothing that would warrant framing her for murder. She thinks about Lizzie Glover, but she's still never met the woman so it's unlikely Lizzie knows anything about her and, besides, if she was going to frame anyone, it would be Dean.

"It must be whoever killed Taylor," she says. "I think Steve's right about that. This piece of shit knows we're looking for him and he doesn't like it. Maybe he chose to frame me instead of Dean, assuming I'd feel threatened enough to back off the case. You saw Taylor's injuries. You know we're dealing with a psychopath who's capable of anything. And one that does *not* like women."

"He probably has mommy issues," says Maggie. "A lot of men do." She looks up at them. "Sorry, just my two cents' worth."

Dean nods. "I agree with Eva. I think if we find who killed Taylor, we'll find the link to Trey Peterson." He turns to

Maggie. "What about the two balloons we gave you? Did they have any prints on?"

Maggie shakes her head. "No. But they did each have a piece of paper inside them."

Eva leans in. "A note from the killer?"

Maggie snorts. "No. Coupons. Two of us can now visit the Haunted Asylum for half price."

Eva feels stupid and avoids Dean's stare. She knows he thinks she's being paranoid about those annoying clowns.

"I checked them both for saliva first," says Maggie. "But they must have been inflated with one of those balloon pumps as there was no DNA on them. They also have no fingerprints on them at all, so they're both clean. Whoever inflated those balloons used gloves. Which in itself is odd."

"Not if it was a clown," says the captain. "Don't clowns wear gloves?"

"But we've searched the Haunted Asylum and there was nothing untoward there," says Eva. "Apart from the actual employees, that is. I wouldn't be surprised if it's all linked somehow. It's too much of a coincidence for a new haunted attraction to open in the same week as a dead body is mutilated and a young girl is beaten to death."

"Young girls get beaten every day so that's not unusual," says the captain. "But the mutilation is different. I don't think the two cases are linked, despite the timing. Is there anyone else new to town?"

Eva thinks of Jake and she shares a look with Dean. "The Hope Center is new," she says. "But the owner's doing some good work from the looks of it. He's loaded too, so he has too much to lose to go on a random killing spree."

Dean chimes in. "Marty said the bowling alley re-opened while I was away. Who owns that now?"

"A woman. Astrid something or other," says Steve. "But that re-opened last summer."

There's a knock on Maggie's door. It's Sheila. "Am I interrupting something?"

"No, come on in," says the captain.

Sheila squeezes in. "I've got the autopsy report here for Taylor. I thought you might want to hear my findings as soon as possible."

Captain Brown nods. "Go ahead."

"She died from a post-traumatic subarachnoid hemorrhage. It happened fast, with a typical severe headache beforehand." She pauses. "I want to be clear about something. This hemorrhage was the *direct result* of her head injury. A direct result of the attack."

Eva lowers her eyes. These results won't bring Taylor back or diminish her suffering, but her killer has more chance of getting a life sentence now. If they can catch the guy.

"Did she have any defense injuries or DNA under her fingernails? Anything that can help us identify who did it?" asks Dean.

Sheila looks at Maggie who shakes her head. "No," says Sheila. "Maggie sent some scrapings off for testing but the lab didn't find anyone else's DNA, which suggests she didn't attempt to defend herself. She just let it happen." Her voice falters.

Eva can't look at her. She has to remain composed, but it's hard because Taylor must've thought her life wasn't worth defending.

Steve puts his arm around Sheila, but she pulls away. "I'm fine. I never normally let these things get to me, so I don't know why I'm getting so emotional." She dabs her eyes with a tissue. "It must be because I knew her alive for a short time."

"Or maybe you're just human," says Dean.

She doesn't react. "Her prints aren't on our system and as no family members have reported her missing, I don't know how we'll ID her." She sighs. "I'll write up Trey Peterson's autopsy report this afternoon, but I can tell you he died from a couple of deep stab wounds to his chest. One of them pierced his heart. He was dead before he was cut open, which is something, I guess. His organs were disturbed but none were missing. He had no defense injuries either, so he never saw it coming. Toxicology results will take some time to come back."

Everyone remains silent for a minute as they think about how he died. Eva's thoughts are clouded by the fact someone's blaming her for this.

"If they cut him open *after* they killed him," says Dean, "doesn't that suggest the murder wasn't about Trey? If they wanted to hurt him, they would've cut him open while he was alive. And the fact he was killed on *your* couch means this is more about you, Eva."

She nods. "Let's drive up to see Danny's mother. We can give her the news in person and she might know who would've wanted to kill her partner. He must've had enemies or some link to Maple Valley. Also, we can get his cell phone number from her and pull his records to see who he was talking to the day he died."

Dean nods. "Steve, have you got her address?"

"Here you go." Steve tears a page from his notepad and hands it to Dean.

As Eva's about to leave, Captain Brown stands up and stops her. "Actually, Detective, I can't let you interview anyone related to the victim."

"What? Why not?" She realizes it's because her prints are on the knife. That could look bad for the department when this goes to trial. It could look like she's trying to frame someone else for a murder when the prints and location of death suggest she committed it. Especially as there's a witness willing to lie about seeing her do it.

Captain Brown looks sympathetic as he says, "The family and the media would have a field day if they knew your prints are on the murder weapon and that I'd let you talk to the grieving partner. I'm sure you understand."

Sheila raises her eyebrows. She wasn't here for that revelation.

Eva looks at Dean and feels helpless. He looks like he's trying to think of a way around it.

"What if she waits in the car?" he says.

Captain Brown shakes his head. "Sorry. It's not happening. We all need to do this right. Otherwise, it could lead to an appeal if the prosecution ever secures a conviction for this. You have to remember, Eva, I'm in a precarious situation right now. I should probably be interviewing you for this murder."

Eva can't believe her job and possibly her freedom are on the line. For now, all she can do is work behind the scenes on Taylor's case while Dean visits Trey Peterson's partner. She thinks of Jake at the community center. Maybe she can jog his memory for anything he's forgetting about the night Taylor was dumped. He's the only person who was nearby around the time she was found.

As everyone filters out of Maggie's office, Eva follows Dean to their desks. She doesn't want to be here so, as it's meant to be her afternoon off, she decides to leave. She needs to check in on Scully anyway.

"I'm leaving for the day. I won't get in your way, Dean. But keep me updated."

"Are you okay?" he asks, his eyes full of concern.

She nods.

"Would you feed Mulder for me? I'll check in on him in a couple of hours." He digs out his spare key from his coat pocket and hands it to her. "I'll see you at mine tonight."

She leaves without responding. She needs to get away from Dean and this place for a few hours.

CHAPTER THIRTY-ONE

Eva throws her bag onto the passenger seat and gets into her crappy car. She pulls away from the station, probably too fast, and turns her radio on full blast, even though she doesn't recognize the singer or the song. She thinks about why she moved here in the first place and realizes she's probably made a mistake. George was right. He warned her she was being too impulsive. She was running away from everything that happened back home; from the corruption at McArthur PD to the marriage that turned out to be a sham.

Maple Valley seemed so normal at first. She was excited to be starting over in a town where no one knew her husband or her undeserved reputation at work as a troublemaker. After meeting the MVPD team when Dean was in the hospital, and seeing how they all rallied around him, she was looking forward to working in a supportive environment at last. But it seems Captain Brown might have to suspend her if she and Dean don't find an alternative suspect fast.

Where would that leave her? Out of money and eventually homeless. She'd have to move back to Colorado to be with George.

"Oh shit, George!" She'd forgotten to call him back after he left her five messages earlier. He doesn't always appreciate the fact she has to put work first.

She pulls into Dean's driveway and lets herself into the house. She hears the kittens but she doesn't know where Dean left them. The kitchen door is closed so she opens it gently and the meows get louder. Her heart melts as she spots them, and she feels her blood pressure decreasing already. Maybe the experts are right when they say pets are good for you.

She thinks they must be hungry so she prepares their food. They eat it fast, on the breakfast bar. She makes herself a sandwich and watches them as she eats. Mulder finishes his food first and then pushes Scully away from hers so he can eat that too.

"Hey, you. Don't be greedy." She moves him back down to the floor and he heads straight to their litter box.

When Scully finishes eating, she does the most adorable full-body stretch and then tries to jump into Eva's lap. Eva lets her cuddle while she finishes her sandwich. Scully's purring relaxes her.

After playing with both kittens for a while, realizing they'll chase anything that moves, Mulder starts yawning and Scully uses the litter box. It must be nap time, which is good because Eva wants to visit Jake Andrews.

She puts Mulder in one of the beds Maggie gave them and closes him in the kitchen. Scully's coming with her because once she's seen Jake, she should probably go and check out her apartment. If it's ready, she wants to sleep there tonight and not wait until tomorrow if she doesn't have to. If it's not ready, she'll probably have to waste more money on a hotel for the night. She doesn't want to stay with Dean again. She's relying on him too much and she needs to get her head together.

She puts Scully in the pet carrier, on a fleeced blanket, and gathers all her own things from her overnight stay. Once everything's packed, she locks Dean's house, gets in her car, and sends him a text.

Fed Mulder. He's sleeping now. I'm taking Scully with me. I'll see you tomorrow.

She doesn't wait for his response. Instead, she heads to Jake's.

* * *

When Eva pulls into the parking lot outside the Hope Center she spots Jake's blue pickup truck among the scattered cars.

It looks as though a class has just finished as several people are leaving the building. Jake follows them out. She watches as he helps an elderly lady into a waiting cab. He helps buckle her into the backseat and closes the door, waving as the cab drives away. Then he walks to the front entrance. It looks like he's locking up.

Eva gets out of her car and approaches him.

"Detective Valdez!" he says with a warm smile. "Nice to see you again."

The last time she saw him he asked her out for a drink. She'd told him that wouldn't be appropriate right now, what with them investigating a crime that had taken place right outside a building he owns. She doesn't suspect he was involved but it still didn't feel right. Now, after the day she's had so far, she'd love a drink with him.

"I'm not here as a detective so, please, call me Eva. I wondered if you've got time for that drink you offered me?"

He looks surprised but his smile widens. He has perfect straight, white teeth. "That would be great. As you know, we do coffee and soft drinks inside. Or were you thinking of something a little stronger?" He looks at his watch. It's still the afternoon.

She thinks about taking him to the Tavern, but she doesn't want anyone to see them. It could add fuel to the fire if news gets out about her prints being on the knife and then she's spotted drinking in the daytime. She has to be careful right now.

"Are you closing this place for the day?" she asks.

"Just until later. A couple of exercise classes are scheduled for tonight, but we have a few hours."

"Good. Do you keep liquor in your apartment upstairs by any chance?" She has a feeling he doesn't drink alcohol. Otherwise, he wouldn't look as good as he does.

"I have some beer in my fridge. Would that do?"

She'd prefer something stronger. "That would be perfect." She smiles at him and they have a weird moment.

"Okay, come on in," he says.

"I just need to get something from my car." She runs back and pulls the pet carrier out.

Jake looks amused as she approaches him. "Who's this little guy?"

"This is Scully. Sorry, we come as a pair now. She's sleeping so she won't be any trouble." Scully looks up, yawns then stretches one paw before returning to sleep.

Jake leads them inside and locks the entrance closed behind them, shutting out the strong wind and dark rain clouds. He doesn't bother putting the lights on downstairs, which is already losing the winter daylight even though it's only midafternoon. She follows him into the reception area and up some stairs to his apartment.

"Of course, if I knew you'd be seeing my apartment I would've cleaned up," he says, as he lets her in.

She looks around, intrigued. It's much tidier than she keeps her apartment, so he has no reason to be embarrassed. Each shelf is covered with plants and books, and each wall is covered with paintings of all different sizes. They could be in Manhattan, it's that trendy. She can tell he has money because the place is effortlessly stylish. It's completely different from Dean's house, where everything looks like it's been well-worn. Not that that's a bad thing. Dean doesn't care if she spills pasta sauce on the rug. Well, he hasn't spotted it yet so maybe he will once he knows about it.

She places Scully's carrier on Jake's coffee table and walks to the window, to see how much of the road he has a view of. He has a good view. Better than she expected from what he told them. "Are you sure you didn't see or hear anything on Sunday night?" She turns to face him as he hands her a bottle of beer. He looks disappointed. He must think that's the only reason she came to see him. She realizes she needs to work on her people skills.

"I wasn't up here," he says. "I was downstairs getting ready to lock up, remember? Take a seat."

He motions to his couch which is leather and expensive looking. He has a desk in the corner of the room with two screens and a laptop sitting open. He quickly switches it all off and she wonders what he doesn't want her to see.

"Did you design this building?" she asks.

He sits opposite the couch in a matching leather armchair. "Not the building, really, just the layout. I told the contractors what I needed and they did a great job. I did furnish the apartment myself though, so if you don't like it, that's all me I'm afraid." He sits back, getting comfortable.

"It's nice. And modern," she says. "Much better than my place."

"Do you live in town?" he asks.

She takes a sip of beer, wondering how much to tell him. "Actually, I'm probably your nearest neighbor. I live above Frankie's Diner, the other side of those woods out there." She gestures to the window. Then she watches his face for a reaction. Does he watch the local news? Will he realize it was her apartment where a man was found dead three nights ago?

"Really?" he says. "I haven't eaten in Frankie's yet because I feel like they wouldn't offer any healthy options. Am I right?"

She laughs and relaxes back on the couch, relieved he hasn't made the connection. "Yeah, there are a lot of high-carb meals on the menu. But he does off-menu requests too and all his food tastes better than you'd expect. Frankie's sweet, once you get used to him. Actually, he told me he thinks you're running some kind of cult."

Jake smiles. "I get that reaction a lot. But have I tried to sign you up for communal living yet?"

She snorts. "It would probably be cheaper than my current rent."

Jake puts his beer on a coaster on the oak coffee table and gets serious. "I'm assuming you didn't come here to talk about food and rent. Is there something you need?"

She sips her beer. "I don't know. I've had a really bad day, and days like this make me think about everything that's ever gone wrong in my life, you know?"

He nods.

"You said you lost your fiancée when she was in her twenties. I lost my husband last November."

He leans forward. "I'm really sorry to hear that. Losing a partner is one of the worst things that can happen to you, after losing a child."

"How did you cope with it?" she asks.

Her cell phone rings. It's Dean. She declines the call. She doesn't want to talk about work. She wants to sit here in Jake's warm, comfortable apartment, talking to an attractive stranger about everything that's wrong with the world.

CHAPTER THIRTY-TWO

Dean pulls up to the address Steve gave him for Shannon Mallory. He switches the engine off. It took him over an hour to get here and a quick look around the neighborhood tells him all he needs to know. Shannon's house is surrounded by empty homes with broken glass in their windows and graffiti covering the exterior walls. Next door's yard is full of rusting cars missing their tires.

The sun emerges from behind the clouds as he walks up to the small wooden house and pulls open the screen door, or what's left of it. It's hanging on by just one of its four hinges. He knocks hard on the door beyond as he can hear a TV blasting from inside. It sounds like kids' cartoons. Danny must have siblings.

A dog barks loudly from inside and after a minute or two a skinny woman with dyed black hair approaches him. She has a cigarette hanging out the side of her mouth and Dean doesn't think she's sober.

"Who are you?" she asks, through squinting eyes.

"Hi. I'm Detective Matheson from Maple Valley Police Department." He flashes his badge but she doesn't even look.

"Never heard of Maple Valley."

"It's just south of here."

"Have you found Danny? Is that why you're here?"

He hesitates. "I don't have any news on Danny, no. But I'm here about your partner, Trey Peterson."

She looks surprised and takes the cigarette out of her mouth for the first time. "Trey? He's the one who took Danny. I'm sure of it. Probably just to piss me off."

Dean doesn't want to deliver the bad news on the doorstep like this. "Can I come in for a minute?"

"No, you can't. Just tell me what you've come here to say. I'm busy."

Dean's used to this reaction. His time in uniform saw him verbally abused on a daily basis. One older lady had even spat in the coffee she offered him. She thought he didn't see it but he'd had a hunch she'd do something. She had mean eyes that didn't match her friendly demeanor. He waited until she left the room to feed the coffee to a house plant.

He takes a deep breath. "Okay, if you're sure. I'm here because Trey's been found dead. He was found in Maple Valley on Tuesday night."

Only a slight flicker of emotion passes her face. Not sadness, more like surprise. "So the son of a bitch finally got what was coming to him. What about Danny?"

He expected her to be a little more upset. Judging by her reaction, they must've had a love-hate relationship. "There was no child with him, I'm afraid."

She takes a long draw of her cigarette and then drops it on the ground, squashing it underfoot. "Well, that's the end of that then," she says.

"What do you mean?"

She immediately lights up a fresh cigarette, blowing smoke right into Dean's face. "I've been kicking that asshole out every year since I was sixteen. But I always took him back. I guess that won't be happening again. I can sell all his shit now. God knows I could sure do with the money. Out of interest, how'd he die? Was he shot? I'm assuming it wasn't suicide. He's not the type."

Dean considers not revealing what condition Trey was found in just yet, but he needs to know if Trey had any enemies capable of such a savage assault. "No, it wasn't suicide. He was murdered. In fact, his body was mutilated. We don't know why yet."

He waits for a reaction but all he gets is raised eyebrows. "Shit. Well, it's his own fault."

"Why's that?" he asks, not quite believing she's not upset by this news.

She shrugs. "He was always in trouble. He had a drug habit he couldn't afford. And he liked sleeping around. I'm pretty sure some of those girls weren't even legal. I know I wasn't when he first met me. Maybe some girl's daddy found out." She pauses. "When you say mutilated, is that a polite way of telling me he was castrated?"

Dean tries to think of the scene in Eva's apartment. He thinks the victim was intact in that area but he can check with Sheila. Shannon may be onto something there. Although they're not sure whether Taylor's death is related to Trey's, she was obviously young. So, if Trey did like young girls, maybe he crossed paths with her at some point. And maybe someone in her family found out about it and decided to put an end to it. Vigilantes. It's all the rage at the moment. Dean's aware of the pedophile hunter groups online. They think they're helping the police but a lot of the time they're just making things worse. Trey doesn't have a past record of sexual assault, but that could just mean he's never been caught.

"No, I'm pretty sure he was intact in that region. But he was slit open from his chest to his stomach." He pauses. "Know anyone who'd want to do that to him, Ms. Mallory?"

Finally, she reacts. *"Slit open?"* Her eyes widen and her hand starts shaking so badly that she struggles to get her cigarette in her mouth. "I don't know no one like that, but he might. Like I said, he was always in trouble. I don't know what he was doing down where you're from though. Sounds like he had a wider circle of shit going on than I ever realized."

Dean looks back at his car to check it's still there.

"Does he have any family down there?" he asks.

"He doesn't have family anywhere, apart from me and Danny." She suddenly looks aghast. "What if he had Danny with him when he was murdered and whoever killed him took my boy?"

Dean thinks about it. None of the witnesses eating at the diner that night reported seeing a boy. But then, none of them reported seeing the victim, either. It was dark and wet outside, so they wouldn't have had good visibility of the parking lot. Frankie doesn't light it up at all, despite Dean's advice over the years.

"Have you heard from Danny at all since he ran away?"

"Nothing."

"What about your other kids? Have they heard from him?"

She looks taken aback. "What other kids?"

"I heard the cartoons coming from inside and I just assumed Danny had siblings."

"No," she says. "We only had him. I had to have my lady parts removed after the birth. Little son of a bitch tore me up good and proper while he was inside me. The cartoons make me feel better. They're all he ever watches."

Dean's surprised she doesn't get emotional talking about her missing son, but she could be numbing her pain with drugs. "I need Trey's cell phone number so we can pull his records and see what he was up to the day he died. His phone wasn't with his body."

A tall white male approaches them and pushes past Dean. The stench of marijuana envelopes him. He stands next to Shannon and puts his arm around her shoulders like he owns her. She obviously moves on quick.

"This man bothering you, sweetheart?"

"No," she says. "He was just leaving."

Dean holds out his hand and the man is surprised into shaking it. "Detective Matheson. Just updating Ms. Mallory on her partner's death."

The man flicks his long, greasy brown hair out of his eyes. "Trey's dead?"

Dean wonders whether he's acting or whether he genuinely didn't know.

"He was murdered, apparently," Shannon says.

"No way?"

"Can I take your name?" asks Dean.

"Why? So you can pin this on me?" He snorts. "I don't think so. Come on Shannon, it's starting to smell of bacon out here."

"I don't know his cell number," says Shannon. "He had more than one phone and he was always changing them. That's got nothing to do with me now he's dead. Leave me out of it." She turns to go in. "Don't come back unless you've got my boy with you," she says over her shoulder.

They retreat into the house and slam the door closed behind them.

CHAPTER THIRTY-THREE

When Dean arrives back in Maple Valley, it's dark and blustery out. He tries calling Eva for the second time but she's not answering, so he figures she wants some space. His phone buzzes with a text from Jones.

Get over here. There's someone I'd like you to meet.

On his way to Jones' place, he stops by his house to pick up his kitten. As he bends down to greet him, Mulder runs over and claws his way up Dean's pants to get to his face. "Wow. That was painful," he mutters.

Mulder starts purring and rubbing his face on Dean's.

"I missed you too, buddy. Come on, let's go and introduce you to your older brother."

He looks around for the pet carrier and realizes Eva must have taken it, so he finds a shoe box instead. He throws the lid away, puts some newspaper inside, and carries Mulder out to the car in it. But Mulder doesn't want to be contained. He tries to escape for the entire car journey, meaning Dean has to drive with one hand.

"Next time I pull over a suspected drunk driver I'll check if they've got a kitten on their passenger seat first," he says to the tiny black feline, who meows loudly at him in response.

When he reaches Jones' house, a car he doesn't recognize is parked in the driveway.

Jones opens the front door as Dean approaches. "What the hell have you got in there?" he asks, looking at the shoe box.

"I'll show you inside." Dean enters the living room and spots Rocky lounging in front of the fireplace. The big dog wags his tail and softly barks, but he doesn't get up until Dean puts the shoe box on the floor.

Dean sits between Rocky and Mulder, in case they don't get on. "This is your new little brother." He strokes Rocky's head and the dog licks his face in greeting.

Rocky looks at the kitten. His ears go up and he looks at Dean as if to say *what the hell is that?*

"I know, I know. He's no dog, that's for sure," says Dean. "You'll have to be gentle with this one."

Rocky's massive head leans into the shoe box and Mulder backs away slightly. As Rocky starts sniffing him, with Dean holding his collar — just in case — Mulder leans in and touches Rocky's nose with his paw, batting it a few times. Then he rubs his face against the dog's.

Rocky jerks back, with a bewildered look, probably wondering what the hell is happening. Mulder climbs out of the box, walks over to the dog, and tries again. He starts chewing on Rocky's velvety ear until the dog licks his head. Rocky's tongue is so big it knocks the kitten over. Mulder gets straight back up as Dean pulls him away.

"Okay, that's enough for now. Let's give the little guy some breathing space."

"Why did you get a kitten of all things?" asks Jones. "I assumed you'd get another dog now you're staying in town."

"I had no say in the matter. Maggie Summers forced them on us."

"Us?"

"Yeah, Eva's got his sister. They're called Mulder and Scully. I wanted to name mine Bullet, but she wouldn't let me."

Jones laughs. "It's like you pair have skipped the sex and gone straight to the marriage part."

Dean realizes there's jazz music playing, and he spots two whiskey glasses on the coffee table with a selection of chips and dips. He looks at Jones. "Are you on a date?"

Jones laughs and claps him on the back. He turns the stereo down and Dean hears someone singing along in the kitchen. It's a male voice.

"George, get your ass out here!"

A voice from the kitchen shouts, "I'm coming, I'm coming! Give me a chance. Didn't I tell you I've got a bad hip?"

Dean smiles as George appears. He looks to be in his late sixties, with a full head of graying hair and the start of a beer belly.

"Well, well, well!" says George. "You must be Eva's new partner?"

Dean shakes his hand. "And you must be Eva's foster dad?"

"Guilty as charged! Let me take a look at you then."

George steps back and gives Dean the once-over. It makes him self-conscious and he looks at Jones, who's laughing.

"I'm just trying to assess whether you're the kind of guy who can protect my little girl, that's all," says George.

Dean scoffs. "Are you kidding? She doesn't need any help in that respect. In fact, I'm hoping she'll protect me."

"Oh, don't let her fool you. She's like a Mentos. Tough on the outside but soft and chewy in the middle."

"Yeah, if Mentos carried guns! Right, Dean?" Jones laughs.

They all take a seat and Jones pours Dean a whiskey. It seems rude not to accept it when they're both in high spirits. "When did you move in?" he asks.

"Yesterday," says George. "I wanted to surprise Eva by doing it without her knowledge. Now I'm settled in I've been calling her all day but she's not picking up. Jones has been very hospitable."

"Why doesn't anyone call me Harry?" says Jones.

"Doesn't suit you as well." George winks.

Dean's concerned that Eva didn't even pick up for her dad.

Rocky walks over and leans against George's legs. "Look at this dog. He loves me!"

Dean looks at the potato chip covered in guacamole that's hanging precariously from George's hand and he knows Rocky's just waiting for it to fall on the floor. But he doesn't want to burst George's bubble, so he doesn't say anything.

"Is that your cat?" asks George.

Dean realizes Mulder's walking around, sniffing everything. "It is. Eva has one too. We were talked into it by our forensics tech."

"No kidding! Eva never had a pet when she was growing up. She always insisted she didn't like animals." He turns to Jones. "I think it's because she's afraid of dogs."

"You don't say?" says Jones.

"She got bitten as a teenager. It was just a small nip, but it put her off dogs for life. She had nightmares for a while."

Dean's surprised. She warmed to Rocky when they were in Colorado, although now he thinks about it, it did take a while.

"She's a sleepwalker too. Although I think that's got more to do with clowns and the movies she watches."

Dean leans forward. "What is it with Eva and clowns?"

George's smile fades. "You've noticed? Let's just say she had a bad experience."

"What happened?" asks Jones.

George takes a deep breath. "Don't ever tell her you got this from me, but she was adopted once, when she was six years old, by a single lady called Dana. I was told by child services that Dana was the first person Eva had ever truly bonded with. She'd had trust issues growing up, because of being given up as a baby and not knowing anything about her real parents. Anyway, Dana arranged for a clown to attend Eva's ninth birthday party as a surprise. So the clown turns up, does a few magic tricks, and then gets caught by Dana molesting a kid in the bathroom."

Jones shakes his head.

Dean can't believe what he's hearing. "It wasn't Eva, was it?"

"No, thank God. Dana pulled the kid away and started screaming at the clown to get out of her house. She threatened to call the cops so the guy panicked, pulled out a knife, and stabbed her repeatedly in the chest. Apparently, Eva witnessed the whole thing. She phoned the police immediately and the guy was caught running down the block, covered in blood. When the police went into the house, Eva was cradling Dana's head in her lap. But the woman was already dead."

"Oh my God." Dean understands why Eva was hesitant to call her kitten Scully now. He downs his drink.

They all sit in silence for a moment.

"What happened to the clown?" asks Jones.

George sips his drink. "Eva testified at his trial, and because she was so compelling, he got the death penalty. But he's still on death row in San Quentin. It's been twenty-three years, and I know Eva still checks on him to make sure he hasn't been released on appeal."

Dean thinks about how hard Eva's life has been. She's suffered more loss than him, yet she never talks about any of it. "Courts aren't any place for kids," he says quietly. "They're bad enough for adults."

"But don't dwell on that," says George. "She's not one to let the past control her so don't treat her with kid gloves. She came to us in her teens and my wife Mary suggested she get some therapy to talk about Dana, but Eva rebelled pretty hard." He laughs. "My wife and I learned early on that Eva's headstrong and will do the complete opposite of whatever you suggest. Wait until I tell you about her first boyfriend. Man, that kid was a douche! And she only dated him to piss me off."

Dean smiles. He listens in as George starts telling them all about what Eva got up to as a teenager.

CHAPTER THIRTY-FOUR

The next morning, Dean still hasn't heard back from Eva so he decides to treat her to breakfast. He parks outside the diner and sends her a text, letting her know he's ordering them breakfast downstairs. He knows she can't resist food and coffee, no matter what kind of mood she's in. He doesn't blame her for being angry about being framed. He's been there himself when he was accused of his wife's murder. It made him feel like everyone he worked with turned against him and he was shouting into a void where no one was listening, despite knowing him for so long.

Eva replies by saying she'll be there in ten minutes. He's relieved. Part of him wondered whether she was okay. With a killer on the loose, she needs to accept she's vulnerable right now. Not that he'd ever dare say that to her.

After he places the order, he grabs a booth. He watches a car pull into the parking lot. It's Camille's. He's not heard from her since she made a pass at him so he's wondering if this is going to be awkward. He watches her get out of her car and enter the diner.

She places her order before turning to survey the room. When she spots him in the corner, she waves, so he smiles and she comes over. "Morning, Detective."

"Hey. How are you?"

"Good, thanks. Just getting some breakfast before I start work. I'm glad I bumped into you because I wanted to say it might not be a good idea for me to list your house. That's if you ever make up your mind about selling it, of course."

He nods. "I understand. To tell you the truth, it could take me months to be in a position to move, so it's best I don't waste your time."

"Good, I'm glad we're on the same page." She changes the subject. "I was just reading about the murder that happened upstairs. It made me so afraid I've started locking my doors even when I'm in the house."

"I'd recommend you do that anyway," he says, "whether you're in the house or not. I know I do."

She nods. "I know, I know. But I get complacent. I feel like nothing bad could happen in a friendly town like this. Until I read that article, anyway. You didn't get the call-out to the dead person, did you?"

She seems naive. Does she really think a town like Maple Valley has a huge selection of homicide detectives to choose from? "I did, yeah," he says. "But don't worry, my partner and I are on the case. The killer won't be free for long."

"But I *do* worry," she says. "It's like something off of TV. Where do you even start in a case like that? I mean, I've watched *CSI* a few times, but I wouldn't have a clue!"

He drinks some more coffee. She's nice, but he can't figure out if she's for real or not. He realizes there's something about her he doesn't trust. It's just a gut instinct.

He spots Eva's car pulling into the parking lot. He hadn't noticed it wasn't already here. He stares past Camille's shoulder and watches Eva get out. She's wearing the same clothes as yesterday and she's holding the pet carrier. She rushes out of view, presumably heading upstairs to drop Scully off.

Dean wonders where she's been all night. He knows it's none of his business but he can't help it.

Camille follows his gaze and spots Eva just before she disappears. "I'll just grab my breakfast and be out of your hair." She heads to the counter.

Dean notices Laurie walking away from the diner, carrying cleaning products out to her truck. She must've finally finished upstairs.

Camille leaves the diner just as Eva enters. They share an awkward greeting and Eva gives her room to pass.

A waitress comes over with their food. Dean thanks her as Eva sits opposite him.

"How's it going with your realtor?" she says. "You know, I could swear I've met her before somewhere."

"I'd be surprised if you have," he says. "She's from LA."

"She just looks familiar." Eva tucks into her eggs without saying anything else.

Dean stares at her, considering whether to ask if she had a good night. He's trying hard not to get too involved in her business.

She looks up at him. "Come out with it, Matheson. Whatever's causing you to stare at me."

He puts his cup down. "Where did you get to yesterday? I tried calling more than once. So did George."

She looks surprised. "How do you know that?"

"Because he moved in with Jones two days ago and last night I was treated to an evening of *Eva Valdez: The Teenage Years*."

She chokes on her eggs and puts her cutlery down to catch her breath. "*What*?" She looks genuinely alarmed.

"He wanted to see you but you didn't return his calls. Where were you?"

She sips her coffee. "That's none of your business. I'll call him today. I can't believe he moved here without telling me first."

"Well, maybe if you paid him some attention, you'd know." Dean's just repeating what George said last night.

She rolls her eyes. "Oh great, he's recruited you as his number one fan. Now I'll get no peace. Enough of the guilt trip already. I said I'll call him today. I'll visit after work, too." She keeps eating.

Dean recalls the humorous stories George told him last night and he has to hide his smile behind his coffee cup. "He's an entertaining guy."

"Just never repeat whatever he told you about me and take it all with a pinch, no, make that a *handful*, of salt," she says. "He likes to exaggerate and embellish. It makes for a better story. He really should've been a journalist."

"Okay, whatever you say." He decides not to let on that he knows about what happened to Dana. "But seriously, where were you last night? When you have a killer trying to frame you for murder, you really need to let me know you're okay. We're partners, remember? I'd like to think you'd be worried about me if I went AWOL?"

Her phone buzzes and even though it's upside down on the table in front of him, he can see Jake's name flash up. She pulls it away and slips it into her coat pocket without reading it.

Dean doesn't feel like smiling anymore. She must have spent the night with him. He's surprised. He didn't think she was up for dating anyone yet. Jake's okay, but he almost seems too good to be true. He's also younger than Dean and a millionaire who supports good causes. Who can compete with that?

She ignores his comment and pushes her plate away. "I need to grab a few things from upstairs."

"Fine. I'll come with you." He stands. "I want to see how good Laurie's team were at cleaning up."

* * *

Dean looks around her apartment in awe. "It looks like nothing ever happened in here. The walls are clean, the carpets are clean . . . Even the kitchen is clean."

Eva replies from her bedroom where she's getting changed. "It's amazing, isn't it? They even cleaned inside the oven. Not that I'll ever use it."

The apartment smells strongly of chemicals and there's a note on the coffee table advising Eva to keep the windows open for as long as possible whenever she's home.

He spots Scully wobbling around the floor before she climbs the armchair with her claws. He crouches down to stroke her. "Hey, Scully." She looks at him like he's a complete stranger before she curls up on the cushion to sleep. Dean smiles as he stands. "Have you noticed how cats prefer to sleep in the daytime instead of at night? It's exhausting."

Eva appears from the bedroom looking confused.

"What's the matter?" he asks.

"Nothing. I'm just missing a dress."

"Really? You think one of the cleaners stole it?"

She shakes her head. "I doubt it. I wore it to Jones' retirement party so it needed cleaning. Would someone really steal a dirty dress?"

He'd hope no one would be that desperate to get something for nothing. "It's worth asking Laurie about it. She might not be aware she has a thief on her team."

"Mmm, maybe. Or maybe it'll turn up."

"When's the locksmith coming?" he asks.

"Frankie's organizing that. All I know is it's sometime today. He's paying for a new front door too. Says he feels guilty someone was able to get in so easily."

Dean's glad Frankie's taking his responsibility as a landlord seriously.

"So what was Trey Peterson's partner like?" she asks.

He's surprised it's taken her this long to ask. "Oh, you missed a treat. She's a real doll."

Eva picks up on his sarcasm. "That bad?"

"I know we're not meant to judge people but, man, she was a piece of work. She hardly reacted at all to the news her partner was dead. Until I told her he was cut open. That shook her a little, but not as much as it would a normal person."

Eva frowns. "Even if they didn't love each other anymore she should've been shocked. Was he even living with her and Danny?"

"It's hard to tell because she wouldn't let me inside the house. And I'm pretty sure she's already moved on to a new man. She said Trey was involved in drugs and liked young girls, so she wasn't surprised he was killed."

Eva rests her hands on her hips. "Young girls? Do you think this could be linked to what happened to Taylor?"

"It's possible. But Shannon didn't know what he was doing in Maple Valley. She said he didn't have any relatives here." He sighs. "And Cedar Falls PD hasn't located Danny yet. They don't think he was with Trey at any point as they both disappeared at different times, so they're treating Danny's disappearance separately from Trey's murder."

"This just gets weirder and weirder," she says.

"I know. It's so frustrating. I feel like we should have someone in custody for Trey and Taylor's murders already, but we're still no closer to figuring out what's going on."

Eva laughs.

"What?" he says.

"You're so impatient! Being a detective is about the long game. It's not like on TV where witnesses come forward straight away, or you conveniently find a bag of all the evidence needed to convict someone. It's a puzzle we need to put together, and we can't do it by ourselves; it takes a whole team. But don't worry, we'll get there." She brushes her hair as she talks. "Let's face it, we both have something to prove to Captain Brown, so we *need* to do this. But I've got news for you, Matheson — it won't be a quick process because it never is. However, in my experience, the longer it takes to catch someone the better case you have by the time it reaches trial."

Dean thinks about it. She's right. He's being too impatient. He's just worried about the killer striking again in the meantime.

His cell phone rings. It's Captain Brown. "Hey, Captain."

"Matheson. Are you with Valdez?"

"Yeah. Why, what's up?"

The captain hesitates before continuing. "It's Emily Gordon. She's been attacked."

Dean's heart skips a beat. "Is she alive?"

Captain Brown sighs. "Yeah. She's been in surgery to fix some internal bleeding but she's in recovery now. No one knew her identity until she came around in the recovery room and was able to tell her doctor her name. She's only managed a few sentences so far. She said the attack happened at about eleven last night, when she was walking home from the diner."

Dean wonders why she was hanging around the diner that late. Frankie's closes at ten most nights. He realizes his first instinct was right: she's prostituting herself. Maybe she was beaten by a john or her pimp. That could be what happened to Taylor. They could have themselves a guy who likes to pick on working girls.

Dean feels defeated. Emily's life wasn't supposed to turn out this way.

"Now listen to me very carefully," says Captain Brown. "I need you to get to the hospital right away, but you can't take Valdez with you."

He's confused. "Why the hell not?"

Brown lets out a deep breath, like even he can't believe what he's about to say. "Because Emily told her doctor it was Valdez who beat her."

Dean looks at Eva who's buttoning a clean shirt and waiting to hear what's going on.

She whispers, "What is it?"

"Oh, come on!" Dean explodes. "Captain, you know that's a lie, right? That can't even be possible."

He thinks about how Eva wasn't answering her phone last night. He pictures her arriving home this morning in the same clothes as yesterday. Where was she all night?

"I'm sorry, Matheson. I know you and Eva are close and you trust her, but it's time for me to interview her."

Dean's heart sinks. She's not going to take this well at all. This could be the final straw that makes her leave town.

"With all due respect, Captain, that's bullshit. You're going to lose her if you go down that route. I know her, she won't stand for it. And neither will I. Are you ready to lose two detectives over false allegations?"

Silence from the end of the line.

Eva perches on her coffee table. She's clearly shocked at what Dean's saying but not fully understanding.

Dean wonders if he's pushed his luck with Captain Brown, but he has to take a stand. This is ridiculous and no matter how concerned he is for Emily, he can't let her ruin Eva's career. He needs to speak to Emily himself, as Ryan obviously didn't get through to her.

"Look, Matheson," says the captain. "I don't like this any more than you do but if I don't interview her, I'll have the DA on my back accusing us of favoring our own. And what if this gets out to the media? Can you even imagine the shitstorm that'll follow? No. I've got to follow procedure. Tell Valdez she needs to be in my office in the next half hour. Otherwise . . ." he hesitates. "Well, you know the rest."

Dean ends the call and slowly stands up. Eva copies him. He's so angry he could throw his phone across the room, but he knows the captain's right.

He looks her in the eye. "I've got some bad news."

CHAPTER THIRTY-FIVE

Eva doesn't react how Dean expects her to. She sits down. There's no fight in her.

"You have to tell me where you were last night," he says. "You need witnesses and an alibi to get you out of this."

She's looking at her hands. "I don't have an alibi. I was alone last night, just . . . not here. Laurie's team were cleaning until late, trying to get it finished for me."

He crouches down in front of her and puts his hands on hers. "Eva? Look at me. I don't care where you were or what you were doing." He thinks of Jake. "But you need to tell the captain because otherwise, it's going to look bad."

She's so quiet. He doesn't like her this way. He'd prefer she was throwing things and yelling at him.

Impulsively, he says, "I'll say you were with me. I mean, you did stay with me the night before so it's not that much of a stretch."

She looks at him, surprised. "You would lie for me?"

He nods. "I know you didn't do any of this." He can tell she's seriously worried she's going to be arrested for murder. He's reminded of the man who was staring at him outside the police station, and possibly at the hospital too. He was tall and slim. It could've been Jake. And now he's trying to get close to Eva. Maybe he's trying to distract her from what he's doing.

Dean isn't sure. It sounds far-fetched, and Jake has a lot to lose if he's caught. He's got a good set-up here. At least, that's how he's made it look. Maybe his church, or community center, is a front for something else. Maybe he doesn't even own it.

Dean's going to need to dig into Jake's background. Maybe he'll find a link to the Haunted Asylum too. The balloon on Eva's door bothers him. She could be right about the employees at that place. One or two of them could be former felons, helping Jake or someone else to frame her.

He needs to visit Emily immediately and find out why she's saying these things about Eva. Find out who's putting her up to it.

"Come on," he says, standing. "I'll drive you to the station."

She stands. "I won't make you lie for me, Dean. I can handle myself and I've done nothing wrong. I'll tell the captain where I was. But I think we should visit Emily first. Maybe if I spoke with her and made her see how wrong she is about me, she'd change her story?"

Dean's shaking his head before she even finishes her sentence. "No way. There's absolutely no way you should be talking to Emily. She could say you tried to attack her again in the hospital. You need to stay as far away from her as possible. Besides, if you don't speak to Captain Brown within the next—" he looks at his watch "—twenty minutes, he's going to send someone to bring you in. You can bet your ass Miller would volunteer for that. Don't give him the satisfaction."

She nods, resigned to her fate.

They hear a commotion outside. Voices and vehicles. Car doors slamming. Eva walks to the window and peers out. "Oh, God." She turns to face him. "This is bad."

Dean passes her to look for himself. There are two news trucks outside with reporters gathering.

"How did they find out?" He turns to face her. "Grab your things. We're getting out of here."

"What about Scully?"

"She'll be fine. She'll probably sleep all day. And if you're arrested . . ." He pauses and then shakes his head. "I don't even want to think about that."

Dean leads them down the apartment's external steps, covering both him and Eva with a large umbrella. Out of the corner of his eye, he notices Camille standing a short distance away, among a crowd of onlookers emerging from the diner. It looks like she's filming them on her cell phone.

"What the hell?" he mutters. He pushes past the reporters and is about to open the car door for Eva when they both notice the yellow balloon tied to his windshield wipers.

Eva groans.

Dean spins around. He wants to ask if anyone saw who put that there but he's being filmed. Eva slips into the backseat of his car as he pulls the balloon off and throws it into his trunk. He ignores the reporters' questions and jumps into the driver's seat, starting the engine.

"Stay down, Eva. Don't let them get a photo of you."

He looks behind him to reverse out of the parking lot. He can't believe it when two cameramen chase his car. "This is insane," he says.

He speeds away, heading to the station. When he's clear of the news trucks, he tries to drive carefully but fast. He notices a man by the side of the road. He's just standing there, not moving. It's the guy from the diner; the Michael Myers wannabe. He seems to focus on Dean as he passes, watching his car until he's out of view. Luckily, Eva doesn't notice him as she's looking down at her hands.

Dean needs to find out who owns that place as these balloons are turning up in all the wrong places and it's starting to feel threatening.

"Call George," he says over his shoulder. "Tell him and Jones to meet you at the station. You need someone with you. I've got to speak to Emily as soon as possible to get these allegations dropped." He doesn't know whether Emily's condition is serious enough to kill her, and it's not a risk he's willing to take.

Eva looks up as he glances in the rearview mirror. She looks dazed, like she can't believe this is happening to her.

"Emily must've called the media," she says. "Why does she hate me so much?"

Dean bites his tongue. He doesn't think it was Emily. The only person to gain anything from the media knowing Eva's a suspect is the killer, because it will divert attention away from him. In the meantime, he's free to escape. Or keep on killing.

He watches as she puts her phone to her ear. It doesn't take long for someone to answer.

"Dad?" she says.

Dean's never heard her call George dad before.

"I need you to meet me at the police station. Ask Jones to take you. I'm in trouble, and it's bad."

Dean can't hear what George says in response but it must be brief.

"Thanks. I'll be there in five minutes. And, Dad?" She hesitates. "Don't believe what you see in the news."

Dean doesn't know what to say to make things better, so he just drives faster.

CHAPTER THIRTY-SIX

Eva waits out front for George to meet her, not wanting to walk into the station alone. She's hoping Jones comes along too, as Dean said he'd be helpful.

She looks up at the sky, which is bright white. It looks like it's about to snow. She wishes she'd grabbed some warmer clothes before she left. Her hands are trembling with fear. She tries not to think about where all this could lead if Emily doesn't change her story.

The sound of a car speeding way too fast reaches her. Eva wonders if the press has made it here before George and Jones. She watches the black car approach. It looks like it's going too fast to be coming in here but at the last minute, the driver makes a sharp turn. The car's tires skid and screech as it just makes it into the parking lot.

Without slowing down, they drive straight into a parking space and, with more tire screeching, perform a dramatic emergency stop. Despite everything that's happened in the last hour, Eva smiles. She'd recognize that erratic driving anywhere.

Both car doors open and the loudest rap music she's ever heard outside a bar hits her. It only stops when the engine's switched off. As George and Jones get out to walk toward her, they look as if they're twenty years younger than they actually are, fired up by the urgency to get here and kick some ass.

She hasn't seen George since she left Colorado a couple of months ago. Her shoulders relax with the relief of having him here.

Grinning from ear to ear, he leans in for a hug. "I had two media trucks riding my tail so I had to drive erratically to make them fall back."

Jones snorts. "If you hadn't shouted 'Leave my daughter alone, assholes!' out the window as you passed them, they wouldn't even have known who you were. One of them ended up sideways on the highway, blocking both lanes!"

George shrugs. "It's not my fault young people can't drive properly. Besides, the rap music made me drive faster. We've gotta find a way to switch that stereo off for the ride home."

Eva has to swallow a lump in her throat. The sight of him, and knowing he'll be on her side, makes her choke up. "Thanks for bringing him," she says to Jones.

"Trust me, I had no say in the matter," says Jones. "One minute I'm sitting on the couch watching re-runs of *Columbo* and the next I'm clinging on for dear life beside this guy, thinking my days are numbered." He chuckles. "Anyway, what's the problem and where's Dean?"

She doesn't even know where to start and before she opens her mouth, the two media trucks that were following George arrive. "We need to get inside," she says, as she nods in their direction.

George and Jones simultaneously turn to face the trucks. Before George can do anything crazy, Eva pulls him inside the station.

As she leads them to the offices behind the front desk, there's not a single person in the station who doesn't look at her. Probably because Marty's live streaming the local news on his computer and most of the team is watching the drama unfold.

"Look at that," says George. "We're on TV."

She watches as Jenny walks over and switches Marty's monitor off. Eva smiles at her, to show her appreciation.

Captain Brown comes straight over to them. "Thanks for coming in, Valdez. I appreciate this is a difficult situation for everyone. Nice to see you, Jones."

"Captain," says Jones, as they shake hands.

"And who's this?"

Eva says, "This is George, my foster dad."

George looks at her. "It's been eighteen years since we took you in. I think you can drop the foster bit now, Eva."

"I've told you before," she says. "When I meet new people in your presence, I want them to know why I don't look like you." Her face reddens and she feels like an embarrassed teenager again. "Would you concentrate on why we're really here, please?"

Captain Brown has the good grace to ignore the family drama. "Pleased to meet you." He holds out his hand and George shakes it.

"So how come my daughter isn't listed on your website yet? She's been working here a week already."

Eva cringes. This is *not* what she needs right now. "George, leave it. Please."

He must sense her discomfort as he backs off. "Okay, okay. I'm obviously just here to look pretty. Got it."

"I appreciate you both attending with Eva," says the captain. "But I'll need to interview her alone."

The two older men share a look.

"Interview her?" says Jones. "For what?"

Captain Brown motions to his office, and Eva's relieved to do this behind closed doors. Although the team has stopped openly staring, they're now pretending to work, which is worse. The only person who isn't pretending is Officer Miller. He sits facing them with a smirk on his face, happily listening to every word. She can tell he's going to have a sarcastic comment for her when everyone's out of earshot.

"What are you gawping at, asshole?" says George as they walk past him.

Eva smiles to herself.

"Hey, show a little respect. I'm a cop," says Miller.

George squares up to him. "Yeah? Well, I'm ex-military. Want to take this outside and settle who deserves the most respect?"

Eva notices Marty laughing. In fact, everyone seems to be enjoying the show. "George!" she hisses. "Get in here."

Jones pulls him by the arm and they all enter Captain Brown's office.

"Sorry I don't have enough seats," says Brown as they stand in front of him. "So I'll get straight to the point. Eva? Emily Gordon says you attacked her last night at around eleven o'clock when she was walking along Main Street. I can't give you any more information than that. I suggest you hire an attorney so I can interview you."

She turns to Jones, who looks like he's considering everything.

"Is there any evidence Eva did it?" he asks.

The captain shakes his head. "Not yet. I don't know how much you know about the guy found in Eva's apartment?"

George looks confused. "What guy?"

"I'll explain later," she says. "It was a dead guy. My prints are on the murder weapon and this Emily girl says I killed him."

"Bullshit!" he says.

"Captain," says Eva. "I didn't do this. I don't know how plainer to put it."

Captain Brown nods. "Then I suggest you lawyer up and stay away from the media. Don't speak to anyone at all. Not even to deny it. We'll speak to the press on your behalf. You need to take my advice and lay low after our interview."

"You can stay with us," says George.

She thinks of Dean's spare room and would prefer to stay there, but it looks like Captain Brown knows what she's thinking.

"I wouldn't recommend staying with Matheson. He could inadvertently feed you information about the case. That wouldn't look good. And the media would love to imply my two detectives are sleeping together. Unfortunately, sex sells."

She feels helpless, but she's determined not to show it. She looks at Jones. "Know of any good lawyers around here?"

CHAPTER THIRTY-SEVEN

When Dean quietly approaches Emily's hospital bed, he's relieved to find she doesn't look as bad as Taylor did. In fact, she barely looks bruised. There's a little discoloring to her jawline, but that's all he can see. He realizes this might not have been done by the same person who hurt Taylor.

She doesn't look well though. Before he entered her room, Dr. Armstrong told him the operation Emily had overnight was an attempt to repair her ruptured spleen, but it couldn't be saved. She also has three cracked ribs, so he knows she's not lying about being attacked and it can't be self-inflicted.

He looks at her nightstand and sees her belongings: an iPhone, a red lipstick, a single house key, and a wallet. The wallet looks stuffed but he can't tell whether that's a wad of cash or coupons without betraying her privacy and opening it. If it's money, he can rule out robbery. When he looks closer, he can see the corner of a condom wrapper poking out.

His heart sinks. He looks out the window, wishing there was something he could do to help her. Snow gently settles around the glass panel.

Emily opens her eyes and stares at him, so he smiles. "Hey. How are you feeling?"

She doesn't respond so he takes her hand, which is warmer than his. "Emily, talk to me. Yell at me. Anything but silence, please."

Emily pulls her hand away and grimaces as she tries to sit up without hurting her ribs. She takes a sip of water, then settles back and looks at him. "Why are you here?"

"I heard about the attack and I'm worried about you," he says. "You need to tell me who did this so we can stop it from happening to anyone else."

She sighs. "I've already told your department who did it. That woman you work with. She jumped me from behind."

He's taken aback for a second. She's sticking to her story. "Then tell me exactly how it happened so I can investigate it properly. Eva's not involved in the investigation so you can trust me. What were you doing outside the diner that late?"

She rolls her eyes. "Like you're going to investigate your partner. You just want to be able to blame someone else. You need to realize what kind of monster you're working with. Just because she's pretty doesn't mean she's innocent. I think we both know you're not the best judge of character." She looks him directly in the eye, goading him about Lizzie Glover.

She has every right to, seeing as Lizzie killed her mother and Dean didn't even know until it was too late. But it still hurts. "Emily, listen to me. I get that you're mad at me for not staying in touch with you when I left town. I'm sorry about that, it was lousy of me. I should've checked in more, but I only just found out Derek left too. I thought he was taking care of you, and I was processing everything that happened to me. Trying to start fresh. But I'm back now and I can help you more."

She's not convinced. "You took my dog too, but I never see him with you. Did you drop him off at the pound on your way to Vegas? Was he too much hassle for you too? Whatever you did, I'm guessing you dumped him as quickly as you dumped me."

She has tears in her eyes and Dean suddenly realizes the impact it made on her when her mother died and she was placed in foster care. When she was growing up, the only people she'd see regularly were Dean and her social worker, Derek. Her mother isolated her because she was an addict who became deeply paranoid of outsiders. The only companion Emily had in that house she shared with her mother was Rocky.

After her mother died, her foster carers made her give Rocky up, Dean moved away and then her trusted social worker left town. Is that what all this is about? She feels abandoned so she's taking it out on Eva to get back at *him*?

"I'm sorry," he says. "You're right to hate me. I should've stayed in touch and brought Rocky to see you. I've taken care of him as much as he's taken care of me. He's got some health issues now he's older, so he's recently gone to live with my closest friend. He's happy there, I promise. I can bring him in to see you whenever you want."

He can sense the conflict between who she is and who she's trying to be. He suspects she would love to be reunited with Rocky, the only real link to her childhood, but she also wants to pretend she's too old to care about that kind of thing. So he doesn't wait for her to reply. "I'll bring him in tomorrow morning. He'll be happy to see you. Be prepared to get squashed though. He has a thing for sleeping on people's beds and he's not exactly light."

She looks at him like she's trying to judge whether he's lying. Then she looks away. "Whatever. It's too late now. Everything's different."

"Of course everything's different," he says. "Life moves on, and people come and go, but that doesn't mean you don't have people who care about you."

A man appears at the door. He looks about the same age as Dean but shorter and more casual in his appearance. He has shoulder-length, messy brown hair which is covered in a sprinkling of snow. "Who's this guy, Emily?" he says.

"Nobody," she says. "He's leaving."

Dean shakes the guy's gloved hand. "Dean Matheson. Are you Ryan?"

"The one and only," he says, with an enthusiastic shake, making the fake Rolex on his wrist rattle. He rubs his hands together, then brushes off the snow from his shoulders. "I should probably ask you to leave. Unless . . ." He looks at Emily for a reaction.

"I'm tired," she says.

"Sure," says Ryan. He looks at Dean. "I'm going to grab some coffee to warm up. Do you have time to join me?"

Dean nods. He can tell he won't get anywhere with Emily today. "I'll be back tomorrow, Emily. And I'll bring Rocky."

She doesn't respond.

Ryan leads him along the hallway and down a flight of stairs to the hospital's cafeteria. "Take a seat. This one's on me." He goes to order their drinks.

When he comes back, he sighs as he sits next to Dean who's checking his phone for an update from Eva. There isn't one. He wants to know how her interview is going.

"The way Emily tells it, your partner beat the shit out of her," says Ryan. "That's pretty messed up, man. Does she have rage issues or something?"

Dean's so exhausted by all this that he doesn't even get angry. "We both know Emily's lying. She's protecting someone else. Did you know she's prostituting herself?"

Ryan's mouth widens in shock. His laid-back demeanor changes for the first time. Dean's glad to see he cares.

"Why do you think that?"

"It's obvious," says Dean. "Why else would she spend so much time walking around that part of town at night? It used to be notorious for prostitution. I think she's either covering for a customer or for her pimp."

Ryan shakes his head. "No way. She's too good a kid to fall into that game. And she's got herself a good set-up now Jake Andrews is helping her settle in with that family. She wouldn't want to risk that."

Frustrated, Dean says, "So where does she get her money from? Who bought her that iPhone? Someone's exploiting her and I need to find out who before she gets into serious trouble."

Ryan appears to think about it as he drinks his coffee. "She has a friend, Tiffany. I think I mentioned her before?"

Dean nods. "You said Emily had fallen in with the wrong crowd. Is that Tiffany?"

"Emily hangs off her every word. It's a damn shame, but I've tried everything to separate them. Tiffany's heading for jail time if she's not careful. I just hope she doesn't drag Emily down with her."

"Why? What's she doing?

"Tiffany's been known to hang out with some shady characters, according to some of my other kids. Not that they'll name anyone, of course. That's why I didn't want Emily getting involved with her. But they're thick as thieves. I can always tell when she's been around Tiffany because she swears more and gives me major attitude. I guess it's not too far a stretch to assume Tiffany's got her involved in something and now she's in over her head. She's just not made for that life."

Dean gets his notepad out. "What's Tiffany's last name?"

"Sanders. She doesn't have a fixed address but Emily told me recently that some nights she sleeps behind the community center you told us to visit. Apparently, Jake's been feeding homeless people in the evening with his coffee shop leftovers." Ryan shudders. "If I'm honest, he gives me the creeps."

Dean's surprised. "Why?"

Ryan leans back in his chair. His cell phone rings and when he checks the caller ID, he shakes his head and pockets the phone, carrying on without answering it. "In my job, maybe even more so than in yours, I don't know, you learn to suspect guys like Jake. Guys that appear too good to be true. I mean, he says he's loaded, he moves to a small town to help the locals — who he has no relationship with whatsoever as far as I can tell from asking around — and the young girls appear to love him. I know Emily's face lights up when she sees him. I don't get to spend much time with her because I have to split my time between twenty-three other kids." He pauses. "I don't know, maybe I'm just jealous of the guy or something. But it makes me nervous when young girls sing an older guy's praises. Know what I mean?"

Dean knows exactly what he means. Child sexual exploitation thrives on relationships between adults who have money or power and young people who have neither. The fact that Emily owns the latest iPhone and has what looks like a stash of money in her wallet suggests she's being exploited by someone. He makes a note to discuss Jake with Eva. She knows him better than he does. "Do you know who Tiffany works for?"

Ryan shakes his head. "Not officially. I have my suspicions though. Have you ever met Beau Lachey?"

"Skylar Hutton's boyfriend?" Dean's had dealings with the couple in the past, when he was in uniform. They're drug dealers and Skylar's clever about it. It's hard to pin anything on her. Dean always thought she was wasted on Beau as she's clearly the brains of the outfit.

"Right. I've seen him with Tiffany more than once. But she's not one of our kids so it's none of my business unless I find out he's abusing her in some way."

"How old is Tiffany?"

"Difficult to know," says Ryan. "I've only spoken to her once but I'd say she's the same age as Emily, maybe a little older. Hard to tell with the amount of makeup she wears." His cell phone rings again but he makes no moves to answer it.

"Could that be one of your kids?" asks Dean.

"Nah, it's the boss. Always hassling me for something."

"Has Emily not told you anything about Tiffany?"

"Nah, like I said, they're thick as thieves. They spray-painted *Tiffany & Gordo* all over my car once. Took two hundred dollars to get it removed." Ryan laughs like he doesn't mind at all. "It's like they were too dumb to realize they were incriminating themselves."

Dean sits forward. "What does Tiffany look like?"

Ryan sips his coffee and thinks about it. "Scrawny. Brown hair."

Dean grabs his cell phone and opens the photo he took of Taylor before she died. He shows Ryan. "Is this her?"

Ryan's face drops as he takes in the terrible bruising. Then a sign of recognition flashes over him. "You know what? I think that is her. Is she here?"

Dean stands. Finally, they have an ID for Taylor: Tiffany Sanders. "Don't you watch the news?" he asks.

Ryan shakes his head and sighs. "Used to all the time when I was a rookie social worker, but I got tired of finding out one of my kids had run away . . . or worse. I never had any downtime, so I had to stop watching. Life's a little easier without it."

Dean can understand that. "Well, she died. A couple of days ago. She was beaten by someone and left for dead outside the new church."

Ryan's genuinely surprised. "No way? Shit. I guess I'll have to break the news to Emily."

"I'd prefer it if you'd let me do that when I come back tomorrow. I'll have Emily's dog with me so it might help her cope. Will you be keeping an eye on her today?"

"Of course. I've cleared my schedule so I can stay here all day."

"Good. I better go." Dean leaves Ryan seated, finishing his coffee and looking a little shaken at Tiffany's death. He's probably thinking the same as he is. Emily could be the next girl to die.

CHAPTER THIRTY-EIGHT

Eva's exhausted. She's arrived home after spending four hours in the small, claustrophobic interview room with Steve and Captain Brown, denying everything she's been accused of and trying to make them see sense. Her new lawyer, Gloria Olson, seemed pleasant enough, but there wasn't much she could do for her at this stage.

The worst part for Eva was having to explain her whereabouts last night. She hopes they don't tell Dean she had to sleep in her car after realizing she didn't have enough money to waste on another hotel room. After she left Jake's place at around six, she checked whether her apartment was ready, but Laurie's team hadn't finished yet. They still needed masks to shield them from the strong fumes of the cleaning materials they were using.

Eva didn't want to ask Dean for help. She should be able to take care of herself, and normally, she can. It's just that Frank's death left her with a lot of unexpected bills and a reduced income. Something no one ever tells you is that death isn't cheap. She has enough to get by until she gets paid for the first time, but not if she spends it on hotel rooms.

So she did what she used to do when times were hard: she'd found a quiet corner of the mall's parking lot and stayed there all night. At least she had Scully for company. She only got out of the car for coffee and to use the nearby gas station's restroom. Scully was happy enough, spending the time when she wasn't sleeping, sniffing around the car and sitting on Eva's lap, providing more comfort than Eva could ever have expected from an animal. It was cold, but Eva had taken a blanket and cushions from her apartment with her and used the car's heat every time it became unbearable. Scully had her fleeces and Eva's body heat, so she was fine.

The spot she'd parked in was shielded from the weather by a brick wall to the front and large trees to one side. The sound of the trees rustling in the wind had woken her a few times but the night had passed pretty fast considering she was limited to one sleeping position; propped up on the backseat.

The captain had been kind about Eva's predicament, not showing shock at one of his detectives sleeping rough. He's going to pull the CCTV from the mall to corroborate her story, so she feels confident she'll be back to work in no time. As long as Emily stops making harmful accusations.

For now, Eva's suspended because her prints are on the knife that killed Trey Peterson, but she hasn't been charged with anything yet, thankfully.

Gloria kindly dropped her at home when her interview was over but she suggested she doesn't sleep at her apartment tonight, in case the reporters return. Eva agreed. She's only dropped in to collect Scully, some clean clothes, and her car.

Scully is curled up in exactly the same place they left her in earlier, on the armchair. Eva crouches in front of the chair. "Hey, little lady. Did you miss me?" She scoops her up and Scully immediately starts purring, in between cute high-pitched meows.

"Oh, I know! It's your dinner time, isn't it? Mommy got home just in time." She kisses the top of her head and places her on the litter box to make sure she empties her bladder before they go out. She watches as Scully crouches down but when she stumbles over the side of the litter box, finished, only two tiny stones are wet.

"That's the smallest pee I've ever seen!"

She squeezes a sachet of kitten food into a saucer and lets Scully eat while she texts George to thank him and Jones for supporting her today. She reassures him she'll be fine tonight by telling him she has somewhere else to stay, but she doesn't say where. Then she sits on her armchair and calls Dean to update him. He answers on the second ring.

"Finally!" he says. "How did it go?" He sounds as exhausted as she is.

"Suspended with pay. But no charges, thank God."

He sighs. "I'm sorry you're suspended. That sucks. Are you staying with George tonight?"

"No. I can't face it. He'll be giving me advice all night and I just need a break."

"So stay at my place," he says. "I'll be home from work in a few hours and I can stop for some tequila on the way?"

She laughs and it feels alien to her face. She's been frowning most of the day so far. "That's really tempting, but actually I'm going to stay at the community center." He doesn't reply and for some reason, she feels horrible. "Jake's offered me his spare room, plus, you know, there's a coffee shop right downstairs. How can I resist that? You need to up your coffee game if you want to compete with Jake."

He laughs, but she can tell it's only half-hearted.

"Nothing's going on," she explains, even though he hasn't asked. "He's just being cool and helping me out. Captain Brown told me not to stay with you because you could inadvertently feed me information about Emily. I think he's right. We've got to clear my name in a way that leaves no ambiguity."

Dean sighs again. "I guess you're right. Can I at least tell you what I think about Emily's accusations?"

She hesitates, but could it really do any harm to hear it? She could do with some insight into Emily's reasons for accusing her. "Sure."

"It's a long story, but all you really need to know is that I messed up and now she's blaming you, to get back at me. It'll all make sense when you know the backstory."

"But what about Trey Peterson?" she asks. "Do you think she really knows anything about it or was she just accusing me of his murder to piss you off?"

"I don't know yet. I'll ask her tomorrow. I need to ask about her friend too."

Eva's confused. "Who's her friend?"

"Oh shit, yeah, you don't know. I've finally managed to ID Taylor. Her name was Tiffany Sanders and she was a friend of Emily's. She was involved in drugs and prostitution, but never arrested for anything which is why her prints aren't on record. It sounds like it was just a matter of time until she was. I've managed to track down her grandmother. She was devastated when I told her. Sobbed so hard I thought she was going to pass out. She said she raised Tiffany since she was ten years old, after her mother died of cancer."

"Did she have any idea who would kill her?" asks Eva.

"She said Tiffany had gone wayward in her teens. She stopped coming home and told her grandmother she was living with a boyfriend."

"How old was she when she moved out?"

"Thirteen."

Eva gasps. "You're kidding?"

"Nope. The grandmother got CPS involved to try to get Tiffany to move back home. The social worker's report she was given said the unnamed boyfriend was the same age as Tiffany and they were living with his parents. They said it all looked above board, so she had to stop trying to get her to come home. The grandmother heard rumors from her neighbors that Tiffany was turning tricks. She last saw her four months ago, by chance, and said she had bruises on her. She wouldn't talk to her grandmother for long because she was paranoid and thought she was being watched by her boyfriend."

"Is there a father in the mix?" she asks.

"No. Her grandmother said Tiffany's father wasn't a part of their lives and he moved overseas years ago."

Eva sighs. "We need to find out who Tiffany's boyfriend was. It must be him who beat her."

Dean agrees. "It looks like a case of either domestic violence or child sexual exploitation, so it's probably not linked to Trey Peterson's murder. I think I have someone in mind."

"Who?"

"Beau Lachey. He's a local drug dealer and Emily's social worker has seen him with Tiffany before. I've spent the afternoon watching his place because I wanted to see if any other teenage girls are hanging around him, but nothing so far. I'll find out whether he's involved when I go back to speak to Emily tomorrow morning. She doesn't know her friend has died yet, so I've got to break that to her."

Eva sits back in her armchair. "You're going to be busy. And while you're busy, who's looking for your old friend Lizzie Glover?"

"Well, actually," he says, "I was hoping you wanted a side project while you're off work? It'd be better than watching daytime soaps."

She smiles. That's exactly what she was thinking. But she'll have to do it undercover seeing as she's currently suspended, and they've been told to leave it to the FBI. "I can do that. I want to speak to some of the employees at the secure unit for myself. I know Jones interviewed them a while back, but I'll pretend I'm a visitor to try to get more out of them. In my experience, there's always one gossip who likes to tell everyone's secrets and Jones said he can get me in with no questions asked."

"Okay, good. Just don't let the captain find out," he says.

She smiles. "He'll never know."

"Could you also look after Mulder for me?" asks Dean.

"No!" she says, exasperated. "Stop trying to offload your responsibilities, Matheson! You need to bond with him. He's your son!"

"Whoa! Okay, crazy cat lady! I wouldn't go so far as to call him my son but, whatever. I like him, I do . . . when he's not tearing up my furniture. But I just never seem to be at home anymore. It's why I need to downsize."

"Has your sexy realtor listed your house yet?" she asks. "What's her name? Cameron?"

"Camille. No, she's not working for me anymore."

Eva wonders if he's already slept with her and now things have turned awkward. It sounds like that's how things usually go for Dean. "Let's hope she doesn't go fatal attraction on your ass. She seems the type."

Dean laughs. Just as the conversation comes to a natural close, she realizes she's yet to thank him for trusting her over Emily's accusations. "Dean?"

"What? You change your mind about the tequila?"

She smiles. "No. I just wanted to say thanks for sticking by me. I mean, yeah, this is all your fault because every woman in your life seems to have a problem with you, and for some reason, I'm paying the price, but anyway, thanks."

"You're welcome. Just . . ." He stops before finishing.

"Just what?"

"Just be careful around Jake."

"What do you mean? You're not jealous, are you?" she teases.

He doesn't reply right away. It makes her wonder if he knows something she doesn't.

"Probably," he says. "I mean, have you seen the guy's jawline? I can't compete with that."

She laughs as she ends the call. It's a relief to know Dean will help her clear her name.

* * *

Eva arrives at the Hope Center just after seven that evening. As Jake shows her the spare bedroom, she wonders whether she'll actually sleep in there. He hasn't made a move on her, but the last time she was here they got into some deep, personal conversations. She told him all about Frank and how badly that ended, and he told her about his late fiancée, who passed away after suffering a stroke four years ago. He seemed genuinely upset. Now they've shared this stuff, she feels like they have a connection.

"The bed in here is rock hard, I'm afraid," he says. "You might get a better night's sleep on the couch."

She smiles. "Hey, I'm just grateful to have somewhere to spend the night."

"Why don't you want to sleep at your place?" he asks. "Not that a murder in your apartment isn't enough. I wouldn't want to sleep there ever again."

She considers telling him everything that's happened, but she's too tired and she doesn't want to think about it. "Yeah, it's basically that." She looks up at him as he's about six inches taller than her. Which makes him about three inches taller than Dean. "Plus, I'm afraid of the dark."

Jake smiles and takes a step closer to her. She can smell his aftershave and she has to resist touching him. It's been over six months since she last slept with anyone, and that was Frank. He was the only man she'd been with in five years. This probably isn't a good idea considering they live in the same small town, but if things go wrong, she's not opposed to leaving town and starting over somewhere else. She thinks of Dean, which is annoying because she doesn't want him in her head right now.

Jake reaches down and pulls her face to his. They kiss. But it isn't what she had hoped it would be. He's clumsy and it's a little awkward at first, with neither of them relaxing into it.

She pulls away. "Have you got anything to drink?"

He looks surprised. "Er, no, sorry. We finished the beer the other day. I'm not much of a drinker, really. I have soda though?"

Her heart sinks. She doesn't think she can sleep with him stone cold sober. For some reason, that kiss has put her off. He must see it in her face because he offers to take a ride to the nearby liquor store. She's relieved. "That would be great. Get whatever they have as long as it's strong."

"Sure." He looks a little worried. He might think she has a drinking problem or something, but he grabs his keys and leaves for the store.

She sighs. "That was awkward." Why does she feel like she wants to get out of here? She can't just leave while he's not here, so she decides to wait and try again after a few drinks. Maybe she just needs to relax. While he's gone, she thinks about looking around his apartment, maybe opening a few drawers. Nothing too sneaky. But when she looks up at the corners of the room for cameras — a force of habit, given her job — she notices a small round security camera high up on the wall above the front window, facing the living room.

"That's weird. Who films their own living room?" she mutters.

She sits on the couch, feeling like she's being watched. He better not have one in the bedroom. She wonders if it's there because he's worried about being robbed. He does have a lot of expensive items. She wishes he told her she was being filmed the first time she came up here. It makes her feel uncomfortable that he didn't disclose it.

Her mood turns sour. She looks around. His computer screens are switched off again but the power lights are flashing. Is he hiding something? It makes her wonder why he chose Maple Valley if he's as loaded as he makes out. He could be living in a mansion in California, or a penthouse in New York.

She realizes then that something doesn't add up. She's been too quick to believe his claims about wanting to help those less fortunate than him. And wouldn't a millionaire be a better kisser? He must have had his pick of women over the years, with his money and looks, so he should have more game than he has.

She stands up, not sure what to do next.

CHAPTER THIRTY-NINE

After watching Beau Lachey's trailer for hours, Dean learns that his girlfriend Skylar no longer lives with him — and neither do their kids. He isn't surprised. Skylar was always the entrepreneur of the family. The last time Dean got called out to their place they were living in an impressively large house on the other side of town, all thanks to Skylar's well-earned drug profits. Now she's gone, Beau's back to living in his old trailer park.

Apart from a few males coming and going, not one female visits him. When it gets dark, Dean calls it quits and drives home via the Haunted Asylum. This is the second night it's been open and MVPD hasn't received any reports of suspicious or criminal activity, only complaints from locals about loud noise.

He pulls into the parking lot and is surprised by how many people are lining up outside. Dean watches the actors terrorizing the crowd as they wait to go in. He hears screams and laughter in equal measure. He walks up to the entrance. The heavy metal music is back on and even louder than when he and Eva were here the other day. Matt's on the door, letting people enter in small groups before halting the line.

He looks at Dean and rolls his eyes. "Not again! What are we doing wrong now?"

"Nothing." Dean has to shout to be heard over the music. "I need a list of your employees' names and dates of birth."

Matt sighs. "Sure, whatever."

"Do you do background checks on the people you hire?"

"Are you kidding me?" says Matt. "This kind of place has a high employee turnover so it would take up too much of my time to do background checks on everyone. I ask for one reference from their last employer but if they can't produce one it doesn't usually stop me from hiring them if they seem otherwise legit. Most people fake their references anyway."

Dean knows they're not obligated to perform checks, but for a job like this, it would be wise. After all, people — and mostly young people, judging by the crowd — are entering a building designed to confuse and isolate them in the dark, with masked strangers. What's to stop the actors groping the customers as they pass? Or worse.

"I'd strongly recommend you start performing checks," he says. "In the meantime, get that list of employee names to me ASAP." He passes Matt his contact details. "Unless you want me to come back and shut this place down."

Matt holds his hands up. "I'll get it to you. Just stop hassling us, man. It's bad for business."

Dean's seen enough for today. He drives home.

* * *

After taking a quick shower, with Mulder closed in the bathroom with him so he can't get into any trouble, Dean grabs a beer from the fridge. He sits on his couch, ready to start planning what he needs to do tomorrow to progress the homicide investigations. Mulder's climbing the drapes again and Dean can't be bothered to get him down. He figures the cat will get bored of it eventually.

He sifts through his mail. Among the utility bills is a letter from his life insurance provider. His stomach flips as he opens it. This can only be about Linda. They both took out life insurance when they bought the house, and he didn't even think about claiming it until Jones talked him into it. Jones reminded him how costly it had been for Dean to cover all the expenses that were accrued from sorting his brother's funeral and estate. John hadn't had life insurance and with their parents being long gone, Dean had been responsible for paying for everything.

He hasn't thought about Linda's life insurance for a while. The company had a copy of her death certificate so it should have been an open and shut case, but they wanted to speak to the medical examiner who performed Linda's autopsy. Dean never questioned why. He just gave them Sheila's contact details and, as Sheila never mentioned it to him, he just assumed there was nothing to worry about.

For some reason, he feels the need to stand when he reads this letter. It's longer than the others they've sent so he's hoping it's the last one he gets.

> *Dear Mr. Dean Matheson,*
>
> *In respect of your claim for life insurance after the unfortunate passing of your wife, Linda Jayne Matheson, we are pleased to inform you that you are entitled to the award of the sum listed overleaf. This will be paid to you within the next 28 days.*
>
> *However, we regret to advise that your statement claiming your wife was pregnant at the time of her death has proven to be inaccurate.*

Dean stops reading. "What the hell?"

They've got to be wrong. The night she died Linda told him she was carrying his baby. They were considering whether to get back together, for that very reason. His whole body suddenly feels cold.

There's obviously just been a mistake, that's all. Sheila can confirm Linda was pregnant. He can't let it stay recorded on a legal document that she wasn't pregnant. This isn't about the money; it's about accuracy. His baby died with Linda, and he grieved for them both. That baby needs to be recognized and remembered.

He has to swallow the lump in his throat. This is stupid. Why's he letting a clerical error get to him? It'll get sorted out, but he could really do without this crap. He reads on.

> *Dr. Sheila Didcott, Medical Examiner, has confirmed your wife was not pregnant at the time of her death, nor was there any question of her having been pregnant in the months leading up to it. Her medical records indicate she had previously been pregnant several years ago but suffered a miscarriage. Therefore, the amount you will receive is solely in respect of Linda Jayne Matheson.*

Dean's stunned. Linda lied to him about being pregnant to make sure he took her back after revealing she'd been cheating on him for two years. His ears ring and his heart thumps hard in his chest as he realizes she caused him so much extra unnecessary pain.

"What was she *thinking*? Why would she do that?"

He falls onto the couch and holds his head in his hands. Then he thinks of Sheila. She's been lying to him all this time.

He grabs his cell phone and calls her immediately. She takes a while to answer.

"Hey, Dean," she says. "You're not still at work, are you?"

"Why didn't you tell me?" He tries hard not to shout.

"Tell you what?" She pauses. "Oh, no." She knows exactly what he's talking about. "Dean? Who told you? Was it Eva? Or the insurance company? Have they written to you?"

He stands. "They're saying Linda wasn't pregnant. Is that true?" Then he realizes what she just said. "What do you mean did Eva tell me? How would she know?"

She hesitates. "Oh, Dean. I'm so sorry. Please hear me out. At the time I didn't know what to do. You'd taken John's death so hard and we had all that crap going down with Lizzie Glover, so I didn't want to add to your stress. And then after all that, there just wasn't a right time. I mean, how could I tell you there was no baby and that your dead wife had lied to you?"

He's seething. "So there wasn't a right time to tell me, but you found time to tell Eva? Thanks a lot, Sheila."

He hangs up and throws his phone on the couch. The urge to get wasted right now is stronger than his common sense. He stops and sinks into the couch. He hears a thud on the floor by the window. Mulder's no longer on the drapes and within seconds he's run over to Dean and climbed up the couch to sit on his lap.

* * *

Twenty minutes later, Dean finds himself crouching in the dark between John and Linda's graves. He hadn't meant to come here. He fully intended to buy some liquor and get drunk, but for some reason, he ended up here instead. It's wet and windy but Dean doesn't bother pulling his coat hood up. This kind of sleet gets you soaked no matter what you do. It runs down his face as he looks at their headstones.

He wishes he could talk to Linda, to ask why she felt the need to lie about something so serious. What would have happened after a few months back together when there was no growing bump? She would have been found out. It was so stupid. And desperate. Maybe she thought she could pretend to miscarry, or get pregnant for real in the meantime. She didn't even love him anymore; she'd admitted that. She never admitted who she'd been having an affair with but he found that out after her death.

He shakes his head. They were both so stupid back then. So immature.

The ground is cold beneath him so he stands just as the sleet turns to snow. It reminds him of his time in Colorado and he wonders whether he should have stayed there instead of coming home. It appears he can't trust anyone here, not even Sheila.

Feeling calmer than earlier, he looks around, wondering what to do next. He spots movement off to the right, under a streetlight. It's a cell phone's flashlight pointing at him. He's being followed again.

“Who’s there?” he shouts.

The person turns and runs away. Annoyed, Dean chases them. As he almost catches up, they suddenly stop running and turn around to face him.

It’s Camille.

“What are you doing here?” asks Dean. “And don’t give me any crap about going for a late-night walk. I’m not in the mood to be lied to today.”

She catches her breath and then tries to give him an innocent look by lowering her eyes and talking quietly. “I’m sorry. I just wondered who you were visiting. I like you and I—”

He doesn’t let her finish. “Cut the crap, Camille. I said, tell me the truth. Unless you’re visiting someone’s grave, you’re talking bullshit. Why are you following me?”

Her innocent demeanor changes in a second. First, she looks surprised by his attitude, then she looks determined. “Look. I have a proposition for you. It could make you a lot of money.”

He’s confused. “What are you talking about?”

She hesitates. “You’re not going to be happy when you find out, so let’s get a drink and I’ll tell you everything. It’s too cold out here to talk. I’ll meet you at that awful diner you’re so keen on.”

She walks off so fast that he doesn’t get time to ask anything else.

CHAPTER FORTY

Dean pulls into the diner's parking lot and looks up at Eva's apartment. It's 9 p.m. and the lights are off. She's with Jake Andrews. He hopes she knows what she's doing trusting Jake so soon after meeting him. Hopefully, Emily's social worker is wrong to be suspicious of the guy.

As he enters the diner, he spots Camille sitting in the corner. It's Saturday night so the place is busy with teenagers on dates.

"Deano!" shouts Frankie from the kitchen. "Have you come to spend Saturday night with me? I'm flattered." He wipes the grease from his forehead.

Rachel and the other waitresses are busy serving customers.

Dean barely smiles. "Hey, Frankie. I'll be over in the corner." He nods to Camille just as she looks up and notices him. "Can I get a decaf coffee?"

Frankie looks over at Camille, puts two and two together, and gets seven. He touches the side of his nose. "Say no more. I get it. But I hope Detective Valdez doesn't find out. She's pretty feisty, you know?"

Dean shakes his head. "We're just partners at work, Frankie. Nowhere else."

"Whatever you say, my friend. Whatever you say. One decaf coffee coming up."

Dean weaves through the tables and sits opposite Camille. She puts her cell phone away. "Well?" he says. "I'm listening. But keep it brief, I've had a bad day."

"I'm glad you came," she says. "Are you getting anything to eat?"

"No. This isn't a date."

Frankie interrupts and places a vanilla milkshake in front of Camille and a cup of coffee in front of Dean. Then he adds one slice of tiramisu. There are two forks on the plate. He winks at Dean and walks away, looking happy with himself.

Camille's about to pick up a fork so Dean pushes the plate away.

"You have exactly two minutes to explain why you were following me, otherwise I'm going to arrest you and you can tell me with your attorney present."

She looks shocked at his impatience, but he's not in the mood for games.

"Okay, here goes." She takes a deep breath. "I don't work in real estate. I'm a TV documentary producer."

Dean's confused. "What? Then why the hell have you been trying to sell my house?"

She winces. "I haven't. That was a little white lie. I'm actually in town to make a documentary."

He feels himself tense. "What's that got to do with me?"

She picks up her milkshake and takes a long sip through the straw. She won't meet his eyes.

"Camille? Get to the point."

She sits back and glares at him, defiant. "I'm making a documentary about you."

He blinks. Then he laughs. "What? That's ridiculous. I'm a nobody."

She leans forward, suddenly animated. "Are you kidding? You were an attractive young cop who was fooled by one of New Hampshire's most notorious female serial killers! Then you left town for a year, catching Colorado's worst child killer in their recent history, and now you're back where it all started, but this time as a *detective*. And the cherry on the cake is that your new, sexy female partner is suspected of murder! Now, tell me how that won't make excellent TV viewing?"

She doesn't wait for an answer. "Actually, it was originally going to be primarily about Lizzie Glover, but after speaking to the locals I've realized you're far more interesting. You and I could make a lot of money from this, Detective. I could write a book to go with it, and you could be *famous*! That's if you cooperate with me and fill in the blanks. There are quite a few at the moment." She pulls a laptop from her bag. "I'll pay you, of course, for your side of the story. You can even play yourself if you want. I mean, with your brooding good looks, the camera will love you."

Dean's aware his mouth is wide open. He doesn't know whether to laugh or flip the table. It's probably a good job it's screwed to the floor.

Camille sits back and crosses her arms, looking pleased with herself.

It's the self-satisfied look on her face that does it for Dean. He slowly stands, trying to contain his anger. She tricked her way into his house. He thinks about the kitchen drawer that was left open a few days ago. She's been snooping — no, more than that — she's been reading his personal documents while he wasn't there and without his permission, just so she can make a documentary about him.

He thinks about their kiss and shakes his head. She actually came on to him to get closer to his story. Thank God he turned her down. This would be even worse if he'd slept with her. He knows he has to get away from her immediately or he's going to cause a scene. "If you go ahead with this crap, you'll be hearing from my attorney."

She fixes her eyes on his. "Would that be the same attorney Detective Valdez is using, or one who worked with your crooked brother at the corrupt DA's office?"

Dean stares down at her, seething. How dare she mention his brother? And to call John *crooked*? There's so much he wants to say to her right now. John wasn't crooked — he was an amazing lawyer. He was a flawed person like everyone else around here, but he took pride in his work. Where did she get that from? Has someone been smearing John's reputation? Is this town not content with talking about him that they have to bring his dead brother into their gossiping? He realizes everyone around them has stopped talking. He doesn't look around, but he knows they're being watched.

His body trembles with anger but he doesn't want to react. That's what she wants. Whatever he does next she'll use against him in her ridiculous documentary. He leans forward. Quietly he says, "Don't you *ever* talk about my brother again. He's dead. He's off limits."

He turns away and walks through the packed, silent diner.

Rachel holds her arm out to stop him as he reaches the exit. "Dean? What did she say about John?"

Rachel dated his brother. She knows he was a good person.

Frankie joins them. "My God, you look like you've seen a ghost. Was it the tiramisu?"

Dean needs to get out of here. He turns to them both. "If you really care about me, don't let her in here again. She's about to take me and John down."

They gasp.

Dean walks outside to his car. He has to resist the urge to punch something. John's a raw nerve for him. And if Camille goes ahead with the documentary, it could be the end of Dean's career as a detective.

CHAPTER FORTY-ONE

Dean considers going home to his empty house but he drives to Jones' house instead, still pumped up with unspent adrenaline. Jones knew his brother and he'd be as outraged as Dean is about what Camille just said. When he gets there, Jones is happy to see him.

"Dean! Come on in."

"Sorry to turn up this late."

His anger must show on his face because Jones notices. "What's going on? Is it about Eva?"

He sighs. "No, she's fine. She's staying with a friend tonight. Where's George?"

"He's already gone to bed," says Jones. "Today's excitement with the media chase wore him out."

Dean thinks how lucky Eva is to have a parent, or any family member, to fight her battles with her. But he suspects Jones would do the same for him, even though they're not related.

Rocky yawns loudly. He's in his new favorite place, spread out in front of the fire.

"What can I get you to drink?" says Jones. "Is it too late for coffee? I don't have any decaf, I'm afraid. Barb always remembered to keep some in for you but I just forget every time I go to the store. Sorry."

Dean sits on the floor and lets Rocky put his giant head in his lap. It's not long before the dog turns onto his back to get a belly rub. Dean feels like he's starting to calm down now. "Got anything a little stronger?" he asks.

Jones smiles broadly. "George and I finished the whiskey last night, but I've got some vodka somewhere."

He goes to the kitchen and Dean listens to him opening and closing cabinets until he finds it. He brings the bottle into the living room with two glasses. As he pours their drinks, Dean thinks about how to tell him the ridiculous news that someone's making a documentary about him. He downs the first drink and holds his glass out for another. Jones doesn't comment.

"Did you ever meet Camille?" Dean asks.

"Your realtor?"

He nods.

"No, but Eva told George she thinks you're sleeping together."

Dean shakes his head. "No. I'm not sleeping with her. There was something about her I didn't like, but I couldn't figure out what. Well, now I know." He downs his second shot. He's going to have to take a cab home.

"What?" Jones is intrigued. "Don't tell me she's a killer?"

Dean scoffs. "No. Not this time. She's making a documentary about me. About everything that happened with Lizzie Glover."

Jones gasps. "You're kidding? Is she allowed to do that?"

"Probably. She also accused Eva of being a killer, so someone's been talking to her about the Trey Peterson case." He pauses. "And then she mentioned John."

"*What*?" Jones stands up, angry. "Who the hell does she think she is?"

Dean shrugs. "She called him crooked. What do you think she meant by that?"

"Crooked?" Jones looks puzzled. "*Crooked*? Are you sure she used that word?"

"Yeah. When I threatened to contact a lawyer, she asked if I'd be using the same attorney as Eva, or one who worked with my *crooked* brother and the *corrupt* DA."

Jones sits down. He looks stunned. "The DA's corrupt for sure but John was above board. I don't get it. She must think she has some dirt on him. Or maybe she's fishing for dirt, trying to judge your reaction to the suggestion?"

Dean thinks about it. It could be that. But the pit of his stomach tells him she's learned something about John that isn't true. "There's something else," he says. "Tonight I found out Linda wasn't pregnant when she died."

Jones looks at him open-mouthed before downing his drink. "I can't believe she lied. I know that's going to eat you up inside, so why don't you look at it a different way?"

"How?"

"Well, you didn't lose a child. Sure, you've been grieving unnecessarily, but isn't that better than actually losing a child?"

Dean looks into his glass and thinks about it. Of course, Jones is right, as always. It's far better that there was no child involved in all that mess. He feels a tiny flicker of hope in his chest. He thinks about what it will be like when he does finally have children in the future, if he ever settles down with someone else. At least that experience won't be spoiled anymore, by thinking of the child he thought he'd lost.

Suddenly, George appears in the doorway. "Let me see if I've got this right. Some TV producer is looking to take down my daughter in a documentary?"

Dean feels bad that George has to worry about this now too. And he doesn't know how to break it to Eva. She has enough on her plate with her suspension and trying to clear her name. "The documentary is about me and presumably how incompetent I was as a cop. But, yeah, she mentioned Eva too."

George considers this. "And your brother? Who, I'm presuming from your reaction, is no longer with us?"

"Right." He looks at Rocky who's snoring loudly. Dean doesn't think he'll sleep as peacefully as the dog tonight.

George sits next to Jones on the couch and pours himself a vodka. All he says is, "Huh."

"What are you thinking?" asks Jones.

After downing the shot, George smiles. "I'm thinking we should have some fun with this broad."

Dean shares a look with Jones. "How do you mean?" he asks.

"Well, she's obviously looking for information about you from the locals and someone's feeding her bits and pieces. But how about she meets two old guys with nothing but time and information on their hands? How about we feed her some information that's too good not to use in her documentary?"

Jones smiles, getting where George is going with this. "Right. We could steer her in the wrong direction and make her look like an idiot. Discredit her. I mean, I used to work with you so she won't be able to resist my input. And I was Lizzie Glover's arresting officer. She'd listen to me."

Dean watches them scheming and he smiles at the matching glints in their eyes. He's glad George moved in. They've quickly become a pair to be reckoned with. It also means Eva's more likely to stay here, once she's cleared her name.

He stands up, gently lifting Rocky's head off of him. "Whatever you pair get up to, just promise me you won't make things any worse."

They look at each other and laugh.

"Is it okay if Rocky stays at my house tonight?" he asks. "Emily Gordon wants to see him so I promised I'd take him to visit her at the hospital first thing tomorrow."

"Sure, that's fine," says Jones. "Is she still insisting Eva was the person who attacked her?"

"She is, but I think I can change that tomorrow. Or at least, Rocky can."

He grabs his keys and is about to order a cab when George offers to drive him and Rocky home. "I've only had one shot," says George. "Besides, you're on Eva's side. Which means you're part of the family now."

Dean's glad he came here tonight. He no longer feels like his life is falling apart. He can get through this. He's been through worse.

As he and Rocky head out to George's rental car, he notices an SUV speeding away from out front. "Did you see that car?"

George looks around but it's already gone. "Want me to chase them?"

"No, that's fine." He's hoping it wasn't Camille following him again, but it wasn't her red Nissan. As George starts the engine, all thoughts of being followed are replaced with the loudest rap music he's ever heard. He winces as he covers his ears.

Rocky barks as George turns the stereo off. "Sorry, guys! Happens every damn time."

Dean's ears ring all the way home.

CHAPTER FORTY-TWO

Including tonight, it's been six sleeps since Danny last slept in his own bed at home. And because of the basement incident, he's not allowed to sleep on the couch downstairs anymore. He has to sleep in Miss Livingstone's bed while she watches him from her armchair in the corner of the room. It's creepy and it makes him want to cry.

Tonight, he decides to make a list of everything that's good about living with his teacher, to help him feel better. Only in his head of course. He would never risk writing anything down. He lifts his head from the pillow and checks whether she's still awake.

Her face is lit up by the glow of her iPad. It makes her look like she's just a head without a body because the room is so dark.

"Go to sleep, Danny-boy," she says. "Don't worry. Mommy's still here watching over you."

Why is she saying his mom's here when she's clearly not? He sighs. Living here is exhausting. He's constantly trying to work out what she's talking about. Danny realizes he's thinking about the bad things, not the good.

Okay, the good things . . . He likes that he gets to eat whenever he's hungry. His mom never has enough money for a lot of food, and by the end of the week they live off basic cereal for all three meals. Sometimes without milk. Miss Livingstone loves the smell of junk food so he likes that he gets to regularly ride to fast food restaurants with her and see the outside world. She makes him wear sunglasses and a baseball cap but he doesn't mind. He likes that she's got a good sense of humor sometimes. She pretends to be the characters in the stories she tells and she puts on funny voices for them. That makes him laugh and stops him thinking about what happens to the characters at the end of the story.

What else? He struggles to think . . . He likes living in this big house because it's warm all the time. He hasn't been cold for ages. The beds have thick comforters on that keep him really cozy. He also likes that his dad isn't here to beat him. But he doesn't want to think about that.

Despite all these things, he thinks he'd still rather be sleeping in his own bed tonight. Living with his parents is turning out to be better than having Miss Livingstone watching him constantly and behaving strangely. He knows what to expect at home. He's learned how to stop his dad from getting angry with him, and where to get food when he can't bear the pain in his stomach anymore. Miss Emilia from across the street will always feed him a sandwich if he pulls weeds from her front lawn.

Danny feels for the watch he's hidden under his pillow. He found it in Miss Livingstone's purse when she was in the shower and he was looking for the door keys. It's his dad's watch. He knows because his dad once showed him the engraving on the back, which Grandpa had done for him. His dad said it's the only item Mom isn't allowed to pawn because it's his favorite possession.

What Danny doesn't want to think about is why his teacher has it and why the leather strap has a dark brown stain on the back of it. She must have visited his house and stolen it. Maybe she went to reassure his parents that he was safe. Maybe she paid them so they wouldn't come looking for him. He can imagine his mom selling him. She'll do anything for money. He wonders if Miss Livingstone told them he was naughty and snuck into her basement.

Oh no! He thought about the *basement*!

He squeezes his eyes shut, to try to stop the images of the dead man flashing back to him. He doesn't want to see him again, but it's too late. He sees the dead man's blood all over his foot and remembers that awful smell. He starts retching and can't stop. It makes him panic.

"Danny? What's the matter?"

Miss Livingstone rushes over, picks him up, and feels his forehead. She quickly carries him down to the kitchen, his least favorite place after the basement. As he stands on a footstool, hunched over the sink with the faucet running, the man's smell is stronger than ever. Does she not smell it? Why isn't she spraying an air freshener or something? He realizes he has to say something, even though he knows it won't go well.

"Miss?" He turns around.

She's leaning against the dining table, sifting through her big box of pills. "Yes?"

"Do we need to tell the police about that man?" His voice sounds squeaky to his ears.

She raises her eyebrows. "What man is that, Danny?"

He cringes inside and his throat goes dry. He knows he should stop right there as there's something wrong with her if she's going to pretend the man doesn't exist. Danny can't stand that smell for many more days. He can't stay here if he has to eat in this kitchen. Maybe if he annoys her enough, she'll take him back to live with his mom and dad.

"The man in the basement," he says with a shaky voice. "Maybe the police could take him away for us?"

His knees are shaking now, so he holds onto the sink to stop himself from falling off the stool.

She looks surprised. Then she nods in agreement. "You know what? You're right. Dr. Livingstone was silly to fall down those stairs. It's time we got rid of him."

For some reason, this scares Danny more than when she pretended he wasn't there. He doesn't know who Dr.

Livingstone is, or was, but he's starting to think he didn't fall down those stairs through his own bad luck.

She approaches him. "You can help me," she says, with a twisted smile. "Would you like that, Danny? Would you like to help me scrape Dr. Livingstone from the floor like a cockroach off your shoe?"

Danny can't help it. He screams, turns to the sink, and brings up everything he's eaten today.

CHAPTER FORTY-THREE

At ten a.m. on Sunday, Eva's driving with the heat turned up, but it's temperamental like every other part of this aging vehicle, so it still feels cold. She slept at her apartment last night, not wanting to take things further with Jake after their disastrous kiss and after noticing the camera in his living room.

It was a little awkward when he arrived back with a bottle of liquor and a smile on his face, but he'd been a gentleman about it when she lied and told him she'd been called into work. He told her she was welcome anytime but she doesn't think she'll be visiting him again in a personal capacity.

Now, after leaving Scully curled up on her bed, she's on her way to visit the secure psychiatric unit that held Lizzie Glover. It's been snowing all night so the roads are treacherous. She's passed state troopers forcing people to the side of the road to clear their vehicles of heavy snow. She can't believe people are stupid enough to drive like that.

As she approaches the secure unit, she follows the signs for visitor parking. Once parked, she gets out of her car and treads carefully, trying to avoid ice, and heads toward the visitor's entrance. The intercom asks who she's there to see and she asks for Brent Mitchell, just as Jones told her to.

Apparently, Brent has a deal with Jones and was happy to let him in without permission from the unit's manager when he would come to check on Lizzie.

She's buzzed in and joins a line of other people waiting to visit the inmates. As she waits for Brent to appear, she looks around the reception area. Out here it looks like any other hospital, with its white tiled walls and matching floors, and disinterested employees. But ahead of her, she can see the metal detectors and security guards waiting to frisk everyone. If she has to go through a metal detector her gun is going to get the party started and she'll be escorted out within minutes. She knows she shouldn't have worn it, but who enters a unit for the criminally insane without protection?

After a minute or two, someone tugs her arm. She looks around and has to move her eyes upward. Brent is extremely tall, with a blank face and big wide eyes. Jones didn't tell her Brent was an inmate. Or maybe this is just how she imagines the inmates to look.

"This way," he says.

She follows him through a door behind the reception area which takes three keys to open. No one looks at them. None of the employees show any interest in her at all. It's no wonder Lizzie was able to escape.

"I know what you're thinking," says Brent, walking slightly ahead of her and without turning to face her.

"Oh yeah? What's that?"

"You're thinking this unit isn't secure because I'm letting you back here," he says. "But in actual fact, you're only one of two people I've ever let in. And none of the other employees would dare do this." He stops and she almost walks into him. "Detective Jones asked for my help. I've known him fifteen years and he's as good as they come, so I trust him. If he wants me to let you speak to the other employees undercover, then I'll do it. But don't go thinking we don't run a tight ship around here, Detective. Because it's tight."

She raises her eyebrows. "So tight someone recently escaped."

He winces as if he's been hit. "That was our first escape in fourteen years. She couldn't have gotten out without someone helping her. When an employee betrays our trust like that it makes us all a laughing stock. You've got to find the person who did it. They'll be fired immediately. I'll personally make sure of it."

He opens a door that leads to what looks like a cafeteria, presumably just for employees. He hands her a clipboard with a legal pad and a pen attached. Then he motions for her to go in. "Just don't tell them you're a cop. Tell them you're here to discuss employee satisfaction, equal opportunities, that kind of thing."

He's about to leave so she grabs his arm. "You seem very knowledgeable, Brent. Care to hazard a guess who helped Lizzie escape?"

His face is blank as he says, "If I knew that, I wouldn't have needed to let you in. I'll be back in an hour."

He slams the door behind him, making some of the employees look up from their food. They must be on their breaks. She looks over at a man who immediately pretends he hasn't noticed her. He's warming his hands on a hot drink and reading a gun magazine. The smell of coffee is overwhelming in here and it's been at least a half hour since Eva finished her last gas station coffee.

"Hey," she says to him. "Do you have a minute to answer some questions?"

He gets up to leave. "No. Break's over."

She's not going to let him walk away. He looks guilty of something. "I'm from Human Resources so I'd suggest you sit down and talk to me."

He hesitates before rolling his eyes and sitting back down. "What is it this time? I don't want to give half my salary to starving kids in Africa, thanks."

She doesn't know what he's talking about. "I'm wondering how happy you are with the safety and security procedures around here." She takes the lid off the pen and starts writing. "What's your name?"

He doesn't answer so she copies it from his name tag. "Max McCann. Okay, and you work in which department?"

"C block. With the women."

"You must feel pretty secure around a bunch of women?" she asks, looking for a reaction.

"Are you serious?" He snorts. "They're worse than the men. They don't wash, they spit on you, and they rub themselves all over you because they're always horny. It's a disgusting side effect of the medication some of them are on."

She hadn't expected that reaction. "So how do you keep them off you?"

He immediately looks down at his hands with a look of shameful defiance.

She realizes he hits them. *What an asshole.* She needs him to confide in her so she can't react with disgust. "It would be understandable if you used force. I mean, that's expected in this job, isn't it?"

His eyes light up. "Exactly! That's what I tell the others. But some of them get off on the attention. The losers who can't get a woman in real life."

Jeez. This is worse than she was expecting. She notices a man staring at her from a distance. He's a little overweight, with brown curly hair and he's wearing thick glasses. When he sees her looking, he rushes away.

"What would you do if an inmate asked you to let them out?" she asks. "Or maybe give them a little bit of freedom? You know, nothing serious. Just an extra half hour out of their room?"

Horrified, Max says, "I would never allow that! I'm not like those morons." He motions to a table about ten feet away where three guys are sitting around laughing. "Don't make it obvious you're looking at them. They hate me. They say I'm too strict and I need to lighten up, but that's how we got into this mess in the first place."

She sits up straight. "What mess would that be, Max? Do you mean the recent escape?"

He looks at her properly, trying to weigh up how much to say. "If you don't want that to happen again, you need to put everyone through security training again. Everyone's too negligent around here. We're lucky she didn't stop to kill any of us on her way out."

She thinks she can ask him the next question without raising any suspicions about why she's really here. "That sounds like a good idea." She writes it down. "I think you're right. People are getting too complacent around here. I'll get something booked in. Is there anything about the way the inmate escaped that you think made it easy for her? Do we need better locks, or more security guards?"

He laughs, which surprises her. "No. What we need are professional doctors. They're worse than anyone else here."

She stops pretending to take notes. "Really? So you're saying the doctors are inappropriately involved with their patients?"

He must realize he's said too much as he gets up. "What did you say your name was again?" he asks.

"Eva."

"I never said you could quote me on any of that. Just get the training booked in. And hire better doctors while you're at it. We seem to get all the crap ones here. Some of them only last a month. You can't blame them; it's not easy working with these people. They go off with stress a lot too. Dr. Livingstone's been off sick for six weeks now, and you can bet he's on full pay. I'd never get away with that."

He scurries away, avoiding eye contact with the other employees. Eva recognizes Dr. Livingstone's name from Lizzie's progress reports. She wonders if he's off work because he's embarrassed he got it so wrong about Lizzie's progress. It doesn't look good for his professional reputation and, if she kills again, he could be sued.

She sighs and turns to the table of men in front of her. One of them is wearing a white coat over a shirt. He looks more like a doctor than the others. He has that air of authority about him. He's also speaking louder than the rest of them and lapping up the attention from his sexist jokes. She gets up and walks over to them. Two of the three men at the table excuse themselves. Just the doctor remains, and he's grinning at her.

"Got a minute?" she asks. "I'm from Human Resources."

"Sure, sit down," he says. "I always have time to talk to pretty ladies."

"So I've heard."

He slicks his hair back but doesn't say anything.

"I'm here to do a survey on risk management. I understand it's easy for an inmate to escape, and management is concerned that employees are at risk of serious harm, given the nature of the people we're dealing with."

He takes a sip of his coffee.

She looks at his name tag and makes a note of his name: Evan Tanner. "So, Dr. Tanner. Any opinions or suggestions?"

"Oh, I've got plenty," he says with a smirk. "How about I tell you about them off the clock, over a drink tonight?"

Before Eva can reject him, a woman runs in crying, "Tommy's dead! Oh my God, he's *dead*!"

Eva jumps up and runs to the woman. "Where?"

"Don't make me go back there!" says the woman, covering her eyes.

Eva grabs her arm. "Take me to him. You don't have to look at him again."

The woman whimpers as she leads Eva through a hallway behind the kitchen. No one follows them.

"Is Tommy an employee?" asks Eva.

"He's one of the cleaners. He has a janitor's closet back here."

Eva stops her. "Don't go any closer, I've got this. Just go and call the police."

The woman spins around, crying as she runs.

When she's out of sight Eva pulls her weapon and slowly walks toward the janitor's closet. With no windows back here, the hallway is dark, but there is light coming from within the room. She holds her gun out as she turns the corner.

She doesn't need it. The heavyset man who was staring at her in the cafeteria is definitely dead.

CHAPTER FORTY-FOUR

At the hospital, Dean gets some good luck. The nurses taking care of Emily are charmed by Rocky and they agree to let Dean take him in to see her, as long as he's quiet and he doesn't scare anyone. Some people may believe pets don't belong in hospitals, but the amount of faces that light up as they pass the patients suggests otherwise.

Dean's keen to see if Emily will open up to him now Rocky's here. He knocks on her door, which is wide open. Emily's lying still and staring at the ceiling but she makes an effort to sit up when she sees him. He has Rocky hidden from view for now.

"Are you well enough for visitors?" he asks.

She nods and, as Rocky walks around the corner into full view, Dean spots the young girl he once knew. Her eyes open wide, but not as wide as her smile. Rocky stops a few steps away from the bed, not yet aware of who he's visiting. He looks up at Dean, probably wondering why he's been dragged here when he could be asleep at home.

"Rocky!" says Emily.

The dog looks up at her, his tail wagging slowly at first until he fully recognizes her. Then he tries to launch himself onto the bed but it's too high for his arthritic hips and immense weight. Dean pulls the visitor armchair close to it and lifts Rocky onto that instead. From there, Rocky makes it onto Emily and he goes straight for her face, licking her all over. His tail is wagging so hard that it hurts Dean when it makes contact with his arm.

He steps back to watch them together and has to swallow a lump in his throat. He feels guilty for taking Rocky away from her but he has to remind himself it was either that or let Rocky try his luck at an animal shelter.

Emily's openly crying and rubbing her face over Rocky's.

"I can't watch," says Dean, pretending to wipe tears away. "It's like that show where they find long-lost family members and reunite them. Gets me every time."

Emily laughs through her tears.

Finally, a laugh. He's relieved. He might be able to salvage their friendship.

A female nurse walks in and stops, raising her eyebrows at the dog. "I know we said your dog could visit but he's going to crush your ribs, Emily. And watch the wires."

"Sorry, that's my fault," says Dean. He moves the IV drip out of Rocky's way. Rocky settles next to Emily on the bed. He stares up at her with his tongue hanging out.

"It's meant to be shower time now," says the nurse. "Your hair could do with a wash."

"Can I just have ten minutes with her first?" asks Dean, trying to convey with his eyes that he's here on important police business, not just to reunite Emily with her dog.

She smiles. "Of course. I'll go and see Mr. Patel from next door first. He needs a sponge bath. Lucky me!"

Dean laughs and watches her leave. When she's gone, he pushes the door closed and sits next to the bed.

"How are you feeling now?"

Emily looks away from Rocky for the first time. "It's painful when I cough, sneeze, move, or breathe." She smiles sadly. "I'll be fine."

He feels for her. "Here's my number. If you ever need me, call me."

She looks at the piece of paper he hands her. "Calling is old-fashioned. Are you on Snapchat?"

He laughs. "What, at my age? Why would I be on Snapchat?"

She smiles. "I like it because whatever you say or send is temporary. I'll probably text you if I need you. I don't do phone calls."

"I feel so old," he jokes. He's not sure how she'll react to being questioned about her allegations but time is against Eva. With both the media and Camille gunning for her, Dean needs to get at least one allegation against Eva dropped.

"Emily, are you ready to tell me what happened to you? I'll believe whatever you tell me and I'll investigate it thoroughly. I just need to know the truth. It's the only way to stop what happened to you from happening to someone else."

She looks away and bites her bottom lip as if considering whether to keep up the pretense of claiming this was Eva's fault. She strokes Rocky's head but she doesn't say anything.

"I met Tiffany, you know?" he says.

She looks at him. "Where is she?"

His heart sinks. She really doesn't know. She can't have seen the photo they put out of Tiffany when they were still referring to her as Taylor. Or maybe she did and she didn't recognize her friend because of the injuries. He reaches for her hand. "Tiffany was badly beaten. Her injuries were severe. She was brought in here, and at first, she was doing surprisingly well."

Emily's gaze is intense. She's hungry for information about her friend.

"That's why I haven't seen her around," she says. "I thought she was murdered in some cheap motel somewhere, or she'd run away with some weirdo. Is she still here?"

Dean leans forward in his seat and squeezes her hand. "No. I'm really sorry, Emily. Tiffany died of her injuries."

The hard expression instantly returns to Emily's face and she turns away from him. He knows that look from other kids who've been let down by the system or their parents. It's a front to protect them from what they're feeling. She's going to act as if she doesn't care. She even takes her hand off Rocky.

"I need to know if the person who beat her was the same person who beat you," he says. "And you're not going to like this, but I know for a fact that Detective Valdez wasn't involved at all in Tiffany's injuries, so I need to know who did it. At the moment, we don't have anything to go on other than the fact she was dumped outside the church."

Emily's head snaps up. "The church? Shit."

"What is it? What's going on there?"

"I can't say." She sits up straighter and looks nervous. "You don't understand. Until you're in our situation, you never will."

He hates it when people talk in riddles. It wastes so much time. "Then make me understand, Emily. Do this for Tiffany and all the other kids who are probably being exploited by this person. Who is it? Who's in charge of whatever you're involved in?"

She looks at him. "It's really unfair to put me in this position. To make *me* the one who has to speak out. No one's spoken out for me!"

He nods. "Trust me, I get it," he says gently. "But think about it, if someone had found the courage to speak up before now, you and Tiffany wouldn't have gone through any of this. She'd still be alive. *Someone* has to do it, or it will never end. You'll never be free of them. You have the power to make it stop."

Emily looks down at Rocky, who's starting to snore. She strokes his velvety ears and bursts into tears. She sobs so hard her whole body shakes, moving the bed. Rocky snaps awake and looks up at her.

"I'm so sorry you're in this situation," says Dean. "I didn't want this for you." It's hard to watch someone struggle like this.

When she stops crying, she says, "Did Tiffany say anything about me?"

He tries to think. "She was suffering with amnesia because of her injuries. She didn't remember anyone in her life." He pauses. "Emily, what was she involved in?"

Emily uses some tissues to wipe her face. "She did whatever she needed to do for money and food."

"Is that what you do?"

She looks ashamed. "When you don't have any money, you have to do whatever you can to survive. I'm not proud of it, but it's no big deal. I'm basically an adult."

He shakes his head, angry that someone's had this effect on her. "No, Emily. You're not even seventeen. You're not an adult and you don't have to act like one, no matter who's trying to tell you otherwise. Please, tell me who hurt you."

A tear rolls down her face. "I can't tell you anything."

"But why not?"

She looks up at him with more tears in her eyes. "Because you'd never speak to me again if you ever find out what I've done."

He's surprised, but he doesn't show it. That's not what he expected her to say. "Don't be stupid. There's nothing you can do that would make me think any less of you."

She's shaking her head. "There is." She pauses before looking up at him. "Because it's about you." She starts sobbing again and the nurse returns, giving him a hard look.

He pulls Emily to him and hugs her gently, trying not to hurt her ribs. Dean knows he can't push her any further today. She's distraught but he doesn't understand what she means.

And what's with that damn church, or community center, or whatever it is? He realizes it's time to focus his attention on Jake Andrews.

CHAPTER FORTY-FIVE

It's getting dark, and Dean's feeling pretty miserable. After visiting Emily earlier, he dropped Rocky home to Jones and declined an offer to go in and hear George's plan for Camille. He wasn't in the mood, even though he's grateful they're trying to help him. The problem is, he's not convinced they won't make things worse by trying to feed her false information, but he decides to leave them to it. He figures it'll be difficult to make things worse when someone's hell-bent on making a documentary about all his past mistakes.

He's spent all afternoon at the station, concentrating on finding out more about Jake Andrews. A criminal background check told him the guy doesn't have a record, but he's found articles online about a legal argument Jake had with a former friend. The friend accused him of stealing his website idea and making millions from it. From what Dean can tell, it looks like Jake settled the case out of court. It shows him Jake's not the angel he makes out but, other than that, he appears to be clean. Without any evidence he was involved in Tiffany's death, Dean can't officially dig too deep.

Matt from the Haunted Asylum emailed the list of employees Dean asked for but most of them are difficult to trace. He's convinced they're not using their real names, which means one or more of them could be trying to hide the fact they're convicted felons. But, again, without a real reason to bring any of them in, his hands are tied for now. The owner of the asylum appears to own three other haunted attractions around New England, with no criminal record. He lives in Boston and has no link to Maple Valley.

Dean moves on to check what Beau Lachey's been up to lately and finds out he's doing the same as usual: dealing drugs and being anti-social. He's had a few arrests and a short stay in jail but that's it. He could've been dealing drugs to Tiffany before she died but there's nothing to suggest he's a pimp, or that he has anything to do with underage girls, so it's looking like that theory's another dead end.

He gets up to make himself a drink and finds Steve in the kitchen. The awkwardness between them is still there but Dean's still none the wiser about what caused it. He figures it's best not to know.

Steve turns around with a cup in his hand. "Did Detective Briggs manage to get a hold of you?"

Dean nods. "Yeah, it was about Trey Peterson. Turns out he doesn't know much about the guy so they haven't been able to figure out any prime suspects for me to interview. Danny's still missing so they're taking that more seriously now, even though his mom never calls them for updates."

"They don't think he just ran away anymore?"

"No. They're working on the assumption he was abducted by Trey's killer, so they wanted to know what we know. Briggs told me a teacher from the boy's school wants to speak to the police about his concerns about where Danny might be, so Briggs is meeting with the teacher tomorrow morning. I've agreed to go along with him."

Steve nods. "Let me know what happens."

Dean heads back to his messy desk, feeling weighed down by the amount of paperwork that covers it. He misses having Eva to talk things through with and he's feeling the pressure of trying to solve these cases by himself.

Just as he's thinking of finishing for the night, Captain Brown calls him into his office. Dean wonders if it's about Eva but when he notices Officer Miller's in there, his gut tells him he's about to get some bad news. He's starting to wish he'd left work sooner.

"Take a seat, Matheson. You're going to need it." Captain Brown nods to the seat next to Miller.

Miller smirks and Dean can see the gum he's chewing. He can't even bring himself to sit next to him. "I'm fine standing."

"Suit yourself," says the captain. "Well, you're a smart man. I'm sure you know what I'm about to say. We're a detective down. The media and the DA are on our backs and we're going to be in for a shitshow if we don't find who killed Trey Peterson. We also need to exonerate Valdez as soon as possible and find out what happened to Tiffany Sanders. You need help as you can't do this alone. That's got nothing to do with you being a new detective, so don't take it personally."

Dean does take it personally. He doesn't think Captain Brown would've given Detective Jones someone to help him when short-staffed.

"While Valdez is suspended, Officer Miller here will be on detective duties."

He can't even bring himself to look at Miller. "Understood. Is that it? Can I go now?"

Captain Brown shakes his head. "Come on, you guys. Can't you get over this beef? It's been going for years."

"Hey, I'll work with anyone," says Miller. "I'm not the one with the problem."

Dean silently rages, but he won't give Miller the reaction he wants.

Captain Brown tries to engage Dean. "Don't you two have any mutual ground? Anything in common?"

Miller laughs. "Sure we do. We'd both like to bang Valdez."

Captain Brown immediately stands up and shouts, "Do *not* speak about another officer in that way ever again!"

Dean barely hears him. He's across the office and punching Miller in the face before the captain can even finish his sentence.

Brown pulls Dean away by his arm after just one punch and then Steve's in the room, pulling his other arm.

"Get out of here, Miller! Before I fire your ass," says the captain.

"Fire me? I'd like to see you try." He has a bruise already forming around his jaw. He turns to Dean. "You cracked my tooth, you son of a bitch!"

Steve pushes Miller out of the room and slams the door shut behind him. "For Christ's sake, Dean. Why do you let him get to you?"

Dean's surprised when Captain Brown stands up for him. "He had it coming, Sergeant, trust me. That man's a piece of shit and he's skating on thin ice. But you can't do that again, Matheson. Show some damn professionalism. You're a detective now."

Dean rubs his sore knuckles. Miller's bonier than the last time he hit him. "Come on, Captain! Why him? Why can't you promote someone else? What about Jenny or Marty?"

Captain Brown doesn't like being told what to do. "I think that's my decision, Matheson. He has experience, and I thought it would bring out your competitive streak."

"Listen," says Dean. "I don't need any more motivation than I've already got. They got to Emily Gordon this time and someone's framing Eva. Trust me, that's enough. I will find out who's doing this, but I'll work better alone than with that jerk."

Captain Brown sighs and pushes some paper around his desk. "Look, you don't have to physically work together. Tell him what you need him to do. Send him off on errands. Use him. This is your investigation, so you're in charge."

Dean knows this is the best he can hope for. "Fine. But make sure he knows that."

He pulls the door open and leaves. Miller's nowhere to be seen. Marty gives him a thumbs-up from behind the front desk.

As Dean returns to his desk, Steve approaches him. "I don't appreciate you upsetting Sheila, man. She was in an impossible situation when she found out Linda wasn't pregnant."

Annoyed, Dean sighs. "Great, so you know about that too? Does everyone else around here know?"

Steve stands his ground. "She only told Eva because they were drunk. She said a lot of things she shouldn't have that night." He doesn't elaborate. "And she only told me after you called her about it. She was distraught about what you might do to yourself. I had to calm her down."

Dean feels like a jerk. He knows Sheila couldn't win in that situation but it was a shock to find out so long after it happened. "I'm sorry," he says. "I'll apologize to her. I just didn't like finding out from the insurance firm and I reacted badly. Tell her not to worry about it."

Steve nods. "She was just trying to do the right thing." He walks away.

Dean doesn't like the simmering tension between them. They used to be close, but now it feels like they just work together.

As he grabs his things, he notices a text from Eva saying she's outside his house and needs to talk to him. He leaves the station and heads to his car. He's not looking forward to seeing her as he didn't do a very good job of getting Emily to retract her allegations. Although he's still hopeful she'll be thinking about it after his visit. Especially now she knows what happened to Tiffany.

CHAPTER FORTY-SIX

Dean's still fuming when he pulls into his driveway and spots Eva standing beside her car. He tries to brush off what just happened so it doesn't ruin their evening. "Aren't you cold out here?" he asks, getting out of his car. It's snowing again.

"Yeah, but I didn't want to just let myself in. Hurry up and open your door! Oh, and I brought two friends." She waves a bottle of tequila in front of his face and gestures to the pet carrier.

He smiles as he lets her into his house. Just seeing her lowers his blood pressure. She's the only person who understands what it's like to work with someone they can't stand, although he has to admit that Detective Garner was much worse than Miller.

He changes out of his work clothes and into a T-shirt and sweatpants before joining Eva in the kitchen. He doesn't bother asking if she wants coffee. He automatically puts the coffee machine on and then turns to face her. She's taken a seat at the breakfast bar where she's placing Scully next to Mulder. The kittens sniff each other and Scully starts rubbing her face over her brother's. Dean prepares food for the kittens and they both eat hungrily.

"So what did you want to tell me?" he asks.

"I had a great morning at the secure unit," she says with a smile. "The guy Jones put me in touch with let me into the employee cafeteria and I found out not many people take security seriously there."

Dean's glad to see her smiling. If he were in her position he'd be wallowing in self-pity. Although, he's learning that doesn't get him anywhere. "Go on, then. Tell me everything." He pours two coffees and stands in front of her at the breakfast bar.

She notices his swollen knuckles and reaches out to touch his hand. "What happened here?"

He shakes his head, dismissing it. "Just Miller."

She raises her eyebrows. Her hair is tied back and she's wearing a sweater that's too big for her. She looks great. He knows he's not supposed to think about her in that way, but he can't help it.

"You can tell me about that later," she says. "We need shot glasses."

He turns around and grabs two from a cabinet behind him. She pours them each a shot of tequila and they both down them. It's exactly what Dean needs right now.

"Okay," she says. "So do you remember someone called Dr. Livingstone?"

"Wasn't he one of Lizzie's doctors?"

"Correct."

While she talks, the kittens try to jump off the breakfast bar so he places them on the floor, letting them explore. Mulder heads straight for an empty box next to the trash. Dean watches as he crouches inside the box, hiding from Scully and wiggling his ass. Scully walks past, completely unaware he's there until Mulder jumps out at her, landing on top of her head. She shakes him off and runs into the living room.

"Well, the doctor has been off work for a while now." She sips her coffee and then pours them another shot of tequila. "His wife has been phoning in sick for him, probably because he's been professionally embarrassed by Lizzie's escape."

"Let's go into the living room," says Dean.

She takes the bottle and glasses with her. Dean picks Mulder up but he wriggles in protest. He seems to hate being picked up. Dean has to let him perch on his shoulder as he walks into the living room. Mulder jumps off before Dean has a chance to bend nearer to the couch, and the cat immediately starts with the zoomies. He's running back and forth around the living room, ending in his favorite place: halfway up the drapes. Scully silently watches her brother's antics before cleaning her face.

"I think there's something wrong with mine," says Dean.

Eva laughs. "He's going to be more trouble than mine, that's for sure."

He lights the open fire before taking a seat on the couch, one space away from Eva.

"So I'm going to pay him a visit at his home tomorrow," she continues. "I have a hunch there's a link between Lizzie escaping and him going off sick. Maybe he feels guilty or something, I don't know. I just think it's worth following up. I mean, the guy probably knew her better than anyone else by the time she escaped."

"But Jones and the FBI already interviewed him straight after she escaped," says Dean.

"I know, but I think he could fill in some blanks for me and he's had a lot of time to think about it now. He saw her almost every day during her incarceration so he must know something, right? I know he refused to say much to Jones and the Feds because of patient-doctor confidentiality, but maybe he's feeling different these days."

Dean finishes his coffee. The tequila mixed with caffeine is starting to give him a nice buzz. "Isn't that pushing things a little far, to visit his home? I mean, you're meant to be suspended and he's a professional, so he'll probably ask to see your badge, which I assume you had to hand over to Captain Brown."

She pulls a face that suggests she hadn't thought of that. "Okay then, come with me and do the talking. You can show him your badge."

He thinks about whether he'll have time because he needs to be at Danny's school in Cedar Falls at nine a.m., and he remembers what the captain said. He wants the two recent murders wrapped up as fast as possible to get the focus off of MVPD. He's not going to like it if Dean suddenly switches to looking for Lizzie Glover. "I shouldn't. Captain Brown might suspend me too."

She looks disappointed. "Okay. Well, anyway, that's not even the most interesting thing that happened today. While I was at the secure unit, one of the employees decided to kill themselves."

Dean leans forward. "Are you serious? What did you say to him?"

"I hadn't even spoken to him!" she says, amused. "He was one of the cleaners. And I was the first person on the scene after he was found."

"How did he do it?" he asks.

"Hanged himself."

Dean thinks about what started the whole business with Lizzie Glover two and a half years ago. It was the woman they found hanging in the Maple Valley woods. This is much more like her MO than Trey Peterson's murder. Could she be back? Out of hiding at last? Or was the guy overwhelmed with guilt for helping her escape? "Did he leave a note?"

Eva nods with a satisfied smile on her face. "Sure did. And you, my friend, are never going to guess what it said."

Dean thinks about it. "How about: 'she made me do it'?"

Eva looks impressed. "How did you know that?"

"Was he overweight with dark hair?"

She nods. "Right. So he was the one who shot you at Barbara's funeral?"

"Maybe. Do you have a photo?"

She gets her phone out. "Of course. I took it before I had to get out of there. I couldn't risk being found by the local police as they wouldn't be happy with me investigating while suspended. I also took a photo of his note. It was poking out the pocket of his coveralls."

She gives Dean her phone. He looks at the dead man. His face is bright red and his swollen tongue is sticking out of his mouth. His eyes are open but glassy and bulging from their sockets. Dean didn't get a close look at the person who shot him at Barbara's funeral, but he saw him approach from across the cemetery. He thinks this is the same guy.

"He's still fresh."

"I know," she says. "I saw him about ten minutes before he did it too. He was staring at me in the cafeteria."

Dean's mind is racing. "He must've known you were a cop." He reads the note.

She made me do it. She told me to poison the drinks. I didn't know it would kill that nice volunteer lady. She made me shoot the guy at the cemetery too, but I wouldn't have killed him, I'm a good person. So I'm sorry about that. I thought she was my friend. But I didn't help her escape. I knew that would be terrible for everyone. She's not a good person. Please take care of my parakeet. Tommy.

"So he didn't help her escape." Dean thinks about what he's reading. "He doesn't name her though?"

"No. But it's pretty obvious," says Eva. "Tommy must've panicked when he saw me at his place of work. He must've thought I'd come to arrest him. I don't know how he knew who I was though. I wasn't at Barbara's funeral."

Mulder suddenly jumps through the air from the drapes, landing on Dean's stomach. He runs away as Dean hunches forward in pain. "Shit!"

Eva laughs. "Come on, that can't have hurt. He doesn't weigh anything!"

"He got me right where I was shot. It's still painful."

"Probably because you opened it so many times trying to be a tough guy! Let me see how it's healing now." She sits forward.

Dean stands and lifts his T-shirt, exposing the raised pink scar on his abdomen.

"Damn, Matheson." Eva stands and lifts his T-shirt a little higher. "You've got abs! Why have you been hiding these bad boys?"

He drops his T-shirt and sits back down. "It was easy to stay fit living in Vegas. They won't last much longer if I don't start working out again soon." He pours them both another tequila.

"Urgh, working out." She collapses onto the couch. "Just the thought of it makes me hungry. Do you have anything to eat? I'm starving."

He gets up and heads to the kitchen on autopilot. He's thinking about how everything that's happened over the last seven days all fits together. He's sure now that the person who attacked Tiffany and Emily is different to who killed Trey Peterson. And he'd go so far as to bet that neither of them has anything to do with Lizzie Glover. She doesn't work like that. Trey's murder was messy and over the top. Taylor's was brutal. Dean thinks their killers are male.

He hands Eva a family pack of potato chips.

Her eyes light up. "Awesome, thanks."

He sits down. "We'll have to notify the FBI about the link between Tommy and Lizzie. But I think she's gone from New Hampshire."

Eva nods. "I think you're probably right. I know she's meant to be crazy but she'd also have to be stupid to stick around here and risk re-arrest, and we know she's not stupid. I couldn't stand one day in that awful place so I don't blame her for getting out. And there's always someone stupid enough to fall for a killer, I mean, just look at all those weirdos who write to death row inmates. It looks like Tommy was easily manipulated, but there have been no attempts on your life since the funeral at Christmas. That was almost three months ago." She sighs. "But I'd still like to speak to her doctor. We need to find out who helped her escape. They need to be fired and charged with something."

Dean leans back and sighs. "This is exhausting. My mind never stops trying to link everything together."

"Welcome to the life of a detective," she says. "Here, have another tequila. That'll help."

They tap their shot glasses together. "Cheers."

"Mind-numbing TV also helps," she says.

She switches the TV on and Dean wonders whether she'll stay the night. Before he can ask her, he recognizes the person talking on the news. He gets a sinking feeling in his stomach. It's Camille.

CHAPTER FORTY-SEVEN

"Hey, it's your realtor!" says Eva. She feels a little drunk now and nicely relaxed. She likes it at Dean's house. She can be herself here.

"This is bad," says Dean, as he turns the volume up.

They listen as Camille talks to the presenter.

"Filming isn't finished yet," she says, "but I've put together a little teaser trailer for your viewers so they can see what to expect. It shows just how interesting this story is and how hard it is to believe."

The female presenter smiles. "The old adage of truth being stranger than fiction comes to mind! We'll run the teaser trailer in just a second but I have one last question. Where have you got all your facts from and is Detective Matheson a willing participant in the documentary?"

Eva looks across at Dean. "What's going on? Why's your realtor making a documentary about you?"

He cringes. "I'll explain in a minute. I can't believe she's going ahead with it."

"Oh, the residents of Maple Valley have been extremely helpful," says Camille. "In fact, today I've secured interviews with two people who were involved in finally catching Lizzie Glover. They worked closely with Officer Matheson, as he was then, so their insight will prove invaluable. But Dean himself hasn't been so forthcoming, unfortunately. When I asked him to be involved and to have a chance to put across his side of the story, he basically threatened to sue me. In my experience, only people who have something to hide react in that way."

The presenter turns to the camera. "Well, here it is folks. The trailer for Camille's forthcoming documentary: *Lust, Lies, and Homicide.*"

Dean winces next to her. "That's what she's calling it?"

Eva can't tear her eyes away from the screen. How did he not tell her this was being made? She's on the edge of her seat and suddenly remembers where she knows Camille from. "It's *her*!" she says. "I knew I'd seen her before. She was the interviewer on a documentary I watched about a serial killer from back home. She went to death row to interview him and you could tell she loved every minute of being at the prison and talking to a child killer. What was his name? Oh yeah, Tate Spencer. You'd think she was in love with him the way she flirted on camera. It was sick. She got trolled on Twitter for it."

Dean doesn't reply.

The trailer starts and Eva realizes they're using an actor to play him, and not one with a very good likeness. As they watch the actor driving around in a police cruiser, the narrator explains what the documentary is about.

'Maple Valley, New Hampshire. After the devastating impact of what happened in 2016, there's a new detective in town. Local man, Dean Matheson, wasn't an obvious choice for Maple Valley's newest homicide detective. In fact, his own life could be described as a car crash waiting to happen. But, fresh from catching one of Colorado's worst child killers in recent history, the ex-Maple Valley PD officer was quickly promoted upon his return home. This is all the more surprising considering he used to be in a sexual relationship with New Hampshire's most notorious female serial killer, Lizzie Glover. As if that wasn't enough, he's now working alongside Detective Eva Valdez, the main suspect in the recent mutilation of Trey Peterson. This is

the story of how a small-town cop became immersed in lust, lies, and homicide."

Eva gasps when she hears her name and Dean reaches for the remote. He turns the TV off and kneels down in front of her. "Are you okay?"

She's stunned. "That bitch! What does she think she's doing comparing your life to a car crash? Doesn't she know that's how your wife died? She can't do or she wouldn't have used that term, surely?"

"Don't worry about me," he says. He's gone pale. "I'm just sorry you're being taken down with me."

She doesn't even want to think about how they'll portray her. "Was she lying to you then? About being a realtor?"

He gets up and sits next to her on the couch. He reaches for the tequila bottle and forgoes the glass, taking a slug straight from the bottle. "Yeah."

She's glad she was here for his first viewing of that. If he was alone, he might have packed up and left town in the middle of the night. "You didn't screw her, did you? Is that why she's doing this? Did you not return her calls or something?"

"No," he says. "I didn't sleep with her, although she came on strong."

"Really?" She's intrigued. "How strong?"

"Like, *real* strong. She would've gone ahead with it too, just to get her story."

"Don't be so surprised," says Eva. "Male journalists do that too. Someone I worked with at McArthur PD fell for this guy. He promised her marriage, kids, everything, and they were together for almost a year. Turns out he was a journalist trying to get the inside scoop on a homicide case we were investigating. Some of them are assholes."

Dean shakes his head in disgust. "I think she was even snooping around my house, reading my mail and shit. But thank God I turned her down."

She thinks about it and then smiles at him. "So you *can* keep it in your pants? Well done, Matheson. You're finally acting responsibly. I'm proud of you." She takes the bottle off him and drinks a mouthful.

"Gee, thanks."

"What? I assumed you two were sleeping together. It's good to know you can see through women like her now. It means you've learned from the whole Lizzie thing. As for me being in that stupid documentary, they better get Jessica Alba to play me, or I'm complaining to the network."

"I was thinking a young Eva Mendes would be perfect as you," he says.

She pretends to think about it, secretly flattered. "Hmm. I'll take that. Who should play you? Because that guy looks nothing like you. You're taller, with more hair and less of a beer gut. I'm thinking someone like Henry Cavill would be good." She makes a thinking face. "Or . . ."

He looks at her and smiles. "Go on."

She realizes she's paying him a compliment. "On second thoughts, maybe Danny DeVito would do."

He laughs.

She turns serious as she thinks aloud. "How much damage could this show do to us? I mean, the press will probably increase the amount of attention they pay us from now on. I won't be able to work undercover any time soon."

"I know." He sighs. "It's going to make everything harder. We'll be scrutinized. I'd be surprised if someone doesn't start calling for you to be arrested for Trey Peterson's murder. Just be prepared."

Her stomach flutters with nerves. The thought of being arrested for murder is scary, but she knows she didn't do it. Having said that, it doesn't mean she can't be found guilty. She's seen more than enough corrupt murder trials in her time as a cop. "So what's our next move?"

He fixes his eyes on hers, and she doesn't know if it's the tequila, the close proximity, or his blue eyes, but she wants him to kiss her. She knows it would be disastrous for their working relationship but they may not be working together for much longer if she gets sent down for this.

She gives him the bottle and moves away a little. His lips are looking way too good right now.

"We need to start with Emily," he says. "If we can at least get her to retract her allegations, that's one less thing that can be used against you. I visited her this morning."

She raises her eyebrows. "And?"

"She's involved in something more serious than she can deal with, but she wouldn't tell me who's behind it all. I saw a spark of the old Emily though, so I'm hopeful she'll see sense soon. I'll try again tomorrow." He runs a hand over his hair. "I had to tell her Tiffany was dead. She was really cut up about it, and she was shocked when I told her Tiffany was dumped outside Jake's place." He pauses. "I don't know how well you've gotten to know Jake yet but I'm starting to suspect he's involved in Tiffany's murder."

Eva thinks about the camera in Jake's apartment. Their awkward kiss. The way he appears too good to be true. "I don't know him well at all, so if that was your way of asking me whether I've slept with him, the answer's no."

He looks away. "I think we should be looking more closely at him. He doesn't have any witnesses to confirm his alibi for the exact time Tiffany was found. And Emily's social worker mentioned Tiffany would sleep outside Jake's building some nights. If Jake knew her, he could've let her in after everyone left on Sunday night, attacked her, and then dumped her out front. Maybe he was paying her for sex."

Eva's stomach turns at the thought. She didn't realize Jake knew Tiffany. He said he hadn't recognized her from the photos Dean took. "But why would he dump her there? It's obvious the police would want to question him about it."

"Maybe he ran out of time, or she escaped from him before collapsing. I don't know. I need to question him. I'm also going to see if he'll let us search his building without a warrant."

"Do it," she says. "I get the feeling something's off about him too." She yawns. "Can I crash here tonight? My apartment's cold and still smells of bleach. I know Captain Brown said I shouldn't, but I don't care anymore."

He smiles. "Of course. Anytime."

She stands and looks for Scully who's curled up in front of the fire with Mulder. "Thanks. I've got a bag of clothes in my car. I guess I should grab them and hit the sack. We're going to be busy tomorrow."

Dean looks up at her. "If that's what you want." He hands her the bottle of tequila and their hands touch.

She takes a final drink. Then she heads outside before she does something she'll definitely enjoy but probably regret.

CHAPTER FORTY-EIGHT

Lizzie is livid. Last night, she watched the announcement about a TV documentary that's being made about her and Dean Matheson. The bitch who's in charge of making it has it all twisted. She keeps referring to Lizzie as a serial killer. She can't believe no one understands why she killed those women. Dean should never have testified against her. He should have made everyone understand her reasons for killing. She needs to make him understand properly this time. It's the only way they can be together.

She knows she scared Danny by smashing the house up after watching it but anger is a side effect of all the drugs they fed her in the secure unit and now she's getting them out of her system, it's messing with her hormones. It's been almost a year and a half since she was found guilty of murder with diminished responsibility and locked away in that pathetic psychiatric unit. The ignorant employees pushed so many pills down her throat that it's no wonder she gained weight so quickly and that her head was messed up. But once she met Andrew Livingstone, one of her doctors, and he started to express feelings for her, she knew she could manipulate him into stopping her meds.

He abused his position by taking advantage of her when she was drugged and vulnerable, and his falling for her wasn't planned, but it was certainly useful. He didn't know it, but she was in control the entire time. Not like those other zoned-out pushovers on the ward who were too dumb to realize they were being abused. He was so desperate for a woman that when she outwardly reciprocated his feelings, he overlooked all the ethical and practical warnings about getting too close to a patient. Especially a patient who's also a convicted murderer.

Not that she *is* a murderer. Society just didn't appreciate what she was doing.

Thanks to Andrew, she has somewhere to live. Somewhere to hide. She thinks the FBI got close once, just after her escape, but recent media reports suggest they're working on the assumption she's left the state, if not the country. She feels like she has some breathing space now and, since she's come off the meds completely, she's already losing the weight she gained. She can also think clearly for the first time in a long time.

Before she escaped, she told Detective Jones that she was waiting for Dean to come back and marry her, but she doesn't really believe that. She just knew it would mess with Dean's head. Last time she messed with his head it made him sloppy at his job. That's what she's hoping for again, now he's returned. Part of her knows she should leave the country and never look back, but she feels linked to him. Like their destinies are entwined.

Her feelings confuse her. She's meant to be out for revenge, not falling in love with him. She struggles with knowing which of her emotions are real sometimes. It's a result of her terrible upbringing and she hates it.

After smashing the house up and having slept on it, she's no less angry about the documentary than she was last night. If she's on TV, the hunt for her will intensify, with more risk of her being found. With that in mind, she realizes she needs to go to work today in case her absence raises questions. It's Monday, and she called in sick last Thursday and Friday as she had to scrape Andrew's remains from the basement floor and discard them in the Chase River.

So far, no one at the school has shown the remotest bit of interest in her because of how plain she looks and how private she is. Her wig, glasses, and weight gain have helped with that. Andrew provided her with an excellent fake reference so the principal snapped her up at the interview. She doesn't think any of them will figure out her identity but it's not a risk she can afford to take right now.

She's been wondering what Dean thinks about the impending documentary. It won't be good for his new career.

Danny walks into the living room and notices she's getting ready to go out. "Are you going to school today?" he asks.

"Yes."

"Can I come? I miss my friends."

She takes him by the hand and sits him in front of the TV. "No, Danny. If you went to school that woman you used to live with would come back and take you home with her. You don't want that now, do you?"

He looks up at her with tears in his eyes. His bottom lip is trembling.

"Oh, for God's sake!" she spits. "I saved you from a life of misery with them and this is how you repay me? Well, you better snap out of it, Danny-boy, because you don't want to make me angry."

He wipes his eyes and she feels a little sorry for him. She can see he's at least trying to be good. It's her job as his new mother to show him patience. She kisses his cheek, even though it's probably covered in kid germs. "Don't worry, Danny. Everything will change soon. We'll leave this awful state and start over, somewhere new. You might even have a new daddy soon, depending on how things go. We'd be a proper family then and we can move somewhere where no one knows our old names." She smiles. "Have you picked your new name yet?"

He looks away. "I'll let you choose."

She smiles at him. "Good boy. Right, I've got to go to work and then to the supermarket. I'll be back this afternoon. Don't forget to do your schoolwork. I'll be checking it later." As she walks away, she says, "I've left you some sandwiches in the fridge. The bread's a little moldy but it's still perfectly edible. Have a good day!"

She doesn't wait for his response. Today's going to be busy for her. It's always exhausting pretending to be like everyone else.

She makes sure to lock the door behind her.

* * *

When she arrives at the school, she has to check in at the office to let Leanne, the secretary, know she's back from sick leave. The annoying, curly-haired woman is sitting at her desk but she's not working. She's reading a true-crime book. It has a photo of a mean-looking man on the front, in black and white. Obviously a serial killer. Leanne's probably lapping up all the gory details of someone else's death. People like this make Lizzie sick.

She notices one of the third-grade teachers is sitting in the principal's office. She can see them through the glass behind Leanne's back. They appear to be having a serious discussion. "Is everything alright with Mr. Dutton?" she asks. "He's not in trouble, is he?"

Leanne glances behind her. "He wouldn't tell me what he wanted to see the principal about, but I've been told to let them know when the police arrive."

Lizzie feels a jolt of electricity. "The police?" Her voice is too high-pitched. "What are they coming here for?"

Leanne shrugs. "If I had to guess I'd say it's for an update on poor little Danny Mallory. I just hope he hasn't been murdered and dumped in the woods somewhere. You know, after being *molested*." She drags it out like it's her favorite word.

That's exactly what you hope has happened to him, you voyeuristic bitch. "What time are they due?"

"Any minute now."

The bell rings.

"I better get to class." Lizzie quickly turns to leave the office. She knows it won't be MVPD coming to see the principal as this town isn't in their jurisdiction, but she doesn't want to be around any law enforcement officers. You never know who might've watched last night's news coverage about the documentary.

Just as she reaches the doorway, a short older man in a cheap suit walks toward her. She can tell he's a cop just by looking at him. He has that curious look in his eye, like he's trying to figure out if she's on *America's Most Wanted* list. But that doesn't spook her — all cops have that look. Well, the good ones.

He realizes he's in her way so, to be gentlemanly, he stands aside to let her through the doorway. Doing this reveals the person standing behind him.

Lizzie almost gasps.

It's *Dean*.

CHAPTER FORTY-NINE

Dean's reading a text message from Jones as he follows Detective Briggs into the Mill Brook Elementary School office. He accidentally bumps into what he has to assume is a teacher on her way out of the office. He looks up. He doesn't see her face but she has long, black messy hair and she hurries away, probably late for class since the bell just rang.

"Sorry, my fault," he says to her back.

She waves her hand in dismissal and keeps walking.

An overly tanned man with gray hair steps forward and smiles at them. "Thank you for coming, Detectives. I'm Principal Whiting." He shakes their hands and leads them into his office.

Dean smiles at the administrator on his way past and she winks at him. He wonders whether he imagined it but when he turns back, she smiles widely. He turns away and closes the principal's door behind him.

Principal Whiting has an exhausted look about him that suggests the teaching profession hasn't been kind. He introduces them to Mr. Dutton, who looks like he's fresh out of college. Dutton seems a little overwhelmed at being in a room with two detectives. He won't stop messing with his tie.

Principal Whiting obviously enjoys hosting visitors as he wastes a lot of time shooting the shit and telling them about how great his school is. Not wanting to seem rude, they both oblige him, but Dean's focusing on the snow hitting the office window and worrying about the drive back to Maple Valley if the weather worsens. It's a good half hour before the principal's ready to start talking about why they're all here.

Detective Briggs shares a look with Dean and then uses a natural pause in Principal Whiting's narrative to lead the questioning. He crosses his legs and faces the young teacher. "So, as I understand it, you have some concerns about someone who works here. Is that correct?"

Mr. Dutton enthusiastically nods. "That's right. There's nothing specific about her that I can put my finger on, but I've always felt that something wasn't right about her."

"Who exactly are we talking about?" asks Briggs.

"Oh, sorry. I mean Danny's teacher. She's actually a supply teacher while Miss Vickers recovers from her nervous breakdown, so she's only been with us since January."

Dean raises his eyebrows. He's heard stories about teaching being a difficult profession these days, but could a class of second graders really cause a breakdown?

"But you see," Mr. Dutton continues. "I've overheard the children in her class talking about her and it made me start watching her a little closer."

Detective Briggs uncrosses his legs and tries to get comfortable in his plastic seat. "So give me some examples of what you think isn't quite right about her," he says.

Mr. Dutton looks to Principal Whiting for reassurance, which he provides. "You can tell them anything you think is helpful, Jeremy. Don't hold back."

Dutton nods. "One of her students, Johnny Laverne, has been pushed by her on a couple of separate occasions."

"Physically pushed?" says Detective Briggs.

"Right. The other children were talking about it. If I'd seen it myself, I would've reported her immediately. The children said he was even pushed against a wall on one occasion.

He didn't get upset because, well, he's a bully, so he's pretty tough on the outside. I mean, he's horrible to some of the younger kids so maybe that's why she pushed him, to get him away from someone. But also, well, she's very odd."

Principal Whiting grunts in agreement.

"In what way?" asks Briggs.

"Well, she won't let anyone get to know her. Don't get me wrong, she comes alive around the children and a lot of them love her, but she's not so good with the rest of the faculty or with the parents."

Dean interjects. "Being shy isn't a crime, Mr. Dutton. Some people prefer to remain private, which I have to say is refreshing in this social media-obsessed world."

Mr. Dutton nods. "Yes, but she's incredibly awkward and no one can figure out her accent. She seems local one day and not so much on others. We've all tried to get to know her better, but she's a little weird."

Dean hears car tires skidding outside, followed by doors opening. He thinks he hears a dispatcher on a radio.

Principal Whiting agrees. "I've recently had a complaint about her. She told Annabelle Gibson's parents that if Annabelle ever arrives at school with another bruise on her, she'll personally see to it that they get what's coming to them."

A ball of dread builds in Dean's chest. "Are you saying she actually threatened the parents?"

"Well, allegedly," says the principal. "We have to be careful because some parents are real assholes who probably *are* harming their kids, so they make up all sorts about our teachers to deflect attention from themselves."

"But have you ever had any safeguarding concerns about Annabelle?" he presses.

Mr. Dutton nods. "Yes. She has a social worker and I believe they're working with the family to overcome the mother's anger issues."

Dean jumps out of his seat and feels sick. He doesn't want to believe where this is heading but he has a horrible feeling about it. "What's this teacher's name?"

Briggs looks up at Dean with a confused expression, probably wondering what he's getting excited about.

"Her name's Linda," says Mr. Dutton.

Dean's stomach flips. *Linda*. The name of his dead wife. "Linda what?"

"Linda Livingstone."

He immediately thinks of Lizzie's doctor. *Shit*. Then he thinks of the woman he bumped into earlier, the woman with the bad hair. Was it a wig?

The sound of approaching sirens distracts him.

He pulls out his weapon. "Where is she right this minute? Take me to her classroom." He turns to Detective Briggs. "Pull your weapon. She won't go down without a fight. They're talking about Lizzie Glover."

Detective Briggs' eyes light up and he jumps out of his seat. "Holy shit! She's working as a *teacher*? Are you sure?"

Just then, Briggs' cell phone rings at the same time as the school fire alarm goes off. They listen to the sound of more sirens fast approaching outside. They look out of the principal's window and Dean spots a police officer in a bulletproof vest with a loudspeaker standing behind the open door of his cruiser. More officers arrive behind him, all armed.

"Attention!" the officer announces. "This is the Cedar Falls Police Department. Reports suggest there is an active shooter at large in your school! Teachers; follow your active shooter drill. Lock your classrooms. Everyone get down. Do not leave your classrooms until a police officer arrives to escort you! I repeat, do *not* leave your classrooms. The school is in lockdown!"

Dean's arms cover in goosebumps. This is his worst nightmare.

He looks at the others in the office. Everyone is frozen in fear. "I didn't hear any gunshots. Did you?" He hears kids crying in the distance but that could be a reaction to the sirens.

The principal is completely white. "What do we do?"

"Stay here," says Dean. "I'm going to take a look. Where's her classroom?"

"Last class on the left at the end of the hall."

“I’ll answer this and find out what’s going on,” says Briggs, pulling out his cell phone. It’s still ringing.

Dean looks at him and realizes he’s just as scared as the teachers. But he’s a cop. He should be coming with him. He has to hide his contempt. “Fine. I’ll expect backup when you’re done.”

As Dean leaves the office, gun raised and hyper-alert to everything around him, he notices the administrator is hiding under her desk. She’s crying, and not quietly. He puts his finger to his lips to indicate she needs to be quiet.

He pokes his head into the hallway. It’s completely empty apart from a row of lockers on either side. The school alarm is louder here. It’s piercing his brain with every wail.

Just then the door to the boys’ restroom opens and Dean spins around at the sound of it, keeping his weapon raised. He comes face to face with a very young boy, about six years old.

The boy sees Dean’s gun and bursts into tears.

Dean runs to him, picks him up, and takes him back into the office, shoving him under the desk with the administrator. She hugs him as Dean leaves to find the shooter.

CHAPTER FIFTY

Emily's alone in her hospital room wondering whether she has to stay here much longer and what her next move should be when she receives an unwelcome visitor. Having had a lot of time to think about everything Dean said to her, she's been dreading this moment.

"How are you?" her visitor asks, as he checks behind to see if anyone noticed his arrival. He approaches the bed.

"I'm fine now," she says. "I don't know why they don't let me leave already. I want to get back to work."

"That's what I like to hear," he says, as he reaches for her hair and tucks it behind her ear. She wants to pull away from him in disgust, but she can't. She needs to keep up the pretense of working for him, of admiring him, until it's time to get out of this town for good. She thinks about Tiffany. It's too late for her, even though she was the tough one, the one who showed Emily how to exist with no family and no support.

She knows now that he killed Tiffany and she wants to make him pay for it, but she has absolutely no power to do that. The best she can do is get away from him before he does the same to her.

He leans in and kisses her on the lips, smiling at his ability to do whatever he wants because she remains silent.

"You need to get out of here today so you can meet me at the church later," he says. "You've had enough time off and I've got clients waiting to meet you. You're losing money for both of us while you're in here. Besides, with Tiffany gone, you need to recruit her replacement. How about that nice religious girl from the family who's taken you in? She always has a big smile for me when I see her. She's practically begging to join us. I can see it in her eyes."

His suggestion makes her feel sick, so she doesn't look at him. There's no way she's dragging someone else into this. "I'll see what I can do. I want to be back at work. I need some new clothes."

He laughs. "Oh, come on, Emily. That's not the only reason you do it. You've already proven you would do anything for money. But I know you enjoy the attention, especially when it comes from me."

Emily's face burns with shame. When she first met him, she was attracted to him, probably because he was so nice to her and showed her affection. She actually thought he was her boyfriend, as well as Tiffany's, because of the way he treated her; showering her with gifts and praise, showing her off to other men like him, and filling the void where her family should be. Her mother was only ever interested in getting drunk and high and she's never had a father or siblings. The closest she ever got to having any male figure in her life who showed her what real kindness was, was Officer Dean. But he left town a broken man, abandoning Emily without a second thought.

It wasn't long before she met this man in front of her, someone who was offering protection in a different way. She can see now that he took advantage of her and Tiffany. He's like the reverse of a superhero: by day he wears a mask of responsibility and kindness, but by night he prostitutes the vulnerable. He makes money from them in all kinds of ways. It didn't take long before she saw his darker side and then she experienced it for herself, which is how she ended up in here. He may be charming but it's all an act. He can go from affectionate to murderous in seconds. That's why she has to keep up the pretense around him. For now, at least.

She thinks about Dean and wishes she could confide in him. If it was just this asshole sitting next to her to worry about, she'd probably do it. But it's not. She's been sucked into someone else's vendetta, someone far worse than him. She feels stupid for getting involved. Especially as Dean had always been so good to her. But he left her and never looked back, which is something she'll have to do before he finds out the truth.

"You don't have to worry about me," she says to her visitor. "I'll be back at work tonight."

CHAPTER FIFTY-ONE

When Eva wakes the next morning, Dean's already left for work so she showers, feeds Scully, and then decides to visit Lizzie's doctor. Dean may have advised her not to visit Livingstone while she was suspended, but she's got nothing better to do. She woke up to a text from Frankie, warning her about several reporters parked outside the diner, waiting for her to appear. Probably because of Camille talking about the documentary on TV last night.

The drive to Cedar Falls is pleasant. The snow has stopped and the sun has appeared, although it's still bitterly cold outside as Eva gets out of her car after the hour-long drive. She walks up the slippery path ahead and knocks on Livingstone's front door. She takes a step back to look up at the house. It's large and detached, with a landscaped front yard and mature trees surrounding it. He must earn a good income working at the secure unit.

A silver Mercedes sits in the driveway but no one answers the door. She figures if he's genuinely ill it could take him a while to get downstairs so she knocks once more. This time she hears a voice on the other side of the front door but she can't hear what they say.

"Hello?" she says.

"I don't have the key," says the voice. It's a young boy.

"Is Dr. Livingstone in?" she asks.

There's no response.

"Are there any adults in there with you?" She tries again.

A sharp female voice comes from behind her and makes her jump. "Would you like to come in?"

Eva didn't hear her approach. The woman moves in front of her and puts her key in the lock. Her hair disguises her face but Eva can tell she's panting, like she's just rushed from somewhere. She turns around and notices a Ford is now parked sloppily behind the silver Mercedes.

"I'd like to speak to Dr. Livingstone if he's available. My name's Eva Valdez."

The woman doesn't turn around to look at her. Instead, she opens the front door wide and invites Eva to follow her. "Of course, come on in. I'll make us all a drink."

Eva steps inside the house. It's hot in here. The heat must be turned up high. It also smells bad, like there's been no fresh air in here for a long time and no one's emptied the garbage. It's *really* bad.

"I'm Linda, Dr. Livingstone's wife," the woman says as she tidies her coat and scarf away. "And this is Gage, our son. Gage? Make our visitor comfortable while I fetch us some drinks."

She walks into the kitchen, leaving Eva alone with the young boy. He looks nervous. He comes over to her and takes her hand, leading her to the couch but when they sit down, he doesn't let go of her hand. He sits close, too. He's wearing a blue baseball cap that covers his eyes.

"Hi, Gage," she says. "How come you're not in school today?"

Linda returns and puts a tray down in front of Eva that has three glasses and a bottle of soda on it. "Oh, he's got a cold. Come here, Gage."

The boy gets up and stands in front of Linda, who bends down and picks him up, resting him on her hip like he's a toddler. Eva looks up at her and gets a good look at her face for the first time. It takes everything in her power not to pull her weapon.

After hearing all the stories about Lizzie Glover, Eva did her own research. She watched the news reports and looked at photos of the woman taken at her murder trial. She was slim and attractive at the time she committed her crimes and was sleeping with Dean. That's not the case anymore. This woman standing in front of her is wearing a good disguise, with the wig and the glasses, and even her American accent fooled Eva at first — but only until she saw her face. It's the eyes that give her away. Something is lacking in those eyes. Not compassion, because Eva knows this woman thinks she kills for the right reasons. She can't put her finger on it.

Eva leans forward to pick up a glass and she pours herself some soda, but she has no intention of drinking it. She's not going to meet the same fate as Jones' wife. She thinks about the name Lizzie's given herself. Linda was Dean's wife's name. This woman really is obsessed with him.

"There's a lot of that going around. I guess it's just that time of year." Eva smiles up at them both.

She wonders who the child is, but she can't get a good look as Lizzie has turned his face into her shoulder. As far as she knows, Lizzie never had children. The boy's sucking his thumb like he's self-soothing. She wonders then whether Lizzie knows who *she* is. Tommy, from the secure unit, had shown some kind of recognition of her before he hanged himself, so it's probably best to assume that was because Lizzie warned him that the police would come for him one day.

She desperately tries to think how best to handle this situation. She'll probably only get out of here alive if she can convince Lizzie she hasn't recognized her. She swallows. "I was hoping Dr. Livingstone was around, and I want to be completely honest," she says. "I'm a detective from a town south of here but I'm suspended from active duty at the moment so I shouldn't actually be working. I don't have my badge or my service weapon on me."

Lizzie's expression doesn't change but she relaxes her grip on the boy ever so slightly.

Eva's telling the truth. She did have to hand in her badge and gun, but she's carrying her own gun now instead. Fully licensed and all above board. "So he doesn't have to talk to me if he doesn't want to. I'm only here to ask a few routine questions about an employee who sadly—" she stops and lowers her voice so the boy doesn't get scared "—took his own life recently."

It takes a few seconds for Lizzie to react. She's obviously trying to make sure she plays this right too. Her eyes soften. "Oh no, that's terrible! My husband will be so upset."

Eva notices she doesn't ask who it was.

"To be honest, Detective," says Lizzie, "I think he's probably too sick for that kind of bad news. As soon as he's better, I'll get him to give you a call, so you don't have to travel up here again. Do you have a card you could leave with me?"

"I don't, actually," says Eva. Her heart's thumping harder than ever, making it difficult to remain breezy. She knows exactly what this woman's capable of. "I'm new in my job so nothing's been arranged yet. But I can write my number down if you have a notepad?"

That will involve Lizzie taking her eyes off of her. Eva needs time to pull her gun out, but the woman has the boy in her arms, shielding her. She's not stupid.

Lizzie doesn't move. Her eyes harden. "So you're new there but you've been suspended already? Oh dear. That's not good, is it? Are you one of those dirty cops we hear so much about on the news? They're everywhere apparently. You can't trust anyone these days, least of all the police."

Is this bitch seriously taunting me? "No, I'm being framed for something a deranged killer has done. Actually, what am I saying? All killers are deranged, obviously. I mean, no sane person would think they have the right to end another person's life, would they?" Eva laughs. She knows she's playing a dangerous game, pissing off a serial killer, but she doesn't like the smug look on her face.

"It depends who you listen to," says Lizzie slowly. "My husband actually works with convicted killers, and he's told me all about research that suggests someone who takes another's life for the right reasons is actually highly intelligent and more compassionate than those who stand by and watch grievous acts of psychological harm befall a person, especially a child."

"Is that right?" says Eva. "I'd like to see that research. But who would actually stand by and watch someone suffer without trying to do something about it?"

Lizzie's face twists into an angry mess. "Who?" she says with contempt. "Are you really that naıve? The social workers, the child protection judges . . . The *police*!"

Eva knows she can't win an argument with a crazy person, but she can't help it. "All those people you listed are bound by laws and procedures. There's only so much they can do, legally, to have a lasting effect. It doesn't mean they don't care."

"Exactly my point," says Lizzie with a smirk. "There *is* only so much they can do legally. Which is why, according to my husband, some people are justified in taking it upon themselves to act as angels of mercy. To end a child's suffering in a way that no court can ever undo. In a way that means no parent will ever be able to hurt their own flesh and blood again. Most people think killers kill for the thrill, and that has been proven to be the case for some — usually men — but others kill to protect the vulnerable because they can't stand by and watch children suffer. They're *good* people."

Her eyes are shining as if she's giving a sermon to a Sunday congregation. She's holding the boy so tight he's squirming. If only Eva could grab him. She has to do something because if she walks away from this house, which she thinks Lizzie will let her do to save herself, that boy doesn't stand a chance. Adrenaline floods her body, but she doesn't know how to use it with him in the way.

The boy suddenly removes his cap, letting it drop to the floor. Eva immediately recognizes him from the photo Steve showed them. It's Danny Mallory. That means Lizzie killed Trey Peterson. That Lizzie *did* go to her apartment.

Shock makes her body sweat. She thinks of the mess in her apartment, Trey's mutilated body. She takes a deep breath, trying to remain calm. The stakes just got higher. She has to get Danny away from this killer before it's too late.

"I've never once stood by and watched a child suffer without intervening," says Eva as she slowly stands. "Which is why I have to take Danny away from you."

Lizzie seems to come back to reality. Her eyes clear. She puts the boy down on his feet in front of her and holds onto his shoulders. She stares hard at Eva. "You're fucking him, aren't you?"

Danny gasps at the foul language and looks up at Lizzie.

Okay, so she's dropped the pretense and the fake accent. Eva's glad. She prefers to face things head-on. She has to make Lizzie so angry she'll forget about the boy.

"Who, Dean? Of course I am," she says with a smile. "We're having a great time together. We talk about you a lot. Or should I say we *laugh* about you a lot. While we're in bed together. He thinks you're a psycho and, having finally met you, I'd have to agree."

Lizzie cackles. "I know what you're trying to do but it won't work. I'm more intelligent than you. You see, I'm a psychiatrist, and you can't outwit me. I don't think he's sleeping with you at all. He's waiting for me to come back."

Eva smiles broadly. She's making this so easy. "Listen, asshole. Number one: you're not a psychiatrist, you're a serial killer with nothing but serious mommy issues. And number two: if he was waiting for you, the sex that *we* have wouldn't be as intense as it is. When he looks at me with those blue eyes of his, it's like you never even existed."

The look on Lizzie's face is priceless, so she continues. "I read all about your upbringing, you know? About your mother. It's no excuse for your actions. You're not saving those kids. You're no angel of mercy. It's the complete opposite; you do it because you have a God complex and a bitter, black heart."

Lizzie's face reddens. Beads of sweat pop up on her forehead and she's squeezing Danny's shoulders with pent-up rage.

"And you seriously believe Dean would want to get involved with a murderous bitch like you?" Eva laughs at her. "You're even more crazy than your mother, and that's saying something."

Lizzie lunges for her as Eva hoped she would, but she pulls a carving knife from her dress pocket. She must have taken it from the kitchen when she went to fetch the drinks. Eva should've known she would be armed but judging by the intense hatred on Lizzie's face, it's too late to reach for her gun. All she can do is try to turn away from the impact.

The boy cries out in shock as Lizzie forces the knife through Eva's shoulder.

Eva screams as Lizzie pulls it out. The pain is sharp but fleeting because of the adrenaline rush. Thoughts of Frank run through her head. He was killed in the same way. Is this what he felt?

Somehow, she doesn't drop to the floor. She forces her good arm up into Lizzie's face and uses the palm of her hand to punch her nose upward. Lizzie retreats, screaming, while holding her hands to her face. She drops the knife and blood pours out of her nose. Eva witnesses enough to feel satisfied that she's done *some* damage, at least.

Danny runs for the front door and opens it wide.

Eva can't let him go. But as she watches him, something crashes into her head and the room turns black.

CHAPTER FIFTY-TWO

It takes Dean an hour to get untangled from the tight security at the school. The active-shooter call was a hoax. The worst kind. He tries not to think about those poor young schoolchildren who were genuinely in fear for their lives. Even the teachers were shell-shocked. It must have been Lizzie, buying time to escape from him.

The thought of having been so close to her that they actually touched makes him feel sick. Although he didn't see her face, he should have known it was her. He should have felt it. He runs to his car, jumps in, and pulls out the address the administrator gave him for Danny's teacher.

Someone must have notified the press because news trucks speed into the area. He needs to get out of here before he's caught on film. He doesn't want Camille and her crew to have any footage of him that she can use for her ridiculous documentary. As for Detective Briggs, he can go to hell. He was useless.

Although every second counts, he needs to update Eva. He speeds away from the school with one hand on the steering wheel and calls her with the other. He doesn't know what her plans are for today. She was still in his spare room when he left for work this morning.

When she doesn't answer, he tries again. Still no answer. He leaves her a message.

"Eva, it's me. I've just discovered that Lizzie Glover's been working as Danny Mallory's teacher, so she must've taken him. She just fled his school. I have her address, so I'll message it to you. Meet me there and call Steve or Captain Brown. Let someone know where we're going and arrange for backup."

He messages her the address and then punches Lizzie's zip code into his GPS. It tells him she lives a ten-minute drive away. She's had a good head start thanks to the drama at the school, but she probably still needs to go home to collect Danny before she tries to get away. Unless she decides to leave him behind, but Dean doesn't think she will. He needs to get to her before she escapes again.

When he arrives on Lizzie's street, he's careful to stay back and park behind a row of cars, far enough away from her house that she won't spot him but close enough for him to assess the situation. He'd like it if Eva had time to get here before he approaches the house, but a look at his phone tells him she's not on her way yet. He tries calling her again but there's still no answer. He wishes she'd stop disappearing on him.

He looks at the house. It's nothing special. There's a red Ford parked out front but all the blinds are closed. Is she watching out for him from behind them? She could be armed. He's strangely nervous at the thought of their inevitable showdown. This could finally be the end of all the toxicity.

Now he knows she has Danny Mallory, it's logical to assume she was also the person who killed Danny's father. Danny must have been abused or neglected by his parents. Dean thinks of his visit to the boy's mother and realizes that, if Shannon's behavior is anything to go by, those parents were never going to win any parenting awards.

Something comes to him. If Lizzie killed Trey Peterson at Eva's apartment, why did Emily Gordon say she saw Eva there that night? Was Lizzie dressed as Eva? It's possible she would do that, as she's obviously been using disguises to get around. Lizzie was close to Emily that night, she could've killed her too if she'd seen her.

But then why did Emily say that it was Eva who beat her? Was that Lizzie too? Or was Emily lying about being there? He considers the possibility that they got all this wrong. They were looking for a violent man for Tiffany's death and Emily's injuries. Could it all have been Lizzie?

Suddenly, the realization of the alternative hits him. The last time he visited Emily, she was distraught that she'd betrayed him in some way, and seemed to think that what she had done was so bad he'd never speak to her again if he found out.

Has Emily been working *with* Lizzie? His body goes cold at the thought. Did Lizzie manipulate Emily into lying about Eva? He doesn't want to believe she would agree to that. Not after Lizzie killed Emily's *mother*.

He needs to speak to Emily as soon as he gets out of here. Assuming he gets out alive.

CHAPTER FIFTY-THREE

Danny's never been more scared in his life. He's also never seen his teacher like this before. She reminds him of the big bad wolf. Her nose is dripping with blood and she's pulled her hair off. Even though she still has hair underneath, tied back into a ponytail like the girls at school, she looks different now. Younger, but scary. She's pulling their visitor across the floor by her head, but it's leaving a large smear of dark red blood along the wooden floors.

Miss Livingstone is talking to herself. "If she thinks she's going to ruin this for me, she's got another thing coming! I won't run anymore. I *won't*! She's the one who needs to go, not me. If she came alone that means no one else knows she's here." She turns to face Danny and suddenly screams, "Gage, open the basement door!"

Danny freezes, unable to do anything. He just wants to go home.

"For God's sake! Do I have to do everything myself?"

She drops the lady's head with a loud thud and strides to the kitchen to open the door to the basement. Then she pulls the lady along by her hands this time. When she gets her to the top of the basement steps, she's panting. She turns and looks at him, but her eyes aren't her own anymore.

He's trying really hard to be brave right now.

"Danny?" She smiles at him but it's not a smile he ever wants to see again. "Come here. If you help me with this, I'll let you keep your own name. Would you like that?"

He would. He doesn't want to be called Gage. He nods ever so slightly.

"Good boy. Now I just need you to help me roll her down the stairs, okay? She won't feel a thing, I promise. It's already too late for her. Then I'll order us some pizza for dinner. Your choice. Okay?"

Something inside tells him it's wrong to do something bad in order to get something in return, but he wants to get back to normal and that means hiding this lady and pretending nothing ever happened. Not that he thinks he'd be able to eat anything right now.

He walks over to them both.

"Great. You push her from here, her hip. I'll push her shoulders. After three. Ready?"

He nods again and looks down at the lady's face. Her eyes are closed and it doesn't look like she's breathing. She's bled so much that he knows she can't still be alive. But at least she doesn't look like the man who was in the basement. Not yet, anyway.

Miss Livingstone counts down and they both push really hard. The lady goes over the top of the stairs and they listen to her fall. She doesn't cry out in pain. There's just silence when she reaches the bottom.

Miss Livingstone stands up and wipes her hands on her dress, but she doesn't even try to wash the blood off her face.

"Right. Pizza time!" She crouches down in front of his face, so close he wants to take a step back. "And then we'll go for a drive because I need to buy some rope. I have a surprise for you. Would you like that, Danny? *Would you*?"

Danny can't hold his fear in any longer. He screams.

CHAPTER FIFTY-FOUR

It was a false address. Of course it was. The old lady who answered the door looked terrified when Dean explained who he was and why he was there. She let him inside to look around in case anyone was hiding there, but of course they weren't so he'd scared her for nothing. Lizzie's never been to that address in her damn life.

Dean gets back into his car and punches the steering wheel. "Dammit!" He has no idea where she's gone, and he doesn't know what to do next. He just knows he needs to get a hold of Eva before she turns up at this poor woman's house, all guns blazing. He tries calling her again, but there's still no answer so he has to leave a message letting her know about the false address and that he's on his way back to Maple Valley. He considers notifying the Feds next, but something puts him off. He wants to find Lizzie Glover himself. He calls Jones instead.

"Hey, Dean. How are you?"

He sighs. "Not great. Do you or George know where Eva is?"

He hears Jones question George in the background. Those two always seem to be together. "No, George hasn't heard from her today. Is there a problem?"

He doesn't know, but he doesn't want to worry George just yet. "No, I'm sure she's fine. I'm just waiting to meet her and she's running late. Probably stuck in traffic. No need to worry George."

"Gotcha," says Jones. "Hey, we saw you on TV last night. Well, the guy playing you. He's not exactly your doppelganger."

"Yeah, I know. We saw it too. Luckily, Eva didn't seem too cut up about being dragged down with me."

"You were together last night?" asks Jones.

Dean can tell he's getting the wrong idea. "She stayed over, that's all. In the spare room." He then has to listen to Jones repeat this to George.

Jones laughs at something. "George says he's going to pick out a tux."

Dean frowns. "What for?"

"Your wedding!"

He rolls his eyes. "Okay, I'm going to hang up now."

"No, wait! I wanted to let you know we're both meeting separately with that producer, Camille, today. She doesn't know George and I know each other. We're going to lead her on a wild goose chase."

Dean doesn't know whether to laugh or cry. "Okay, well, you two have fun."

"And guess what I found out?" Jones continues.

"What?"

"You're not going to like this and don't do anything stupid, but Miller was the person who told the press that Eva was a suspect in Trey Peterson's murder. He told Camille and she did the rest. That's why they chased Eva down the other day. The son of a bitch tipped them off."

Dean's grasp on his phone tightens. "How do you know that?"

"Frankie saw Miller and Camille whispering to each other in the diner. He said he knew Miller was up to something because he looked smug afterward."

Dean's in an even worse mood now. He already knew Miller was a piece of shit, but he never thought he'd release confidential police news to the press. This will be the end of his career in law enforcement. Dean will make sure of it.

"But don't get caught up fighting with him again," says Jones. "George is going to take care of him. After all, it's his daughter Miller's messing with now."

He hears George shout "Asshole!" in the background.

He decides not to tell Jones about Lizzie just yet. This is something he'd like to face without Jones this time. It's something he has to do, to prove to himself that he can finish it. Although, he'd like to have Eva with him as backup.

That's if she ever returns his calls.

* * *

Instead of driving straight to MVPD when he arrives back in town, Dean heads home first to see if Eva's there, but she's not. There's no sign of her, so he drives to the hospital to visit Emily, hoping to drag the truth out of her in case Eva's thinking of doing the same thing. He doesn't want to believe Emily would conspire against him and work with Lizzie Glover of all people, but he also can't hold it against her. She's a kid and in way over her head.

Besides, she could know where Lizzie's hiding.

Just before the turn-off for the hospital he drives by a bunch of actors from the Haunted Asylum. He only recognizes the young girl in the porcelain doll mask. They're all handing out flyers to passers-by but most people are giving them a wide berth because of their masks and outfits. He wonders whether Eva might have returned to the Haunted Asylum or whether she's dropped the notion that someone who works there is involved in all this.

Now he knows Lizzie has Danny Mallory, Dean's convinced no one else was involved in Trey Peterson's death. He's still not sure who killed Tiffany though.

When he reaches Emily's room at the hospital, someone else is in the bed. Dean checks the room number and then looks in again. A family is surrounding an older man. One of the relatives looks up at him just as Dr. Armstrong walks past.

"What are you doing here?" she asks him.

"I wanted to speak to Emily Gordon." He hesitates, fearing the worst after what happened to Tiffany. "She's okay, isn't she?"

"I think so," says the doctor. "She left this morning. We weren't ready to release her, but she went without telling anyone."

Dean could be too late. She might have skipped town. "Did someone pick her up?"

She shakes her head. "Not that we noticed. I'm not too worried as her injuries weren't life-threatening. I was waiting for a psych evaluation for her though, because she appeared to be suffering with bad anxiety."

Dean rubs the back of his neck. "So you don't know where she went?"

"I'm afraid not. Sorry, I've got to see my next patient."

She walks away, leaving Dean clueless as to his next move. He needs to make sure Emily's protected in case Lizzie decides she's disposable now.

As he heads downstairs and out of the hospital lobby, he pulls his phone out and calls Emily's social worker. He answers almost immediately.

"Ryan here."

"Hey, it's Dean Matheson. Did you know Emily's left the hospital?"

Ryan sighs. "No, I didn't. I haven't had time to visit her today because of drama with another kid on my caseload. He's stealing from us and refusing to admit it so we're one call away from turning him in to you guys. Do you know where she is now?"

"No. I was hoping you would."

Ryan seems distracted and Dean can hear paperwork being moved around. "I'm due in court shortly for a child protective order hearing. All I know is she didn't want to stay with the Johnsons anymore, so they've given up on her. My guess is she's with that Jake guy at the church, or whatever he calls it. We all know it's a damn church; he might as well be upfront about it."

"If you hear from her, tell her to call me urgently."

"Is she in trouble?"

"No, not at all," says Dean. "The opposite. We need to make sure she's safe. I'm starting to think she's involved with someone even worse than I originally thought."

"Whoa, that's not good."

"Exactly. I'll go to the church, but keep a look out for her and tell her she can stay at mine for now."

Ryan hesitates. "I don't know if I can approve that, to be honest."

"What do you mean?" Dean's incredulous. "You'd rather see her on the street and at risk of being beaten to death?"

"Hey, don't yell at me! It just doesn't sound like a good idea to me, what with you being a single older guy and all. Plus, you've got a bit of a reputation. I saw that producer talking about you on TV."

"Are you serious?" shouts Dean.

"Yes, I am! You also work with the cop who's suspected of murdering that guy. I mean, it doesn't look good to an outsider like me."

"You know what, Ryan? Go to hell." Dean throws his phone into his car in frustration. That damn documentary is already causing problems.

CHAPTER FIFTY-FIVE

When Dean arrives at the station, Jenny approaches him, fresh back from patrol.

"Hey, Dean. I've been watching Beau Lachey's comings and goings like you asked, but he's not doing anything out of the ordinary. He's actually not even dealing at the moment; he's been spending time with his kids instead. I'm sure it won't last long though."

Dean's certain now that Beau's not involved in exploiting Emily and Tiffany. "Okay, thanks for checking. Could you chase up the parole officers of the recently released sex offenders I emailed you about, and see what those guys have been up to since their release? They were supposed to get back to me and I asked Miller to chase them but he's not going to be able to now."

"Sure."

"Also, do you know of anyone who's been selling girls around here lately?"

She shakes her head. "We haven't had any reports of prostitution for a long time. Oh, by the way, someone called in about recognizing Tiffany's photo in the press."

He frowns. "Really? What did they say?"

"They said they'd seen her hanging around at the church a lot at night, with a couple of other teenagers."

Dean thinks about Jake Andrews. He must be the ringleader. Why else would he be attracting teens at nighttime? It's time to update everyone on what's happened today.

"By the way, I saw them talking about the documentary on TV," says Jenny, looking embarrassed for him.

Dean's heart sinks. Is there anyone who didn't see it?

"And I've just seen Detective Jones talking to that Camille woman in the diner," she says. "I know he would never say anything bad about you so I'm assuming he's telling her to watch her step?"

Dean sighs. "Something like that. He says he's going to lead her down the wrong path, but I don't know how he intends to do that. To tell you the truth, I think I'd rather not know."

"Oh!" She looks relieved. "Good. It's just that I overheard him telling her not to trust anything Officer Miller tells her because he's been diagnosed with a mental age younger than his physical age, and the only reason he's on the force is as a favor to his wife." She laughs. "He said we all pretend he's a cop so as not to upset him, but really he's never been a cop and his badge is a fake one we had made up for him."

Dean surprises himself by laughing. After the crap day he's had so far, it feels good. "That's great. Miller's going to blow a fuse when he hears that."

Jenny smiles. "She was lapping it up. I'm pretty sure it's going to make it into her stupid documentary. Either that or she'll just disregard everything Miller's told her about you."

Just then, Miller walks in, pulling up his trousers by the waist like a hobo with no belt.

"What have you got for me?" he asks Dean.

Dean ignores him and finishes with Jenny. "Keep an eye out for any girls hanging around parking lots. Emily Gordon's gone missing and I want to locate her fast. I'm going to ask Captain Brown for a warrant so I can search the church."

"Sure thing. I'm heading out again now. Catch you later." She walks out past the front desk.

"Next time bring me back some coffee, sweetheart!" Miller calls after her. She doesn't even react.

Dean wonders if anyone around here ever talks to Miller. Does he even pick up on their hostility or is he completely oblivious?

"Well?" he says to Dean. "You're meant to keep me in the loop, hotshot."

Dean clenches his fists. "Come with me."

He leads Miller to Captain Brown's office and knocks on the door. Steve's already in there and they look like they're deep in conversation.

"Captain?" says Dean. "I have an update on several things. Would you and Steve join us in the conference room?"

They get up and follow him out.

Dean calls Marty over. "Would you grab Maggie for me? I have an update and she should be present. You too."

"I'm on it." Marty goes to find her.

"This better be worth my energy," says Miller, as he sits on a table in the conference room, biting his fingernails and looking uninterested.

When Maggie and Marty appear, Dean closes the door behind them.

Steve and Captain Brown stand with their arms folded. Everyone's looking at Dean. He realizes this is the first briefing he's ever given as a detective. It makes him feel self-conscious but only because Miller's probably waiting for him to make a mistake. He wishes Eva were here, and then he remembers he's still not heard from her. He glances at his cell phone but he has no notifications.

He takes a deep breath. "I've had a busy morning. First of all, Emily Gordon has discharged herself from the hospital and disappeared. She's not suffering from anything life-threatening, but I believe she's being controlled by someone and she's working as a prostitute. It's pretty obvious she lied about Eva being the person who attacked her—"

"How is it obvious?" Miller interrupts.

Dean doesn't respond. "And I think I can persuade her to withdraw that allegation as well as the allegation that Eva was the person who killed Trey Peterson."

Miller's shaking his head. "You're crazy. You're blinkered by the fact you're screwing this broad to see who she really is, just like last time!"

Dean feels a surge of adrenaline run through his chest. He's close to hitting Miller again, but he refuses to risk his job for this dick.

Maggie rolls her eyes. She's obviously figured out Miller's an asshole too.

"Miller? Shut the hell up or get out. I'll only tell you once," says Captain Brown. He turns back to Dean. "Do you know why she would make those claims in the first place?"

"She's mad at me for leaving town and not staying in touch. She lost a lot of people all at once and it's probably why she had to turn to prostitution. Her foster carers kicked her out, leaving her homeless and vulnerable to exploitation. And she feels like I stole Rocky from her."

Marty reacts. "But the dog would've gone to the pound if you didn't take him in. You did her a favor!"

Dean shrugs. He's not going to speak poorly of Emily.

"Teenagers see things differently to adults," says Maggie. "If she was feeling rejected, it would've been easy for her to misinterpret everything and feel unloved. It's a delicate time in a young person's life."

"Yeah, so delicate she likes to give blow jobs to random johns in parking lots," quips Miller.

Maggie gasps but instead of everyone looking at him, they turn to Dean for his reaction. Steve steps forward, ready to stop Dean from lunging.

Dean won't lunge. He's just biding his time. But if Eva were here, she'd have Miller on the floor right about now. "Also, I have reason to suspect Emily was being manipulated by an old friend of the department." He pauses for effect and everyone looks at him. "I've located Lizzie Glover."

This time it's Marty who gasps.

"So why isn't she locked up downstairs then?" says Miller. "You didn't let her sweet talk you into getting away again, did you?"

Dean's getting better at ignoring him. He just sounds like an annoying fly that needs to be swatted.

"Where is she?" asks Steve.

"She's been working as a substitute teacher at Mill Brook Elementary School in Cedar Falls." He waits for them all to recognize the school name and put the pieces together.

Captain Brown is the first to react. "Well, I'll be damned. Does she have Danny Mallory?"

"We have to assume she does. But before I knew all this, I was at the school to interview a teacher. While I was there, Lizzie walked right by me."

Miller laughs. "You let her walk by you without arresting her? What kind of detective are you?"

"Officer Miller! Get out of here! Now!" Captain Brown explodes.

"No. Stay where you are," Dean says to Miller. "It's fine." Dean gives him a hard stare until Miller looks away and the smirk vanishes from his face.

"Lizzie's disguising herself. She looked like a much older woman because she was wearing glasses, a wig, and baggy clothes. And I didn't see her face. It wasn't until after speaking to the teachers that I realized who she was. As I was about to pull her out of class, the local police turned up responding to reports of an active shooter at the school. We were locked down for over an hour until they confirmed it was a hoax, giving Lizzie time to get away. I went straight to her registered address, but it was fake."

Steve whistles and shakes his head. "Man, you were so close! That must be hard to swallow."

"It's not a great feeling but I know we'll get her." Dean faces Captain Brown. "Do you want to notify the FBI and let them take over?"

Captain Brown thinks about it before answering. "Do you think you can finish this?"

Dean doesn't hesitate. He looks him directly in the eye. "I want to more than you'll ever know."

He nods. "Well, you know, today was supposed to be my day off, so let's just say I was never here. I never heard a word that just came out of your mouth. I mean, how can I tell the FBI something I didn't hear?"

Dean smiles.

"I can only wait twenty-four hours though. We can't risk losing her again and the Feds have more resources than us."

Dean feels both relieved and uneasy at the same time. He wonders if he's set himself up for another fall. "Based on something Emily said to me, I think Lizzie's been tricking her into making these false allegations against Eva. I think she took advantage of how Emily was feeling about me. I just need to find Emily to confirm it."

"So did Lizzie Glover kill the guy found on Eva's couch?" asks Maggie.

"I believe so. He was Danny's father, and she has a thing against abusive parents. It sounds like Danny didn't have it easy at home. I'm surprised at the method she used to kill him though. It doesn't seem like her."

"She was covering her tracks," says Marty.

Dean nods. "Eva tracked down an employee from the secure unit who confessed to poisoning Barbara and shooting me. Tommy something."

Captain Brown steps forward. "I guess I'll have to ignore the fact that Valdez is working while suspended. We need to bring him in."

"We can't," says Dean. "He's dead. He killed himself at work."

Brown sighs. "Shit. Do we know where Lizzie might be headed?"

Dean shakes his head. "No. But she must have Danny with her, which means we need to tread carefully."

"You think she'd kill a child?" asks Maggie.

Dean stops to think about it. It would go against everything she believes in. "I really don't know. But I don't want to risk it. We need to lure her into a false sense of security."

"Call me stupid, but there's something I don't get," says Maggie. "What's the point of what she's doing? I mean, why here? And what does she actually want?"

Dean flinches when everyone turns to look at him.

Miller's the first person to say it. "She wants *him*."

CHAPTER FIFTY-SIX

Emily feels like she has no choice. She needs the money. After leaving the hospital she hitchhiked to the Hope Center where she's now sitting out back, not knowing what to do. The last time she was here, Tiffany was with her and they were hiding from work, even though they knew the consequences. It's just that some nights — hell, every night if she really thinks about it — it's a tough job to face and Tiffany was growing tired of it. She had been so badly treated by clients that she feared for her life.

That was the last time Emily ever saw her. She'd been on her way to quit and she wouldn't let Emily go with her, probably knowing she was facing trouble before she could break free for good. Emily was planning on doing the same thing but she wanted to see how it went for Tiffany first. Now she feels guilty that they didn't make a stand together.

She can't believe she'll never see her friend again.

It's getting dark now but she's paralyzed by doubt. It's drizzling but not wet enough for her to try to find shelter elsewhere. The snow from earlier has melted. She's partially covered by the center's roof.

Tracy, one of the employees from the center's coffee shop, comes out with a bag full of garbage. She spots Emily and waves. Emily ignores her so she goes back in without coming over, but within minutes the owner comes out to see her.

Jake pulls his coat over a thick jumper and then he pulls a woolen hat out of one pocket, and a pre-packed sandwich out of another.

"Hi, Emily. How are you feeling?" he asks. "I thought you might like something to eat. I hope you like cheese."

He hands her the free sandwich. The small gesture opens the floodgates. She buries her face in her hands and sobs for what feels like an hour. Jake sits next to her and hugs her to him. She welcomes the warmth. He doesn't say anything at first, he just lets her cry. After a while, her tears turn to sniveling, and she regains her composure.

"If I knew you hated cheese so much, I wouldn't have bothered!" he jokes.

She laughs. He hands her a pack of tissues, which she uses to clean up her face.

"Want to come inside? It's warmer. I'll get you a hot drink."

She can't do it. She can't give in to the kindness. Because if she gets used to the warmth, the free food, and the people who care, it will make it so much worse when she has to return to the cold, the scraps, and the people who use her. She'd rather stay hardened, like Tiffany. That way you forget people like Jake and Dean exist and you crave them less.

She shakes her head. "No, but thanks. I'm just going to sit here a while longer."

He gives her his gloves and slips his coat over her shoulders. "Keep these until you get your own. It's going to be cold tonight."

Tears form in her eyes again. He slips his hat onto her head and she can feel his body heat in it.

"I'll leave the back door unlocked until midnight. There will be a blanket on the couch near the coffee shop. Please feel free to sleep inside tonight. You don't have to stay out here and you don't have to go anywhere else. There are people willing to help you, Emily. Good people. Just stop telling yourself you don't deserve it."

She looks down at her hands, unable to speak. She'd love to believe him, but he doesn't know her. He doesn't know how she's helped a killer frame an innocent person.

The thought of Lizzie Glover makes her check her phone for notifications. Her Snapchat has been silent ever since Lizzie stopped needing her to lie about Dean's partner. When Lizzie first approached her, Emily was badly shaken by the encounter. Lizzie found her alone by the side of the road, waiting for business. She hadn't recognized the woman at first, and even when she did, she didn't run. She had nowhere to run to. No life worth protecting.

Lizzie talked Emily into getting in her car and she apologized for what happened to her mother, while trying to make her see that it was better for Emily to grow up without a mother like that.

Emily thought living with a drug addict was better than being used as a prostitute, but she'd just had a bad experience with a client and she wasn't looking forward to sleeping with another stranger so soon, so she stayed in the warm car and quietly listened to her mother's killer.

Lizzie went to great lengths to point out how badly Dean had let her down by leaving town and never checking in on her. By taking her dog and almost getting Rocky killed. She said Dean was the reason Emily was in her current situation.

Emily shakes her head at the memory of it. She was so naive to listen to a convicted killer. She would've turned her in if Lizzie hadn't been holding a knife during the entire conversation. Eventually, Emily agreed to lie about Eva Valdez, just to get Lizzie off her back. They exchanged contact details and whenever Lizzie wanted anything from her, she'd use Snapchat as the temporary messages would be impossible to show anyone unless the police seized her phone, which Emily couldn't risk because of what she does to make money. Her phone has a lot of her clients' numbers in there, along with all the sleazy messages and photos she's forced to exchange with them. If Emily wanted to expose Lizzie, she would've had to expose herself.

As Jake disappears inside the building, she makes her mind up. She's going to make enough money tonight to get out of Maple Valley. She's not going to give anyone her earnings this time; she's going to keep everything. She doesn't want to be here when Dean realizes she's been helping the woman who tried to destroy him. She has to leave this town for good. She stands up, pulls Jake's coat on, and leaves the community center.

It's time to go to the church.

CHAPTER FIFTY-SEVEN

Dean knows Miller's right about what Lizzie wants, and the smug look on his face when he says it pisses him off.

"I have a question for you, Miller," he says.

Miller looks shifty all of a sudden. His narrowed eyes dart from Dean to Captain Brown. He's not used to Dean actually talking to him. "What?"

"Why did you tell a TV producer that the fingerprints found on the knife that killed Trey Peterson belonged to Eva?"

Captain Brown's head spins around to face Miller. "What's that now?"

Miller looks incredulous but his face turns bright red. "I don't know what you're talking about, Matheson! You're out of your mind. Have you been drinking again?" He laughs, but it's not convincing.

"I have two reliable sources," says Dean, "that you were involved in a cozy conversation with Camille in the diner just minutes before the press arrived to hound Eva."

Miller moves toward the door. "You're crazy! You've always had it in for me and now you're blatantly lying!" He turns to the captain. "Come on, Captain. You don't believe this crap, do you?"

Captain Brown looks furious. Dean can see the vein in his temple pulsating. He's intimidating when he's angry and Dean spots Marty backing away.

Steve shakes his head. "Why does it always feel like you're working against us?"

"Because he is," says the captain. He walks up to Miller's face until they're nose to nose and Miller is backed against the door. "Give me your badge and your gun. You're fired."

Miller swallows hard. "Come on, Captain! We can work something out. I didn't tell that woman anything, we were just shooting the shit! Ask her if you don't believe me."

Somehow, Captain Brown moves even closer to him. "Don't make me repeat myself."

Miller moves away from the captain and pulls his service weapon out. He hands it over and then throws his badge across the room. He pulls the door open wide. "You'll be hearing from my attorney. And you," he points to Dean, "You better watch yourself, asshole."

Dean can't help it. He laughs. "Is that supposed to be a threat?"

Miller looks like he wants to spit on him. Instead, he storms out and they watch him grab some belongings from his desk.

When he's gone, Maggie lets out a deep breath. "Wow! That was better than an episode of *Law & Order*! Good work, Matheson. I might enjoy coming to work now, without that jerk hassling me every day."

Dean shrugs. "He did it to himself. I don't know why he even joined law enforcement. He's never enjoyed working here."

Captain Brown turns to Dean. "Where's Eva? I think it's time to reinstate her. Providing you can get Emily to withdraw her statements."

Dean checks his phone. Still nothing. "No idea. I'll go find her, then I'll track Emily down. Also, I need a warrant to search the church as I strongly suspect the owner is the one who's been exploiting Emily and Tiffany Sanders."

"What church?" asks the captain, confused.

"The Hope Center."

Captain Brown thinks about it for a second, before nodding. "I'll organize it. In the meantime, stay away from Miller. He'll probably try to get you to hit him so he can sue all of us."

Dean agrees. "As far as I'm concerned, he doesn't exist."

"Good. Everyone else, back to work."

CHAPTER FIFTY-EIGHT

Dean drives to the diner to see if Eva's returned to her apartment. It's almost seven o'clock and it's dark and wet out but her lights are off. Only the diner below is lit up. He heads inside to see if Frankie or Rachel have seen her today.

As he enters the warm diner, he quickly looks around but she's not in here.

"Hey, Dean. What can I get you?" says Rachel, holding a handful of dirty dishes.

"Have you seen Eva today?"

She thinks about it. "I don't think so, but then every day feels the same in here so maybe she's been in and I didn't notice. Frankie? Have you seen Eva today?"

Frankie pokes his head out of the kitchen. He's sweating profusely, trying to keep up with the orders.

"I haven't seen anyone today, I've been busy! You think this food cooks itself?"

Dean's concerned now, but he's not sure if he's crossing some line by trying to track her down. She's entitled to privacy, but she could at least text him to let him know she's safe.

"Can I get coffee to go?"

"Sure thing," says Rachel.

Dean sits at the counter. He has so much to do he shouldn't waste time on coffee but it'll help him concentrate. It could be a long night. He needs to find Lizzie. His heart pounds harder than usual. He just wants to get this over with once and for all.

Speaking to Dr. Livingstone might be a good idea now Dean knows Lizzie's still in New Hampshire. He might have some insight into where she's likely to be hiding. He doesn't have any contact details for the doctor so he googles the secure unit's phone number and hits call.

When someone answers he says, "Hi, I'm Detective Dean Matheson from Maple Valley PD. I'm after a phone number for one of your doctors."

There's a slight hesitation from the switchboard operator. "If you give me the name of the doctor and your cell number, I'll text you that number once I've checked your credentials."

"Great, thanks." Dean gives the man the details. "It's urgent, so as fast as possible would be good."

"It always is. Would you like his address also?"

Dean thinks about it. If the doctor doesn't answer his phone, he'll have to drive back up there. "Sure, that'd be good."

"You should get the text in about five minutes."

"Thanks." He ends the call.

Rachel puts a coffee down in front of him. "We've banned that producer from coming in here. She won't get any information from us."

"Thanks, Rachel. A documentary about me and my brother is the last thing I need."

"What's John got to do with Lizzie Glover?"

Dean takes a deep breath. "Absolutely nothing. Camille implied he was a crooked attorney, but I have no idea what she's talking about. She's obviously trying to find dirt where there isn't any, to make her show more appealing to the network."

Rachel puts her hand on his. "Oh, Dean. You really can't catch a break, can you?"

He nods. "It feels like that some days."

His phone buzzes with the text containing Dr. Livingstone's contact details. He grabs his coffee and stands. "I've gotta go."

He hurries to his car, but he stops when he hears a rustling noise in the woods next to the parking lot. It makes him spin around. He notices a figure running away, farther into the woods. It looks like the same person who's been following him recently; a tall, slim male. He drops his coffee and runs after him.

"Stop! Police!" He doesn't draw his weapon yet, but he will if this guy doesn't stop.

The man is faster than Dean and within minutes Dean can't tell which direction he ran in. It's too dark. He stops and tries to slow his breathing so he can listen for any sign of where the guy went. While he waits in silence, his phone buzzes again. He retrieves it from his pocket and looks at it.

I need help. I'm at the church. Please be quick. Emily.

He doesn't hesitate. Dean runs back to his car and speeds off in the direction of Jake's place.

The whole building is in darkness when Dean arrives. He runs to the entrance but it's locked, so he runs around the back to see if that's where Emily is. There's no one there, just an empty sandwich wrapper.

He tries the back door and is surprised when it opens. He slips inside and as his eyes adjust to the dark, he can hear the faint sound of music, presumably from the apartment upstairs. That's where Jake must have Emily. He uses his cell's flashlight to search for the staircase that leads to the apartment. When he finds it, he runs up, pulls his gun out, and quietly tries the door handle. It opens so he enters.

"This is the police! Put your hands where I can see them!"

Jake's relaxing on his couch. He looks half asleep and Dean can smell marijuana. He rushes up to him, flips him over, and cuffs his hands behind his back.

"Where is she?" he shouts.

Dazed, Jake says, "Who? Where's who?"

"Emily Gordon! Where is she?"

Jake stutters, "I, I don't know. I haven't seen her since earlier. I swear!"

Dean was wrong. Emily's not here. "She said she's in trouble at the church. Could she be hiding downstairs?"

Jake tries to sit up. "I keep telling people, this isn't a church. It's a—"

"Yeah, yeah, a community center. Got it." He checks her message. It definitely says the church.

Dean thinks of the only other church in town, the one his parents used to take him and his brother to when they were kids. But that's boarded up and ready for demolition. It's on the other side of town, near the Haunted Asylum. He suddenly realizes he's made a potentially deadly mistake. Why did he never think of that church before?

"Because Tiffany was found outside this one," he mutters. "Shit!"

He runs back downstairs and hears Jake shout behind him, asking to be released from the cuffs. He'll have to wait. Emily's life is at stake.

CHAPTER FIFTY-NINE

Emily's trying to keep the situation calm, but she's in way over her head. He's holding a knife to her throat. Her ears are ringing from his punches. She's never seen him this angry before. His last beating was just a warning, not like this. Now she knows what Tiffany experienced before she died.

All she can do is wait, and hope that Dean saw her text. She thought he'd be here by now. It's making her wonder whether she can rely on him after all. After everything he said to her at the hospital, she thought she could. Tears stream down her face but she daren't make a sound. She knows it doesn't take much to make this guy mad, and she thinks having to listen to her cry would push him over the edge from just threatening to kill her, to actually doing it.

"Why did you tell him you're a prostitute?" he screams at her. "He would never have found out if you hadn't told him. You've ruined everything for me!"

"I didn't tell him anything!" says Emily. "I promise you. I would never do that to you. You know I love you." Just saying it makes her feel sick but she's in survival mode. She'll tell him anything he wants to hear.

He pushes his nose against hers and she can feel his breath in her mouth. "If you loved me, you wouldn't be talking to the cops about me behind my back."

She closes her eyes. Dean's not coming for her. He'd be here by now.

"Are you screwing him? Is that your game? Giving him little freebies on the side because he's a cop? Well?" He removes the knife and slaps her hard, making her head spin to one side. She can handle the physical pain, that fades, but she doesn't think she can handle the pain of rejection anymore.

"You're nobody without me. Don't you realize that?" he shouts. "Don't you realize that working for me pays for your lifestyle? It pays for things like your fancy iPhone, which looks completely out of place on a nobody like you, by the way. Your mother was scum and so are you, Emily Gordon. People can see it with one look at you." He turns away from her, running his hand through his hair.

She nods. He's right, of course. Her mother was scum. And so is she.

When Dean brought Rocky in to see her at the hospital, Emily could have cried for days. It didn't feel like a happy reunion; it just reminded her of everything she didn't have as a child. It was horrible to see Rocky with a graying muzzle. He's an old dog now. But Dean was the same person as when she last saw him. When Emily felt in danger at home, or felt like her mom was going to die, she usually phoned the police, even before her social worker. It was nearly always Dean who came to take care of her while her mom was taken away.

When she saw him again for the first time, she remembered all this. How caring he'd been. She wishes she hadn't treated him so poorly, remembering that he lost his wife just after she lost her mom.

"You need me, Emily! And you need to work harder tonight. I'm going to give you to three guys and then you need to find us more girls. Now Tiffany's gone, we need someone else on the team. The others don't work as hard as she did."

Something in her shifts. She realizes she's never going to get away from this man as long as she lives. She doesn't care if he kills her. It would be better than living like this. When he leans in to start ranting at her again, she lifts her head and spits in his face. "You're nothing but a monster who gets his kicks from controlling young girls."

He steps back and touches her spit. His eyes are wide with shock.

"Pick on someone your own size!" she screams. "Oh no, wait. You can't, because you're a *loser*!"

She's sobbing now because she knows what's going to happen next. And she's right. He lifts his knife.

CHAPTER SIXTY

Dean parks outside the derelict church and doubts whether he's right about this. It looks empty and it's mostly boarded up, with a caved-in roof. It's not until he hears Emily scream that he knows he's in the right place.

He runs toward her voice but it's dark and the rain is pelting down hard, making visibility poor. He pulls his gun out and tries to find his way around this dangerous shell of a building. It's been closed for years, and no churches have opened in the town to replace it because Maple Valley folks aren't the most religious bunch of people. Those that are choose to attend the larger churches in neighboring towns, or modern community ventures like Jake's place.

He steps over broken floorboards and rotting roofing until he hears a man's voice and realizes he's found them. He peers around the corner and can see someone standing in front of Emily, blocking her from his view. He can't tell who it is, just that the guy's agitated.

Dean steps out. "Stop! Police!" he shouts over the rain.

This isn't the man he saw in the woods at the diner earlier, the one who's been following him. This man is shorter, and he doesn't look around at Dean. He lifts his arm and Dean spots his knife. He's going to stab Emily.

Dean doesn't hesitate. "Emily, get down!" When he has a safe shot, he fires his weapon. It hits the guy in his shoulder from behind. He drops the knife and stumbles forward, pushing Emily onto the ground.

"Get off me!" she screams, as she struggles out from under him.

Dean rushes forward and pulls her away, but she immediately collapses again. She's hyperventilating.

"Emily, try to calm down," he says. "Try to slow your breathing."

He moves toward the man, who is face down and still.

"Be careful!" shouts Emily. "He killed Tiffany!"

Dean can see blood through the guy's jacket. It's being washed away by the rain. He wasn't shooting to kill, but he wonders if he misjudged it. He pulls him over by his shoulder, exposing his face.

"Ryan?" Dean's shocked. And disgusted. Ryan's meant to protect kids in Emily's position, not exploit them.

Ryan's eyes are open and he's breathing. If Dean can get an ambulance out here fast, he could make it. He picks up the knife so Ryan can't reach for it and calls the station. Dispatch pick up immediately.

"It's Dean. I need an ambulance and backup at the old Grace Baptiste Church on Witcham Street. I've shot a suspect. Ryan Scott. He has a shoulder wound and needs immediate medical attention. We also have a sixteen-year-old girl with injuries. Emily Gordon." He doesn't know what injuries yet. "And send someone to the Hope Center to uncuff Jake Andrews. He's no longer a suspect." He ends the call.

"It would be you, wouldn't it?" says Ryan. He's speaking so quietly that Dean can barely hear him over the rain.

"You were meant to protect her," says Dean.

"So were you." He coughs. "Besides, she asked for it. She loved the attention."

Dean's so disgusted he wants to punch him, but he knows he can't. "You're going to pay for this. And for Tiffany."

Ryan laughs weakly. "No one cares about these kids. Did anyone turn up to claim Tiffany when she was in the hospital? No. Because she was a waste of space. Will anyone believe Emily on the stand? No. Because she's a sex worker. I gave her a chance to make money and do something with her life, which is more than you ever did for her."

Dean doesn't hold back this time. He punches Ryan hard in the jaw. His fist vibrates with pain but it's worth it. Ryan turns away and groans. Dean steps back.

Emily hugs him. "Thanks for coming," she says into his neck.

He hugs her back, relieved he got here in time.

She takes a step back and looks up at him. Her eye is swollen and she has a bloody lip. "I'm so sorry," she says. "I've got to tell you what I did." She starts crying.

Dean holds onto her shoulders. "It was Lizzie, wasn't it? She killed Trey Peterson and she made you lie about Eva?"

Emily slowly nods, looking ashamed. "I'm really sorry." She breaks down.

He hugs her to him again. "It doesn't matter, Emily. It's not your fault. None of this is your fault."

Within five minutes, Jenny and Marty show up, sirens blazing and skidding to a halt nearby. Dean explains what happened as Jenny cuffs Ryan. An ambulance turns up a few minutes later and the crew rushes straight over. Dean's exhausted. He's been running on adrenaline all evening and could do with something to eat.

"How did you get here so quick?" he asks Jenny.

Jenny looks at him. "We were on our way to another call-out. A woman's been found hanging in the woods."

Dean freezes. His ears start ringing and his stomach feels like lead. "What did you just say?"

"A suicide. Female. That's all we know so far. Want us to leave you here while we attend that?"

Dean thinks of Eva. And how she's been out of contact all day. Then he thinks of Lizzie. How she framed Eva for murder. How she knows Dean's onto her. A suicide in the woods is how all this started, two and a half years ago.

Goosebumps cover his entire body. This can't be happening. She wouldn't dare.

"Dean? Are you okay?" Jenny looks concerned. "You look like you need to sit down."

"I'll go to the woods," he says, barely audible. "You take care of these two."

"Sure. We'll follow them to the hospital. I'll keep you updated."

Dean isn't listening. His legs shake as he heads to his car. He feels completely numb because he knows what he's about to find in the woods. And it's going to destroy him.

CHAPTER SIXTY-ONE

The rain is pelting down so hard Dean's windshield wipers struggle to keep up. All the way to the woods he keeps telling himself how strong Eva is. How she could easily overpower Lizzie if she needed to. Eva's the toughest woman he's ever met and if she can't escape her, no one can. But these thoughts aren't helping him because he knows how insane Lizzie is, which means she's capable of anything. She's unpredictable, which only adds to the danger.

His hands shake as he tries not to crash in the rain. He skids around corners and shouts at other drivers to get out of his way. He doesn't even know why he's rushing. If there really is a woman hanging in the woods, she's already dead and nothing he can do will bring her back.

He tries to console himself with the thought that it could really be a suicide. It could be Lizzie hanging there. Could she have decided living on the run was too much? Especially with how close he came to finding her.

No. It doesn't work. He knows she values her life too much to kill herself.

He glances at his cell phone and tries calling Eva one last time. He slows down his driving so he can make the call. It rings out. Until it's answered.

"Hello, Dean."

His blood runs cold as he recognizes the British accent. He swerves the steering wheel in the wrong direction by accident and almost drives into a tree. "Where is she?" he says, trying to stay calm.

She laughs, but she sounds unhinged. "You know where to find us."

He realizes now that he can't change anything. He's too late to save Eva. Something inside him shifts and he knows this has to end. He refuses to play her games, so he hangs up on her, determined to kill her for what she's done.

He drives his car as far into the woods as he can get, feeling like he's been here before, because he has. He abandons it when it can take him no farther. He's surprised his legs are functioning as they move him forward. He knows exactly which tree he should be looking for and he heads straight for it. Dean tries to think of nothing as he walks. He should call for backup, for an ambulance, but he can't do it. He has to face this alone. It has to end. Tonight. He can't live like this anymore.

As he locates the huge maple tree that held Lizzie's sister, he spots the body hanging from it. It's not moving at all. He stops walking and looks at the victim's feet. Last time, they were shoeless. Not this time.

Dean collapses onto his knees. He can't bring himself to move, not even to look up. He thinks about how Eva was only living here because of him. He was blind to the danger he'd put her in. He tries to slow his breathing but he's on the verge of an anxiety attack. His chest feels constricted.

He hears rustling leaves and can tell someone has approached the tree through the bushes, just ahead of him. He looks up.

The woman from his nightmares appears. She's smiling. She looks different from the last time he saw her; she's heavier and she's aged a lot. Her nose is badly swollen and he thinks he can see dried blood on her face. That can only mean that Eva fought back. She tried her hardest to stay alive.

He tries not to think about Eva's last moments, not until he's dealt with her killer.

As Lizzie steps out of the shadows he notices she's not dressed for this weather. It's then that he realizes she's wearing the dress Eva wore to Jones' retirement party. The one that went missing from her apartment. It doesn't even fit her.

He shudders. His whole body is trembling. "You killed her!" he shouts.

She looks surprised. "Of course I did! What did you expect me to do?" She starts walking forward and she looks genuinely pleased to see him, as if she's going to receive a warm welcome.

"Back off!" He pulls out his weapon.

She stops and frowns. "What are you doing? Don't you understand? I'm ready for us to be together. I'm even willing to overlook what you've done to me." She pauses. "Dean, we're linked forever. You know that."

Dean shakes his head. He can't believe the level of her delusion. "I don't want anything to do with you."

He can just make out the falter of her smile.

"But imagine the good we could do together. I could save so many more children with you on my side." She becomes passionate, warming to her foolish idea. "Now you're a detective you could dispose of evidence, turn a blind eye, and help me! You're in law enforcement to help people, aren't you? Think of the children. There are so many children growing up with monsters. It's not right, Dean. You must see that?"

He can't stop shaking his head. There's no reasoning with her. She's too far gone. "No. This is all about you and your mother. You need to stop trying to get back at her and let it go. You've already killed her, for God's sake! What's it going to take for you to move on?"

She looks at him, unable to comprehend what he's saying. She won't accept she has unresolved issues.

She takes a step forward. "I'm sorry Tommy shot you. He was only supposed to graze you. That's the problem with using lunatics to do your bidding. They always take it too far."

"He was an employee," says Dean. "Not an inmate."

"Actually, he was an ex-inmate. The secure unit likes to hire the more sedate inmates after their release. Cheap labor, I guess, all under the illusion of helping the vulnerable members of the community."

Dean stares at her in disbelief. She still has a superiority complex. "And what about Jones' wife? What possible reason did you have to kill an innocent woman?"

Lizzie looks away, conflicted for the first time. "She was a difficult one. The first person who didn't deserve to die. She wasn't even a mother." She stops and looks at Dean. "At least, not biologically. I know you loved her, but I couldn't get to Jones. He'd stopped my work by putting me away. He didn't even listen to what I was trying to do, he just condemned me on the spot! Everything was black or white with him, but life's not like that, Dean! If it was the world wouldn't need people like me." Her eyes are shining. "You weren't here anymore. I needed to bring you back to Maple Valley. So his wife became collateral damage. I'm sorry about her. I truly am. But I knew if one of them died you'd come home. You're so predictable. Just like tonight. A woman hangs in the woods and you come running. You always want to save everyone. Everyone except me." She pauses and looks at him, confused. "Why won't you save *me*, Dean?"

He shakes his head. "Because you're beyond redemption." He walks toward her so he can be closer when she tries to run. He feels for his handcuffs but they're not there; he left them on Jake. He forces himself to look up at Eva as he passes, which is when he notices the hood over her head.

"Why did you do that?" he asks. "Can't you even look your victims in the eye as you murder them?" He feels his energy draining from him and he's overwhelmed with despair. He can't believe things are this bad. He thinks about George. How is he going to explain this to him?

Lizzie looks up at the body. "Hanging's an ugly way to go so I was trying to spare Danny the awful sight."

Dean looks at her. Danny? He'd completely forgotten about the boy. Is there still time to salvage something from this? "Where is he?"

She looks to her right and motions someone over. "Come on over, Danny. Come and meet your new father."

Dean feels a whole new level of alarm. Does she really think the three of them can be a family? He realizes she no longer has any grasp on reality. She's much worse than last time.

The boy steps out of the darkness, so slowly that Dean wonders if he's going to refuse.

"Danny?" he says. "Come to me, not her." Lizzie isn't carrying any weapons so she can't hurt him.

"I can't," he says, teeth chattering. "She'll hurt me." He looks at Lizzie.

"Whatever makes you think that, Danny?" She laughs, incredulous.

Danny looks at Dean. "Because she's bad. She killed Dr. Livingstone. And she stole my dad's watch."

Dean's heart sinks. Just how many people has she managed to kill while she's been on the run? "Where's Dr. Livingstone now, Danny?"

He looks scared. "He's in the river. But I don't want to talk about him. Is my dad here? My real dad?"

Lizzie softens. "No, Danny. I killed him for you. He won't be lashing out at you anymore." She looks at Dean. "He made it too easy. I followed him to a bar and flirted with him. Of course, he thought I was desperate to sleep with him so he let me drive him all the way back to my old apartment. He got what was coming to him."

Dean's heard enough. Without hesitation, he shoots Lizzie. He makes it a painful shot, so she can feel half of what he's feeling. The bullet hits her left shin and she screams out long and loud. She sinks to the ground, clutching her bloody leg.

He takes the opportunity to pull Danny far away from her and gives the boy his coat, which swamps him. "Stay here, Danny. Until backup arrives."

The boy takes refuge in the bush he was hiding in before Dean arrived. He's shaking uncontrollably but he's not crying. He keeps his eyes on his abductor.

Dean calls the station. "I need backup ASAP at the Maple Valley woods. I have Lizzie Glover here, injured, and . . ." He stops, trying to fight the sob in his throat. He looks up at Eva's lifeless body. "We have an officer down." He can't bring himself to say her name.

He doesn't wait for the response from dispatch. He ends the call and notices too late that Lizzie's crawling along the ground toward him with a small knife in one hand.

"You're supposed to love me!" she screams, as she stabs him through his foot, twice.

The pain is immense, and he feels the warm spread of blood in his shoe. As he collapses, she somehow manages to get up. She looms over him with the knife, unsteady on one leg.

"No, Lizzie," he pants. "I've never loved you. I should've killed you last time." He watches her pained grimace as she realizes it's over.

"Dean, please?" She slowly lets the knife fall to the ground. "I wasn't supposed to be this way." She sinks down onto her knees, on top of him. Her legs pin him down. "You could still save me?"

He sees pain in her eyes. He has his weapon in his hand but he hesitates to use it, wondering one final time whether she *can* be helped. Whether she can ever escape the curse of her childhood. He knows she's right. Given another mother, she could've been who she was supposed to be, not this bitter, broken woman seeking revenge on anyone who remotely reminds her of the woman who damaged her.

Even after everything she's done, Dean's conflicted. He knows enough about people to know that no one is all good or all bad, but he thinks Lizzie comes close to the latter. Her childhood may have triggered her hatred, but it's not the reason she continues to kill. He thinks about how she used Emily and how she killed Linda, Barbara, and all the others. Finally, he thinks of Eva. He realizes then that she would do it all over again if she could. Because he can't save her from herself.

He extends his arm and places the barrel of his gun against her chest.

Lizzie doesn't attempt to pull away. She just watches, tears rolling down her face.

"You want to go back to prison?" he asks.

She looks at him, understanding what he's asking. Pointing to her head, she says, "Not this one." She slowly lowers her hand and places it on top of his, the hand that's holding the trigger.

Ever so gently, she squeezes.

Dean looks her in the eye as he shoots her through the heart.

After the impact, she falls forward, onto him. He's winded and he doesn't have the strength to push her off immediately. He drops his gun and lies back, gasping for breath, wiping her blood from his face.

Danny's crying now. He stays safe in the bush.

Dean's stunned. By the power of the gun and the way she let him kill her. Her hair is in his mouth and he smells her familiar scent. It makes him retch. He rolls her off of him, steadies himself, and then stands, trying not to put too much weight on his foot.

He looks down at Lizzie. Her eyes are already glazing over. She's gone. After all this time and all the destruction, she's gone. He finds himself hoping she's finally at peace and is surprised by his reaction.

He picks up her knife and his gun and walks to the tree trunk. His foot is throbbing and, although he's trembling all over, he manages to climb the tree. When securely on the thick branch that Eva's hanging from, he uses Lizzie's knife to cut through the thin rope that's holding her up. When he gets through it, her body drops to the ground with a thud.

He jumps down and approaches her, barely containing his grief.

"Look away, Danny."

He doesn't wait to see if Danny turns. Dean pulls the hood off the body and stares. "Oh my God." He sinks to the ground and sobs.

CHAPTER SIXTY-TWO

Dean's in the back of an ambulance, getting his foot bandaged. He's refused to go to the hospital for treatment. There isn't time. He's soaked through from the rain and all he wants to do is collapse, but he can't.

The relief at seeing Shannon Mallory's face under the hood instead of Eva's was overwhelming. He knows he shouldn't be relieved — someone still died and Danny's now an orphan — but he *is* relieved. Of course he is. Part of him knows it doesn't mean Eva's alive, but for now, there's hope, however small.

He feels like he's on the verge of breaking down. Killing Lizzie didn't feel good and he knows he'll see her in his nightmares. He shakes his head. He needs to concentrate on the present. On finding Eva. There will be time to reflect on whether he did the right thing afterward.

Danny's in a separate ambulance with EMTs caring for him. Physically, he looks fine. He didn't see his mother's face when Dean lifted the hood, but he's told them he was there when Lizzie abducted her earlier today. Then he shut down, like he couldn't face discussing any of what he's been through. He didn't react to Eva's name, so no one knows if he's been a witness to whatever's happened to her. The poor kid will need a lot of therapy to get over this. How could Lizzie believe she was helping him?

Dean rubs his eyes. He's trying to think where Eva could be.

"Here, drink this."

Jenny tries to hand him a bottle of water, but he shakes his head. He doesn't want anyone to see how hard his hands are trembling. He slips them into his pockets. He's already getting flashbacks of the look in Lizzie's eyes when she put her hand on his. She chose death, hopeful that it would be better than living with her illness.

Steve arrives and comes straight over. "I've had an update from Marty. Emily's being checked out right now, but she says she feels fine apart from some bruising. The social worker's in surgery. He lost a lot of blood. They can't tell yet whether he's going to pull through."

Dean doesn't care about Ryan's condition. He's finding it hard to focus on anything but Lizzie's face.

"Okay, this is the best I can do for now," says the male EMT, letting go of Dean's foot. "But it's at risk of infection. You know what I'm going to say?"

"I know, I need to go to the hospital. I will at some point." He gently slips his shoe on over the bandages.

Sheila arrives. She runs up to Dean and hugs him. "Would you please stop getting yourself into these situations?"

Dean feels uncomfortable because Steve's watching them. He tries to smile but it feels like he's grimacing instead.

"What's wrong?" she asks.

Steve speaks up. "We don't know where Eva is."

"Shit." She looks at him. "She's a tough chick. She'll be fine, I'm sure."

Dean nods.

Sheila makes her way over to Lizzie's body on the stretcher, unzips the body bag, and looks down at her. "I know this is really unprofessional of me, but I'm glad she's dead."

Dean doesn't say anything. Maybe Eva was right when she said that he was the only person who understood Lizzie.

He can't relax until Eva's found. He thinks about their conversation late last night. She'd had the idea of visiting Livingstone and he'd advised her against it. That doesn't mean she listened to him. Didn't George say she does the opposite of what anyone tells her to?

She's at Livingstone's house. She must be. He tries to contain the feeling of dread that's threatening to consume him. His body wants to move fast but his mind is pinning him to his seat. Can he do this? Can he face the death of yet another woman he cares about?

But she could still be alive.

He forces himself to get up and he staggers to the nearest cruiser.

"Dean? Where are you going?" shouts Steve.

Dean enters Livingstone's address into the GPS and speeds away from the woods.

* * *

It takes him twenty-five minutes to reach Livingstone's house but only because it's nighttime and he drives so fast, with lights blazing. His injured foot makes the drive dangerous, but he doesn't let it slow him down. Livingstone's front door is made of solid oak and it's locked, so he knows he'll never be able to force his way in through that. He picks up a ceramic plant pot and throws it through the front window. The noise is bound to attract the attention of neighbors, but Dean doesn't care. He smashes enough of the glass to be able to climb inside safely. His foot is numb at the moment, but also weak. It gives out from under him after every other step.

All the lights are off in the house. It smells bad. A ball of dread weighs heavy on his chest. Any hope he had of finding Eva alive is dwindling fast.

"Eva!" he shouts. "Eva! Are you here?"

He tries to listen but the house is silent. He walks through the large living room to the kitchen. "Eva!"

He stops to listen again. Faint banging reaches him. He switches on the light and notices another door. He'd guess it's hiding a pantry or a basement. He opens it and tries the light switch but nothing happens. He uses his cell phone's flashlight and lights up the room. It's a basement.

He lowers the flashlight to the stairs beneath him and that's when he sees Eva.

She's completely still at the bottom of the stairs. He has a second's hesitation because his brain is screaming at him not to go down there, not to look. He wants to remember her alive.

He hears a bang at the same time as he sees her hand move.

"Eva!" He runs down the stairs so fast his injured foot gives out and he tumbles down past her, yelling in pain as he goes.

She's moving her hand up and down, trying to make noise with an old can of paint. He gets on his knees next to her, trying to see her face. She looks pale and thirsty; her lips are dry.

"Eva? Where are you hurt?"

She might be too weak to talk. He looks her over and sees her shirt is covered in blood, so he rips it open to identify where she's injured. She's been stabbed in the shoulder. He applies pressure to the area with one hand as he tries to retrieve his phone with the other. He has her blood on his hands so his phone slips and drops to the floor.

Eventually, he manages to call Steve. "I've got her! She's barely alive. Send an ambulance to the address I'm about to text you."

"Understood."

Dean forwards the text with Livingstone's address and then drops his phone. He puts his spare hand on Eva's face and leans in close.

"Hold on, Eva. An ambulance is coming. I'm going to get you out of here. You hear me? You can't die." He chokes back his anguish.

Her cold hand finds his and she squeezes it. She lifts her head barely an inch. She says something but he doesn't quite hear it.

"What's that?" He leans closer to her mouth, to hear her better.

She coughs, then tries again. "I said, it's about time you ripped my clothes off of me."

Dean laughs, more relieved than she'll ever know. He collapses beside her, completely drained of energy. He can't speak.

They lie together in silence until they hear sirens approach in the distance.

EPILOGUE

"I'm going to need more beer for this," says Dean, downing his third bottle.

It's May and almost two months since he killed Lizzie Glover. He's sitting on the armchair in Sheila and Steve's living room. There are no spare seats due to some of his friends from the station joining them. Sheila decided to host a party for the premiere of Camille's documentary, *Lust, Lies, and Homicide.*

Dean only agreed to come because he decided it would be easier to watch it with everyone than arrive at work the morning after and face them.

Jones, George, and Rocky are here, as well as Marty and Jenny. Miller obviously wasn't invited and Captain Brown declined the invitation, saying he doesn't want to know what the damage is so he can plead ignorance to his boss.

Dean's hoping the damage isn't too bad. He also hopes Camille is sensitive to Lizzie's victims and their families.

Eva comes over and perches on the arm of his chair with a bottle of beer in one hand and Scully in the other. Her shoulder healed quicker than Dean's foot, which was surprising to him. He's only just losing his limp.

Scully's asleep with her head on Eva's elbow. Mulder's been chasing Rocky around the house, but they've both called a truce and are settling down on the floor under the TV now. Mulder's massaging Rocky's stomach before he settles down to sleep. He's growing up fast, but his ears and paws still look too big for his small, sleek body.

Dean's been surprised by how much comfort the cat has provided during his recent depression. Just having someone else to take care of gets him out of a bed he'd probably otherwise never leave.

Eva takes a sip of her beer as Marty watches her. "You can share my seat with me if you like." He winks and pats the narrow gap next to him.

"No, thanks," she says. "I might catch something."

Marty laughs. He appears to find insults a turn-on.

Seeing his friends safe and here to support him provides some comfort to Dean, but it's fleeting and quickly replaced by a heavy feeling of dread. He's hoping that, once this documentary becomes yesterday's news, it will be easier for him and the town to move on. Maybe that's when he'll finally relax.

Marty passes around popcorn. He looks excited, like he's here to watch the latest Marvel movie or something.

"I wonder if they had trouble casting someone to play you," he says to Dean. "It must have been pretty tough to find that right level of rugged and doomed! Hey, I bet whoever plays you is jinxed for the rest of his life, you know, like the guys who play Superman."

Everyone laughs, including Eva.

"Don't encourage him, people," says Dean, trying to be a good sport.

Jenny sits next to Rocky on the floor and looks up at Dean. "What do you think about the plea deal Ryan agreed to?"

They've learned Ryan Scott will only serve two years in prison for what he did to Emily. There wasn't enough evidence to convict him of Tiffany's assault or manslaughter. He'll never work as a social worker again and the cash he made from exploiting the girls has been seized, along with any assets such as his Rolex watch, which turned out to be real.

For Dean, two years isn't enough. Kids like this never get true justice and that's why Lizzie felt compelled to issue her own sentences. To make sure the worst people couldn't re-offend.

Emily told him Ryan had been the one trying to confuse them about who attacked Tiffany. He'd phoned in the fake body when Dean and Eva were at the Haunted Asylum and he'd tied the promotional balloon to Eva's front door to make it look like a warning from someone who worked there. He'd even dumped Tiffany outside the community center to make it look like Jake was involved, although he hadn't expected her to die, according to Emily. He's a worthless piece of shit.

"I'm not surprised he took the deal," he says. "Emily's upset but she'll be okay. She has her new job to look forward to."

Jenny seems surprised. "What new job?"

Sheila stands. "She's going to be my new mortuary apprentice. It's just a trial for now, doing all the menial jobs my assistants complain about. Not everyone can handle working with dead bodies, so we'll see how she does."

"That's great," says Jenny.

Dean smiles at the thought of Emily working with them all. At least he can watch out for her better now.

Sheila nods at Steve, who joins her in standing. As he puts his arm around her waist, he clears his throat and says, "While we've got you all here, there's something we'd like to tell you."

Dean stares at them. He can guess what's coming and it makes him think of Linda and what the insurance company said.

Sheila doesn't look as happy as Dean would expect. "We're pregnant!" she says with a shrug.

"Congratulations!" says Eva, who's the first to hug them both. "So that's why you've been throwing up and running out of crime scenes lately."

"It must be," says Sheila. "This certainly wasn't planned, but that's okay. I'll come around to the idea."

As Marty shakes Steve's hand, he says with a wink, "So is it yours or Matheson's? Because I'll need to know who to address the card to."

Eva and Sheila gasp in unison as Dean shakes his head.

"What? It's a joke, people. Can't anyone take a joke anymore?" says Marty.

Luckily Steve takes it well. He doesn't punch Marty too hard on the shoulder.

Dean whispers to Marty as he walks past, "You're going to be the death of me, man."

Marty laughs and grabs some more popcorn as Eva asks Sheila all the right questions about due dates and baby names.

Suddenly, it's time. The documentary is starting. Steve turns all the lights out. It's atmospheric, like a movie theater. Dean's glad as it hides his face.

Dramatic music plays over a scene of a man in a black police uniform driving his cruiser fast down a road that's meant to be in Maple Valley but clearly isn't. Then Camille's voice starts narrating the history of the town.

Dean feels jittery. He stands up. "I need the bathroom."

Marty jeers him good-naturedly as Dean passes.

The truth is, Dean can't bear to watch. He can't bear to relive Linda's death and all the mistakes he made with Lizzie Glover. To an outsider, he's going to look like a complete idiot. And no one knows that more than him.

He walks into the kitchen and leans against the sink, looking out of the window. He feels something at his feet. It's Rocky. He's come to check on him. Dean slides down to sit on the floor with him and Rocky licks his face. They lived through this ordeal together so maybe Rocky doesn't want to watch it either.

Dean starts feeling nervous. This all feels surreal. He was ordered to attend compulsory therapy after shooting Lizzie and although he's been putting it off, he thinks it's time. He feels like he could be suffering from PTSD due to everything that's happened. Killing a convicted murderer didn't make him feel good, and there's been no relief from knowing she's dead. The media have covered it non-stop and Captain Brown's treating him with kid gloves, giving him easy cases to work on. Maybe his team can tell he's suffering. His nightmares are starting to take over, leaving him too afraid to sleep, so it's easy to see he's exhausted.

After hiding in the kitchen for twenty minutes, Jones walks in. He looks like he's seen a ghost.

Dean's heart skips a beat. "What's wrong?"

"You need to come see this."

He gets up and slowly walks into the living room. Part of him wants to leave before it's too late. He wonders how things could possibly get any worse.

He arrives in time to hear Camille talking about his brother over photos on screen of John in college and then as an attorney in court. He angers immediately. "Where did she get those photos?"

He realizes she must have stolen them from his house when she was there alone, supposedly taking photos for the house sale.

"Listen to what she's saying." Jones puts a hand on Dean's back.

"And that is why," says Camille dramatically, "John Matheson's suicide was faked. As a potential star witness in the shocking allegations, John had to go into hiding or risk being killed."

Dean scoffs in disbelief. "What's she talking about?"

Jones leads him to a chair and he automatically sits down.

"She's saying John's not dead, Dean. She's saying something went down at the DA's office and John had to be protected because he could've been a star witness."

Dean starts trembling as his blood runs cold. "No. She's wrong. She's making it up. I saw his body. I had to visit him in the morgue."

He looks up at Sheila, but she looks as shocked as him and on the verge of tears. John didn't die in Maple Valley, so it wasn't her morgue he was taken to.

"Did you see his face?" she asks.

He thinks back to that terrible experience. He was told John had shot himself in the face with a shotgun so there were no features left. The ME had spared him the sight. "No. He was identified by his fingerprints. They covered what was left of his face."

He feels faint and his stomach grows heavy. He looks at the TV.

Camille isn't finished. "I can now exclusively reveal that I have successfully tracked down John Matheson." She leaves a dramatic pause. "And he's ready to reclaim his life."

As everyone gasps around him, Dean leans forward in his seat. He holds his head in his hands. He doesn't know how much more he can take. He thinks of the man who's been following him lately. Dean never saw his face, but he thought he'd recognized his outline, and now he knows why. It was John.

His brother's alive.

THE END

THANK YOU

Dear Reader,

Thank you for reading the third book in the Dean Matheson series. This was originally written in 2019 but I've updated the entire series for its relaunch in 2023, and I've had so much fun returning to Maple Valley after all these years!

If you've followed Dean from the start of his journey, you'll know it's been one hell of a ride for him to get to this point. I hope you've enjoyed being part of that journey so far. If you've started the series at book 3 and want to know what on earth happened between Dean and Lizzie Glover, I highly recommend you read books 1 and 2 to find out! This series is designed to be read in order, due to the backstory.

I get a lot of contact from readers specifically about Dean, with some readers even wishing he was real! I'm glad you're able to look past his flaws. He has a good heart and he's learning from his mistakes as he progresses up the law enforcement ranks. It certainly wouldn't be as interesting if he was perfect at everything. And I don't know about you, but I can't wait to find out what his brother will be like . . .

If you enjoyed this series, you might also like my more recent series which follows Detective Madison Harper and PI Nate Monroe. At the time of writing this letter, I'm currently working on book 7 in that series.

If you enjoyed *this* book, please consider leaving a rating or review on Amazon, Goodreads and/or Bookbub, as that helps it to reach more readers and may result in more books in this series.

Until next time!
Wendy

ACKNOWLEDGMENTS

Thank you to the bloggers and readers who leave reviews for my books and inspire me with your enthusiasm for the series! I know many of you are crossing your fingers for more Dean Matheson books and have enjoyed my Madison Harper series too. Both series remain my priority right now, so keep an eye on my website and social media for updates!

Thanks also to my publisher and editor for allowing me to update this series, it was well overdue.

And thanks to my husband for his continued support.

THE CHOC LIT STORY

Established in 2009, Choc Lit is an independent, award-winning publisher dedicated to creating a delicious selection of quality women's fiction.

We have won 18 awards, including Publisher of the Year and the Romantic Novel of the Year, and have been shortlisted for countless others.

All our novels are selected by genuine readers. We are proud to publish talented first-time authors, as well as established writers whose books we love introducing to a new generation of readers.

In 2023, we became a Joffe Books company. Best known for publishing a wide range of commercial fiction, Joffe Books has its roots in women's fiction. Today it is one of the largest independent publishers in the UK.

We love to hear from you, so please email us about absolutely anything bookish at choc-lit@joffebooks.com

If you want to hear about all our bargain new releases, join our mailing list: www.choc-lit.com

ALSO BY WENDY DRANFIELD

DEAN MATHESON
Book 1: WHO CARES IF THEY DIE
Book 2: WHERE THE SNOW BLEEDS
Book 3: WON'T YOU SAVE ME

Printed in the USA
CPSIA information can be obtained
at www.ICGtesting.com
LVHW090825050624
782318LV00005B/330